A NOVEL

GLOBAL AFRICAN VOICES

Dominic Thomas, EDITOR

THE SHAMEFUL STATE

A NOVEL

SONY LABOU TANSI

Translated by DOMINIC THOMAS
Foreword by ALAIN MABANCKOU

INDIANA UNIVERSITY PRESS
Bloomington & Indianapolis

This book is a publication of

Indiana University Press
Office of Scholarly Publishing
Herman B Wells Library 350
1320 East 10th Street
Bloomington, Indiana 47405 USA

iupress.indiana.edu

This book was originally published in French by Editions du Seuil
under the title *L'État Honteux* copyright © 1981 Editions du Seuil
© 2016 by Indiana University Press

Manufactured in the United States of America

Library of Congress Cataloging-in-Publication Data

Sony Labou Tansi, author.
    [L'État honteux. English]
    The shameful state / Sony Labou Tansi ; translated by
Dominic Thomas ; foreword by Alain Mabanckou.
        pages cm.—(Global African voices)
        ISBN 978-0-253-01925-7 (pbk. : alk. paper)—ISBN 978-0-253-01932-5 (ebook)
        I. Thomas, Dominic Richard David, translator. II. Title.
III. Series: Global African voices.
    PQ3989.2.S64E813 2015
    843'.914—dc23

                                                                    2015021504

1 2 3 4 5   21 20 19 18 17 16

For AME LA YAO, H. LOPÈS, and U. TAM'SI

Together we shall fight

until freedom is no longer

a word buttered with sardines.

FOREWORD

THE SHAMEFUL STATE OR THE PORTRAIT OF THE AFRICAN MONARCH

Alain Mabanckou

Sony Labou Tansi (1947–1995) is widely acknowledged as one of Africa's most talented authors. Although he died at a relatively young age, the singularity, creativity, and pioneering qualities of his novels and plays shaped a generation of literary production and continue to influence contemporary African literature. A cursory glance at the work of such important writers as Kossi Efoui (Togo) or Koffi Kwahulé (Ivory Coast), both of whom have also published novels and plays, reveals traces of this inspiration. Sony Labou Tansi's creative energy was channeled in multiple directions, at times toward the Rocadu Zulu Theatre Company which he founded in the early 1980s, at others toward the six novels he wrote, all of which were published by the prestigious Éditions du Seuil.

Sony Labou Tansi burst onto the French and francophone literary scene in 1979 with his novel *La Vie et demie* (*Life and a Half*, IUP), featuring the emblematic figure of the immortal rebel Martial before whom the relentless efforts of the ruthless postcolonial dictator to liquidate him prove futile. This marked a significant turning point in francophone sub-Saharan African literature in a more general manner, bolstering the importance of the African dictatorship novel. Sony Labou Tansi's political commitment and oppositional nature were the source of constant difficulties with the authorities, but also afforded him tremendous respect and the opportunity to engage with audiences in Africa and beyond that listened attentively to his words.

In his next novel, *L'État honteux* (*The Shameful State*), published in 1981, the figure of the rebel is eclipsed by the dictator, the despot, the African monarch, whose name is Colonel Martillimi Lopez. One day, all his ministers seek private audiences and hand in, one after the other, their letters of resignation, because they can no longer bear the idea of leaving "the country to the children of the children of our children" in this "shameful state." The nation is on its knees, and they don't want to be blamed. The irony is palpable in this unusual turn of events in which the very people who had the most benefitted from the power structure now become conscious of the country's collapse, after having enriched themselves and enjoyed its spoils while the masses languished in poverty. The political situation at the time is of course relevant, and observers were quick to equate the central protagonist in this novel with real-life megalomaniacs such as Mobutu Sese Seko, whose dictatorial rule over Zaire for more than thirty years was characterized by embezzlement, corruption, and widespread human rights violations.

Following in the footsteps of such Latin American greats as Gabriel García Márquez and Mario Vargas Llosa, Sony Labou Tansi applied himself to the task of describing the most salient traits of political intolerance, to exposing the arbitrariness and whims of a monarch, while also highlighting the absurd nature of dictatorial rule. *The Shameful State* offers readers a historical insight into a grotesque and bloodthirsty monarch whose appetite for power proves insatiable. His degenerate behavior is comical, excessive, and ludicrous, but also tragic and apocalyptic when one takes into account the fact that so many African leaders, such as President Gnassingbé Eyadema (Togo), Field Marshal Idi Amin Dada (Uganda), and the self-crowned emperor Jean-Bédel Bokassa (Central African Republic), all closely resemble Martillimi Lopez. In *The Shameful State,* Sony Labou Tansi provides an inventory of the eccentricities of a leader whose acts of sexual debauchery prove to be limitless and who governs exclusively by responding to the urges of his "big herniated greasy balls." Extrajudicial killings, murders, and imprisonment without due process are simply the order of the day.

The Shameful State was written at one of the most tumultuous moments in the history of the African continent. However, over time, this magisterial novel has lost nothing of its innovative merits and initial appeal and remains relevant to a range of political and social realities of the twenty-first century. Sony Labou Tansi has made it possible for us not only to understand better the complexity of Africa and the world today and the incessant ethnic conflict and competition for power, but also to reckon with the latest incarnation of the dictator-monarch who now exercises power in more discrete and discernible ways, perhaps because they too have read *The Shameful State . . .*

WARNING

I've heard it said that the novel is a work of the imagination. Even if that is true, this imagination must still have a place somewhere in reality. One could say that I write, or rather that I cry out, as a way of forcing the world into the world. Your shame of calling things by their name doesn't apply in this instance. In my view, our so-called world is both a scandal and a source of shame, and I am only able to express this through several "ill-gotten words." Ultimately, God alone can decide whether or not a book is great: in my book you will find me fighting for it to stand out. Life is no secret to any of us. *The Shameful State* is thus the summary in a few "ill-gotten words" of the shameful situation in which humanity has elected to live.

Sony Labou Tansi

A NOVEL

THIS IS THE STORY OF COLONEL MARTILLIMI LOPEZ, son of National Mom, our very own matriarch of the nation, who came into the world holding his big greasy herniated balls and exited still holding onto them—National Lopez, younger brother of Lieutenant Colonel Gasparde Mansi. Oh dear! Poor old Gasparde Mansi, Supreme Commander of the Army, ex-President for life, ex-founder of the Rally for Democracy, ex-Commander-in-Chief of the Peoples' Liberty, the late Gasparde Mansi, alas, just like Mom's Lopez, born holding onto his hernia and still clinging to it in the same old filthy way when he died; such a pity!

We set off from National Mom's village and took him on his first ever trip to the capital. He was greeted by a lively crowd, chanting, and saluting cannons; there he was, perched on his white horse Moupourtanka, singing the national anthem. Because white is the color of frankness, and if nothing else, as we shall see my brothers and dear fellow countrymen, he was certainly frank. My brother from another mother, National Oupaka, was galloping along proudly behind him, sharing a horse with Mom, who would probably fall off if she were riding alone on such a beast. To his left, Carvanso, to the right, Vauban. The crowds followed him on foot. We were all convinced that this president was going to be a good one. We carried his kitchen utensils, old fishing nets, machetes, fishhooks, domestic birds, seventy-one sheep, three cases of gourmet Benedicta mustard, eleven Sloughi hounds, his Argand oil lamp, bicycle, fifteen watering cans, slop pail, three mattresses, Arquebus, sieves. . . . And when our brother Carvanso said to him: "Don't worry, Mr. President," he responded: "I'm not so sure; I won't put up with people saying that I embezzled funds." His big magnanimous father-of-the-nation smile extended from ear to ear.

At first glance, you might have thought we were back in the age of caravans, because he'd refused to take an airplane, and so we had to walk, bent double under the weight of his belongings and you better make sure you don't break anything. . . . We sang his praises. Spread our loincloths out in front of him. As he made his way in to the capital, an honor guard stretched out for over eight miles, almost three thousand feet of red berets, a hundred of green berets; he sidled up to brother Carvanso when he saw the soldiers and whispered: "What are they?"—"Infantrymen Colonel"—"Ah, Ok!"

We made our way to the city center via route 15, and once across the Alberto-Icuezo Bridge, reached District 45. Folks were dancing at Delpanso's and he wanted to watch since the dances were different from those he was accustomed to in his tribe. But Colonel Vasconni Moundiata approached the dance floor and bellowed: "Cut the crap, can't you see that the President is here?" Colonel Vasconni Moundiata lost his temper and started kicking the dancers, and five infantrymen charged in and lashed out with rifle butts. We then noticed his father-of-the-nation frown as he motioned to National Carvanso. Carvanso steered his mount over to the white horse and listened attentively: "Shoot these idiots, they're disturbing the people." We applauded loudly: this was the first time a president had done such a thing in the name of the people. We walked over all the dead bodies. One man ran up to him, kissed his national legs and then killed himself, screaming just before taking a nose-dive: "Ah, Mr. President, what a beautiful gesture!" "Go ahead and grant him two national days of mourning," Lopez instructed Colonel Carvanso.

We took him all over the capital: up and down Valtaza, Dorbanso, and Corbanzo streets, to the Graci roundabout, the Opera. . . . Then on to Vatney, the seat of power. Later to city hall, to the Museum of the Nation, the military camps, the presidential port, the Place du 8 juin; we only made it back to the palace at dusk. We walked through all the rooms: the weapons hall, the diamond gallery, the corridor to the Companions of the Revolution, the presidential vault where only one of our eleven presidents had lain at rest because the other ten had been dumped in a mass grave for acts of high treason.

"What's that?"

"That's the map of the country, Mr. President sir."

"Aha! I see! But what are all those blue serpents?"

"The rivers, Mr. President."

"Aha! I see! And these smaller serpents?"

"The county roads, Mr. President."

"And those serpentlets?"

"The borders, Mr. President."

This is when we first heard his big fatherly laugh, and holding on to his sides, he pointed out just how stupid we all were: You've gone and left parts of the nation over in that shameful state in which those "Flemish" left them, you've left parts of the nation as if the pale power was still here. How shameful dear Mom, and you're such a bunch of fools! Hand me some red markers. And he set about redrawing the contours of the fatherland: put those infantrymen to work, and he proceeded to join together four straight lines, leaving areas of the sovereign territory over to our neighbors and taking over some of theirs because, my brothers and dear fellow countrymen, that's the sovereign decision of my hernia: the fatherland shall be square. How could you possibly expect us to live in a crater left behind by the colonizer! What kind of a people are we if we don't even have the freedom to fabricate our own borders? He enlisted the support of the media for this decision of his hernia and that's enough of this crap, and put those infantrymen to work instead of them spending their days mounting girls, clothed and fed by the state, and fucking up the shit and seizing power at the first opportunity. . . . And the sovereign decision of his big, big, big herniated balls was decreed in red ink, sending the infantrymen to the new borders, get the lot of them outta here, because an infantryman is made to fire old boy!

After delivering this first televised message on those god-damn TVs that keep teasing my hernia, he beckoned Carvanso, grabbed him by the shoulders, and gave him a couple of friendly taps: you're going to be my right-hand man, you'll be National Mom's right-hand man, and then he lowered his voice and asked him if, well, you know, it's not that easy being a bachelor these days: my appetite is up, go find me a hooker.

"Mr. President sir, you need to be more careful now with all the media around."

"Fuck the media, my appetite is up. And don't bring me one of those young ones. Those young ones aren't ripe enough."

He ate quickly, barely drinking. He called over the maitre d' to ask him why his meat was bloody. "I'm not a fucking cat, you know!"

"On the contrary, Mr. the *Presidente:* this is civilized cuisine."

"Well what on earth makes you think I'm civilized?"

". . . Ah, Mr. the *Presidente* . . ."

"Just get the hell out of here if you don't know how to cook like we do around here."

We applauded when he appointed Mom as the national cook.

"What about the title *National Hotelier,* Mr. President sir," suggested Carvanso.

"Why's that?"

"It sounds better, Mr. President."

He sounded out the title a few times and said, well, Ok then, you're right, it does sound better. And then came the day when, in front of the parliament, the Chamber of Elders, the diplomats and military High Command, the Apostolic Nuncio, he swore in Mom's name and mine, in the name of the fatherland, "You can trust me, I'll be a good president." He got down from the podium, sporting the colors of the nation, grinning from ear to ear, humming the national anthem, arms raised, hands joined together, escorted only by Mom, Carvanso, and Vauban, making his way through the cheering crowd, past the people dancing, covered in the fatherland's flowers, past the children who wanted to touch his hernia, the mothers who laid down their loincloths on the ground before him, the elders who wept tears of joy: we're going to have a good president, long live Lopez, son of National Mom, long live Carvanso! The air in the streets of the capital, Zappalo, Muerte, Grabanizar, Machinier, and in Passion Place was filled with the smell of palm-waving perspiring dancers and sulfurous gunpowder. He paused to eat and drink as my people do, joined them in my true dances, not like those assholes who imported everything from my colleague's country; I'm staying as I am, I'll eat what we eat here, drink what we drink here. He gathered one hundred and thirty nationals and fifteen former presidents living in exile in the country and I'll show you how we do politics around here; he set about dictating to our brother Carvanso the seventy-five articles that would make up the new "Order of Command": article 1: the fatherland shall be square; article 2: down with demagogy; article 3: National Mom is everyone's mother; article 4: no strikes and no more bullshit; article 5: down with the death penalty; article 6: I'm the president but you can knock me off whenever you see fit. . . . He set about appointing the Council of Ministers. Raise your hand. Who wants to be Minister of Dough? Who wants to be Minister of Stamps? So, who wants to be Minister of Roads who wants to be Minister of Rocks who wants to be Minister of Medication in charge of the status of women? He appointed a Minister of Borders, Minister of Customs, Minister of Transactions, Minister of Debts, Minister of Crops in charge of the forests, Minister of Fishing in charge of wildlife, Minister of Trade Negotiations. . . . But I'm going to be Minister of Infantrymen in charge of the people's freedom. My brothers and dear fellow countrymen, let's get to work. And while they sang the national anthem, he whispered to Carvanso: please, I'm so horny: fetch me a chick.

"Yes, Mr. President."

"And a real chick. How about a White one, I feel like a nice juicy White one."

"Yes, Mr. President."

For five years he managed the nation and the borders and damn those Mihilis who had risen up in the western region. Carvanso will teach them the lesson of my hernia; as for the Bhas who refuse to pay a tax offering, go dish out my big greasy balls, and those Bhozos rising up in the south, go put a curse on them Carvanso! Yes, Mr. President sir! And to relax he had his griot National Thanassi come over, who recounts the famous story of our brother Louhaza who loved his own mother so much and gave her twelve children including Talanso Manuel, National Mom's great-grandfather, a descendant of National Lakensi, founder of the fatherland, and tells the story of Lukenso Douma, founder of a vast kingdom that encompassed the Congo, Zaire, and Angola, and also how Manuelo Otha had founded Tamalassi . . . as well as the story of ex-Colonel Youhakini Konga, now that one's a long story, but I very much want it to be handed down from father to son for eternity, exactly in the way I heard it from my grandmother, the late Gasparde Luna. As he listened, his eyes looked as if they were going to pop out of his head: my God, our ancestors were truly great.

"Yes, Mr. President."

"They were born to shake things up."

"Yes, Mr. President."

"There aren't a thousand ways of being in this world. We'll muddle through somehow. Twenty percent Flemish blood running in our veins, not quite Black enough to be negroes, not quite White enough to be whites, but I'll find a way to shake things up too. . . . There aren't a thousand ways of being in this world."

"Yes, Mr. President."

It all started one May evening at the Alberto-Sanamatouff stadium. On a Tuesday, at that time of day when the sun begins to set, striping the hands of nature blood red, as the nocturnal concert of pulsating insect wings gets underway announcing Africa to the tourists in my colleague's country across the way. At that hour when you found out, as we all did, that Lieutenant Proserdo Manuelio had killed his brother-in-law Jolanso Amelia as he lay in a hospital bed: "After all the blood and sweat I put into making you a lieutenant! So apparently you want to take power? Well here it is: in the barrel of a gun."

Mother of Lopez! He had summoned all my brothers and dear fellow countrymen to this first evening meeting (because there's no time to waste: the nation's business can't wait), and so I'll start by explaining, ah yes, because I need to provide some background and explain the real reasons that motivated my hernia to get involved in power. And no, no, and no, it was not a coup d'état! I rebelled against the central authorities because we couldn't let *you know who* go on pissing on the fatherland, we couldn't let him go on confusing the nation with the legs of his badly fucked mom, a real loser, uncultivated, a rogue like him. It wasn't a coup d'état and he went ahead and pointed to a scar done by *you know who,* and then unbuttoned his fly and showed us another scar on the inner thigh, and several others as well, and then also his puckered ass and told us how, my brothers and dear fellow countrymen, Abbey Perrionni the son of his mother injured him there on the day he was caught with the ex-virgin Gléza Dononso: "This is truly shameful, Captain (that was my rank in those days), shameful that you can't find a real woman to throw your juices at when the streets are brimming with them, and it would be so much better than preying on those nice religious girls." He showed us what *you know who* did to his hernia the day he surprised him in bed with his daughter and well, what can you say, we're only human. I have to show you all these scars so that you can understand that being in power was not some kind of personal ambition of my hernia. Ah my brothers and dear fellow countrymen, I still haven't shown you the full extent of the injuries I sustained on the day when National Loutoulla caught me screwing his wife. . . . And so out came his male junk, ravaged by pock marks and blemishes, and please, don't go thinking I'm crazy: this is where the nation begins.

And that half-wit National Outranso who thinks this is all a big joke: I'm educating our people and all you can do is giggle from under Foni Sènso's beret. You must take me for that ex-President Jlanso Zenno who used to throw himself in front of young girls, with joined hands and hernia: you're a mulatto, mulatto girls drive me crazy. With Africa, clenched between their thighs. But let's get back to the subject at hand and let's not forget what a nasty world we live in: men, ah men! Always trying to conquer the world with their tools. But God rules, ah yes, my brothers and dear fellow countrymen, if we can still breathe this evening as we're breathing it's because God is with us. Because, and the evidence is clear, at two o'clock tonight, *you know who* tried to seize power with the help of a dozen or so little mechanics and a handful of demons who work with those goddamn TVs, what bullshit; do you really think, my brothers and dear fellow countrymen that you can seize power with big plans? But in that gang there was also a woman ah! Mother! And by all accounts she's as beautiful as the Queen of Sheba. And he started fondling his big greasy herniated balls, gently massaging them as we applauded, as our cries made their way to the heavens: Long live Lopez! Long live National Mom! He stroked his hernia in a premeditated fashion, "But before I fully expose them to your anger, my brothers and dear fellow countrymen, children of my loins, let's take stock of the situation: I'm no Gasparde Mansi who got his balls chopped off by some girl because he held sexual audiences in his office, I'm no Oustanno Ludia who killed people as one does a chicken, and I'm certainly no son-of-a-bitch Orenso Gemma whom you made a hero of the nation just because he left behind three hundred and twelve mulatto girls and seventy-five Black ones just like him; I am Lopez, National Mom's son, five years at the helm, now tell me, who have I killed?" We all shouted out: "No one! Long live Lopez, long live National Mom, down with crocodiles."

He was in full flow by now and these occasions meant a lot to his hernia. The story of my hernia is linked to the history of the fatherland, but don't worry, it's not a sad story. I am the spiritual son of Alberto Sanamatouff . . . and the story lasted until three in the morning and my brothers and dear fellow countrymen you come on back now at eleven tomorrow so we can discuss the fate of the mutinous rebels and agree on appropriate sanctions. In the meantime, my hernia is tired. Before we headed home, we overheard him whisper to brother Carvanso: "I'm thirsty, it's tough being a bachelor," and Carvanso saying:

"Mr. President, we have to watch out for the media."

"Ok."

He left on foot, shadowed by his aide Colonel Vauban, in charge of his personal security detail, and made his way up rue Felicio-Danarassi, avenue Panglos, past the Touré-Diakaté Market, then rue de la Pompe, Oreillidos Alley, and recounted the story of ex-Colonel Vadio who did what he did and no one did a damn thing about it, then the one about ex-National Loujango who got a long way in the science of looking the other way and what was done to him? When he reached the Corbanni-Suaze Bridge, he stood there for ten minutes watching the water running below: after all, I'm no Alvaro Diosso who for God's sake managed to study for his thirteen diplomas while president. The people are stupid and will remain that way.

"Yes, Mr. President. But the shirt need not fear the hot water."[1]

His heart filled with shadows, the heart of a prophet, the heart of a father, in the majesty of the human dream, from where you can contemplate our late General Also de Nonso donning his tiger-hunting gear, with full military stripes and plumes, gold tassels, exotic, magical medals heavy as gates, row upon row of military decorations across his chest because my people expect things to be eye-catching; ah Vauban, this is the country for people who are eye-catching. He starts telling Vauban the tragic story of our late brother Grabanizar during the shameful years of the Labinto regime that our people went and made a hero of the fatherland; we live in a nasty country and there ought to be a sign with gold-leaf lettering as you enter the port of Zouhando-Norta: *Nasty country.* That's how it is Vauban, since there are no wars, our infantrymen wreak havoc. Havoc because we're the world center for cowardice, the world capital for shame and sin, because we're the masters of lying and maliciousness Mom. . . . As for Vauban, listening attentively to him, with his pale courage that tried to save the world, you can see how much he loves this land while National Lopez, kaki giant that he is, sporting the nation's drama, the country slung over his shoulder, and that's enough bullshit, up rue Nolavinto, rue Fantar, past the café Les Rate-Bonheurs, over

---

1. Sony Labou Tansi's experimentation with language is a defining feature of his pioneering corpus of works. A range of devices are used, including subversions of well-known proverbs or translations of these from the original Lingala directly into French. Attempting to explain each and every translation choice would be futile. In this particular instance, however, the original French text read "L'eau chaude ne brûle pas le linge," a direct translation from the Lingala "Mai ya moto etumbaka elamba te"—the closest equivalent phrase in English might very well be "Don't let yourself be intimidated."

to the other side of the Place de la Patrie, to the sound of
Plazzinni Delaroux's music, you'd think that Delaroux guy
was French but he's actually the product of racial mixing:
French face, American manners, walks like an Arab, but
with a body typical of our region; today, he's performing in
the Oulanso-Mondia Gardens, in heavily accented French:

> Open your body
> To this fear
> Of the world
>
> The earth is a public good
> But your own turn is now
> So make sure you don't miss it
>
> In life
> Accomplish your part
> In this flesh between heaven and earth
>
> For us the future is now
> Sing your nerves and dance your heart
> There aren't that many ways
>
> Of being alive
> Long live you and so long live me

"My people are so beautiful when they dance to my poems!"

"They are, Mr. President."

Rue Fortio, rue Amela, rue Fontaine, this city, ah this
city, rue Foreman, boulevard ex-Duchaillu. . . . He reaches
the banks of the "Rouviera Verta" and God damn it this
city's stunning at this time of day! He then starts telling the
story of how that pig Oxbanso, on the very day I appointed
him Minister of Imports, tried to sleep with National Mom,
but I didn't kill him for that. You see Vauban, this is Satan's
village, only he whom you love can betray you. . . . His slippers are covered in mud. A dead dog has been abandoned in
the middle of the road; doesn't anyone work around here:

he moves the dead dog out of the way. Zamba-Town, a city in the south, even hotter at midnight than at noon, with its muddy swamps, breeding grounds for mosquitoes, where those who've managed to escape the stifling heat of their hut make love out in the open which is why you can hear the darkness groaning panting weeping and coughing. Zamba-Town, its symbolic hand extended out in peace, rue Gaza and the lingering signs of the latest curfew (now lasting sixteen months). And on the opposite bank of Lake Oufa: the Cité-du-Pouvoir, as exquisite as a love dream, oh how beautiful my hernia is, a monument built to them: thirty-five million dollars and now a patrimony of the state, a valued possession for them to enjoy today and in the future when my hernia has passed away. Well done to the nation!

It's still not quite that hour when the loudspeakers left behind by our late Colonel Pouranta Ponto start pouring my speeches into my people's ears; this innovation is hardly new, it was National Laountia's in fact, and Manuelo Sanka kept it up. Entire districts yelling because people have the shameful habit of changing stations when I speak, I ask Colonel Minister of Borders to install loudspeakers in every district, and to make sure they're all functioning properly while my hernia is at work, because it would be utterly shameful for a people not to listen to their president's speeches; make sure they're installed, Carvanso, and blasting so that they can hear me in their shameful wild animal sleep, so that they can hear me as they mount their wives, curse me and plot against me, as they insult me; at least make sure they can still hear me and let my voice deflower them, if they won't love me at least they can fear me, know me, smell me.

"Yes, Mr. President."

Rue des Toudonides, rue Whitman, rue Delaronzo: Eckerd Drugs, *open till Midnight* . . . his skeletal face starts to look like a mummy, he's scouring the different districts, he can feel a tickle tickle in his hernia, hang in there Vauban and I'll show you this country, fuck yeah: isn't it great here! A light rain had started to fall, wetting his denim uniform, he shrugged his shoulders: ever since I got a taste of that White woman that's all I want now, but tell me, old moldy dick Vauban: Why do you prefer men? And he launches into the anecdote about my war against Russia: eleven months in the rotten forest, without love, soulless, and I swear, Vauban, testicles are the next heart.

It was now Wednesday. The meeting got underway on time. You're going to laugh, yes, for sure you are, because Colonel Martillimi Lopez made Africa and the rest of the world laugh too. No no and no again: I wouldn't have seized your crappy power if my predecessor hadn't taken it upon himself to piss all over the fatherland's business, if he had just left you to starve to death rather than killing you off like rats, if he hadn't squandered seventy percent of the budget on Russian scrap metal. Here, that's the way things are— you visit any household you like at night and you'll hear the story of the late Colonel Martillimi Lopez, Commander-in-Chief of love and fraternity, and each version will have its own tone, saliva, dates, places; each household will allow their imagination to run wild, but this is the true story of the life of Colonel Martillimi Lopez, the son of our National Mom, as it is told by those in my ethnic group, with their taste for myth, amidst gales of laughter, Mom's very own Lopez who now lies in state in a stone casket in the National museum, his right eye permanently open, let him look at the fatherland for centuries to come, watch over us from his father's rotting sleep, let him protect us from tyrants, his dead person's gaze will continue to germinate in the memories of our children's children, it is the very symbol of our past, God is great! And this dead eye that watches over us is a miniature of the nation. No more bullshit, my brothers and dear fellow countrymen: let us love Lopez. He was a hundred times better than Dolsano Maniana is today.

"My hernia is sad today."

He grabbed the sides of his baggy kaki shorts and hoisted them up toward his belly-button, rearranging his big greasy herniated balls in their sack that reeked of corn beer and mustard.

"My brothers and dear fellow countrymen, my hernia is sad today." Not really sure why, but we applauded. That happens when you're in a crowd: one person does something and everyone joins in. Long live Lopez, Long live National Mom! And he says it again: "My hernia is sad." All of a sudden, I'm pretty sure, his handsome face looked much older.

"Ah, Mom! My hernia is sad. All because Cataeno Pablo, that shameful national, that sellout, but how could an insect like that Cataeno Pablo betray us in this way, how could he, how could he? Barely for the price of a tin of sardines, how shameful for us . . ."

Vauban, the head of personal security, stood at his side as he delivered his speech to the nation. His hernia was sagging, giving off a nauseating stench of eggplant and spices, scales were breaking out all over his body in protest at the sweltering heat, and there was also a hint of sugar and the aroma of wormwood, and a smattering of sour urine along with the musty vapors of his nocturnal juices, that kaki odor, a terrible noxious smell. He spoke loudly, our tricolor colonel did, barricaded off from his nights as national lover, conqueror of virgins! Let my people sing and dance: I adore them with the love of a mammal, Lopez one Tuesday night came directly into the world making mystical sounds, right in front of the Pope, and was then raised in poverty and total destitution, National Mom wiped his backside with a hemp rag, just regional Lopez at the time of Sanamatouff, then later Lopez of my ethnic group under Faramento, and today Lopez that my people sing and dance to, Lopez of my people who don't want me to step down because of the prestige I embody, Lopez for peace, after all I gave the people back to the people, the world back to the world, Lopez aimed at swine like Cataeno Pablo, that miserable national *who who who* went into hiding with Laure and her mother, Cataeno Pablo whose meat we were going to distribute here today to those of you at this meeting, to *you the national,* and not to the you of expatriates who shamefully support the rebel command by handing them seventeen Mauser-52 rifles and eleven Sten guns. Come to think of it, is mister the diplomat in charge of the Belgian embassy and all its "flemishings" here today? Close down their diplomacy, close it down right now and take the first plane in the first direction, and if you don't want to, in the name of Lopez, I'll ship you to His Majesty of the shame of the "Flemish" who have always pecked at us, go ahead and close it down, and I'll also ask the whole Flemish colony settled throughout my hernia to leave the sovereign territory and return to their native Flemishything, in the name of the Revolution, in the name of National Mom and in my own name too, and the same decision of my hernia goes for Italy, yes, my brothers and dear fellow countrymen, Italy has also been mixed up in Cataeno Pablo's harebrained nationalist ideas, Italy, and Cuba as well: same crisis, same sanctions, and in two days time, my brothers and dear fellow countrymen, if you lay hands on a "Fleming," Italian, or Cuban, you have my full p . . . , you have my full permission to waste him. To conclude, my brothers and dear fellow countrymen, I'm going to bring out five "Pablosard" rebels captured by the nation's infantrymen, I'm going to have them come up to the mic, so that it's not only my hernia making decisions. I'll ask some questions, and you can decide as to the severity of their actions and the punishment they deserve. (A pause). My brothers and dear fellow countrymen, I'm being told there are in fact six and not five, bring them up. And my God National Mom, what do we have here? This young girl too? No no no: such a delicious creature, but why on earth mother? No no no this can't be so! We've all witnessed his hernia swell when he gets angry, but the swelling quickly dissipated, now come closer my girl, but how on earth does a girl like that, barely twenty years old, with that kind of body, as juicy as they come, and those thighs my God, National Mom, oh my goodness, and those fleshy breasts, a girl who should be able to cage every man in her dreams, imprison every man in her vertiginous bodice and the magic of her thrusts, go figure my brothers and dear fellow countrymen, unless one has been badly fucked, as is often the case for most of the girls in the area near the lake. Just how is it that Flora and the Mona Lisa, brought together in this way, just how is it that such a beauty can come into the world . . . "Like this!" someone shouted out from the crowd. And just like that they were silenced for centuries upon centuries, and that'll teach you to have big mouths and to use them as instruments of hate: get rid of the corpses and go ahead and tell your god-damn TVs that the President's speech claimed several lives.

Under a sun that had become unhinged, in this very same Alberto-Sanamatouff Stadium, National Alberto Sanamatouff that the "Flemish" had incessantly pecked at, God rest his soul! Pecked to death through their local "Flemishings," poor old Alberto, the former conqueror of regimes, Martillimi's former father-in-law, former police chief of his hernia, proud member of the national bureau of hernia sufferers, former Special Representative of his very own hernia to the United Nations, the late-lamented Alberto Sanamatouff, national hero with no other heroism than his "herotic" capacities which, if truth be told, were closer to gushings, and the rumor goes around and around: what a horny devil! With his hellish aptitude for squirting, national tomcat known to all the country's bitches and as you know, as we all well know: shameful lover of National Mom . . .

And he repeats the refrain: just how is it, that such a simple body, such a complete body, with the proportions of an angel, so physically blessed, a body that in the end is frightening because, my brothers and dear fellow countrymen, one can't really tell where it begins and where it ends. He cradles his privates that are beginning to stir: easy now, we're talking politics: you can't chase after two sets of big balls at the same time. Check out that fine-looking ass won't you, it's as enchanting as a campfire. My brothers, such beauty is making me restless. He stuck his enormous hand into his pants and stroked his kaki sack: easy now, we're talking politics. But "they" ignore their master's instruction, and begin to undulate, trickle, to emit a smell because of this ready-made nudity before my eyes. And this is how far Cataeno Pablo has driven the nation: he wanted to turn our girls into weapons, "Over my dead hernia!" Ours is a land of peace and love, we're a people made of love: don't let them sell the skin from our hernias without having killed them first, and he cradles his hernia the same way he had on the day he asked Europe's Cubans that are the British to go back to their small island of misfortune because you have become humanity's biggest mark of shame, more so even than the Jews and the Armenians: you add fuel to the fire of my people. He stuck his hand back in his pants and unconsciously sniffed his fingers openly and for the whole crowd to see, come closer my girl: my dear sweet girl, in the name of the Revolution, in the name of the fatherland, in the name of all our mothers, you're going to ask for the nation's forgiveness. For the forgiveness of the earth that has given you everything, the forgiveness of martyrs and their families, of the Constitution and don't let me forget a special forgiveness for France who helped us capture you, forgiveness also for Amerindia and for Poland, come closer to the mic because you're going to ask for forgiveness as our ancestors did, your hands folded across your chest, your forehead touching the ground, I'm listening, and speak up so that Mom's international news agencies who always misrepresent the events of my hernia can hear you loud and clear . . .

"But Colonel, she can't speak."

"What? Why not?"

"We cut off her tongue because that's what the rebels do to us."

"You're teasing my hernia . . ."

"They cut off Colonel Touvanso Dieu's, they cut off ex-Captain Honse's, they cut off ex-Colonel Fouga's mother's tongue, they cut off the tongue of every soldier in Colonel Letanso's battalion. And one day they'll cut off National Mom's."

"My hernia's blazing . . ."

"They cut off . . ."

"Shut the fuck up, Outranso . . ."

He flew into such a rage, just like he had last year when France celebrated July 14th right here and Mom's my witness it's the French who drove me to taking ex-comrade Armando Mundi! The same rage on November 11th when to my great shame the Germans slept with National Mom.

"I don't understand the people around here: they all think they're the President! Let me remind you: *the* President, that's me. No no and no again: everyone behaves as if everyone were me, but why, why is that? Can't you take the trouble to consult with me first?"

And he goes over to her: "Don't worry, my dear girl, this earth is cannibalistic," and he drapes his kaki jacket over her to conceal the nudity they've ruined but don't worry I will take revenge. He tears up the supposed depositions made by your mothers; fear not, I will take revenge. He tears up your mothers' official reports and the emblem of your mothers' nation, and to hell with the support they've thrown out the window, I will take revenge. He rips up your mothers' beret; I'm going to be a civilian again; he tears off his military stripes, plumes, and tassels, and Colonel Outranso where the fuck are you: present.

"You gave the order to cut off her tongue, I'm going to cut yours off too."

"It wasn't me, it was Darcanio."

"Ah! Well, where's Darcanio?"

"It wasn't me, it was Lafondia."

"Well, where the fuck's Lafondia?"

"It wasn't me it wasn't me it wasn't me ah ah ah!"

He began to strangle him. His eyes bulged bulged bulged. Then silence. Ever since everyone at the High Command thinks he became President . . . and now, what are you going to say to the foreign press, what are you going to say to the Pope and all those diplomats? What will you say to them? You're going to, ah what a load of bullshit! He leaps at him again with that rage that pushes me to turn over power to civilians, he stamps on his testicles because you can't be president after all and make those kind of decisions without my input and isn't it those filthy beasts filling your head with these ideas, with your shameful business schemes but I'll show you, you need people on this earth who know that a president, well, that a president can get angry too. . . . For God's sake you should at least know what your male utensils are good for, at the very least, hold on I'm going to cut them off. But Colonel Carvanso steps in now, take it easy Mr. President sir.

"Ok, fine, I'm going to calm down but not before I've shown him how . . ."

He gently caresses his hernia. Soothes him. Hands him sugared almonds and he gobbles them down. Spoon feeds him a couple of scoops of mustard; easy now Mr. President.

"Ok Carvanso, I'm going to calm down."

His chinchilla is brought in, he places it on his right shoulder and its tail sweeps the ground on the same spot where Lafondia drooled. They fetch his parrot Narka who is able to convert the rest of the speech into birdsong: "*I oyo o io yo!*" keeping the reference to his hernia in Mom's mother tongue. In this same Alberto-Sanamatouff national stadium that the "Flemish" had pecked away at, still full to capacity, under the same broiling sun, the crowd still restless in that one section and the police should be doing their job rather than counting my big herniated balls before they hatch, with all those god-damn TVs aimed at his bitter writings, the sun warming his hernia my brothers and dear fellow countrymen, offering up for the mercy of my people this body the infantrymen ruined. Tears running down his cheeks. And we cry along with him because we know those tears.

"This flesh they have blinded."

"Yes, Mr. President."

"This body made of prime cuts of meat."

"Yes, Mr. President."

"It must be said that the world is a very nasty place."

"Indeed, Mr. President."

"But I'll recast you as a monument . . . my dear tender girl, birthed into this world of the world, intoxicating girl who arouses my kaki juices. I'll recast you woman, a place of worship, radiant flesh: that's the decision of my hernia, you'll be my wife. The bachelor life is over! The crowd at the stadium erupted in applause, but she started crying.

"Did you hear me, I'm going to marry her?"

"Yes, Mr. President."

An eleven-gun salute was fired across the capital and the city rose as one and shouted: "Yes, Mr. President." And then silence. "Quiet, National Daddy is loving his wife." No music. No traffic. The streets were empty. This lasted two days.

"**WHY ARE YOU CRYING MY SWEET ANGEL?** Here, have some mango, drink a little. You are in the palace. Wear this dress. Would you like to dance?". . . He lavished her with jewelry and glee, showed her every nook and cranny of my hernia: he danced in front of her, sang her the songs of his people, and "I promise you I'll love you just as I would have if you still had your tongue, here, have some of this fruit, drink some of this drink." But she kept on crying.

He describes her: full mouth, savage mouth, aching, I'll recast you as a monument, mother of the fatherland. He throws himself at her feet, go ahead and walk all over me if you like. I may be the President but my blood rushes to you: you see? And he tells her how they'll never have a better president in this wretched world; I'm not like that Trimitti Lopez who used to hang them like poultry, or that Luigui Lafundia who used to skin them, and I'm not like Manu-elio Samba who used to feed them to the leopards. He told her of the shameful day when Adamonso Liguas became a Pharaoh, but that, never, over my dead hernia. He started showing off my body that you can see before you with all the scars from my war against Russia, made sure the door was double-locked so that Colonel Vauban wouldn't inter-rupt our afternoon nap. The metal bars. The columns. Im-pregnable stone walls. Cannons, tanks, big ball launchers. All these "utensils" you can see. . . . He gets out his fallacious hernia divorced from the salt and drool of his bachelor nights but there's no longer any question of this. He bathes in eggplant, spices, roots, and leaves; they say it helps soothe hernias. He unloaded his father-of-the-nation juices on her, rotten juices that won't give him a son: I don't understand. He tells her all about Jacqueline Daras that the French sent to chop off his hernia but I forgave them. He explained how, and with whose support, my ex-right-hand man National Yallama attempted a coup d'état, but serves him right: he came up against the people. While he gives her the juices from my mother he explains how the Amerindians tried to throw power into the hands of the late Colonel Vanzio Pablo and my dear girl be good be goooooood. But she kept on crying. For three days and three nights he's tried to console her with his cries and his juices.

"Hold on a second, I need to see National Mom or she'll be worried."

And Mom, here's your child. He gives her a kiss and she starts crying. Don't cry Mom, I'm safe. They aren't going to harm me.

"Well they're not plotting for nothing."

"You know, Mom, I'm a good president. I was elected by the dead and the living, with 99.9 percent of the vote. Please Mom, no more tears. I'm in a hurry Carvanso, come and console her."

"Yes, Mr. President."

He rushes back to her, tells her all about the national historic Colonel Fetranso, child of the nation, hero of the people, but the Germans really did a job on him, and ex-Colonel Fetranso almost became my wife, but you must be familiar with Vauban's proverb: *Live by herniated balls, die by herniated balls.* I beg you, show me your teeth. As enchanting as a campfire. Show me your legs. Show me your heart. My God, you're so beautiful. He tells her all about my first wife who cheated on me with everyone and I sent her on her way yes I did: I forgive everything except for indiscretions of the hernia. One evening I came home from the office and found her with Barbara Janco. "What are you doing

here, Barbara Janco?" He turned around and I put six bullets in his hernia. He coughed up his traitor of the fatherland's blood. But what about her, what am I to do with her?
I'm out of bullets. I grabbed her neck and squeezed it, kept
on squeezing, it was revolting and she puked up her dog's
life. Her corpse even crapped a big hot turd. But you, you're
a real hot one: let's talk about your body, let's talk about
your teeth, let's talk about that passionate throat of yours
that unravels the world. He rushes over to the national radio station and announces his decision—I'm going to marry
her—, he takes care of the invitations himself: France, the
British Isles, the Russian president, those Flemishythings,
the Pope. His guest list includes thirty-seven heads of state
while my people start building the village of my hernia, I
can't get married in this great big shameful palace in which
Tatarasho betrayed the nation by slaughtering all those
people from my Ghozis ethnic group. He transfers seventy
million to the newspapers and let's talk about this event in
historic terms. He signs an order proclaiming July 7th my
official wedding day so that it is recorded that way in the
archives, and then he comes back toward you my paradise,
my heaven and my earth.

"You were there and no one wanted you. But now that
I've chosen you, they will all want you."

He tells her about Bamba Outificanso who betrayed me
with a guitar player. And Léo Levourto who betrayed me
with my cook. What is it you women are after? He told her
how ex-Captain Canza had gotten the woman he loved like
I love you pregnant. And do you know how I found out?
One evening, when I felt like comforting her, I asked her to
show me her breasts. I started fondling them and a white
liquid came oozing out of her nipples. Aha! What are you
going to name the child? *Son of a bitch,* what kind of a moron
does she take me for? How did this happen, how: I haven't
seen you for thirteen months and now you're pregnant. I
was just back from my war against the communists. How
did this happen?

"What are you talking about?"

My anger took over: I cut open her belly and showed her the umbilical cord.

"You women are all the same, that's the truth; you don't want us to confuse you with men. Do you know ex-Colonel Miguel Tournanso? What's up with you, Carvanso, why do you come barging in like that unannounced?"

"Colonel, the nation is in danger: Ayelé Ayoko Tite has risen up and is bearing down on the capital."

"How many men does he have with him?"

"No one really knows, Colonel."

"Bring it on! My hernia is waiting for them. What's a bunch of upstarts straight out of a shithole like Galzarra think they're going do? Let them come." Then he set off across the capital on his big white horse, dressed in the way Vauban dresses, his head held high, a hand held proudly across the chest. We prayed he would be killed during this military campaign and that our virgins would finally be safe from his hernia. Candles were now scarce in Zamba-Town: the people had exhausted the supplies. Cardinal Dorzibanso made a fortune from all the extra confessions he heard. I'm remembering all those *huamani* we burnt at night at all the crossroads, poor plant! We stopped eating meat on Fridays: "Let him die." But he wasn't going to die that easily.

He summoned ex-Colonel Carvanso to make it clear that he wanted the Zamba-Town–Maha railway line cleared for his big balls the week of the wedding; he called Cardinal Dorzibanso to inform him first-hand that you'll be the one to marry us; he sent for his brother same father same mother to remind him to let the authorities know that highways 1, 2, 3, and 4 should be open for my hernia to use, let the Italians know while you're at it that the Three-Continents Hotel should be at my disposal, as well as the beach at Valtaza-Diego; he instructed the Minister of Dough to give National Mom three hundred and twelve million for the catering and to set aside the same amount again for the wedding attire and consorts.

Now hurry up with the preparations. He paraded his hernia up and down the hallways of the presidential palace to check that everyone was hard at work. Hurry up now will you! Ha, if I was Darbanso I'd have you shot at the first opportunity! And what if I were like Manuel Lansio who took the precaution of having two cooked as a way to ensure the third was giving his all! But I'm a good president and you take advantage of that to climb in my pants. Where the fuck is Razo Fansa?

"Right here Mr. President sir."

"I've never quite understood why that parking facility of yours never has the right number of cars available for my hernia to use, but if you stumble this time, you're a dead man."

He has a word with his cousin Martillimi Lavouza who'll never fully understand why he isn't president yet, but if you mess up this time I'll shove the PA system down your throat. He has a word with the Minister of Audiovisuals and National Mom because I'm begging you Mom none of your mommy handmade official invitations, this is how you hold a fork, and the knife this way, the drinking glass like this, hold your napkin in this way and I'm begging you Mom no stuffing your face like a pig, and no grazing like a cow at the table: just remember you're the President's mom.

He drops in on Simone des Bruyères, my babe from Vauban's country, to explain to her why I'm getting married but my heart is still with you I won't stop loving you with an irreproachable love, you are as beautiful as the sun and as copper.

"I want to hear you say I am even more beautiful."

"You are as beautiful as the papaya fruit in my garden."

"Even more beautiful."

"You are as beautiful as the day I was born."

Mother from Vauban's country. Who knows how she came into the world. Love me in the way people love in your country. He buries his face in her bosom and laps up the droplets that have started running. Show me that the world over is still in the world. Be good. And he plants his fallacious hernia in her.

"Gently now, Mr. President."

"You can't make love properly by being gentle. Be strong. Don't be fragile like they are in my colleague's country. I'm handling you in the way we do around here. You see, you see?"

He goes and has a few words with Colonel Isidro who spends the nation's money like he sprays his juices about. He reviews his calendar: Thursday night: rue de la Buomba; Saturday night: Payadiso; Sunday night: the Arcades. . . . He goes to say good night to his little Indian babe you should have tasted her Isidro, sober as you are, you would have given up looking for other women: she handles you like no other. That Senegalese girl Sey is a good fuck too, if only you'd tried her. . . . He has a shot of *sowassi* to give him a little boost. This wedding's the chance to get drunk like my people do. He eats and then vomits. Tell me what my people are saying, Comrade Carvanso, anything.

"They say you're a good president. But you're marrying the one who tried to kill you."

"That's true, Carvanso: she's beautiful in a way no other woman has ever been. She's the Queen of Sheba. Have you seen the hips on her?"

"Yes, Mr. President."

"I'll take her thrusts anytime."

He turned away from Carvanso and took a nice long piss in a flower vase just like my people do, splashing urine on his kaki legs, fermented urine.

"You know, Carvanso, I don't see how the consumption of pussy can possibly interfere with the smooth running of the affairs of the state."

"You're right, Mr. President."

"You must have heard about Louis XIV, and you know Vauban—well, those guys had all kinds of mistresses, and I'm telling you, Carvanso, screwing is the next heart of humanity."

"Yes, Mr. . . ."

This god-damn country where the president is expected to do everything himself. He heads over to see National

Thoulouse, also known as Vauban, head of personal security:

"Is everything alright?"

"Yes, Mr. President."

Since no one is currently engaged in anti-national activities, I head out to the districts to see my people. Without an escort: Vauban though isn't far behind, but don't let anyone see you. And he disguises himself as a peasant so that he won't be recognized and to see what the people are saying about him. He mingles with a group of construction workers and shuffles along with them, trampling the mud and dirt under foot. No one takes any notice of him. He overhears them bickering, singing, and speaking badly about his hernia, saying awful things about National Mom for giving us such a shameful son, National Mom who's still fornicating at her age; they talk about that bastard Colonel Carvanso, of his brother who stashed the National finances away over in Switzerland as if we had no need for money; they speak badly of the infantrymen who have no shame or modesty pissing on the nation the way they do. . . . Blending in with the masses, he just goes along with them, joins in the singing. He's surrounded himself with a bunch of rascals. Nevertheless he sings:

> If I were a little little mouse
> I'd go digging in his big greasy hernia
> If I were a little little cat
> I'd go hunting in his hernia
> If I were a little little flea
> I'd choose his hernia . . .

He sings the chorus with them. His denims are now covered in mud, his heavy artillery dangling about to the pace and rhythm of the tune; those who come over to fetch the mud for the hut they're building are picking up the tune.

"My people are beautiful when they sing."

And he starts singing louder than the rest, introducing words from the national anthem. One guy bawls him out, because who the hell gets the mortar ready with work boots on. But he keeps on singing and steps on the guy who then hurls mud at him. He's got mud all over him, in his nostrils, his ears, his hair.

"Who the hell told you to get the mortar ready with your boots?"

A big muscular guy knocks him down in the mud and they all laugh at him.

"What's the deal with this guy, he's dumber than a woman's backside!"

And only then do they catch a glimpse of his hernia and they're mortified.

"It's . . . it's the President!"

They see themselves at the gallows, facing the firing squad, the infantrymen on their knees with their rifles to the ready waiting for the order.

"It's . . . it's the President!"

That was enough to send them scurrying off in different directions shouting, "It's the President!" Those who couldn't run away threw themselves before him, on their knees, shaking, licking his big greasy herniated balls; they're in tears, begging for mercy.

"This won't happen again. It's Larso Laura's fault for misleading us, it was his song mercy mercy mercy for the sake of our children; it's Larso Laura who's against you . . ."

"You have nothing to fear, I'm the forgiving kind. Because I'm a good president. I'm not like Alto Maniana who used to hang you like monkeys. And anyway, that song is beautiful. And in any case, you can't stage a coup d'état with clay. You can't seize power with songs."

And he massages his hernia.

"I'm not like Sadrosso Banda who put stuff in the eggplant. Nor am I like that Manuelo de Salamatar who drank your blood to make him feel like he was in the world. Almost a gallon of blood every night."

They're singing, but in his honor this time. He shuffles along with them until lunchtime. Then he heads back to his jeep, drenched in mud, and no way I'm washing it off,

I'll get married as you see me now. That's my gift from the people. Where the hell are you, Colonel Thoulouse, oil-rubbed bronze, gray eyes, blonde hair, 5 feet 9 inches tall, lasting symbol of my long and tumultuous cooperation with Europe, 210 pounds of brain and muscle at my disposal, a pederast (every country has its own monuments), and goes home to give National Mom a kiss, you see Mom how the people love me. He teaches her the words to the beautiful song they sang in his honor. The heavens have not been good to him: but they did let him hold on to a lovely national male voice, the beautiful eyes of a wild animal, and his shiny white teeth and goatee. Then, without undressing, his boots still on, grubby, he pounced on his presidential bed and fell like a lion into a deep sleep, sleeping on his seventy-five medals from the war on communism, his hands tightly clenched, fly unbuttoned, a real muddy caiman crocodile, teeth poking out, right hand on his gun, stinking of egg-plant beer, snoring.

"I want to get married in this outfit."

National Carvanso tries to convince him otherwise:

"But Mr. President sir, the Whites will mock you. They'll mock you for sure. Reporters will take advantage of this."

"But Carvanso, the Whites can mock me as much as they like: their very own Louis XIV only washed a handful of times and that was the life of Louis XIV, and then there's Vauban, and Frederic II. He fell into his historian's laughter to describe Catherine of Russia who . . ."

"But Mr. President, I'm convinced they'll mock you, it's in your nostrils, all over your ears."

"It's the mud of the people. Let them mock me. Africa must remain Africa. Yes, Africa must give the world back to the world."

And so, covered in mud, he walked the route past the invited delegations and their representatives. Everyone applauded. He shakes hands with His Majesty of the Flemish and embraces him in the way of the ancestors, leaving some historic mud on him; then the hand of Her Majesty the Princess of Denmark in the way of the ancestors, leaving some historic mud on the back of her royal costume; he embraced all the friends of the people in the way of the people and with the gift of his historic mud. Hey, it's you, my colleague from the neighboring country, and he lets him have some of the people's mud. You can see a faint smile on the face of the people with all these illustrious guests getting a dose of his hernia and local mud on them, on this historic day when I'm marrying the most beautiful girl on earth. And then the delegation makes its way to the exact site where National Mom buried my placenta and no bullshit: this is now a place of worship; then from there on to visit the cathedral my hernia erected thanks to the Good Lord. Next they boarded a plane and headed four hundred and thirty-five miles north of my hernia to see where I will be buried. . . .

Cardinal Dorzibanzo, who's refusing to marry me, is brought in. "Untie him and let him get to work!"

"Mr. President, Dorzibanso says he can't."

"Why the heck not?"

With his torn cassock, bloody eyes, hands tied, his mitre all wrinkled, they bring him before his hernia.

"I'll cut your dick off if you fail me on this."

Ex-Cardinal Dorzibanso asks if, for better, for worse, his hernia wants to take this girl.

"But Dorzibanso, the worst has already happened since the infantrymen cut off her speech utensil; they cut off her kissing instrument."

He gives him his yes, his historic yes and here's her yes, yes for me and yes for her.

"Historic Colonel, Your Excellency, I can't bless this union."

"Watch out Dorzibanso, my hernia is about to explode."

He looked at him with astonishment and said it again: I can't do this.

"You're going to come up against my hernia. And believe me, it won't be like banging on butter, so you'd better watch out: my intestines are growling. You're stirring my kaki nerves and the shame I feel in front of the Whites who'll think I'm no longer the supreme master in my own house. Now just get on with it and bless this union or be prepared to die from this national anger that I can feel swelling. Show some respect for my meat stick that's bowing here before your God."

"Mr. President, I can't bless this union, not with this girl here who's crying when she should be smiling. The Church would be ashamed, our Lord would die a second time of shame. Because, Mr. President, Christ is watching me and I can't go pounding shit into the scars left by the nails; I can't give him piss instead of water."

"Dorzibanso, don't go remaking the Lord in your image. No no and no again: there's no trifling with the bites of a hernia."

He kneels down as he would before the Lord, and begs him: "Dorzibanso, my cheek held out for you, for the love of thy neighbor, if you don't want to chow down on my herniated balls in seven sessions," and then he switches his tone: "You can't do this to me; remember how you became a cardinal with the support of dick, ah, my hernia is sad! We've always been good friends, friends and brothers, try and understand."

But there was nothing to be done, this leech won't go along with him, he mimics the voice, he says things in National Mom's mother tongue and amen! The people answer, amen. Folks didn't seem aware this was a hoax. He paraded his hernia around, his chest tinkling with the medals he had won fighting Russia who came to sell my hernia ideas rather than feeding my people. Ha, my people: we have here the proverbial truth of that *The voice don't make the man.*

Dorzibanso was locked away after the church ceremony to make sure no one would find out the secret of the Mass said in Mom's mother tongue. Then came the big night and the gala where he danced with Princess Honglanni leaving behind his trail of strong sweat and smearing her with mud. He also danced with Colonel Domingo Pinto's ex-wife and smeared the people's mud on her too, as he did with the mayor of Zamba-Town's ex-wife, and Her Majesty the Queen of the Flemish; he danced with all those invited by my hernia and smeared them all with the people's mud.

"This earth will accompany me to the grave."

He also offered General de Laborderie, my first wife's father, the people's mud. As he danced the dance of my people, he distributed mud to all the men. By three in the morning, his hernia really started to reek. Truly nauseating vapors. Enough to make you puke. Stomach-churning. The scales on his sweltering herniated balls secreted a revolting stench. Stale juices. As he danced the dance of my people, a loincloth fastened around the waist, his hernia began to stink in that historic way, giving off a rotten nitrous odor. His brochette of medals chimed away. He sang in honor of my colleague whose country came later than ours. After the big feast and binge drinking where he got loaded the way the people do, he collapsed in an armchair right there in the middle of the party, both hands gripping his hernia.

"Don't disturb him."

In shirtsleeves, buttons in the wrong hole, holding his socks, National Carvanso comes to let him know that Mr. President sir your new spouse has hanged herself.

"What do you mean *hanged*?"

"Yes, Mr. President, she has hanged herself."

"I . . . I don't understand. What language are you speaking, Carvanso?"

"She killed herself."

"My herniated balls have dropped."

He thinks aloud just how magical last night was. As enchanting as a campfire. We danced together. I listened to her heart beating against my chest. Ha, that tempestuous shape of a body. Tender and made in the likeness of a goddess. With lips that incite fear and lunacy. There she stood, well-calculated, designed in the very image of my hernia. With her milk-filled breath, child of my own knotted breath. What do you mean *hanged*? Is what you're saying there true? He sheds real tears the way we do, and it was clear he loved her. He's been bawling for the past six days, drowning in tears and snot, hasn't touched his food, his eyes are covered because I can still feel but I would never dare look at her corpse. Three times now he's tried to kill himself over your body that's punishing me. Each time our brother Carvanso got there just in time. Colonel that I like to call Vauban consoles him. National Mom consoles him.

"I let her have the very best copy I had of my soul."

While the infantrymen were busy handing out black armbands to the people at three hundred coustrani each for the period of mourning, ah National Mom I'm inconsolable: he sets off to Italy, France, and Gainesville on a journey of mourning, ah good God I'm inconsolable! He accompanies her glass hearse all the way to the foot of Mount Fuji. . . . Ah! Then he heads to Tahiti.

"What do you mean, but what do you mean *hanged*? I gave her everything: my hernia, the nation, my heart, my strength . . . I gave her everything, and I mean *everything*. I even threw myself at her feet like a big mistake."

When he returned home, brother Carvanso brought Camizo Diaz before him, who along with thirty-six mutinous infantrymen revolted, such incredible cowardice. To attempt to take power when I'm away, you see how the mice play here? And who's at the head of this mousetrap, no other than that Camizo Diaz whom I personally went and found at the other end of the fatherland, who didn't have the slightest idea in those days as to how to eat a sausage. I promoted him to Sergeant, then raised him to Captain then to Colonel just like everyone else, and this is the thanks I get. And just look at him standing there all naked my brothers and dear fellow countrymen. What more does he have than my hernia?

That section of the crowd that always makes things harder than they need to be shouted out: "The hernia," and Mom's Lopez burst out laughing: "That's it, I'm better now." And he orders Carvanso to cut off Colonel Camino Diaz's speech instrument, go ahead and preserve him in formaldehyde, and have him put up on the wall in my bedroom next to the portrait of Mom, just below the portrait of my late wife Atélu-Léa, who died for the fatherland, hanged by those fucking idiots who wanted me to believe that she hanged herself but what do you mean *hanged*? Now please, let's get the investigation underway.

WHAT WOULD YOU HAVE DONE if I'd been like Yao Tananso, who would call the Nation's Council to an urgent meeting for just about any bullshit reason like when my cousin Zozo Portes Luna "slept" my other cousin Argento Comma's wife? I'm not like Dimitri Lamonso who moved the capital to his mother's village. I'm Lopez, National Mom's son, nothing like Lazo Lorenzo who stuffed three cases of pre-filled ballots down the villagers of Yam-Yako to teach them how to vote. What I offer you is the only country in the world where democracy still means something. You get to ask all the questions, and I get to give you the answers; after all, you've had your Lan Domingo who hid the public treasury under Mom's bed, and that faggot Cornez Caracho who gave all the ministers syphilis. Barça Baldi was the one who started all the financial crimes around here, and didn't you go and make him a national hero? And I'm not like that Valso Paraison who took fifteen years in power to take hold of power. The soccer match opposing Juven National and Anzcox will take place right after the speech, or none of you shitheads would have come to the meeting. You love sport and that's how I got you, and that's enough bullshit for Christ's sake! Then he makes his way back to the palace, on foot, to show everyone that the people have never been against him. Trailed by Vauban, a personal gift from my colleague, in charge of the investigation into the murder of my wife and head of security. He laughs at the thought of poor old Vauban who prefers men even though the whole country is swarming with women who want nothing more than my juices, Vauban with his worn-out backside, he laughs, never, I'll never be like him. And he explains that if the Amerindians became what they are, it's first and foremost because they knew how to handle women.

"What's the latest with the investigation?"

"We arrested a certain Laure and the Panther."

"Good."

"But it would seem, Mr. President, that your life is in danger."

"I want to see the prisoners."

"Yes, Mr. President."

He takes a closer look at the prisoner: "I don't recognize him."

"But National Colonel, it's him."

Handcuffs rubbing against the bone. No skin, no eyes, no lips, no ears, and no more hernia. "I don't recognize him."

"How could you do this to him?"

"He would have done the same thing to you, Colonel, if he had taken power and things had been the other way around."

"Ah, all right then! How are you doing, Campalousca?"

"I'm doing well, Mr. President sir."

"Ah, all right then! But you've lost your skin. You should have known better than to mess with power."

"Mr. President, you know as well as I do that everything on this earth ends up hurting you."

"Why don't you shut the fuck up, Campalousca: you're hardly in a position to be giving lessons. And I never asked you to go off and fornicate with those Amerindians. You wanted to die, well now you're going to."

This is when Colonel National Jescani entered with some very bad news Mr. President. "Speak, Jescani."

"Speak now, will you."

"I need to speak with you in private, Mr. President."

"Don't worry about Campalousca; he's a dead man."

"Even the dead should not hear what I'm about to say."

"Ok."

And so he chased the Colonel he likes to call Vauban out of the room, and he chased National Mom and Carvanso out of the room too. He chased my griot National Thanassi out of the room; now speak Jescani, we're alone.

"Mr. President, the good lord is preparing a coup d'état: because Cardinal Dorzibanso went underground with all those wretched demons from the Sixty-Five prison. Alas, Mr. President: they've gathered in front of the old Sáo Juano Cathedral, singing, and threatening to go on a hunger strike."

"How many of them are there?"

"Maybe as many as sixty thousand."

"They are anti-people: kill the whole bloody lot of them!"

"Yes, Mr. President. But keep a close eye on Carvanso: we came across a rough draft of a handwritten letter at his place. Here it is."

Jescani hands him the piece of paper. He says my hernia is sad. Everyone wants to seize power. And he collapses into an armchair. Why are people like this in this country? Aha! That's Carvanso's handwriting for sure. But I'll let him come to me. He lacks imagination: he wants to be a hero of the fatherland, but trust me, his imagination's not worth ten coustrani. It's always the same with these dickless idiots; they think they can solve every problem with a drop of saliva.

He gets up and walks over to the mirror, takes a long hard look at himself before taking another look at the letter that my hernia got hold of at brother Carvanso's place. No no and no again: you should know better than to mess with words. He looked away quickly, almost as if the sight of his own face made him feel sick.

"I don't get it: even Carvanso wants to overthrow me. He goes to stand in front of a portrait of himself, strokes his big shameful hernia that nature stuck there between my thighs. Fitted frock coat, top hat, medals, gold tassels. Cane in hand. The other hand resting on a child's head. In his mind, this child symbolizes the nation."

"What a damn fool."

Even when I'm right there wearing the outfit of the people. With this body of the people. They can still take me out. Ah, what a load of bullshit. Guzzled by the nation and guzzled by these stupid big herniated balls that get in the way of my old hose. But I, Mom's Lopez. . . . Any other time he would have instructed Vauban or Carvanso to bring him to me and have him explain what's written here. . . . Have him come and explain it with his own drool. So that I could hear him first-hand with my own ears and see him with my own eyes. Ungrateful bandit I even trusted with managing my hernia, managing my conscience. And still, still he wants to overthrow me.

"What a damn fool."

And if only I didn't care for him. If I didn't consider him the obverse of my hernia. But no, I'm not his colleague from the country across the way who sends his opponents off on a helicopter ride with strict instructions for the pilot. I'm not like that other colleague in the country across the way who fornicates with the ministers' wives. I'm human. I respect you all. And that's the thanks I get? You killed my National aunt and what did I do to you? I could have hanged the lot of you. You even killed my National wife.

"What do you think, Jescani?"

Brother Jescani shakes his head and says that Mr. President sir, you're a good president.

"Fine, but what good is that, you still take advantage of me and go waving your male utensils in my face. Now things will be different and I'm going to fire into this mayhem and tough luck for those who perish."

"Yes, Mr. President."

He adjusts his hernia and heads out in the direction of Yambi-City where I had a villa built for my little French lady, a nice White woman who's turning out to be as good as two real Black ones in the business of my hernia. He sets out without any god-damn escort and go ahead and kill me if you so please, I've had enough enough enough! We're not going to run the fatherland as you'd operate a dick. What's wrong with this country in which people refuse to understand that they're not the president? From now on I'll treat you as you deserve to be treated. He spent three days and three nights over at Evelyne Ollayat's place, French woman of my entrails, as spicy as they come; ah Jescani, if only you'd have gotten a chance to taste her. Ah, Mom's Vauban, if you'd been able to taste her, old rusted Vauban who prefers men, what a load of bullshit that is! He tells them the story everyone's heard before, long before my hernia, when a loser like Berthanio became a Pharaoh, and when he made up his mind in the full light of day that the national flag would be kaki. Ah dear Mom, this country has come a long way.

"Mr. President, we found poop in your bed; looks like Laure and the Panther was behind this."

He rushes over to see. Mother of Mom! And there, right there for all to see, on top of the photo of the girl, right in the very middle of the bed, lay a steaming blood-stained turd, with undigested stems of wild fruits protruding everywhere. He stares at this odious turd, studded with peanuts and peppers.

"Am I dreaming?"

"I'm afraid not, Mr. President. What you see there is Laure and the Panther's shit."

"And what the fuck are the infantry guards up to? What in God's name are they doing? Ah, this time I've really had it. And he summoned us all before him: the whole Council of Ministers of my hernia, the female representatives of the national unions for women, youth representatives, the representatives of the High Command of my hernia may God curse all of you. He summoned us all before this anger that's eating me up, diplomats, the Apostolic Nuncio, representatives from the police as well as the gendarmerie, writers, musicians, painters, and no question of leaving anyone out, he summoned us before his kaki heart, and hurry up, the Companions of the People's Action Committee, as well as representatives from friendly countries, along with the entire Supreme Committee for National Democracy. And he checks:

"Who's missing?"

"Everyone's here, Your Excellency."

"Good. Now go ahead and take your damn power. I'm going back to the village to grow macaronis."

He grabbed his eleven pairs of kaki pants, his eleven pairs of slippers, his other pair of work boots and his thirteen Phrygian caps; he picked up all thirteen hundred medals won fighting the communists, the machete Mao Zedong had personally given him and loaded it all into his small truck himself because I see how much you envy the President, he takes his gas lantern, his two mattresses that we had to keep in the palace library; he picks up National Mom's mortars, I can see how envious you all are, the pestles, a millstone, his flask, a gas can, go ahead and take your damn power! He tied up his sheep, chickens, rabbits, hummingbirds, his parrot, his three ducks, go ahead and take your damn power, as he takes down the photos of the girl and those of Mom, he gathers his brooms, he tears up the official document from his oath of office! He tears up the decree that placed him at the head of this chaos of chaos, he tears down the portraits of all your mothers hanging all over the palace walls, he tears out all the pages signed by your mothers in the presidential guestbook. This is when we realized he really meant it, that this wasn't a joke like when National Louvendo threatened to leave, and we threw ourselves at his feet, joined our hands together, and started begging him:

"Mr. President, Your Excellency, please don't leave. You're a good president. You're the country's honor and peace. We started licking his big fat greasy acetylene-drenched herniated balls. Mr. President, please don't go. Please don't go, Colonel."

"Give me one reason why I should stay."

"Yes, Mr. President. It has been said that a bird in the hand is worth two in the bush."

And that's when we caught a glimpse of him again, with Vauban right behind him, at daybreak, making his way down what we called Ofmybigballs Hill, a bird in the hand is worth two in the bush for sure. We saw him again, Vauban right behind him, Vauban who still loved Africa in spite of his skin color, jogging along now, his fly unbuttoned, we watched him open the letter in which the new head diplomat from my colleague's country across the way presented his credentials and you see Vauban they can't do without us. He reappeared at Alberto Stadium, his fly unbuttoned, electrocuting the crowd and making his presentation with his hernia: "The earth will no longer be the earth; it's up to us to get by and figure out how to live on it." He started dancing the dance of my people, eating the people's food, and no more bullshit: I'll drink what they drink. And with brother National Robondia, the Minister of Zippers, shadowing him, we caught sight of him making his way over to District 45 and bringing down those shacks in which women were sprawled out on mats selling their wares. And you should all join me in this task; instead of selling yourselves on the black market, you should make an effort to ensure that men grant you a more honorable place on earth than in these brothels. But you can't help yourselves, so much so that we all saw what we saw when my hernia decided the first time around to close down these shameful houses where you were all busy selling your butts. By will or by force I'll make sure you end up where you belong on this earth. No no and no again: you are not politeness utensils, you are not mere items for consumption: the heart of the earth lies in your entrails, and so, throughout the sovereign territory of my hernia, no more giving women the meaning they give to their bodies.

He gives ex-brother Carlos as a striking example, who gave his life the meaning of his gonads and, well, you all know how he ended up. And he gave the striking example of ex-Cardinal Jullianno Moussa whose privates gave meaning to his life and, well, you saw how far that got him. And there's also the example of my colleague in the country across the way who went and gave his queen gonorrhea and, well, let's not get into that, and you all know how they took revenge . . .

It was at this time that we spotted several trucks heading toward Vatney, the seat of power. We assumed they were carrying weapons and ammunition from Amerindia. But nothing could have been further from the truth. They were in fact transporting mustard supplies. It took us quite a bit of time and science to figure this out: jars of mustard with his portrait on them, made by my new mother-in-law's very own family in Haute-Savoie, because they're going to poison me if I'm not careful. He had just taken Mom's decision that henceforth I would only eat this mustard, I'm done with the dishes my people eat, done with those drinks your mothers prepare and with which you tried to get me.

I GAVE THE ORDERS TO THE FIRING SQUAD that executed brother Esperancio. We had to get out of town. He was speaking. I didn't want to listen to him, but I still overheard what he was saying. I can still hear those words. He started by saying: "God is not serious." Then he repeated it over and over. Almost as if he was trying to convince me.

"Man, ah man, what a fragile creature. Armanda will find another man. They'll live happily ever after. Without me. Far from me. I'm jealous of those who will live on after me. Without me. Far from me. It's almost as if they're taking something from me. But I'm not sure I would be able to say what exactly."

It's that time of day when the early morning fog appears. I went to his cell and handcuffed him.

"Ah, they chose you for this?"

Truth was, I'd chosen myself. Because I didn't want them to chop him up into little pieces like they had done with Colonel Diégo Corso, I didn't want them to tear him in half like they had Dorzibanso. I looked at him: he looked sad, with blurry eyes, a silly grin on his face.

"Are we there yet?"

"Yes, we've arrived."

"Well get it over with then."

He seemed distracted. Then he lowered his head. He said he was jealous of those who will live on. But this time he was speaking to himself. While his buddies were busy digging the hole he'd have to drop into I tried to think about something else.

"Why did they choose you for this?"

He had to ask several times. He needed an answer. But what could I say? He wouldn't let it go. There was no ill intent: surely he must know that the dead are more fortunate than the living.

"Now don't go telling me you volunteered for this?"

"But I did."

"Well, I never!"

I have nothing to say to him. After all, he's dying in a position of strength. I probably could have given him an answer. Have explained myself. That way he would have died in peace. Alas! How can I tell him now? I could have made him feel like a comrade right up to the very end. He asked for a cigarette. I'd never seen him smoke. Never. And in principle this wasn't allowed. I let him have one anyway. He inhaled without looking up. I reminded him a priest was available in case he needed one.

"God is more serious than you are: he wouldn't disrespect a comrade in this way."

He asks for another cigarette, but this time smokes it with his head raised. He's clearly enjoying it.

"So what are we waiting for?"

Does he expect a response or was this just a way of breaking the silence?

"By the way, that hole's not deep enough."

"Ah, Ok."

He seems to handle his words differently than he used to. I don't remember him being like this. He holds his hand out for another cigarette: we're out of them.

"You know, it's not that easy being the one sentenced to death. It's much harder than you could ever imagine. And you can't even tell me what I did to you. And of all people, you're the one volunteering for this bullshit: what exactly did I do to you?"

The guys digging the hole signal that it's now deep enough. It breaks my heart. I can't do this.

"You gotta be brave. We're all the same. If it were me I would have gotten it over with quickly. Most likely would have botched things up. Make sure you do a good job. Be brave!"

He climbed up onto the mound. I thought he was going to turn his back on us as his uncle had done, shouting out, "Shoot me in the back now, you bunch of cowards!" He stared down the firing squad. Do you want a blindfold?

"No, gentlemen."

"How about a blessing?"

"Why do you insist on disrespecting God in this way?"

The guys are ready. All they're waiting for now are my orders. I can't get the words out.

"Attention! Ready: aim!"

Everything's ready, my God everything's ready. Goodbye Esperancio. I want things to be over with quickly. But I just can't do it. I've lost my voice. Esperancio can see I'm choked up and smiles. He was the one to shout "fire" and the guys fired. He fell down. Blood everywhere. We've all seen blood before. But not this blood. All the bullets hit him in the heart. What an exercise! They left a big opening in his back. I closed his eyes. So shameful. So vile. I've killed in Algeria with Leclerc, I've killed in Lorraine, I've killed in Vietnam: that's our god-damn job: to kill over and over again. Look at the blood disappearing. And now which war will you wage, old buddy? You'll be old one day. They'll send you packing with anachronistic medals. Your body riddled with gout. Unless they kill you like this: aim, fire! And you drop to the ground face down in the dirt. He feels like he's about to puke.

"It's almost cowardly to come into the world when the die is cast. Most of you were still breastfeeding when the real business went down. Those of us who are older asked for and obtained Independence, and you have no idea what sacrifices we made, and as thanks all you want to do is execute us. Take a good look at history. I'm the last of a dying breed. There should be a ban on people under fifty holding public office."

Ah, on this September morning. He was having his morning dose of Bénédicta mustard, straddling his little French woman Evelyne Ollayat with his big kaki privates, as furry as ever, and those shiny white teeth we were all so fond of poking out. They announce the arrival of Colonel Juano Jeriano Ombra.

"Tell him to wait a few minutes."

"Mr. President, he says it's urgent."

"He's not the president, I am."

Without warning he enters the room. And there he is: drenched in his hateful and angry sweat, no longer wearing his eternal uniform, his eyes bloodshot just like his father's were when he was alive, disheveled hair, buttons undone, Colonel Ombra, a disgrace, standing in front of me with lint from his bedding and smears from last night in his beard, I don't understand, and, Mom, his fly wide open but what on earth has gotten into you? You've even managed to put your slippers on the wrong feet.

"Mr. President, here's my resignation letter."

"But what's going on Jeriano Ombra; why are your eyes bloodshot, but Mr. President, here's my resignation letter."

"But what resignation? I trust you, hold you in esteem and you have everything you could possibly hope for at your disposal: money, cars, villas."

"There's no going back, Mr. President, I'm here to hand you my resignation because one day, we will have to leave the country to the children of the children of our children."

He sets the letter down and leaves. Fine: I'll find someone willing to. . . . Then they announce the arrival of Colonel Fonsio, National Minister of Infantrymen, and I'm handing you my resignation because we will have to leave the country to the children of the children of our children. Then they announce the arrival of Colonel Tounga, and I'm handing you my resignation, and he sets down his letter and takes off without even turning around to check whether my hernia is about to leap on him, at which point Lieutenant-Colonel Vansio Fernandez enters to hand in his resignation because we will have to leave the country to the children of the children of our children but not in this shameful state, and even you my son Giovanno Lanza, followed by my son Fentas Manuello Couba, and you my son that I appointed general only the day before yesterday, and you, and you and you? One by one the whole government appeared before my hernia to leave the country to the children of the children of our children of my shame, what a woeful lot! And all the military leaders who want to leave the country to the children of the children of our children, same for my fourteen fortune-tellers, my twelve cooks, Aunt Outézo Jelia, both uncles, and my sixty-seven illegitimate children. His office now looks like a garbage can, every kind of paper, every color, crumpled, crossed out, chewed up, anxiously torn up, grubby, but we want to leave the country to the children of the children of our children. His throat swells with anger. I don't understand the people around here. National Mom came to comfort him. But he sees Jescani enter: they close their eyes.

"No, anyone but you, Jescani."

"That's right, Mr. President. Anyone but me. You and I gave birth to the nation. I am with you."

National Letanso appears holding onto a piece of wrapping paper dripping in sauce, stinking of butter and onion, covered in scribble done with an eyeliner pencil, and Mr. President I'm handing you a collective statement of resignation from the guards who've decided to leave the country to the children of their children. He pulls up his zipper so that his twelve mistresses can pass before him with their kids tightly wrapped on their backs, Glézani leading the way, her face flushed with anger, drooling, haggard, as if she hadn't brushed her hair in years, hands shaking with contempt, a resolute look in the eye, she couldn't stop the tears from running:

"Why are you crying, Glézani, my love?"

"Mr. President, here is our resignation. Here it is." Soaked with snot, all chewed up by the rats that have infested the palace, she hands it over to him with the same hand she washes her genitals with. "Can't you use the other hand?" No question of changing hands. This says what it says. And just like that, he was handed one resignation after the other all day long, and National Jérica came and threw a letter right in my face, but don't worry, I will take revenge. Do as you please, I'm the one in a position of strength. If fifteen thousand guys have to be shot so that another fifteen thousand can live, so be it! "And you of all people, Jérica, that I picked up on a street corner. Alas, on this earth, no one owns anyone. You would have died of hunger and scabies out there in the bush." Toutansio hands him the resignation from the mayor's office. And Savouansi Luigi Portes comes in with the resignation that's preventing us from getting electric power tonight. And yet, that's also right when Carvanso came in with a handful of infantrymen who'd joined forces with Vauban's men.

"Colonel, we've remained loyal to you and together we will subdue the traitors."

"Ok."

We've retaken control over the radio station Ok we've retaken the prison Ok we've retaken the armament store Ok we've retaken the June 11th camp.

"God is with us."

We've retaken Gatansi Bridge we've retaken the train station and the capitol building.

He places his hand over his heart. Slowly moves it toward his herniated balls that are arousing his fleshy pole. But it's time to go and see my people, and we saw him head over to District 45, guided by the sound of drums. He goes to bang their daughters to celebrate the triumph of his hernia over the forces of evil. He brands the fiancée of our poor old brother Yohassi Loma with his sour juices. And as he passes, the people ask:

"Mr. President, I haven't eaten for three days."

"Ah, Vauban, give him three hundred coustrani."

"Mr. President, I want to purchase a plot of land."

"Vauban, give the guy seven thousand coustrani."

"Colonel, my wife left me."

"Vauban, find him another wife."

"Colonel, when it rains I have water running into my home."

"Ok, I'll send someone over to lay asphalt."

"Colonel, the infantrymen raped my daughter."

"Alas, there's nothing I can do about that: infantrymen the world over are there to fuck. Tell her to wash herself and forget about it. That's the only solution."

"But Mr. President, she wants to commit suicide."

"What? Just because of that?! Tell her to wash herself old man, and to use warm water if she prefers."

"But she only got married yesterday and then they raped her. A poor guy like me. Where am I going to find the money to pay back her dowry?"

"Vauban, settle this issue."

No no and no: I'm not like that ex-your bastard Sarnio Lampourta who drank *muelocco* all day long, and had to smoke cannabis before he had the courage to speak to the people. I'm not like Houtanansa who built stadiums as if the people could eat his mother's balls, I'm not like Dartanio Maniania who left behind a country with neither head nor balls and that you went and made a hero of the people, who managed to rack up a foreign debt of some ninety-nine billion, but you still made him a god-damn hero of the nation just for hurling his shitty juices in your wives' entrails, how shameful; I'm not like Caranto Muhete who gave all the members of his clan positions in the army so that he could hold on to the power to kill, I'm Lopez of the people and there aren't a lot of ways of being president, there's one way for God's sake one way and he pointed to his zipper. We cheered loudly. And I swear on my hernia that I would never kill someone just for being reasonable and you can take my word for that, reason is sacred; and I'm talking about the reason of reason not that of folly, go figure my brothers and dear fellow countrymen, go figure how someone like Hugo de Lafundia that we appointed child of the nation, mourned for a whole month, even buried him three times over to prove to his mother's dumbasses who asked for the return of his remains that we had buried him, yes, in this country of mayhem upon mayhem in which you can't even be sure whether you'll be buried; we buried him with all his military stripes and all his medals, we sang the national anthem and it was as enchanting as a real camp fire; now go figure why anyone would come and bother my hernia in the name of his death: well let me tell you, he hanged himself right when my hernia was about to find out that he was the one who killed the woman of my heart. And he shed real tears over this girl I had loved but that the "Flemish" pecked at. Brother Carvanso wiped away the drool and snot running from his face.

"Mr. President, be especially careful with the Amerindian press."

All this is as sad as crab stock. As sad as a dick infected with bilharzia. He replaces the customary minute of silence with a minute of his hernia, because one must cry in remembrance of lost loved ones, instead of having a good laugh in private, instead of keeping quiet like some dunce. Ah, that national moment for crying, when cheeks glisten in the midday sun, let us give the juices from our eyes the same respect that we give the national juices with which we impregnate our sisters. And the eyes redden, the snot starts to run. The nation has to tighten its heart and soul. We cheered loudly. Long live National Mom's Lopez. He shows us once again how he forgives those who massacred my aunt. He steps down from the podium and walks off rubbing his eyes. He clears his large nostrils noisily, flicks his snot on Colonel Carvanso, I'm sorry my brother, he passes his hands over his eyes then strokes his hernia and wagging tongues would have it that his heart had dropped into his pants. He walked back to the palace. Kissed Mom. Look at this bunch of grovelers but I'm not going to fall for it: if my hernia dropped dead you'd have a good laugh over me just like you did over National Salamanso, and I know it was you lot who just yesterday were licking his hernia. It's written in your eyes, it's written on your foreheads, it's written in your blood: around here, no one likes leaders. He spent the rest of the day in bed crying over his dead aunt. Vauban and Mom bent over backwards to try and cheer him up.

"I loved her you know."

"Yes, Mr. President."

"So don't waste your breath trying to comfort me."

And so he cried over his dead aunt in the way that people here cry over their dead aunts. Unless you're Satan, you can't even hurl your own piss without it coming back to splash you in the face. But I love them. But it's not always funny: sometimes they kill my people to thank me. Too bad for them: the fire next time.

"Lafonsia came to tell me that he had a dream that I would die on Monday."

"Set his grave on fire, Colonel."

"What kind of a world is this in which the dead return and bother the living? I buried him in the way I may one day be buried. I even handed some dough to his seventy-one mistresses . . ."

"Mr. President, those are state secrets."

"I don't agree—the best way to hide things is to show them. I'm going to tell you, my people: all those guys except for myself and Mom have stashed away a pile of dough in Switzerland, billions of coustrani they've sent over there to keep Europe moving. That's why I'm going to reshuffle my hernia, right here, for all of us to see: who wants to be Minister of Trade Negotiations? Ok. And what about Minister of Infantrymen . . . now *that's* democracy, and let's be honest: Who wants to be Minister of Youth and Sports? . . . How about Minister of Diplomas?"

By the evening he was slumped down in his favorite official chair and the visitors kept coming: Mr. President, Vauban informs him, the French want to drill for uranium in Valanta.

"How much are they offering?"

"11 percent."

"Ask for 29 percent."

"The Italians want to fish off the coast from Watangotta."

"What percentage?"

"21 percent . . ."

"That won't do. Tell them we want one out of every three fish they catch."

"The Russians are prospecting for oil in Moudan."

"Out of the question: they're far too dumb in any case."

"But Mr. President . . ."

"Out of the question, I said."

He shows his zipper to Jouvanso who's busy gawking at power and stirring up the tribes in the south and I'm here to tell you in person so that you know that my hernia is angry. Our brother Jouvanso scratches his head. But he says it again: my hernia is angry because you still haven't stopped confusing the fatherland with your way of pissing.

"Where's my younger brother Ravou del Cosso?"

While he strides across the palace, Mom watches him, smiling: my son is so very beautiful. He'd be even more beautiful if it weren't for that hernia swelling up his pants, without that smell of eggplant, and without all that mud from the people. He runs into National Yoha who tells the future using cowrie shells: everything looks good, Mr. President. Ok. Everything looks good, but from what I can predict, death will come on a Monday morning, on the leaves from a Kapok tree, and it will be a woman. An extremely beautiful woman.

"Are those predictions correct?"

"I've never been wrong. A very young woman will slit your stomach open while you sleep, all the way from the solar plexus to the groin, somewhere between nine and ten o'clock. She'll cut out a piece of your large intestine."

"If I was Dananso Lopez, I'd get rid of all the women."

And National Yoha cries along with him, out of male solidarity, with their kaki hearts, those equally kaki juices leaking out, if that reading is correct, but I'm the guardian angel of women, and he tells him all that I've done for them, but who'll take over my hernia, who will be in power after me? National Colonel, the reading says it will be a woman, and he starts barking like a real dog, ah how shameful, how shameful Mom, ever since the earth has been the earth, ah Maman, my hernia is confused, but I won't respond like Tistano Rama who handed over power to a cow, I won't do things in the way that shameful Larabinto did, who gave up power without so much as a tip, without even a sham election, he went and stuck authority in the mouth of a mute, a bonehead, a total loser like Zibanto of my hernia, he stuck it right in his mouth, here's my body and here's my hernia, go ahead, feast on them, he was speaking of the time when testicles were the national dish throughout the sovereign territory of my hernia, but I, Lopez, National son of Mom, came along and said enough with all this bullshit, over my hernia will I ever be like that ex-*you-all-know-who*, never will I be like that ex-National Levando who sold women by nationalizing all the brothels, and he told the story of that shameful ex-Levando, from beginning to end, but the people sing my praises in the streets, in stadiums, in their homes, and the different neighborhoods and districts, the countryside and the forests are abuzz with my name, for once that God has sent us a good president and the churches are packed, and we make our way over to him, en masse, some of us to catch a glimpse of his national hernia and a quick sniff of their sweet and spicy smell, others to admire his trademark leopard-striped costume soaked in the people's mud, spread loincloths and palm leaves out in front of him, shower him with flowers and song and the poor lay down on the ground in front of him so that he can walk over them, up you get now my people, there's a stampede to lick him, to drink his sweat and the juices seeping from his hernia, and he says all this is as enchanting as a campfire, as beautiful as the day I was born when Mom got all torn up pushing me out of her entrails, men, women, and children carry him on their back, he stops off at this little hut that looks like the one in which he was born, he asks to drink the people's water, to eat what the people eat, that overly spicy soup with cockroaches swimming in it because it hadn't been properly sealed, he sucks on the cockroaches before discarding them as the people do, he gulps down their beers, whips out his meat stick to piss like the people do, coughs and spits in the way the people do, ah good God that feels good, as enchanting as a campfire, everlasting beauty, he danced their dances, all of Zamba-Town is with him as he parades his hernia around in the ancient manner, he leaps on that girl, ah it's Vauban who said it best: the Black woman knows how to turn her B-side into an A-side, and as always sings him his favorite childhood lullaby: be good, be good . . . be good for my little banger, with his big greasy hernia hollering for blood, that's what happens after fifteen years of leadership under a loser like Almanzo who thought it was enough to have a bunch of infantrymen on the side of his hernia to be able to assert your authority, and "Go to sleep my little banger, go to sleep my sweetheart," and the masses join in singing the song to my greatness, and they're singing lullabies in the factories, in the garrisons, in the hospitals, as they carry him you can hear, "Go to sleep now my baby, go to sleep now my baby . . ." but that's enough bullshit! He jumps off the person carrying him, my people the party is over, go back to work, we've quite a bit of catching up to do on the other hernias in this world, our breathing should be full gallop, our words full gallop, sleeping, eating, our poets should write and think full gallop, and where's the Minister of Dough, right here National Colonel, now gallop! Enough with this bullshit of allocating half the budget to "firing utensils"; where's the Minister of Infantrymen, right here, National Colonel sir, now listen carefully: the national weapon throughout the sovereign territory of my zipper shall be the machete, that's enough messing around trying to sell Europe's skin without having killed it first; Minister of Roads! Present! Now gallop, Minister of Purchases! Present! Now gallop, Minister of Rocks, Present, now gallop, Minister of Medication! Present! Minister of Society! Absent, ah, now there's one who thinks he can . . .

tough shit for him: I'm giving his job to Mom; she knows all those plants that heal, she knows what cleanliness is and the cost of prescription drugs, those who are absent will regret it, I'm handing over the Ministry for Primary Schools to National Carvanso, the Ministry of Stamps to National Lanza, my fellow comrade National Narso will be Minister of the Countryside in charge of water and hunting, now gallop my brothers, excavate, dig, rummage, leave no place unturned my hernia is likely to visit or revisit; Carlos Pedro same father same hernia walks in crying his eyes out, covered in snot, disheveled, drooling; what's wrong Carlos Pedro of Mom? His eyes redden, he furls his brow, speak, my brother, I've never turned down any of your requests, nor has my hernia, I'm on your side, you're my little brother and, Mr. President, it's so shameful: my wife is sleeping with some infantryman called Tannanso Hussoto, please, National Colonel, do something to get me out of this shameful situation! Ah, sex, sex, these matters are the toughest to deal with, but what do you expect me to do Carlos Pedro, this is what the country has become, our dreadful snobbery: everyone desires what their neighbor desires. And he reeled off the names of all the shameful couples who got together deep in my herniated balls, those bitter couples: National Captain Garcia Lorenso who's sleeping with the wife of my National cousin Gabrielo Folo, my cousin National Darmansi who's sleeping with the wife of my other cousin Isidro Martillimi Zola, ex-Lieutenant-Colonel Sarvanso Tiya who's sleeping with the wife of the Minister of Shots, and as you can see for yourself, Carlos Pedro, the list goes on and on, seventy pages with the names of someone's wife who's sleeping with someone else and that's only for Zamba-Town, and Colobra's list, and all that you can see written here, but, National Colonel, I'm going to commit suicide if you don't do something to get me out of this shameful situation, I'm going to kill myself just to get myself out from under this shame. The tone of his voice is tugging at my hernia, I feel sorry for him, really sorry, but I can't go around ordering women to take their legs seriously, you can't order someone to love you, ah what a terrible waste a dick can be! And he gets a call that evening: National Colonel, your brother Carlos Pedro has hanged himself, ah that's too much. He goes to visit the corpse. The corpse continues to beg him: please do something to get me out of this shameful situation, his eyes bulging, fresh bloody tears, his tongue hanging out, blood leaking out of him, his balls exposed because he went and hanged himself naked, and his shit all over the place staring me down like no one has ever done before. All right then, I'll have his rival executed, it's ugly, real ugly, but if you want to live here, then you have to be tough in the art of looking the other way, and he adds: National Damanso, I'm appointing you minister, he looks at him, yes, you, Minister of Testicles, it's ugly but we can't do without such a position any longer, shut your eyes and nominate your advisory team, and make sure you impose stiff fines for adultery and that the proceeds go directly to the State, and he gives the personal example of his hernia that has never secreted anything but rotten juices but that always ends up being blamed for each and every pregnancy, and those women are birthing kids with no hair and no hernia, now that's enough, things have gone too far this time! He tells him about the latest pregnancy Laura of my shame has gone and pinned on my hernia and when the child was born it turned out that it was a little "Flemish" lad, and no, he wasn't kaki like me, and they'd had me go out and buy baby's bottles and all that other crap for nothing.

He smiled his big smile because we'd arrived, and Vauban, get to your post! Standing outside his little French woman's house, the woman God spent years crafting, he cleared a chunky appetizing glob from his throat and yelled out "Hurray for the fatherland!" then rang the doorbell, the door opened, he shouted "Long live you and long live me!" hide me in your body, National, you that throb in my heart and soul, it's total mayhem out there hide me in your belly, are you ready? Yes, I'm ready, "Long live you, and yes, long live me!" he squirts especially for her this warm version of my juices, and right as he does this he exclaims, "Hurray for the fatherland!" all Vauban can hear are his national male yelps, his kaki father's wheezing and be good, oh be good, all night long he hears the limpid croaking of a national toad clothed to carry out my duties as mammal of the nation, oh be good, be good, you can hear the hiccups and snorting between the sounds of straining bodies, then a meow, a moo, singing during the act, he asks her how she can be so wild and yet still be his at the same time, with all this chaos, double-locked, your belly as your belly punishes sabotages annihilates; call me "zipper-breaker," yes Colonel, call me the "night-breaker," yes Colonel; my dear girl the wind is in my sails, yes Colonel, handle me like you handle your lips, Ok Colonel, make me afraid scatter me all over like confetti, yes Sir, no no and no, over my dead hernia will I ever be like that Zalo who gave orders from his ass, I beg you take those words back, I'm taking them back, Colonel, oh yes be good so that I don't have to come across that awful world of theirs anywhere on your body, that I don't come across their shit in your entrails, ah the sun is about to rise, the night is for my hernia but the sun belongs to the nation, and he gets dressed in a hurry, where are you, Vauban, we're leaving. They make their way back down the hill, he takes his hand in his, ah Vauban, that girl is *terrific,* she's intoxicating, she adds a touch of flesh to the flesh, she really brings you into the world, into the world for good, what an art, what technique, she sets your heart and soul on fire, she dissolves your heart in the blink of an eye, that's what having balls is like my friend, balls that turn into another heart, ah Vauban, not like that bullshit of yours preferring men, she irons her odor into your flesh, for eternity, let's find a place to hide, I don't want the people seeing the other side of my hernia. They hide long enough to let Reverend Father Jean Garbani pass on his way to say Mass to the patients at my National sister's same father same mother Martillimi-Tezo Hospital, they reached my official village, him with his fly unbuttoned, the fatherland is waiting and he speeds up, he steps on a banana peel and falls on his belly filled with pleasure, gets up and quickens the pace until he gets to his office; the fatherland is waiting for me, he welcomes my colleague's envoy with his fly unbuttoned, he welcomes Cardinal Ourvanso with his fly unbuttoned, he holds audiences for visitors up until eleven o'clock, then National Carvanso comes to inform him that Mr. President you've left it unbuttoned ah Mom and he zips it, stained by my shame, with leopard patches from the people's mud, with my hernia reeking of acetylene and eggplant, a personal gift from my colleague. My brother, same hernia, Tino Garage Martillimi comes to tell him: Mr. President, you forgot to comb your hair, and shows him the armband I'm wearing in remembrance of the one who hanged himself and that my hernia can't seem able to get rid of the shame that comes from dying like a woman, may God take your soul he was less of a coward than the rest of us, and he started telling the story that you have to write down without leaving out the smallest detail he started with the kaki era the national era when the Minister of Testicles transferred twenty one billion coustrani to the State because brothels make huge profits, and get a patent on prostitution throughout the sovereign territory of my hernia, that's my supreme decision! We'll impose a tax on polygamy impose a tax on homosexuality you hear me Vauban we'll impose a tax on spending the night away from home and so on, because no no and no again sex is not an object of courtesy: it is the State apparatus.

Old man, we're no different than other men on this earth, and so why should we specialize in the shameful consumption of women, and he parades his hernia around just like all those who will try their best to contravene the measures I've implemented; he parades his hernia around to let women know that it is for you that I'm doing this because you are women in the same way that National Mom is, and consequently I cannot accept that men keep you in this state; yes, it is for you that I'm fighting, I need your support in this war that even God approves of; he brought them all together in the hut reserved for women, and what happens with your legs is a top priority, he gathered them

ah for God's sake help me and he read aloud some poems by
my official poet:

> Be beautiful be beautiful
> but it's strong we want you
> the very strongest of you
> with a strong heart and strong eyes
> beautiful but strong with all your blood.

He asks them to sing the hymn of praise especially for
the women that until today had been little else than a stupid
soul in a stupid body, but let us sing the hymn to women
in its real version, not the one instituted by the enemies of
our people.

> To bring the world
> into the world
> now be a shapely woman . . .

Shit, people have got to stop speaking like that colonel of
our shame who betrayed us by saying that the social place
of women the political place of women is the zipper and
the mattress. All the women applauded, sang his praises,
they made him forget those kaki days when he used to say:
"Only two people on this earth are friendly, my hernia and
my mommy, the rest despise me, the rest betray me." They
spread their loincloths out in front of him, National Colonel, son of National Mom, they refer to him as Mom's only
son in spite of the rumors that go around and around again
in that poor woman's thighs, in spite of all those wicked
tongues wagging and calling her the national whore, mother of twenty-seven illegitimate children all with herniated
balls; they set off with him to tear down the brothels because down with shame, hurray for White hot women! And
so it was the season when National Mom's child went, with
the Minister of Testicles Colonel Estanso trailing him, from
district to district, from one township to another, smash-
ing down buildings! But Colonel, don't you know that sex
is the poor man's Bible—who said that? Shoot him, we're
here to destroy, so destroy! He was covered from head to toe
in ash, snot, and drool. Destroy, destroy! All these shacks

of my shame in which women sell themselves on the black market, going from door to door, he painted the legal notice himself: *Tear down*! And the infantrymen came along with him and helped him tear down the structures. He preached the Gospel according to his hernia: *Thou shalt not sell your legs*, and he gave them the following demonstration: the world shall become nothing but chaos, but screwing shall be the next heart.

————————

Poor Colonel Martillimi Lopez: he invites them all in to show them the big turd I found in my special mug, and he has them all take a sniff; that's the smell of the fatherland, inhale, inhale!

"Colonel, said National Torezo, Minister of Raw Materials, I also found a turd in one of my mugs."

"Me too."

"Me too."

"Shut up!"

National Loyejo said: "Mr. President, I found a turd in my bed."

"Me too."

"Me too."

Lajao found a turd in his caviar.

"Me too."

"Me too."

"Can't you just shut up. You're deafening me with your nonsense. Find those responsible; find them."

National Vouna found a turd in his noodles—how revolting. Find those responsible; find them. Vangadio found a turd in his jacket pocket—find them; Mahoungou spotted a turd right in the middle of the dish his cook was about to serve his guests—find them instead of busting my eardrums. He asked Vauban to play his flute to calm me down. And National Vauban, excellent charmer of hernias that he was, played some tunes from the foggy country. One by one the members of the government withdrew, in silence. Only little Glemabar stayed behind, young and timid as he was he didn't want to offend Mr. President, Glemabar the Minister of Rocks; my poor child you can go ahead and follow the others. But Vauban jumped on him to satiate his twisted balls that preferred men.

"Help, Mr. President, help!"

"What's gotten into you, Vauban? Get out of here and go and court him in your quarters."

But Vauban is deaf to the president's call; he's already off rutting. What are you doing? He grabs him by his pony-tail: and our brother Glemabar's complaining in some kind of technical jargon: stop, Vauban, stop.

"Every country has its own monuments."

"That may be so, but not this one."

Glemabar comes out covered with bite marks from your dog who's not ashamed to bite and I swear to you, Mr. President, sir, that one day I, Glemabar, son of my mother, I'll make sure he curses his mother. Lopez laughed his big fatherly laugh. What, my old friend, can we do to Vauban? He's not like us who have no other monument but our shit. Vauban is Vauban. The science of guns runs in his veins. Don't waste your time, Glemabar: he'll kill you. But Mr. President, I'll have him curse his father's juices. Ok: but if you kill him, I know my colleague won't come asking me to settle things all because of some sexual misunderstanding.

"Now you choose to show up, National Zabouni?"

"Yes, Mr. President."

He grabbed hold of his ears in the ancient manner. I think it's your racism that pushes you to do these kinds of things, but I'm telling you that 20 percent Portuguese blood hardly makes you a full-fledged Whitey. And come to think of it, what stops me from being racist too: I've got 11 percent "Flemantation" running in my veins.

There's a termite mound of fecal matter on his bed. All over his bathtub and in every room in the palace. Find those responsible, for God's sake, find them. For six months the town is invaded with your mothers' shit but don't worry I will take revenge. And still every indication is that Laure and her mother were behind this, but don't worry, I will take revenge. Cardinal Zino.

"Present."

"Please, come here before my hernia, and look at what your church has been up to. And in a country in which 80 percent of the population are Catholic? People turning our temple to shit. How can this be?"

And so, for nine months, every morning and every evening, he found his share of shit in every room in the palace. Find those responsible, find them. One morning, Jescani showed up with some scrawny kid, fifteen years old, in his birthday suit."

"What does he want?"

"Mr. President, it's him!"

"What do you mean it's him?"

"Laure and the Panther: the crapper."

"No way!"

He claps his hands and bangs his feet to try and scare the kid. The boy's shaking like a leaf. He's afraid, really afraid. The president smiles at him to reassure him. He hands him some candy, some cookies. Lets him stroke his big greasy herniated balls. Maman, this child is beautiful. He gives him some jam. He's really enjoying all this food.

"Thank you, Mr. President."

"So you do know I'm the President?"

"Yes, Mr. President."

"Now tell me: where do you get all this raw material from?"

"What raw material?"

"Where do you get all the shit from?"

"But what shit, Mr. President?"

"All the shit you've been sending us."

"I really don't understand what you're saying, Mr. President. This is the first time I've ever been to this town."

"At least tell me your name is Laure?"

"Laure and the Panther. I chose that nickname because it had a good ring to it."

"What do you want me to do," brother Jescani asks.

"Kill the child: but you'll see, Laure will still be there."

They hanged the kid, but the following day there was more shit than ever before all over town.

"That's what I was saying: stop killing people for no reason."

"Mr. President, we'll bend over backward to . . ."

"Yes, but while all this has been going on, where exactly have you been bending over? Forget it, it's too damn late now."

He summons Cardinal Nola so that he can see things firsthand and tell his God that now, it's too late. And you my colleague from the country across the way rolling in medals won ferreting around up young girls' skirts, he summons Mr. La Huenta, Global Special Representative for Peace, and Cardinal Rabougla. And let's hope this is the last time we have to discuss this. First you told me that it was my ex-brother, same hernia, so I had him shot on the spot, right in front of you, then that it was ex-Major Mourtani Diaz, and I had him hanged right in front of you. I slit National Darsano's throat because apparently he was Laure and the Panther, and now you're telling me you'll bend over backwards: well it's too late you've let the shit take over and so here's my response. He pulls back the curtain to reveal one thousand two hundred and sixteen place settings with napkins in the fatherland's colors. He shows them the spoons, the bread, and the forks, roaring, "Hurray for the fatherland."

"Minister of Energy: please start. Let us make love, because hatred is far too expensive!"

The phone rings. Hello! My hernia is listening. Mr. President, Laure and the Panther has just blown up our colleague's embassy. He remains speechless for a while. His hernia trembles with anger and shame. He smokes a whole cigar before reacting. Shit! He's concentrating his efforts. Mom!

"Did you at least recover the body of the chief diplomat?"

"Mr. President, the chief diplomat is alive."

"Ah, it's better when they're alive. Send him over immediately."

He gets up as a way of showing compassion when Jean from my colleague's country arrives. My condolences. But you need to know that you're partially responsible: when I've asked for money in the past to improve security you've always been stingy with us. The phone rang again at that moment: Mr. President, Laure and the Panther just wasted all of your National Aunt's family.

"What the fuck are the infantrymen doing? What in God's name are they doing?" I get it: instead of watching over the fatherland, they're busy mounting women. Now you'll consume me in the state you've put me in, because he's just found his dog Daorfa in the kitchen with a bullet in the ear. He fell into a fit of rage. "This time the fire. Tough shit for you: no more the Lopez you can sing to, dance to, and love. Now it's Lopez in Greek sauce who's off to my colleague's country to learn to fly, smoked Lopez who returns to the country and summons the Minister of Ammunition: I'm demoting you from Colonel to Sergeant." He proclaims the country's flag kaki like his dick, makes arrangements for my beloved dog's funeral, dead for the fatherland, gun in paw. "National Icuezo, what set of big balls have gotten you all in a huff?"

"Colonel, do you remember the fortune teller's prediction?"

"What prediction?"

"Remember when you were warned you would die on a Monday after a dog's death . . . Merline Amarco came up with the same prediction."

"And why are you only telling me this now?"

"Because, Mr. President sir, in this country, only those who have nothing left to lose may speak the truth."

"Ok, you need to be downgraded all the way to the end: I'm making you Petty Officer Second Class: who killed my dog?"

"Colonel Danielli Doutranso."

"Why did he do that?"

"Remember Merline's very first prediction: you were only a child at the time, running around with all the other kids from the village with your dicks out, your belly button filled with mud; Merline rolled his cowrie shells and predicted you would one day become president and also that you would die: after a dog."

This is when the phone rang: "National Colonel, our ex-brother Jean de la Patio has taken up arms against the fatherland. He's marching on the capital. He has already blown up Golbazdi Bridge and the Fosio train station. He's recruiting civilians en masse. He's taken control of the local radio station in Novaya Cierta."

"Teach him the lesson of my hernia."

THEN THEY TALKED ABOUT MERLINE. He heals the sick. He attends to mad people. He revives the dead. Mr. President sir, he's the real deal. He can lay hands on the blind and restore their sight and help a paralytic walk again. Once a *big man* in a tiny little neighborhood in Zamba-Town, he's known today as Merline throughout the city. Merline for the Whites, Merline for the Blacks. He owns a donations store and another that sells hallucinatory plants. He's even healed real cancer sufferers, Mr. President. He can also tell the future. Fine then, bring him to me.

Colonel Jescani, where's Merline? He's right here, Mr. President. He laid his hands on the epileptic guy who came along with brother Corbanso, a direct nephew of Martillimi Lopez: now you are healed, Quatro Terozo. He laid his hands on Colonel Cabio Fourazo's son, and on the Urban Commissioner of Zama's three nieces. Ok, I can see you're pretty good. He paraded his historic hernia in front of the prophet, shaking off the historic mud from his scales that he shows off as his proudest medal, a gift from the people. It soothes my nickel silver heart. On this Monday evening he's parading it about delightedly; he decides to take Merline to the edge of Lake Oufa, over by the presidential village, and his hernia is giving off that smell of acetylene. He presents him with Mom's version of this meat that's eating me up. He tells him how brother Anafonso Louma died unexpectedly, and how brother Rodimos Sama died unexpectedly and how they'd found his corpse, they'd chopped off his dick and stuck it in his mouth and only then called to let his mother and children know, those nasty men! I don't understand the people around here. He started telling him that other story that you must have heard before, the one about brother Yuda Wassamba who died unexpectedly. And the one about National Sanamatouff. And Darbanso that we made into a national hero, also died unexpectedly. How shameful it is to die in that way: but I, Merline, I want to know. Ah, Mom's Merline, you must be happier than the President. You have your others. Your real others: all I have is Mom and my hernia. And he shows him his national marcher's thighs. You want everyone to love you, but everyone is envious of you. You can go searching for a smidgeon of pity, the smallest touch of pity: but they're all as hard as rocks around here. He tells him about his badly spread juices, there are no secrets between us, but oh how they treat me! Be gentle, Colonel, my hernia is yelling out "be good be good"! Come on, Colonel, don't go blowing up my entrails and I'm ashamed, Colonel, you're crushing me don't break my ribs now. He tells him about the piece of ass he just had over there in that run-down neighborhood and who says I make her want to laugh. He shows him his fifteen pounds of malformed herniated testicles, but that's not why I had you come over; what I really want to know now is how it's all going to end. You revived Captain Lapourta, you healed Colonel Juani of his epilepsy, and Damouta the madman is no longer mad, Oufanso the deaf-mute is no longer deaf-mute, and Kamato the blind man is no longer blind. I'll give you an official residence, official car, you'll have an official body, and your mother shall be an official mother. But I want to know *how, when* and *who* . . . I don't want anyone healing my hernia; it's all I have in this world. I'd feel so alone without it, we love one another, we understand one another: it gives me sound advice. Not like those *filii da puta* who only love me so as to better blow me. He tells him how Mom could very well kill herself if someone goes and kills her child just like they killed my National Aunt; she loves me more than life itself. And he tells him about the sixty-three illegitimate children he sired and how they'll probably butcher them just like they butchered our late brother Lola Dosmento's children, and my son-in-law Gomez who'll commit suicide if they kill me.

"Prevention is better than cure."

They went and cut open the hernia that brother Zola got from stamping on Colonel Martinez Lahounto's balls, and if you had seen how they dissected him you'd never eat meat again.

"National Colonel, hand me a ten-coustrani coin."

Shit. The proverb will be fulfilled: *The rich man can't find a needle to pass through.* He sends Jescani to search up and down the palace for a ten-coustrani coin. But no one has one. He sends him out to check in the stores but no one has one. He sends him to the markets. You're just a bunch of idiots, get out of my way, and he makes his way all over town searching for one; but no one has such a coin, and the rumor starts: the country's had it, the President's looking for a ten-coustrani coin. Everyone starts hiding their coins because his hernia should just have produced several at a time. He heads over to the central bank and has them make one especially for him. Here's one, Merline.

"Thank you, Mr. President. Now repeat after me five hundred and eleven times the prophet's words: '*Coulchi coulcha poumikanata,*' and then you'll repeat the response from the gods the same number of times: '*Kalmitana mahanoman-chi lusata.*'"

He repeats the words but it's too complicated for him; he tries again but he just can't do it. Try this, Mr. President, place the coin in my mouth, and now in yours, repeat God's words, think of National Papa's face, but I never knew the guy, Merline. Well then think of Mom's face, Ok, I know Mom, now swallow the coin. Look for it in your next stool and bring it to me so that I can read your future on the coin.

"How shameful, Mom."

He ripped his throat swallowing the coin. The coin gets stuck in the laryngeal inlet and he collapses and falls into a coma. His hernia gives off a sour smell. The top experts from my colleague's country are called to his bedside. The people fill up the churches, every morning and every evening; they have but one single prayer: *Please our great God, let him die.* Colonel Jescani is secretly celebrating. He's already scribbled down his list of appointees, he's written a draft of his inauguration speech and of his oath of allegiance, instructed brother Darso Lamondia to prepare a new draft of the constitution. In short, he prepares a draft of his power. . . . He's been in a coma for three weeks now. Then it's six weeks, two months. And so Jescani decided to bury him. He had him placed in a marble casket, our French brother Jean de Rochegonde's ultimate masterpiece. A golden shroud is draped over the body and diamonds sprinkled over him. The coffin is then moved to the cathedral in Mom's home village, a few infantryman assigned to watch over him, and enjoy your death now, Colonel.

"But he's not dead," said Merline.

No one believes him. Because, after all, there aren't a thousand ways to die. In spite of his second eye that won't close, in spite of the occasional stirring of his hernia, there aren't eleven ways to die. And brother Jescani divulges the new constitution, beginning with plans for a new palace, and I won't be like National Lopez who remained a colonel: I'll be promoted to Pharaoh. He pardons all thirty-nine thousand six hundred and twelve prisoners and sends all the students they drafted as infantrymen back to school. He gave Lopez Belinda to his cousin Sabrossa who'd always fancied her; he gave Oustano his wife back because Lopez had taken her in a shameful and inhuman manner; he distributed all the concubines because he's no longer here to love you like a pack of animals. He renames the streets, markets, the university, National Mom Hospital, the traffic circle of my hernia.

"My brothers, we've been mucking around long enough: now it's time to get serious."

Meanwhile, in a heavy sleep, Mom's Lopez continued to exhibit the splendor of his hernia. Over in a corner of the cathedral National Mom grieved bitterly over her puzzle son, ruler of his hernia, in charge of zippers, savior of legs. Let him parade it before God the Father, God who should have mercy on a poor old lady like me, from whom they've taken away all the chauffeurs and official cars, and cast off in the countryside. Poor National Mom, she has become dirty and bitter. Smelly, flea-ridden, blind. Riddled with gout and moth-eaten. Up until this day when the shroud stirred. Both eyes looked up again at the fatherland and at Mom, why are you crying?

She ran all over the village letting out cries of joy and went crazy.

He made for the airport on foot. People fled before him.

"Don't run away, I'm your president."

"Don't run away, it's the president."

He shows them his big herniated testicles. You see, it's really me. But they continue to flee. He boards a twin-engine plane and flies it himself all the way to Zama, where he holds a two-hour meeting: I'm not dead, I'm alive. Then he takes off for Zamba-Town with brother comrade Lobito who brings him up to date on the situation and explains how that gang of scoundrels seized power.

"Jescani made Mom cry, he hanged your son and killed sixty guards."

"I'll make him eat seventy versions of my hernia."

"Outranso went out dancing the day of your funeral."

"Sixteen versions."

"Carvanso's been sleeping in your bed."

"He'll eat eleven copies of my dick."

He told him all about His Excellency the Italian Ambassador who celebrated his engagement the day of your funeral. Yes, Ok, I'll set aside twenty copies of my prick especially for him. He hands them out right, left, and center. The twin-engine plane landed in Alberto-Sanamatouff Stadium, kicking up a cloud of dust on those brothers and dear fellow countrymen that had come to greet him. He jumps out of the plane, raises his hands, and the crowd goes wild. They start singing and yelling: "Long live Lopez! Long live National Mom!"

"The first thing we're going to do is exact revenge on those traitors; there will be plenty of time for talk later. We'll sing later, we'll dance later, bring them to me. And no death sentences. How many of them are there—pick them up one by one."

And he heads off to find Jescani who's supervising the construction project for the new palace: you don't even watch the news, you dumbass! You didn't even know I was back. Jescani can't believe his eyes. He walks over to him, kneels down, places his head against his hernia; he must be dreaming. But then there's all this historic mud. And that terrible smell and noxious air and that acid burning away on those big kaki herniated balls. It can only be him. What will become of me? Help! Help me my people, help me prisoners! His calls are met with silence and he starts to snivel: please, have mercy on me, Colonel! Spare me, I'll be more loyal than ever. He licks his hernia and his boots, quakes with fear. He runs his tongue over the tip of his hernia.

"Show me your male utensils."

He drops his pants. Here they are, Colonel. I don't want to die.

He licks his medals.

"Please, Colonel, let me live."

"Fine, but I'm taking your male instruments: it's for them you seized power."

He chopped off his bat and balls. Now open your mouth nice and wide: and he ordered him to eat them raw right there and then if you don't want me to fetch my PA system. Eat 'em up, old boy. How do they taste?

"They're sweet, Colonel."

Thanks to you, Merline, I know who my friends and enemies are. I can't thank you enough. He gave his shit a good rummage but still couldn't find the coin. He splashed around, blowing, searching, sniffing: where the hell can it have gone? It's got to be lost somewhere in my hernia. He squeezes out another turd. Still no sign of it. He calls Merline: "Where has it gone?"

"Don't worry, Colonel, it's a good sign: if it's taking it's time to come out that means your story is unprecedented."

He continues searching for it in his historic turds for three years. Ecstatically. With his big old sensible head. All his visitors, minister so and so, His Excellency, the top diplomat, left with the smell of acetylene on them. They suspect it's the aura of "the one that sleeps in that big old prick." But you're mistaken gentlemen: that's the perfume of his historic dung, but don't say a word to anyone: it's a State secret.

"Now, Merline, I want to know how much time my hernia has left."

"All right, Mr. President. Shall I recall the coin?"

"Well, let's give it a few more days."

What you see over there, that glistening layer in the distance, well that's Lake Oufa. He's deep in his tropical sleep. God is great! Here comes Vauban: he prefers men. Your women are out of the question. He listens to the badly tuned flute played by the toads on this July evening. You can see the lights from Mom's village reflected in the thick grass where they haggle at night. Crazy Mom is singing our songs, mimicking the animals. She throws her loincloths at her son: let me show you where you came from. Mom! She calms down. Everyone forgets she's gone crazy. Except at this moment during dinner when she pokes her hand in her plate. The people witnessing this think that God is great. The television serves up other images of crazy Mom's face, after Lopez has spat out the yolk of his sludgy saliva, compared with the newspapers from my colleague's country that make all kinds of wild claims.

"Mom, wait for me, I'm just going to have a quick chat with Liz Traomar, ex-Captain of cruelty Farfaro Mundi's daughter. He shows her the wound, you can see ah a cat scratched me when I was a kid. That's why I kill every cat I come across, the same reason why I accidentally killed ex-Captain Vacha Gonzalès who was trying to steal my cat. Chit chat, chit chat, and more chit chat before he finally presented her with his father of the fatherland juices. Then he left, trailed as always by Vauban, down rue Loumaza, rue Ourtani-Gento, across Jescani Place—change that name and get a move on! Ah, Vauban, how hideous ignoble of you to prefer men: men trampled by your penis. Do you think you can create a third sex?"

Merline Amarco, my hernia's going to jump at your throat if that coin doesn't come out soon. But Merline's not listening to him. He's saying his prayers, but there are no *Our fathers* nor any *In the name of the Son and of the Holy Spirit.* Only other names. God Améliana, God Bourkanazar, Cabornica Donso, Vatourios Alimatès, Bonilo de la Cuenta, Mourdiba Fananso. . . . My hernia's going to jump at your throat. But he goes into a trance.

"Merline, quit playing the fool. Stop acting like a child." He jumps at his throat.

It's raining this morning. This is the first time it has rained like this during the month of April. And Merline shouts out: "Everything is swaying, everything is swaying." Lopez gets up and goes out into the rain. No more. No no and no. No more killing people. After thirty-nine years in power. He walks on. The rain drops look like silver pellets on his mustache hairs. No more. That's what he was saying when he got to us. He pulled up a chair in front of the fire place. He asked for some hot water. He mumbled to himself as he sipped it: no more. He looked up and saw Krachna. Mother of Mom: who does this beautiful thing belong to? He caressed her legs and started singing her this beautiful song:

> If what he wants is your body
> first we'll head
> over to the palace to pick up my hens
> and then roam the crowds.

But if he's left wanting more
from this bodily fusion
then we'll go off and sing those profound songs
in a tune that will mine the map of the world

He told him the story of National Voldani who was president-for-life for fourteen weeks. She's beautiful, Mom, she's so beautiful. He touches her lips. He feels her breasts: you're trembling. I'm leaving now, but I'll be back. He leaves her the money of his hernia that never managed to give me a true love but I'll be back. He strokes her chin. Stay right here: I'm going to bring you gifts. My God how beautiful she is. She warms my entrails. She ignites my blood. He rearranges his hernia and rushes off.

The next day we saw him come back, bowed down under the weight of a massive pile of flowers, with Moupourtanka close behind pulling a wagon stacked with gifts and Vauban, grinning:

"Where is she?"

"In prison, Mr. President."

"No!"

"She came here to hide but the infantrymen found her."

He grabbed hold of his hernia like he always did when he got mad. Maman of my mom, no way! He drops the flowers and tell me, is there a phone in this place?

"No, Mr. President."

"They're going to ruin her again, this poor girl that warms me up. They're going to ruin her. He runs off. Maman of my mother, if they ruin her I'll blame the nation. He raised the alarm. Get those god-damn TVs over here so that I can address the nation."

"Mr. President: she was the one who hanged your girl-spouse with the tongue cut off. It was her sending over all that shit. Mr. President, she's Laure and the Panther we've been looking everywhere for."

"No way. She turns my heart white hot. Where is she?"

He hands him Court order number 425/71/LMZ of November 21, 1971. What's this bullshit, and he tears up the piece of paper. What a bunch of dumbasses: you really are stupid: the soldiers, civilians, the whole lot of you. My hernia's the only ones to reason in this country. And Mom's Carvanso arrives with some good news:

"Mr. President, we put in call to the execution squad. She's still alive."

He drops to his knees and starts praying: God is great, God is God. Tears of joy. God is God. Next to his kaki dick his herniated balls have started to swell. And brother Carvanso that had planned everything introduces him to Vermoz Diaz's other daughter, in the end they are almost identical, and in any case, in front of women, his hernia's blind. She is covered in gold for the introduction to make her glitter, her breasts laden with diamonds: here she is, Colonel. He takes one look at her and smiles: do you mistake me for the legs of your wives?

"No, Mr. President."

"Well then where the hell is she? Where is the real girl of my white hot entrails? Are you trying to keep her to yourselves?"

"No, Mr. President."

"Have you killed her?"

"No, Mr. President. But she has become 'a stupid soul in a stupid body.'"

"Ah? What the hell is that supposed to mean?"

"The infantrymen don't always behave like gentlemen, Mr. President."

"I want to see her."

He couldn't believe his eyes. Mother of Mom: man has become a butcher. I can see that it's her, but what on earth have you done to her? Where there had once been skin he now saw bone, and where's all the flesh gone? He saw bones where there had once been breasts, where's all the flesh gone? Instead of a vagina all he could see was a big blue gaping hole. She had no lips, no eyes, they had peeled away the skin from her head and back. He spent the next three days in his room staring at her and crying over those bones that kept breathing thanks only to the will of God. All the while a battalion of doctors and assistants did all they could to patch her back together again, attempted to reconstruct her as woman:

"I don't understand the people around here."

They grafted some of National Loutanso's muscles onto her; after all, he was the one who supervised the torture. If you need more muscles take his wife's, and if that's still not enough take his mistress Adinonso.

"Yes, Mr. President."

"Make her beautiful, as beautiful as she used to be."

"Yes, Mr. President."

"Her body is a temple for me. Make her as beautiful as the sunset. Make her eternally beautiful. Give her eyes as blue as the ocean is at noon. With long, thick black hair, just like a campfire. Give her the breasts of the most beautiful girl in this town."

"Yes, Mr. President sir."

"Give her the longest, brightest, whitest teeth in the world."

He stayed at her bedside for seven long days. Once she starts showing signs of recovery he gets up: the nation needs me. He kisses her and off he goes, with Vauban right behind.

He has the shameful Colonel Juano Maturias brought in to ask him how much were you making when you were a shameful instructor and how much are you making now that my hernia made you a colonel; I went and dropped sixteen thousand coustrani your way instead of the forty or so pebbles you were bringing in as a sorry-ass instructor. You were born an instructor and you were likely going to die one without National Mom's pity. And what the fuck are you doing hanging out with those chumps from the union you gather every night at Darlanso's. He had Henri Delapour brought in, my cousin who'd better think twice before handing me his resignation that smacks of his wife's juice: but I'm keeping you on in your position and quit your bullshit. And the next time you fuck up I'll pull your pants down and spank you like I used to when you were twelve years old.

"Yes, uncle."

"Now get lost and quit betraying your tribe. And don't forget, the fire next time."

Then Colonel Dani Jango is spotted coming in with all his responsibilities as Minister of Dough wiped away by his hernia, you can see him carrying his pile of college degrees: "I got them at the University of Paris III, and then there are those I got in California." He's all wet and sticky from the tears and snot, Mr. President sir, have mercy on me: because I've got a White wife, and how on earth am I going to hold on to her if you deny me your love. Mr. President sir, you've had White ones before, you know what they're like. Stop crying, Dani Jango, he ripped up his diplomas because it's with those useless pieces of paper that you're ruining the fatherland, now stop crying: I'll take your White woman off your hands and I'm going to pass her on to your cousin National Yosua who can take care of her because you don't want those women thinking we're poor. He tells him the great story of my late fellow Marco who came to Dilolo when I was still only Regional Lopez: he handed me five thousand coustrani now find me a woman Lopez find me a woman for the five nights I'll be in this shit-hole of a town where the only distraction is pussy. I look around a bit and come up with Lola Pinto, give her five hundred coustrani and let her know the president needs you. She let him have five nights of gonorrhea and I'm the one who ended up in prison. He adjusted his historic mud. That's right when Colonel Darso Lopez was introduced, in tears, fly unbuttoned, hair disheveled.

"Why are you crying my brother same mother?"

He wipes away his tears. He wipes away the snot and buttons his fly. Why are you crying? And answers, a quaver in his voice:

"The rebels have taken National Mom."

"Oh, shit!"

He fell into the nearest chair and Carvanso go fetch my pain killers. He grazes on them, grinds his teeth. Get me some mustard. He scarfs down twelve jars.

"Our Lord Jesus Christ, what have I done to deserve this? I'm nothing like that Toutanso who pilfered and stashed away all that dough in Switzerland. I'm not like that Carlos Dantès who killed off half the Khas tribe in two years of my hernia."

"Don't worry, Mr. President, we'll find her."

"Yes, but they're going to rape her. How shameful for me."

He gnashes his teeth and starts crying because I'm sure they're going to rape her. And that shame will be part of me. He summoned the ambassador from my colleague's country and told him about this shame they're going to rape her. He summoned the top diplomat from the country that's staring at me over there: you must have heard all about my shame; now it's up to you to do something. He summoned the Apostolic Nuncio so that you can tell Jesus Christ's father-of-the-nation that the fire is now. He has Vauban come in with your three thousand Cubans of Europe and for the first time in the history of my hernia he's wearing his armor, asks the General Treasurer to join him because, in case there's a coup d'état, then let the people eat shit. I headed for the bush. But first he closed the palace gates himself because in this country you can't trust anyone. The gates will be closed on the government and all those in the High Command for the entire time the war against the rebels lasts. He takes the keys with him. And if anyone so much as flinches, National Lavotou, blow the whole fucking thing up. Yes, Mr. President sir.

The generals' wives express their relief. They're all there: Armando Liz Agonashi, Sobra Ikesse, Laura Paltès, Lavinia, Flaura Nantès, Mryama . . . together they piss the juices from his hernia in the flower pots as revenge for all the scorn heaped on their legs. They get crazy Mom out of the place they've been hiding her and dress her in the clothes of her wretched son who makes them suffer so. They make her wear feathers in her hair and dance her wretched son's dances. Glénazar has her wash her sanitary towels because those are your son's juices. They're all busy jabbering away.

They talk about his big herniated testicles in front of her. They ask her to sing as they burst into laughter. They hide her under their dirty laundry, get her out again, lock her in a cupboard, dress like her son and "Come on National Mom, be scary! Dance those ancient dances for us." They strip her clothes off and stare at the trail that produced such a shameful son. They paint her completely red and then smear her with the mud from around here so that you too can be historic. "Come on, be scary, National Mom, be scary!" They tie dolls around her waist. They make her tell the shameful story of her son. They make her wear the medals won in her war against Russia and repeat her son's speeches as if we were in Alberto Stadium. Then one day he came storming in, followed by Vauban and Carvanso, thanks to his talking parrot Narka who kept squawking "My aunt Léonidas that the women have hidden away in the palace in a cupboard in a cupboard in a cupppppbbbbboooaaaarrd!" Riding high on his savage anger he swings open the palace gates and there they all are right in front of him, Mom busy washing your mothers' dishes and sanitary towels. Just you wait and see what warms my hernia. Ah, this anger that cancels out my father's hearts. He screeched like a wild beast. Muddier than usual, covered in grass, roots, bark, sap, smelling of musky backwaters, crabs, minnows, and leeches crawling out of his armor, cobwebs and multicolored bird droppings in his hair, he honors Vauban because you have been historic throughout this campaign but you lot, just you wait and see. He honors Carvanso my loyal right hand man but you lot, just you wait and see. He wrote a check out for eight million coustrani for my colleague who just lost his mother but you lot, just you wait and see. Toussia the French woman came to let him know that she wasn't the one who hid National Mom in the cupboard. Ok, but just you wait and see. He tears up their laundry and even their sanitary towels he tears up their bras and orders them to lie down on their backs, right there, on the carpet. He has six hundred infantrymen brought in and six hundred others from the palace staff and to wash away my shame please go ahead, right here in front of me, now sleep these bitches! Warm them up until they're white hot: you have one week. And that's how the palace was soon filled with joyful juices, with cries of pleasure, men clamoring, "Be good! Be good!" while the women screamed from pain and from shame. He summoned my little Russian girl Donia Lissounaia and I'm not quite sure how to pronounce your name but you need to know I've got six months worth of juices built up in my veins. He summons the ambassador from Vauban's country and the one from my colleague's country.

"Your countries provided support for my hernia; please let your people and presidents know I am grateful."

And he suggested something that's been trotting around in my hernia for a while: the heads of state should consider creating a worldwide federation such as the Organization of African Unity did, because Mom God knows only too well how our populations can hurt us. Finally he makes the decision of hernia: Mom shall be Minister of Customs, she will be the one to pay tribute and pronounce sentences.

That's when someone came to inform him that, Mr. President, some White guy has invented a machine that can tell the future; well, bring him to me instead of having me waste my time in the shitter digging through my turds for Merline's coin. Bring him to me. For God's sake. What's his name?

"Jean Aknin de Rochegonde."

"Is he Flemish?"

"No, Mr. President. He's from our colleague's country."

"Offer him the nationality of my hernia, you never know with those people. And while I'm thinking about it, what ever happened to the girl of my entrails?"

"She died, Mr. President."

"I have no luck: I swear I'll die a bachelor. Because all the ones I want to marry snuff it. Tell my griot to piece together her story; I'll listen to it with the government on Sunday."

Fully clothed and all muddy, he jumped into his big bed, the one shipped in from America. The leeches were busy at work in the lower part of his armor but we was fast asleep, fists tightly closed. Vauban watched over him, seated on the floor at the foot of the bed. He was snoring, lost in dreams of those wild areas he spent six months in searching for Mom. As always, he slept with his eyes wide open, his mouth ajar, his hernia hanging out, and if it weren't for the sinister snoring and the continuous flow of drool fermenting in his mouth, you could be mistaken for thinking he was engaged in some kind of serious thought. A small vapor mist hovered above his hernia, a sort of halo of slime splashed over his thighs. You can see his fingers, raw after eleven years of excavating his shit I'll never find that coin ah Merline. You can see his bedside books: *Salvation Games, Eleven Years of Spoken Power, Artificial Liberties, Behind the Coup de grâce, Care of God . . . , Where there's smoke, there's fire.*

"Aknin de Rochegonde has arrived."

"Have him come in. But I want to receive him in the presence of the Minister of the Future and the Minister of Pornography. Invite the Minister of Infantrymen as well."

"Yes, Mr. President."

And so the nine hundred and sixty-seven components of the machine that could tell the future were brought in, three hundred and twelve for the reading rooms and ninety-three for the light chambers, and then the listening chambers and we started looking at the future of his hernia. And here was Martillimi Lopez, son of National Mom's future, as we read it in our brother Aknin de Rochegonde's chambers. I'm retelling it for you right now down to the last detail and without so much as omitting even a single comma. We saw it up on a big screen. I can't explain the various sequences, I'm not capable of that: I'm just sharing some of the images with you. Without spending too much time on specific details because we saw his future in every detail. My feeling is that only the important points of what we were going to live through in the immediate future were clear, because we could see from the most fundamental forecasts some rather vague events in his life. I should also say that brother Jean Aknin de Rochegonde's machine was silent. However, as events unfold my brothers and dear fellow countrymen, it has become increasingly clear that the machine was spot on, at least as far as the main events are concerned.

A theater company from the town of Yambi-City came to perform in the presidential palace to mark the forty-ninth anniversary of the day when we went to pick him up from National Mom's home village, reenacting the entry of his hernia into the capital. The company was called El Commedia de la Outa. But you can call him El Commedia Lopez. He watches this girl who's dancing like a goddess and that is presenting his hernia with the greatest dilemma it has ever faced and I mean *ever* faced. Stop laughing: when I say *ever* I really mean *ever*. And he parades it about. My God, how beautiful she is, how fleshy. But Mr. President sir, Maria Leontina Chi is the mayor of Yambi-City's wife.

"He can go fuck himself: surely we aren't going to build walls deep down in our hernias just because of some piece of ass, ah Mom look, Carvanso, look how alive this flesh is, how her rump has become a heart, a heart instead of that shameful thing it had always been: I want her, I must have her, or you might as well rip off my prick." "But Mr. President sir, that's brother Yambo-Yambi's wife." He has the Minister of Inter-Civilizational Dialogue come over. "Now sort this out immediately. I can't sleep. I'm not eating anymore: am I to blame if my heart is telling me to love this dancer? It's no longer just a matter of the zipper; I swear Daninso my heart has fallen into her legs."

"Yes, Mr. President."

He writes a three-thousand-page poem in honor of her lips. I can't sleep, I'll never sleep again. I no longer even need your shitty power. No more of that bachelor heart and soul!

———————

They came to fetch the prisoner and ordered him to confess everything. Then he's handed over to "Master Kidney" just so that he understands how deadly serious we are, Master Kidney squeezes his male utensils, crushes his nuts. A thick whitish gel squirts him in the face: his foul salty juices are spurting all over the place. My God, you Bha really are a filthy lot. He slashes off those male instruments that drive you to hatch plots; you want to be in power so that you can help yourself to all the women's legs, to satisfy those tools of yours, but I won't let you have them. He peels off his flesh deep enough so that it won't grow back. He's yelling: "I don't understand." Really? What is it exactly that you don't understand? You were the mastermind behind the grand plot, weren't you? He's tortured using every known technique: the Zourmana and Jean Moulin technique, and all those left behind from the colonial era. Are you going to confess or not? They try the Master Kidney technique. But his screams are too loud. Try the Cabine technique instead: the screams won't be so loud. And it's better anyway since it doesn't leave any physical traces. It works well on elephants and little runts like him. And you'd better start being more cooperative. Who masterminded the plot? His body was in tatters, his flesh and soul all torn up: "I don't understand." Those are the only words he was able to get out. Well you're going to understand, and right now. They shove a big lead ball in his mouth so that you can't start screaming like that again. They work him over real good. If you believe in God, don't go asking him to punish us under the pretext that we don't know what we're doing. I know what we're doing, I do: it's because of pigs like you that my wife has to go and be mounted elsewhere while I'm busy looking out for coups d'état and plots against me; and I know what I owe that kind of pig who's responsible for such a state of affairs. And he punches away. And I love my wife, you know! I should be sleeping at her side at this hour. Doing the thing with her, all night long. But I have no time for humping and then when I can hump, I . . . I'm stiff like one is with a woman. That's how I exercise my male function. Too bad for you: if this is the way you want things to be. He plunges his claws into the prisoner's throat with such force and pleasure you might very well consider it sexual. Plots every day, fine, but when you're in power we all know what you get up to: the women, the cars, the villas, a real civilization of sex, and I'm snatching all these things away from you. And I'd be willing to bet that with an instrument like that you've probably popped a few cherries in your time; well, I'm taking it away from you. For the simple reason that you won't need it in your coffin. Ouama na chrachi! (My God). Now I want you to give me the names of the others in your gang. You're Bha, and the Bhas have a reputation for being caught up in just about every coup. Maybe this will help you understand why when I lay hands on a Bha, I get a "Bhanana." Let's begin with the official report: and hurry up and talk. I've got a list of fifty people I have to interrogate. Well, what did you want to do? Kill all the members of the government, is that right? Well, that's not very nice my brother now, is it? After all, there are seventy-six of them. And what did you plan on doing with the three Bhas in the cabinet? Were you going to spare them? My God, Bha tribalism really is something else! Who masterminded the plot? It was Yambo-Yambi, wasn't it? Ah, that one, he should be killed ten times over, made into soap, or chopped into pieces and fed to the dogs. Now, which infantrymen were going to "bump off" the president? Let's start with the officers: ex-Colonel Pamo? Ex-Colonel Domitri Diaz? Lieutenant-Colonel Suampo, Captain Alonso Rodriguos Nandi? Del Fuenzo or those bastards Sayonso . . . Ourni Toulazo, basically all those "Bhananas," right? And weren't there a few Mihilis traitors in there as well, like that bastard Oursondo Manuel? And what about Proseido Sanchi? And a few of those shits from the south? Tazos Pueblo, for example? Wow, really! And Nouany Eustacho, Zackario Foundou, Toko Marino Mene Marino; well you've certainly made it easy on my hernia as Lopez would say; now sign here. It's your statement and you don't want to sign?

"But I haven't said a word . . ."

"You never interrupted me once: silence means consent. You're going to sign this . . . you don't seem to understand that if you don't I'll rip out your kidneys. So, be wise: do you really want me to slash open your belly just because of a silly little signature?"

"I can't do it."

"Ok, so be it. Have you ever seen your kidneys?"

He rummages rummages and rummages. He insults your badly fucked mother who should have done a better job of raising you like the real mothers around here do. Do your job in God's name, do your job! Around here, doing your job means allowing yourself to be disemboweled. And he does nothing to stop himself from being disemboweled. I'm just doing my job; all you had to do was do yours.

"I fought in the war of liberation."

"Why should I give a fuck about that?"

He wrung him out like an old rag. Opens him up, tears him apart, closes him up again. Man is worthless. It reminds me of the day when I visited some slaughterhouses in California. It was so horrible that I haven't eaten meat since. But you have to be wise around here: because when you make them mad, they just put a bullet in your brain and the official version is that you attempted to flee. That's the version the national radio station will talk about and that's the version your friends will discuss: "How incredibly naïve to think he could run away from those monsters!" And one by one they'll make their way back into their little corner and will soon forget about you: death only happens to others. But I think such deaths condemn humanity to resurrection; for, without resurrection, then creation is nothing but a crime.

Master Kidneys was pacing up and down like a caged lion, dripping with blood, why don't you take a break for a few minutes and then I'll try out a few Pedro Moulinars on you, Blacks have a thick skin, you can't hold anything back, Blacks are like crabs: you can't tell where the head is, so to find it you've got to pound away all over; smokes a cigarette. Throw some water over these dunces! Freshen them up a little for the next session, and you're reminded of Diaz's words in *Hell at Close Range:* "The fundamental contradiction then becomes man's barbarism against man, and this barbarism appears as injustice, exploitation, and through all forms of physical and mental torture. . . ." Someone has poured water over a group of men sleeping; a few of them woke up, others the national radio will say attempted to flee, but in reality, they merely saw their kidneys; but over there, are you still able to look beyond the national radio? Those who fabricate other versions of the story can come over and see their kidneys unless they attempted to flee from over there, and Sarcomata, Karnansar, Laminondo, Famo Rodrigues, Damanta, the universe's monologue, the light's monologue, already there in the horrifying mono-logue of all matter that enters the world. They deflower you, each taking their turn, and you catch Yambo-Yambi smiling at you, you haven't guessed that he'll soon be looking at his kidneys and you smile back at him, "You do know there was never a plot, right?" Yes, I knew that, and he smiles at you again: that's how we die around here, reluctantly, but with a smile on our face, that's the shameful way in which you join forces in the shameful cause of those brought down for high treason, treason of treasons, but who was betrayed? I saw Master Kidneys a few years later. "You remember that whole business about seeing the mote in your brother's eye, but not seeing the beam in your own eye? For the most part my bosses wanted results, and in police work good inten-tions aren't enough; to get results you also needed a good imagination; I mean who, when it comes down to it, hasn't at least once dreamed of having beautiful women, fine wines, nice cars; who hasn't dreamed of having a great life? I was searching, and since things first went to the police chiefs, I just did my best to please them so that things would go smoothly for me. You really have to have fallen pretty far to have the right to rise up again, so I thought about it and threw everything away and left, because my son there is no greater salvation than choice, and barbarism can only end in demise, destruction, and misery. . . ." I continued speak-ing but I had already left. Yambo was sentenced to death posthumously because, thanks to Master Kidneys' report, the national radio decided he had committed suicide in his cell, and Dr. Nourmandi Santos prepared the medical certification of cause of death: Lopez of my hernia stopped off at Alberto Stadium to publicly condemn the man of our hatred mixed in with this heavy anger that's eating me up, Yambo of my bitter entrails, whose plot was to deprive Mom of her national son, Yambo of the legs of every badly fucked girl, who's just gone and killed himself from shame in his cell, and make this long list of curses available to him. I make this other selection available to Mom, with a few left aside for the "Flemish" because once again my brothers and dear fellow countrymen the "Flemish" were pretty useless at hiding their intention to wipe me out so that they could hand power over to my shameful brother Cataeno Pablo; the French have also chosen their man, and so have the Russians and Mom's Latins as well, the whole world wants my demise, and if the head diplomat from the French embassy is here among us today, let me make it very clear that the people's power I incarnate will never leave this sovereign territory of my hernia to go off wandering the hallways of the French Ministry of Foreign Affairs at the Quai d'Orsay and then return and trip over some swine like Cataeno Pablo, and don't let anyone deny me the right to arrange my hernia as I see fit in the spirit of the constitution; he parades it around and coughs up a ball of mucus right into Colonel Vasco Nomini's face who's grinning as I'm talking. And he administers ex-Major Douma do Sabato a slap followed by a spank who's busy staring at a group of high school girls while I'm educating the people, he grabs General Fatassio by the ears who seems to have forgotten that I'm the one around here who hands out military stripes, and then he parades it some more before warning my brother, same father same mother, that I'm gonna make his wife swallow sixteen versions of my dick if she doesn't stop jabbering while I'm delivering my speech; then he turns his attention back to Yambo the biggest bastard ever born into the Bha tribe, national bastard, unfortunate national, civet in perpetuity, traitor from his toes to the hair on his head, and there aren't enough adjectives, my brothers and dear fellow countrymen, him, nourished by my hernia, housed by it, enriched by it, spitting in the hand that feeds him, but he came up against it, he felt ashamed and now he's gone and killed himself with this shame, oh! I'm pretty sure I would have forgiven him, because my brothers and dear fellow countrymen, I am and shall remain a good president, misunderstood, always misunderstood, but I am and shall remain a good president, and to prove this I'll pardon all those condemned to death who plotted against me who hand me a written request for mercy, and he parades it up and down; I said a written request. This was met with cheers and a standing ovation, because my brothers, you won't get another one like me, you won't get another Papa father-of-the-nation, and they applauded, the part of the crowd that always annoys my hernia starts to stir, they've never quite grasped National Mom's son's good will, he talks about the only real difference between humans and animals: animals don't know how to be appreciative but humans do! Animals will forever be ignoble, but not humans. And we're gathered here talking about the request for mercy when Darkans says he won't kneel down in front of his hernia because I want to die with my head held high, Léa also wants to die with head held high, Pereira wants to die with head held high, and I won't go grazing on his big sour herniated balls, that'll never happen; then number fifteen came up: you won't believe me but I'm going to die with head held high, then number twelve: keep talking so that we don't for even a second consider this bullshit. Then number eleven: Lansa Marta, how on earth did you manage to get hold of National Dorsonto's wife? With her of all people, the rectangle was squared, a former nun if you can believe it! Oh, and mark my words, a total waste of time: so frigid it hurts your thing. You know the type, girls that are like a cold dead fish in the sack. The ones you have to rough up a little to get something out of them. Then there's number eight who hasn't uttered a word, give him a minute: now come on children, give your souls a minute, and number nine burst out laughing: we should be thinking of our remains that they won't return to our families, my mother will be forced to cry into emptiness, my wife, my children, my friends, it'll last two or three days, my buddies will stop by for a quick look, Floria will bring something over, condolences for mom, perhaps a little something as well for the kids, but nothing for Elsa because Floria can't stand Elsa, my sister doesn't care for my wife: it's absurd of course, but she wanted me to marry Drobando; Guilliano will also die, he'll fold his arms on his chest because: "I told him to steer clear of those things," poor guy just doesn't get it, he believes everything he hears on the radio, he'll be thinking about it before he heads off, I had a drink with him on the eve of the arrest, we danced quite a bit, and then went to our respective homes around four o'clock in the morning, the roosters had already started crowing, "How could he have . . . ," he'd never fully understand how the national radio reported it; I owe Morna a thousand coustrani, he was going to drop by and pick them up and since he never listens to the national radio, he'll drop by, they'll tell him I'm dead, he won't believe it, but they'll tell him to turn on the radio, he'll shrug his shoulders. Madra, what do you think death is like? Shut the fuck up, I have no specific views on the question, but it's probably something immense, that's all I know. Do you really think it will be immense? I don't really know, but immense was the first word that came to mind; one person's life is worth the same as the whole world's. Cataeno, you who were once president, how does it feel down there in your balls when you're right there? Who cares about all this, why don't we listen to number thirteen's story, the only serious thing in life is ass; men make you spit, let's talk about women, all their brains have gone into their legs, the first one I slept with tasted of cookies, that was back in my dorm in junior high. . . . Keep your boarding school stories to yourself and quit interrupting Cataeno; some guy came in to clarify some of the conditions for a pardon: you have to write down all the reasons that drove you to work with that traitor Yambo-Yambi and don't leave anything out, write down what you think of the president who's agreed to pardon you, and don't leave anything out, and he takes the opportunity to add a few words: you lot that go looking for democracy in your mothers' pussies, it's right here in front of you, but you have to learn to handle it . . . number eleven cried out "Mothers' pussies," and the guy snapped back at him that the way to answer the dead was through silence; then he took off, and Lansa Maria said: democracy my ass . . . and you can tell his rotten decomposing hernia that . . . Lansa Maria, don't speak in that way, some of our comrades might decide to ask for a pardon; and Agostano started screaming like some lunatic: let them go ahead and waste us, let them get on with it. I couldn't hold on any longer, so at around two in the morning I let Lansa Maria know that I wanted to ask for a pardon; he looked at me for a long time, and then said: I pity you; he looked at me some more, he asked me if it was the fear of death that was pushing me to do this, and then his voice thundered: Is it fear or what? But I didn't respond: then I looked at him and said: It's not fear. Well what is it then? The need to speak out! I see, the need to speak out, because you think they don't know we're innocent, let me tell you, my brother, around here, everyone has found a way to get by in the pretend world, to believe in all the pretend things that go on, and they live pretend lives, and in any case you know they won't bother to read your statement, no, my brother, you can't let them start thinking that we need them in order to die. No, my brother, you're going to get us into a shameful situation, you'll bring shame to all those who know we're innocent, but do as you please: in the face of death we all have the right to do what we like with the time we have left: you can't force people to be heroes. You think about all this some more: and then you decide to write: "Mr. President, these are the words of a dead man, and dead people don't know which language they speak and they've no other polite form of address than the

smell of death, and in any case it's awful to have to die because that's what people ask of you, but that's not the question, it didn't take us very long to learn the business of
death; you who are not the president of the dead but rather
the president of living; I hope you will read these lines all
the way to the very end. This would help you see why you
must not only pardon us but also make sure that justice is
served; death is not harrowing for us wretched folk that
have already been written off, we barely feel its touch, and
in any case, I've already said so much in my books, my conferences, during my stint in office and at this hour I should
probably remain silent, but I'm speaking here in a different
voice, yes, Mr. President, you will notice that I'm speaking
here now with the words of a dead person. I've always spoken of love, fraternity, understanding . . . but today I realize
that those things can't just be spoken, they must also be
lived. But today, Mr. President, this is about us, us and this
shameful state (by which I mean state as condition) in
which we find ourselves. It is our country, continent, race
and finally the Black man in general that is speaking
through me. The Black man and mankind in general, mankind in the face of the eternal struggle against natural barbarism, mankind in life with its human dimension, and you
have to listen to this voice, setting aside preconceived no-
tions. You know how those racists present us in their humanitarian dealings: Blacks are made for emotion, not for
reason. And this charge is historically serious. We've been
made to plunge into a wholly shameful historic situation. As
we see it, it is for us to meet the challenge. Only our particular experiences will tell us whether those prejudices
were right or wrong. Ambivalence, Mr. President! Our most
sacred duty is to get rid of our ambivalence before it destroys
us. We entered history after a series of bad dice rolls, and
I'm no longer interested in questioning the image we have
of our own minorities as we spend time deploring the White
minorities, I'm no longer interested in questioning the image we have of our own helmets as we bury the colonial
helmet, I'm no longer interested in questioning the peculiar

way in which we handle freedom, even if the definition is straightforward: He who knows how to handle freedom is human. As things stand today, I no longer need to breathe to be alive, I'd like to remind you that we condemned Malcolm X's death . . . , we condemned Lumumba's death as well as Biko's, while we were busy applauding Yambo's assassination. But who knows the truth about his death, except for my friends and a certain Master Kidneys, who will ever know, who will ever know that Yambo was assassinated? Torture, Mr. President, is torture revolutionary? Is inhumanity somehow humanitarian? Of course, our national radio that treats our people like a horde of forty million toddlers just announced that Yambo had committed suicide in his cell, but I saw what happened, and my brothers saw what happened, and we loathe the national radio. So the big question we're left with is the following: If we are indeed helpless in the face of mankind's fall, just how much longer do we have left as humans? Why condemn the Africa that kills Steve in order to free the Africa that kills Yambo? Am I to conclude then that freedom is not worth fighting for? That the Black man is a false problem? Well if that's the case, then the slave trade probably was as well, and while we're at it, hats off to Hitler and Pizarro, hats off to Auschwitz and to Hiroshima! But in death, Yambo showed me how to see things differently: now I believe in freedom, as the ultimate human dream, as a basic prerequisite for progress, peace, and happiness. Let's not turn freedom into some kind of fool's trap, let's not turn our respect for human flesh into a farce, for in so doing, we would inadvertently be praising Pizarro and Hitler. And Mr. President sir, I know that you're neither Hitler nor Pizarro, that you were averse to the sacrilegious bombing of Hiroshima, I know that you condemn Auschwitz. But Yambo was assassinated: I have no doubt you will hunt down his assassins and bring them to justice, so I'm here to plead the case of all those who were tortured to death, convinced as I am that barbarism will never be humanitarian, convinced as I am that Pizarro was not human. Us Blacks have been historically christened with insults; we have more reasons than others for being human, and we must not only breathe but also function, function so that the race of crocodiles that came into History covered in scales of shame can function. The force of circumstance, everyone knows our origins, and here we are, shepherded along by prejudice. If, on the other hand, you do not resolve to shed some light on Yambo's assassination, it will become customary for people to kill with impunity. And I wanted to avoid raising, Mr. President, my brother, the key question of. . . ." Listen my friends, Cataeno Pablo has asked for a full pardon for all; tear that up, said Zenouca, no, don't, said Lansa Marta, let's at least read it first, then we can decide whether or not we can leave it as a gift to his hernia. Junitas read the fifteen pages while the others listened attentively. Some liked what they heard, others did not; now listen up children, we're going to vote on this so that we can enjoy freedom one last time; if the vote is negative we'll tear up this nonsense, and if the outcome is positive we'll all add our signatures to lend weight to it, and you get it, the dead don't rip each other up like the living do; and the voting begins: nineteen yeas, eleven abstentions, nine nays, you could say the yeas pretty much won, and Lansa Marta has everyone sign the letter. Number sixteen goes ahead and signs, but not without first voicing his displeasure: those people from the area near the lake have such a high opinion of honor, they say that a promise is a heart. And we send the letter. Do you think he will grant it, Junitas asks his older brother Lansio, and Lansio blows up: I don't need it anymore, they've already killed me, they busted my balls. And Agoranti, what will you do if they do grant it? I'd move up north; it's more peaceful there, I'd find some nice quiet spot and plant some corn, I'd tear up all their filthy licentiousness, but why wouldn't you head for the mountains, corn grows well at high elevations; I'm not so keen on mountains, I find them too imposing for my small frame. The preacher abstained on the vote but nevertheless signed the letter, and he said as he was signing, I no longer believe in life, this life! What time do you think it is?

Four forty; just twenty more minutes, twenty minutes is nothing, and Junitas says: We still have twenty centuries ahead of us, we'll clear a sinister hole in the matter, an emptiness that'll throb across the centuries, and he starts spewing out names: Oudramani Motès; Larbacho, Louvoursak, Pedro Mandezo, Henri de Salmata, Patani, Goya: those are some of my ancestors; I'm off to see them.

FOLKS IN MY TRIBE WERE FOND OF SAYING that you got the President you deserved. It was back in the day when we were building the village to which the seat of power was moved, on the exact spot where National Mom had buried my placenta. I'm tired of this rotten place, and I'm sick of this group of Mom's people who keep muddling up the presidents. He'd made our brother Digomar gulp down three dozen bars of toilet soap because you're starting to confuse your presidents. He'd also spat a chunky ball of spicy spit onto the military High Command of my hernia who no longer seem to know in spite of everything that I'm the President; and well, now I've got to keep on reminding you. He was forced to spank the Minister of Trade Negotiations because I'm the President. He'd instructed the Minister of the Media to kneel down right there in front of the people and my hernia because you seem to have forgotten who the boss is around here. He'd hurled a bowl of crab broth all over the minister from my colleague's country who just doesn't seem to grasp that when it comes down to it we're all presidents; during an official dinner he'd tossed a jar of mustard at the head of protocol but, the monkey having skillfully dodged it, alas, it smashed my host in the face. Right in the poor presidential face of Nicolas Laroux Bissi, I apologize, I apologize in the way our ancestors would have done, I'm terribly sorry, here, you can have the head of protocol, take him with you as a political prisoner and do with him as you see fit, because my brother, it's bedlam around here: and we already have our share of people who are a pain in the ass around here. He'd thrown his chamber pot and all the left-over odds and ends from the years of rummaging through his shit for Merline's coin, here, take that in the face with all my roundworms and consorts, Colonel of my weenie and I'm going to have you operated on to see whether you've swallowed one of those pamphlets; he had his ninety-three secretaries operated on for the exact same reason, and you too, National Toussia, for the same reason, get over here so that I can rummage about in you, and he'd really dug deep inside her, and when he pulled his hand out of her vagina he was holding onto a piece of her small intestine. But he still kept boasting about his thirty-seven years in power and going on about how he'd never harmed so much as an ant.

He came over and offered Yambo-Yambi's ex-wife the beautiful poems that my hernia wrote in your honor:

> Let me be
> that beast
> who knows how to succumb
> to the murmur of things
> let me become a land of recall.

Let me love you the kaki way. He tells him about Mom who went crazy because of the fatherland, but this earth looks out onto my heart, I love it just as I've come to love you. Our brother Issa Traba came to tell him: Mr. President, the *Comedia de la Outa* says they can't go on without her.

"That's fine, from now on you'll be the national theater company. You need to know that the President is a mammal just like everyone."

This was at the time when Vauban and he, disguised as Arabs, went into the slum, on foot, and asked around: "Where does Cataeno Pablo live?" "We don't know, sir." Then to a bunch of kids playing in a puddle left over from the morning showers: "We don't know." The young girls sitting in the sand, busy showing each other their privates answered in the same way. Did you see that Vauban; they're already fiddling with those procreation instruments of theirs. He smiles at them but the young girls scurry off, repeating, "We don't know, we don't know." Their parents most likely warned them about Arab merchants selling off girls. And he's there scratching his hernia: My God how beautiful they are. They ask the women busy doing their washing in the Traori Baba Issa rapids the same question, but we don't know, they answer. He asks the woman who's washing some dishes a little further upstream but I don't know she tells them. So he asks the group of men swimming in the green and languid waters, but we don't know. Vauban's eyes lit up, Yum! What a feast, all those nice bums! What ineffable bodies! He swallowed another glob of saliva. He asks the woman who's harvesting her peanut plants on the community plot: "I don't know. . . ." And yet I was told that he lived in this god-damn slum. All the stuff they're carrying prevents them from going any further. Ok then, we'll come back tomorrow. The following day they return to the slum and ask the whole neighborhood the same question again: "We don't know, sir." He hands out three thousand coustrani: "Where is this hut I'm looking for?" "Take a right, then two lefts, you'll see a large palm tree overlooking the lake; make a right, keep to the right until you get to a pile of manure in the middle of the road, you'll see a small pond, take off your pants because the water will come up to your waist, head to the left until you reach the breadfruit tree, you'll see a hut under construction, someone around there should be able to show you the place you're looking for, but who are you? What do you want him for?"

"We're his friends."

They make their way to the hut under construction and ask a young girl who's doing her chemistry homework: "Where is Cataeno Pablo's hut?"

"There's no one by that name in this neighborhood."

He hands her fifty coustrani but Mister there's no one by that name around here. They walk on and ask a group of women, braiding each other's hair, nattering about loin-cloths and husbands.

"Where is Cataeno Pablo's hut?"

"Right in front of you."

They come across his cook.

"Where is Cataeno Pablo?"

"He's taking a nap, sir. If you don't mind waiting."

"I don't have time to wait, go and wake him up."

"But he's going to start bitching."

"Wake him up: I'm the *President*."

And they wake you up. You come before my hernia. You rub your eyes. Hey, Cataeno Pablo: they say you like women. And she claims it's you she loved. I don't get it. After all, you were there when I took her from Yambo-Yambi. And you were there when I went and delivered all those bottles of wine to her father. Are you challenging my hernia? Fine, if that's how you want things to be. Take him Vauban: we'll be better off back at the palace. And for me to be loved I have to throw in a car and a villa, but you dare to be loved effortlessly, what do you have that I don't? I think you'll be better off back at the palace.

My parrot Narka is singing the national anthem. In order to honor the beast, Moupourtanka will be crowned "National Beast." Brother Armane Suaze said: "Mr. President, that really is the last straw." What, how dare you question the decision of my hernia? He produced a forty-eight-page document to prove that your hernia is making a big mistake, ah hang him; that's enough and leave his corpse on display until he's completely decomposed so that the people can see how their enemies end up. Rodriguez Lopez Lavouza will also be hanged for the same reason. And the same goes for Monsignor Mallavra, now send his body over to Jesus Christ's father-of-the-nation so that he can see how I deal with the likes of him.

"Yes, Mr. President."

Shut down all the convents and consorts, move all the nuns into the army at the rank of corporal, and all those bloody priests as well at the rank of sergeant. Let them learn to handle my prick instead of spending their days lounging around. No more blah-blah-blah.

He received fourteen trunks filled with messages of support; now this is the *real* national literature, enough of that bullshit other stuff.

"Yes, Mr. President."

As the saying goes, *You have to run with the pack,* ah how shameful. But brother Jolango who wanted to leave the country to the children of the children of our children comes to lay Mr. President his congratulations on the table, bowing down to the ground. His eyes are red with shame. But congratulations! He is drenched in sweat. But you have to run with the pack. My ex-wife who wanted to leave the country to the children of her mother's children entered, with all those resigning shamefully lined up behind her, but in reverse order this time. Ladies and gentlemen, you cannot change Africa as one does a wife. General Dordobanni, and Fentas Manu, Giovanno Lanza, Vansio Fernadez . . . please accept our warmest congratulations, Mr. President. They all brought gifts for National Moupourtanka, Beast of the Nation, and also for Mom.

Dressed as a prince, the animal was breathing heavily, up there in its official cage, amidst all the gold and diamonds. He was so healthy, majestic, regal, we all thought he'd live for at least two centuries. On this special day, he must have been thinking about the Spanish hills on the mother's side of his lineage, or perhaps even of the village of Loupiac. Mr. Jean Perrier, who prepared his resumé, spoke of Loupiac and the Auvergne region, places where the beast had spent its childhood, in this country where Europe ran like Africa. He spoke of Florence Mensah who watched the beast grow up, and who welcomed me in the same way we do in Africa, and we spent six lazy days together in the same way we do in Africa, to the magical tolling of cow bells, listening to old guys talk about their hemorrhoids in the same way we do in Africa. The only person we were still waiting for was Cardinal Marcinni; I still don't know why he expects me at his age to have to court him, and I'm not Vauban now, am I?

"Mr. President, he's refusing to come."

I really don't get it, his mother went and slept with Mussolini and the offspring ended up a fucking cardinal and if he doesn't want to bear the full brunt of my anger he'd better get his ass over here and bless me! Does he not know the motto: *He needs to come and run with the pack whether or not he agrees with my hernia.*

"But he won't come, Mr. President sir."

"Fine, then bring me his balls."

Here's Cardinal Marcinni. Execute him. And he thunders: "Lord. I die facing this shame." Bang! Eleven cartridge clips to the groin and he drops like a lump of lead into a pool of his own blood. National Yosuah crowns the beast. Then, as always, came the great big feast, followed by dancing, the true dances of the people. Then there was a violent rainstorm. No one left, we're not made of salt after all, and the celebrations continued. God may well challenge us, but we'll hold on tight. So for three days and three nights they drank and ate and danced in the torrential downpour. There was never any mention of giving up. The water came up to their ankles, the water came up to their waist, and still, they kept on going. They danced in the mud puddles, and those who slipped and fell over got covered in the people's mud. He cursed and cursed the rain over and over again. But you could see them all dancing: the ambassadors, the cultural attachés, the military High Command, the people. They all danced in the mud. The Ameridians, who if they so much as balk I'll withhold the oil supplies of my hernia, the Flemish whom I'll eject from the game if they so much as balk . . . the Russians, the Japanese, the folks from my colleague's country . . . they dance the dance of the century, the horse dance . . . the national dance. And you there from my colleague's country that I made Moupourtanka's godparent. They ate and danced until that moment when, Mom I'm dying, Colonel Tuenso shot the beast and ran off shouting, "Hurray for the fatherland!" He left with three jeeps, firing into the crowd and at the infantrymen and shouting,

"Hurray for the fatherland!" They headed toward Rouviera Ourta.

"Colonel, they've taken National Mom and that girl."

Colonel Tuenso, you're really pissing me off, but your day will come and you're going to pay for this. In the meantime I'm going to take care of your brother, your mother, and all your loved ones because infringement is hereditary in our culture. And with this vertical decision of my hernia, that's it, enough with this Good President shit, and too bad for you.

Do you understand Carvanso? When you see these human shits fornicating with your mom, fucking her poor old lady's heart out, fucking her crazy woman's nerves, how can you not think the world is a nasty place? And he cried over my national horse poor old beast dying for the nation, the world is a nasty place Carvanso because the lot of them and I mean *the lot of them* except him Colonel Tuenso that I picked up from the sidewalk, washed, cleaned up, dried off under the sun of my name, ironed up nicely, I had to blow into his lungs to inflate them, he had no idea how to munch on life, I spoon-fed him, showed him how to use his jaw, the correct motion, and all that was left for him to do was to crunch down and you see the thanks I get; the world is a nasty place Carvanso, everyone but him, but no, you must know Mom's proverb: *The finger you nurse may be the one that ends up pulling the trigger that kills you.* . . . And he cries over this nasty world, he cries because I'm beginning to believe in the existence of sin . . . God is right: men are good for nothing but starting fires, century after century, and he parades it about! God is right: we need the Last Judgment, because my hernia cannot understand why you put them on earth and how it is Mom that they've started mentioning your mother's privates, they've started mentioning your father's legs ah my hernia is smoldering loving you and what filthy dog of a response you have for my entrails, what filthy response you have for my fatherly intentions. What an awful brand of meat we are; without me ordering all the shopkeepers and consorts to buy copies of my portrait, where would all the money you have in your cash registers right now have come from, without me ordering all of them to buy copies of National Mom's portrait at the price you all know, without my hernia that is so strong in the art of looking the other way, what would you have in the country's cash registers?

———————

He jumped out of bed and where's that telegram I want to show it to my hernia, the Pope under my hernia, ah what a pleasure, the Pope, Jesus Christ's father-of-the-nation, let him come in God's name let him come and see for himself, and he made his way into town to see the guys fixing the potholes on the public roads, removing the refuse from the middle of the road, draining the backwaters left by the latest tropical storms, and bury that dog won't you, because we don't want Jesus Christ's father-of-the-nation thinking we're rascals, pick up this dead chicken, move that piece of scrap metal, take this away, dig here, fill that hole over there, and by order of my hernia, so that the father-of-the-nation of the Christians doesn't take us for the last of the rascals; he surveyed every corner of the city, from north to south and from west to east, with national fellow Vauban of my trust following right behind the whole time, and by order of my hernia: paint all the huts white, paint the roofs red and the rest white, let's show the world we're an advanced people, and to prepare for the arrival of the father-of-the-nation of Paradise, he ordered only white horses, five hundred stretch Mercedes, five hundred two-door sports cars, we have to save face even if my hernia runs out of money, what would become of us if the father-of-the-nation of Christians took us for a bunch of losers? He invited all the journalists to the Hotel des Carillons and, ladies and gentlemen, go ahead and ask me anything you like about the functioning of my hernia, the functioning of the ministers and the functioning of the people, at this very moment when we're preparing for the arrival of the father-of-the-nation of worshippers, come on, now, the floor is open. . . . Mr. President, National Colonel sir, what do you think of human rights? Aha, now that's a good question, I'll answer that one: Man's first right is his hernia, because ladies and gentlemen it may be shameful but it's the truth, and it's no joke that my emblem is the zipper, and take my word: it is the hernia that make the man, and don't be fooled: when the White man speaks of mankind it is to his hernia that he turns, so don't be fooled . . . your shitty power that I have just seized, have a look how it is hand-stitched with pricks; I think I've answered that question, so go ahead and ask Mr. National Lopez another one. . . . He interrupts him to say to him, dear boy, address me like real people do or get the fuck out of my country, and while you're at it take your hands out of your pockets ah you look like you're proud to be White, but my hernia is laughing at you, because the White man's merit is to have brought the world to the ground . . . and that's not a good question anyway, someone ask a different one; Mr. President, sir ah ah let's not have the same people asking questions all the time, you there, ask a question: Mr. President, sir, why the Pope? That's a good question, I'll answer it: because he at least does not spit in the hand that feeds him, the Pope is a good president, there is no better president than him on this earth, trust me on that, remember how National Tonso gave himself to the Russians and how the Russians wiped him out, and National Matos that had entrusted himself to the Amerindians and they didn't think twice about wiping him out, and Juarioni who went and turned himself into a utensil for the French and they didn't think twice about wiping out, but I'm an instrument of the people, that's it, period, I'm not like that Dartanio Diaz who went and gave a chunk of his bald head to the citizens of that Flemishything and poor old Dartanio Diaz, God rest his soul! And he motioned to Vauban of my mom, check out that girl, isn't she something, as beautiful as four women; and Vauban's already extending his officer of prey's claws, I want her tonight, yes Sir!, but I want her perfectly fresh and with no scratches on her, yes you old devil sir! No bullshit and yes National Colonel, ah Vauban, you see, out of bad comes good, I don't really care for their questions but each time they come here there's always one that's as beautiful as four, who arouses my blood and activates my balls, eh! National Vauban, this beast (he points at his prick) this filthy beast is our next heart, imagine that! And he points at Edouardo Maunicka from the *Tomorrow My Hernia* newspaper, now ask your question, yes, Mr. President sir, what do you think of the financial situation. . . . Ah just the other day I was thinking, no, stop, that's a bad question. . . . The economy is a drink concocted over there in that Flemishy place, what do you expect my hernia to do about it? And Mr. President sir, people are saying that you have purchased several châteaux in Europe? Aha, now that's more interesting, this is a question of space, the Flemish have land under my big sovereign hernia, so we have to have people owning land over there too, and Mr. President sir, what do you think of the death penalty? Lots of good things actually, old chap, do you read the Bible? In any case, the death penalty was discovered by God and he condemned Adam and his concubine, what was her name again? In any case, the death penalty is for women, and for our part, we've replaced it with the male sentence or the sentence of my hernia; it's more refined, more humane, and that makes one hell of a ruckus, because our civilization is a civilization of ruckus, the modern world is above all about making a ruckus; go ahead, ask your questions, this is a democracy and I'll answer them. . . . Mr. President sir, who killed Tarsansio Ahendio? Ah, I'm not quite sure: it was either bilharzia or malnutrition, anyway, let's not worry about our dead buddies: there are still plenty of people alive. Mr. President sir, why do you offer gifts to rich countries?

"Yes, I was expecting someone to ask that question. I give to Vauban's country to show that I too have hands. The hand is a machine for politeness as opposed to the heart and the prick that are political utensils. The hand does not think: it gestures."

Then he took off to repair the potholes, drain the backwaters, pick up the dead chickens, while waiting for Jesus Christ's father-of-the-nation to arrive.

But on the day the Pope arrived in our capital, at dinner time, as he was dancing with the Christian's father-of-the-nation and was teaching him some local moves no not like that Monsignor, like this, with your butt in the air and your thighs unintelligible, as he laughed his big historical laugh because, Monsignor, you're stubborn your rump should be lighter, brother Carvanso, right at the very moment when the service was offered to His Holiness, lifted the national flag that had been draped over the banquet table to reveal a roast. The guests all jumped to their feet and screamed: Oh my God!

Right there on the large plateau were National Mom's legs and head. The legs were crossed and two big red peppers had been placed into the empty eye sockets, and in red ink, on a piece of cardboard, you could read: *He who uses his big herniated balls will perish by them.* Lopez read the words and started crying.

"Death is so shameful."

Rivers of tears started arriving from every corner of the country, measured in cubic feet, dear Mom if only you could have seen, I wish you could have seen how your people love you, death is so shameful. His three-piece denim suit, stained with the people's mud, was now soaked with snot, and his eyes all bloodshot. Don't go bothering me with your crocodile tears. He toppled over the twenty-eight thousand six hundred and forty cubic feet container holding all the tears contributed by the people of the fatherland, the one thousand and forty-nine contributed by friendly countries, the two thousand six hundred and forty-eight contributed by the ambassadors and consorts, the five hundred and twenty-nine from the women, now don't go bothering me with your crocodile tears, he gave a great big kick to the saintly amount contributed by the Pope, toppled over the sixteen barrels gifted by my tribe. She loved you all and look how you go about thanking her. Dressed in that anger we had seen him in back at that time when he had crossed the rue Tarvanso saying out loud: Your Cataeno Pablo, I proclaim him a hero of the nation, your Vermoz Diaz, I proclaim him a hero of the nation, your Yambo-Yambi, I appoint him Minister of the People, just like with your Jango Sunn, Mr. President sir give him the Ministry of Finance as well; ok, fine, why not Justice too, and while you're at it Defense, now those are stories you can run! Defense belongs to Vauban. He cuts off his right hand and gouges out his left eye as an outward expression of grief. Now we'll see what kind of a monster I shall become. And too bad for you: you'll waste me just like you fucked me.

THE SUN IS SETTING OVER MY OFFICIAL VILLAGE, a light rain is falling, deliciously moistening the raincoats the infantry guard are wearing, these guys are the real deal, they know how to protect me, they've often died for me, and thanks to the late Raondo Hugo ex-major of my hernia, child of the fatherland, national hero, who died taking fifteen bullets meant for me. Thanks also to the late Taranos Pourtanso, child of the nation, Commander in the Order of my prick, killed by flying shards of glass from a bomb that was meant for me. Thanks to my late uncle who absorbed the blast from a grenade that was thrown at my hernia, may God rest their souls, may God rest the soul of my sweet little Polish girl Potiask . . . Mom! I have no idea how to pronounce their barbarian Polish words. But Carvanso comes to remind him that Mr. President the traitor Sarmazo Yarmouna's hearing will be held today, the man who threw pamphlets at your hernia, yes, today, a closed hearing in the palace's court-room, but he says no Carvanso, I've changed my decision, because of Mom's journalists who don't seem to be able to understand the aspirations of my hernia, things will no longer be done behind closed doors this is the century of stark-ness, we are the black and white generation, no closed doors in my hernia, we will hear him tomorrow before the eyes and the ears of the journalists, before the eyes and the ears of the television, because this is the century of enlightenment, and he parades his hernia about deliciously, turning it over lifting it up stroking it up and down gently, releasing that noxious odor into the air, with that love for the people that is stuck deep inside me, that squeezes my gut, National Carvanso says: Mr. President, you must be prudent, Sarmazo is insolent, he will do all he can to ridicule us, he will take advantage of your kindness and throw his meat at you, he'll do it, and if he gets a chance to speak, even for five minutes, he'll blow up the nation, he'll get people to take to the streets, let's not take that risk Mr. President; but Carvanso, my son, power thrives on risk, let him speak, in the name of democracy, because you can't have a country brother Carvanso where people shut up, summon the Nation's Council, summon the ambassadors, summon the journalists, all for eight o'clock and good night Carvanso, it's time for me to have my daily portion of mustard. As usual, he takes his mustard with plenty of spices, he drinks his daily eggplant ration, says his short prayer which is really little more than a sigh: "Dear God, was it you that made me kaki" and he leaps onto my little one from my colleague's country, kisses her with the only real hand he has left, stares at her ravaged body with the only real eye he has left, before serving up "the thick yoke of my big herniated balls" in the midst of the thrashings of this tempestuous flesh that becomes tumultuous, with the smell of my presidential sweat mixed in with the odors of the local nights, he serves her the yoke of his tropical heart deep in this love that you know my girl, my child, my little White girl who alas will never be equal to two Black ones when it comes to these things, because around here testicles are built starting in childhood, they're anticipated, and while the mothers in my colleague's country are busy flattening out their daughters, our mothers are rounding them out, encircling them, that's why my dear those White girls are so flat whereas the Black ones are rounded. His face disappears into the hair of my girl oh be good for daddy, be tender, soft, foaming, be "picassoesque," don't be like those *filia da puta* who go fishing for coustranis in my hernia, and he tells her the old

story about his prick, he tells her about ex-so-and-so that
you must have heard of, he tells her about the late Magloire
de Lantana that I found one day deep in my hernia, I asked
how he made such a filthy mistake, and he said: "Mr. President, I apologize if I have offended you." But there are no
sorrys when it comes to the business of zippers: to each his
own pair; he sees himself again body and hernia before the
full Nation's Council; take every historical example sleeping
deep in my hernia, before listening to this scoundrel who
doesn't understand that I'm not like that Jancio Marti who
blew half the Public Treasury on parties and Carvanso I'm
going to appear on television to explain to my people why I
cannot let Darvanzo Manuel whistle at the nation, but National Carvanso tells him that Mr. President sir that's not
prudent. Maybe you're right Carvanso, but I'm a good president and I must do what my people want, that's my duty,
that's my life, and he parades it about in that delicious manner, brother Carvanso, we must teach our enemies a lesson,
a lesson in freedom, a lesson in understanding, we can't be
like Luis de Lamoundia who mistook the nation for his
mother's legs, and, in front of the national press, in front of
the international press who have never stopped blowing
me, he parades it on his desire to teach the world a lesson in
democracy, he parades it in front of those god-damn TVs, in
that special way, while it emits that noxious ammonia smell
and oozes sticky sap; brother National Carvanso come and
read the indictment because he needs to be judged in the
way we judge traitors around here, you need to roast him in
the way we roast traitors around here, and stand up Sarmazo and repeat after me: "I swear by Almighty God that the
evidence I shall give shall be the truth, the whole truth and
nothing but the truth." But Sarmazo just stands there smiling. Now here's one who's going to clash with my hernia if
he's not careful. But Sarmazo continues to smile, dignified,
and he's watching him, whispers to the representative from
my colleague's country: You see how awful people are
around here? He winked at the defense counsel, and whispered to my brother whom I like to call Vauban that the real

tragedy here is that these people confuse the president with their mother, because how else can you explain, my dear friend, that some guy who started chewing on your hernia can start laughing when you come to settle the score. Sarmazo says, "Mr. President, it's time to grow up," he looks over to the diplomats, now gentlemen, it's time to grow up, he tells the journalists, now gentlemen, it's time to grow up, he is greeted with a series of standing ovations in every district, uncontrollable crowds have gathered and stormed the nation's palace where the hearings are being held, and everyone's chanting: gentlemen it's time to grow up, and he thinks this is the end of my hernia. For three days and three nights they laid siege to the nation's palace chanting gentlemen it's time to grow up, a significant branch of the army has joined up with these losers who show no regard for our institutions or the rule of law, who are making my hernia boil, but, Mr. President, it's time to grow up, he speaks to them from the podium, he appeals for restraint and good sense, to the secular traditions of our people, but, Mr. President, it's time to grow up, he calls my colleague: my hernia is in danger, the rule of law is in danger, and my colleague, same hernia, sends him some green berets, nourished with the cadavers of these scavengers who mocked the rule of law, a good week of cadavers, and then things were calm once again and my people must understand why I'm hanging Sarmazo, international opinion does not understand our efforts to safeguard unity, civil harmony and peace, what are you supposed to do with a man who mistook the nation for his mother, my brothers and dear fellow countrymen, Sarmazo is a ferocious beast, even his mother asked us to hang him, his children asked us to hang him, his wife asked us to hang him, because he brought down the nation, what would you have wanted us to do with such a man? And he heard the unanimous clamor from the multitude gathered in the stadium: "Hang him!" Yes my people, you sure know how to appreciate the simple things in life, you are a people made of iron not of lead, and you've made it perfectly clear that I'm not anything like that Mario Lafundia who buggered off to Europe with the National Treasury, I'm National Lopez, Lopez the loved one, praised by all the people, the son of National Mom who is just as loved and praised by all the people, we are the children of forgiveness, but you can't forgive someone like Sarmazo, national vagabond who crisscrossed my hernia in every direction, a Sarmazo like you see him there, right in front of you, an ape of the state, standing naked before you, and the whole stadium shouts out, except for that section that always asks questions, "Hang him!" I hear you my people, but hanging is for barbarians, I can't stand the sight of blood, I hate death, so no death penalty throughout the sovereign territory of the fatherland, we shall only have the "penalty of the hernia." He climbs down from the podium, takes the knife a virgin hands him on a gold platter, places the knife on another gold platter, takes the gloves, ex-Monsignor Lamizo blesses the knife, then he approaches the prisoner and tells him that in the name of the Revolution and in my own name I'm chopping off your weenie. He severed it with one sharp downward blow, right at the base, taking a few hairs off at the same time, and blood squirts in his face, *madre de dios*, what a filthy brand of male you are, you are a brothel, your blood is spicy, he washed his face in a basin one of the virgins was holding wearing red like the others are. He brings the ceremony to a close and parades it around a little to make it clear that the death penalty is for women, what men need is the penalty of my hernia, because it is their shameful male function that is at the origin of all things, it is their hernias that drive them to betray the nation. The death penalty is abolished for all men throughout the sovereign territory of my prick, I'm replacing it with this national penalty. And since then, once a month, he returns to the always packed National Alberto Stadium to hand down the penalty of my hernia to all the apes covered in hair; sometimes there are as many as ten, twenty, thirty, one hundred of them, and he hands them out to them, in front of the eleven virgins who are there to watch the ceremony swallowing their saliva and the old girls who pity all

these weenies that are being wasted in this shameful manner, and some of the women hang around until the stadium
has emptied out and pick up two or three of them as keep-
sakes, immersing them in formaldehyde, drying them out,
or smoking them.

"My God, you're beautiful!"

For three days and three night he served up the most
exquisite versions of his prick and national juices. My God
how beautiful you are! He opens her up and closes her
again. He gets lost in her hair from here, climbs onto her
knees to admire her big eyes and My God how beautiful
you are! He shows her the seven hundred and twelve scars
on his big herniated balls from fighting the rebels and from
the war against the tsarists. He lifts her up onto his shoulders and sets off into the streets, singing her local songs and
the national anthem. He also sings the *Marseillaise* and *La
brabançonne,* songs from my childhood. He runs off the list
of nicknames the kids have given his hernia: Alpine Sea
Holly, National Almond, Louise the Fat One, National An-
selmo, Little Eggplant, Stinky Blue Goulande, She-National.
. . . He tells her how they killed his national parrot because
he kept repeating the code name for a secret plot against
me. He declared for everyone to hear that I'm giving myself
over to you body and hernia. You're beautiful, white hot,
you will move to my country and you will be matriarch
of the nation. But how can I reveal my heart to you, all
my heart in just one word? And they head off down the
street, with her up on his shoulders, him walking and singing the *Marseillaise* and our songs from back home. Paris,
ah Paris. Down the avenue Foch, then the Champs-Elysées,
past the Clemenceau metro station, over to the Place de la
Concorde, through the Tuileries Gardens, along the Seine
River, into the twelfth arrondissement and back along the
boulevard Raspail all the way to Montparnasse, and on
to Saint-Michel, Paris, ah Paris! The Seine River again,
the quai des Orfèvres, Notre Dame Cathedral. They're all
choked up. But he keeps walking because you are more
beautiful than anyone has ever been, and you're a hot one

too, and he starts singing his hernia's anthem in which for the first time, and I mean the very first time, the White woman can bark about being equal to two Black ones. And he contemplates this miracle of concrete and fire, Paris by night, unsuspected navel of the world. A night made up of names and signs, witchcraft names from the world over, Vincennes, the eighth arrondissement, boulevard Masséna all the way to the Porte d'Italie, and these grape bunches of crazy names, salacious names, who reveal their sex thing to him, Gentilly, but the real Paris is in my hernia: he gives her some juices from back home to drink. Paris-Ceinture. Adolphe Pinard. Porte de Versailles, the Seine of Roosevelt, Saint-Cloud, Boulogne, Neuilly, people turn their heads to observe this monster armored with military decorations and covered in mud singing and carrying this very beautiful girl with big green eyes, blonde hair, hazelnut skin, and oval-shaped face on his shoulders; some whisper that this is the return of Jeanne d'Arc, what a striking mount she has chosen! Won't you stop bothering me with all your media utensils: the real living here are the names, and the normal blood of Paris is the Seine. Stop bothering me with all your nonsense, dragging life along by the hair, well I don't believe in your third sex. He pushes aside these male names and these female names: Garibaldi, Sèvres-Babylone, Emile Zola, that name stinks like those hernias from back home, Volontaires, Passy, Trocadéro, République, Nation, Bonne-Nouvelle, Michel-Ange-Molitor, Richelieu-Drouot, my hernia is right: the real living in Paris are the names; meanwhile all the passengers in the metro stare wide-eyed:

"Who on earth is this quarter of a White man carrying this blonde?"

"Er, gentlemen, I've got the same rape utensils as you do."

They head back to the Crillon, the hotel I always stay in, and a telegram from Carvanso was waiting for them: "Mr. President (Stop) country is in danger (Stop)." He pounds on the table and it breaks in half; terrified, the young girl runs off wearing only her underwear. But where are you going, my love? She ran down the stairs as fast as she could, blushing from fear and shame, but where are you going, my sweet love? He chases after her in his pajamas, brandishing his inseparable suitcase used for transporting cash. Where are you going, my liquid? He threads his way between the cars and all the insults from people calling out the names of Mom's privates. "Come back. Come back!" They make it to the flower market and just when he's about to catch up with her he trips over and now there's this vixen standing in his way because Mister you're going to pay me for those! He opens his suitcase and shoves a big bill right between her rotten teeth. He wants to try and catch up with her, but Mister you're going to pay me for those again and again.

"Ok, fine, I'll buy the whole damn market now get off my back," he throws some banknotes up in the air, "Now let me catch up with her." Mom's Lopez now covered in flowers this time my beauty be good after all this chaos with the money in that market of their mothers.

All night long. Not like those colonels of yours after being promoted and he combs over his body: you see that scar there done by the rebels with a white-hot knife. He explains to her why his juices are strong in the way they are strong, but the phone rings ah it's from the country, now speak!

"Who is this?"

"It's me, Colonel Carvanso."

"What's the latest, Carvanso?"

"A terrible thing has happened: Vauban has seized power."

"But which Vauban?"

"Your personal head of security."

"Vauban has seized power . . . but *which* power?"

"*Your* power, Colonel sir."

Mom, why Vauban? He thunders: a Portuguese guy like him, illiterate, a loser like Vauban? Don't hang up, I'm on my way. Ah Vauban, with his silly zipper with neither tail nor head. What on earth is he going to do with my people's power? Ah! He packs his bags in a hurry and walks all the way to the airport, pursued by a pack of journalists stoning

his hernia with questions; now won't you leave me the fuck
alone, you're all the bloody same. He caused havoc at the
airport terminal with the check-in formalities, that's out of
the question, they've seized power in my country so quit
bothering me with your bullshit formalities! Get out of my
way, and he boards his flight, throws himself into a seat,
the plane takes off, one hour, two hours, what the fuck, he
gets up and goes into the cockpit hey you there this thing
ain't a fucking bicycle you know; he takes hold of the controls and too bad for you if you didn't take on enough fuel,
and he flies the plane nonstop to my country, the airfields
are closed but I have to land tonight in Zamba-Town. Under
fire, in the midst of flying bullets, he lands the aircraft, now
in God's name where's the power, where is National Carvanso, he gathers a group of *aventuriers* heading home on
the same DC-10 flight now off we go my friends, I have the
Public Treasury, Carvanso has taken over an army barrack
to the east of town, onward children. They get as far as the
Juando-Delpata barracks, a phone line is set up for him, ah
what a country!

"Hello!"

"Who's there?"

". . ."

"Ah, Ok . . . Very good . . . And Vauban? . . . On the run?
Don't let him get away: I'm hungry."

Then came that shameful day, morning of the nation
when he invited my colleague and all of Mom's European
friends; he invited the "Flemish" chiefs, ah that day, a long
time before his third death, the real one, not all those false
ones; a long time after the attempt by the Russians who in
total agreement with the Amerindians were damn close to
handing power into the hands of my National Aunt (that's
what I call Colonel Loufao who has a woman's voice), he invited the Pope and all the consorts, because this day comes
straight from my entrails, he invited the top diplomat from
the United Nations, and they all drank, ate, and danced the
night away; he even made a point of serving them all himself, with his father's hands, he served them whispering this

thing that they couldn't quite hear or that some heard but without fully understanding what he was saying: "Here, help yourselves, eat, this is Vauban."

I'm not like National Haracho who siphoned off oil money on the quiet and then stashed it away in Swiss bank accounts, which didn't prevent us from making him god-damn father-of-the-nation my God how shameful! And you saw how National Dascano slept all your women, you saw how he used to spend his nights at Lahossia Junior High, how he sired some sixteen hundred and eleven wrecks but you still stuck him in as father-of-the-nation, and now tell my hernia how many fathers you're going to give this poor land? No no and no, I, National Lopez son of Mom, this is what I have to say: "This business of inviting shit has got to stop, and enough of your hernia games: no more father-of-the-nation bullshit, no more mirage-merchants: Hurray for the fatherland! Down with shit and down with bullshit! I'm handing power back to civilians! Infantrymen, return to your barracks with my hernia and wait for war."

Cries of "Hurrah!" could be heard in the stadium and all over town in the way we do around here when someone scores a goal in the championship.

He ended up marrying the girl. We picked up his cases of mustard and his chamber pot just as we had done forty years ago, and accompanied him all the way to Moumvou-ka, Crazy-National-Mom's village, while he, with that big smile on his face, sang the national anthem: "Long Live Lo-pez, down with Carvanso."

Sugar-Hill, May 1st, 1980

SONY LABOU TANSI

(1947–1995) was a Congolese novelist, playwright, and poet whose groundbreaking work transformed postcolonial francophone African literature. He is the author of *Life and a Half* (IUP, 2011).

DOMINIC THOMAS

is Madeleine L. Letessier Professor of French and Francophone Studies at the University of California, Los Angeles. He has published numerous books and edited volumes on the cultural, political, and social relations between Africa and France, and on immigration and race in Europe, including *Black France* (IUP, 2007) and *Africa and France* (IUP, 2013). He is the *Global African Voices* series editor at Indiana University Press.

ALAIN MABANCKOU

is professor of French and Francophone studies at the University of California, Los Angeles. He is a Franco-Congolese author who has received numerous literary prizes, including France's prestigious Prix Renaudot. In 2015, he was short-listed for the Man Booker International Prize. His novel *Blue White Red* (2013) is published in the *Global African Voices* series at Indiana University Press.

0999

CPSIA information can be obtained at www.ICGtesting.com
Printed in the USA
BVOW08s1842231215

430809BV00033B/66/P

Pamela Carlton, MD, a specialist in adolescent eating disorders, is on staff at Stanford University School of Medicine where she developed and currently directs the Adolescent Eating Disorder Parent Education and Support Program. Over the last decade, Dr. Carlton has treated hundreds of children and adolescents with eating disorders as well as guided parents through the maze of eating disorder treatments. She is invited to speak at major eating disorder conferences and also consults with eating disorder programs across the country. Dr. Carlton graduated from the University of Southern California School of Medicine and did her pediatric and adolescent medicine training at Children's Hospital Los Angeles. She lives with her family in Northern California.

Deborah Ashin is a marketing consultant in health care and high-tech with a background in print and broadcast journalism. Ms. Ashin, who has a master's degree in journalism from UCLA, writes about parenting issues and technology. She lives with her family in Seattle, Washington.

Take Charge
of Your
Child's Eating
Disorder

Take Charge
of Your
Child's
Eating
Disorder

A Physician's Step-by-Step Guide to
Defeating Anorexia and Bulimia

PAMELA CARLTON, MD
AND DEBORAH ASHIN

MARLOWE & COMPANY
NEW YORK

TAKE CHARGE OF YOUR CHILD'S EATING DISORDER:
A Physician's Step-by-Step Guide to Defeating Anorexia and Bulimia

Copyright © 2007
by Pamela Carlton, MD, and Deborah Ashin

Published by
Marlowe & Company
An Imprint of Avalon Publishing Group, Incorporated
245 West 17th Street • 11th Floor
New York, NY 10011-5300

AVALON

Library of Congress Cataloging-in-Publication Data
Carlton, Pamela.
    Take charge of your child's eating disorder : a physician's step-by-step guide to
defeating anorexia and bulimia / Pamela Carlton and Deborah Ashin.
        p. cm.
    Includes bibliographical references.
    ISBN-13: 978-1-56924-263-6
    1. Eating disorders in children—Popular works. 2. Eating disorders in
adolescence—Popular works. I. Ashin, Deborah. II. Title.
    RJ506.E18C37 2007
    618.92'8526—dc22

                                                                2006025836

ISBN-10: 1-56924-263-1

9 8 7 6 5 4 3 2 1

Designed by Pauline Neuwirth, Neuwirth & Associates, Inc.

Printed in the United States of America

In Memory of
Rita Ann Walsh

CONTENTS

PREFACE

TO PARENTS AND FAMILIES

I F YOUR CHILD has recently been diagnosed with an eating disorder, or if you suspect that he or she might have one, it's likely you're feeling alone, confused, and powerless. What is this insidious disease that seems to hold your child captive? How did this happen? How can you help her? What exactly is he fighting against? If your child has suddenly been hospitalized, you may be totally baffled as to why you didn't see any warning signs. These feelings are not unusual: being the parent of a child with an eating disorder is, indeed, very frightening.

As an adolescent medicine physician who specializes in adolescent eating disorders, I have worked with hundreds of parents whose children have these devastating diseases. I understand the anguish you feel—the nightmare of not knowing what to do or where to go. In order to provide my patients' parents with the vital information they needed to care for their children, I created the Stanford University Adolescent Eating Disorders Program's Parent Education and Support Program (PESP). This very successful program is one of the only programs in the nation designed to provide parents of adolescents with eating disorders a structured curriculum covering what they need to know in order to be maximally effective in helping their child fight their eating disorder.

Because the PESP is unique, I have been invited to do workshops for parents and eating disorder professionals worldwide on the topic of education for parents of children and teens with eating disorders. In these workshops, I teach professionals how to help parents be most effective in waging battle against their child's eating disorder. And, I teach parents directly.

This book has been designed to follow the PESP curriculum and to answer questions that participants often ask. It is meant to be a step-by-step guide to walk you through the practicalities of eating disorder treatment.

Even with this guide, helping your child fight her eating disorder will not be easy. It is a challenging, complicated process that demands considerable patience and perseverance from all involved. Successful treatment requires a team approach that incorporates parents as well as multiple care providers, including a physician, therapist, and dietitian. I do not use the term "team" lightly. In order for your child to have the best chance of recovery, she needs to be treated by a cohesive team of professionals. This team needs to communicate with each other and use common strategies to achieve mutually agreed-upon goals. Your position on the team is the professional parent. You are the expert in raising your child. You know him better than anyone else in the world, and you are his greatest resource for recovery.

I have had many parents express great concern when I explained their role on the team. They've told me: "You have chosen the wrong woman for the job" or "But I'm the man who got her in this condition in the first place." It is very common to feel demoralized, disempowered, and even guilty when you realize that your child has an eating disorder. As one parent explained to me, "It is the most basic thing in parenting, 'nourish your child.' I am not even able to do that." This is the reason why this book exists. It will give you the knowledge and tools you need to be maximally effective in your crucial role.

Understanding what an eating disorder is and how it can affect you child's body and psyche is the first step in taking charge of your child's eating disorder. Then you can move forward to help manage your child's treatment and recovery. This book will provide you with the information and tools you need to get your child evaluated, set up an effective treatment team, and confidently take charge of your child's eating disorder.

Pamela Carlton, MD

Please note: Throughout this book we will switch gender from female to male and back. This is for ease of phrasing and to emphasize that eating disorders are diseases that affect both males and females. The names and details in case studies have been changed to protect the patient's privacy.

PART ONE

STRAIGHT TALK ABOUT EATING DISORDERS

I didn't realize it was an eating disorder. My daughter's growing anxiety and strange attitudes seemed to be part of other things—because there are always other things. In real life you don't take a fresh look at your child every morning. You aren't looking for symptoms; you are living with a family member.

For years we had been hearing a steady stream of comments about the size of her thighs, the "unhealthy" foods, and our daughter's conviction that she was not "like my friends." For weeks prior we heard increasingly annoyed and irritated statements about each meal: "This tastes bad." "I don't like this." "This is too fatty."

But it took something dramatic to make it all add up in my mind to something different than the rest of teenage angst and anxieties. It took one particular event to make me lift the pattern that was emerging out of the normal chaos and activities of our daily lives and call it an eating disorder.

"Mom, I ate a whole apple."

"So?" I said with annoyance.

"I can see it growing on my arms. It is making me bigger."

Laura Collins
parent
author of *Eating with Your Anorexic*

W E LIVE IN a society obsessed with losing weight, body image, and being thin. Wherever we turn, there are advertisements with ultra-thin models, magazine articles about how to lose 10 pounds, and gossip about an actress who looks "fat" because she went from a size 2 to a size 4. It's no wonder that 11 million people in the United States are diagnosed with eating disorders. Sadly, 95 percent of these are children, adolescents, and young adults. It is estimated that 11 million more people have undiagnosed eating disorders. And at my clinic, we're seeing more elementary school–age children with eating disorders, some as young as 8 years old.

There is a great deal of misinformation about eating disorders, especially that it's "just a phase," "a fad made popular by celebrities," or worst of all, that "She is just doing it to get attention. Ignore it and it will go away." I know, from the parents I talk to every day, that hearing the words "your child has an eating disorder" is terrifying and confusing. One anguished mother told me, "This is something you read about in magazines—how can it be happening to my child? My daughter doesn't look like those emaciated actresses in the news. What's going to happen to her? What can we do?" Knowledge is powerful, and understanding what this means is the first step to helping your child. This section will give you insight into eating disorders: what they are, what medical risks they present, and what might have put your child at risk for developing one.

1

EVERYTHING YOU NEED TO KNOW ABOUT EATING DISORDERS
Definition, Warning Signs, and Diagnosis

Danielle's Story
How can an athlete have an eating disorder?

When I met Danielle, she was a high school freshman and member of the track team. She told me that she had no idea why she was referred to my eating disorder clinic. Danielle had initially seen her pediatrician because she had missed a few periods. Unable to identify a reason for the missed periods, Danielle's pediatrician referred her to an endocrinologist. The endocrinologist noted that her weight was fine for her age, but she was very muscular. He suspected obsessive exercising—a symptom of an eating disorder—might be causing her missed periods.

Danielle, who was very pleasant and happy to speak with me, was totally perplexed as to why she was referred to an eating disorder clinic. She said she was eating well and not throwing up, so therefore, she couldn't have an eating disorder. Her parents were equally confused. Her father said, "How can she have anorexia? She eats healthy food and is in great shape—she doesn't look like one of those skeleton girls."

Upon further questioning, I discovered that Danielle wanted to "prove herself" to the older girls on her track team. Although she worked out every day with the team for two hours, running about five to eight miles, Danielle admitted that she also ran five miles every morning before school. And on days when there were no practices, Danielle still ran five to eight miles; she also did 150 crunches before going to sleep each night.

Even though Danielle had lost 8 to10 pounds over the past eight months, she told me that she felt "good" and had lots of energy. However, at one point she mentioned that sometimes she feels dizzy when she stands up. She also commented that the previous week she almost passed out at track practice but attributed this to having had a stressful day and forgetting to eat her lunch. Her parents reflected that their daughter did seem a bit irritable and wasn't spending very much time with her friends anymore. But, she was still getting straight As, so everything must be fine.

Danielle, however, was not fine; in fact, her periods had stopped because she was significantly malnourished. She was diagnosed with the *female athletic triad*, a form of the eating disorder *eating disorder not otherwise specified*, or *EDNOS*.

Eating disorders are severe psychiatric illnesses with potentially devastating, life-threatening medical consequences. Stemming from a complex web of biological and environmental forces, eating disorders run much deeper than simply a child's desire to lose weight. Most eating disorders reflect a child's coping mechanisms—albeit maladaptive ones—to deal with external stresses.

Typically, an eating disorder develops gradually and therefore is often difficult for parents—as well as doctors—to diagnose. Many of the parents I meet blame themselves for missing the signs that their son or daughter had an eating disorder. Believe me, in most cases there is no way even the most observant parent can immediately recognize that their child has an eating disorder. Eating disorders are insidious and often tricky to identify, especially if your child is going through puberty. How can parents differentiate between a teenager having emotional stress or being belligerent because of hormones? According to one baffled parent, it was a total shock when her active, vital daughter was diagnosed with anorexia nervosa. "It was like my child just fell off a cliff," she explained. Parents of younger children who are diagnosed with eating disorders are especially bewildered: how can an 8-year-old be worried about her thighs? Because people with eating disorders often deny they have a problem and go to great lengths to hide what they're doing, the situation can be very serious by the time your child is diagnosed or the problem is recognized.

Technically, the term *eating disorder* can refer to a full spectrum of eating-related conditions. However, the media—and therefore most of the general public—use the term *eating disorders* only to refer to anorexia and bulimia. And while the media seems focused on the obesity epidemic in this country, incidents of anorexia and bulimia are increasing at an alarming rate. Eating disorders such as anorexia and bulimia are the *third* most common chronic medical conditions among adolescents, after only obesity and asthma. Even though they have serious and sometimes life-threatening consequences, the signs of anorexia and bulimia may be subtle. And, as you will discover, a child with a serious eating disorder can be underweight, normal weight, or even overweight.

In this book, we will explore three eating disorders: anorexia nervosa, bulimia nervosa, and eating disorder not otherwise specified (EDNOS). We will also focus on the "female athletic triad," an increasingly common subtype of EDNOS. While each type of eating disorder presents itself differently, they have many similar medical and psychological consequences.

It's easy to be confused about why the doctor has diagnosed your child with one eating disorder versus another. The reason is straightforward: the doctor's diagnosis is based on very specific criteria defined by the American Psychiatric Association. However, if your child has an eating disorder, don't get hung up on the label. Just because your daughter's doctor

CONCERNS ABOUT WEIGHT and body image are epidemic in our society. In 2003, the Centers for Disease Control surveyed 15,000 high school students in the United States about eating habits. They found that over 44% of them were trying to lose weight (59.3% of females, 29.1% of males). Over the 30 days prior to taking the survey, the following methods were utilized to lose weight:

○ 57% exercised (65.7% of females, 49% of males)
○ 42.2% decreased food/calorie intake (56.2% of females, 28.9% of males)
○ 13.3% fasted (ate nothing) for greater than 24 hours (18.3% of females, 8.5% of males)
○ 9.2% took diet pills (11.3% of females, 7.1% of males)
○ 6% vomited or used laxatives (8.4% of females, 3.7% of males)

doesn't call her condition anorexia or bulimia, this does not necessarily mean that she's okay. I have heard too many parents whose children were diagnosed with EDNOS say, "Thank God. She doesn't have a full-blown eating disorder." EDNOS is a serious eating disorder that can be just as dangerous as bulimia or anorexia.

ANOREXIA NERVOSA

My child's not eating enough: is this anorexia or just a phase?

ANOREXIA NERVOSA, COMMONLY referred to as anorexia, is a very perplexing illness, especially to the outside observer. Although it literally means "loss of appetite for nervous reasons," this is misleading because people with anorexia do not actually lose their appetites—they have lost the ability to allow themselves to satisfy their appetite. Many cases of anorexia begin as a way to gain control over something concrete such as food or weight. Inevitably, however, the eating disorder leads to a complete loss of control. The disease overpowers their mind and makes it impossible for them to make rational choices. They are stripped of the ability to satisfy even their deepest pangs of hunger.

People suffering from anorexia, whether they are young children or adults, restrict the amount of food they eat to dangerously low levels. As their bodies become depleted of energy and nutrients, their brains undergo chemical changes. This distorts their thinking and can compound already obsessive thoughts about food and weight. These changes may also contribute to cognitive difficulties such as slowed thinking, poor judgment and difficulty in making decisions about anything, but especially about food.

For someone with anorexia, eating and controlling food becomes an obsession. Avoiding food and meals develops into a practice of self-restraint. You may have noticed your child developing "rituals" around food: cutting her food into tiny bites; eating strange foods in small amounts or methodically weighing and portioning food. In a desperate search for control, a child with an eating disorder may employ various strict weight-control methods, including severe caloric restriction, intense and compulsive exercise, vomiting, and using laxatives.

A child with anorexia may also become extremely sensitive about being perceived as "fat." People with anorexia often develop very distorted body images and see themselves as "fat," even when they are dangerously underweight. As the disease progresses, anorexia can have other significant psychological symptoms, including depression, anxiety, obsessive-compulsive behaviors, and social withdrawal. Often, a teenager with anorexia will avoid social situations, especially those that involve food.

The changes caused by anorexia can be drastic. The mother of one of my patients described it perfectly when she said, "My child has disappeared and a stranger had taken her place." She then told me about the vibrant, funny, carefree girl who had been replaced by the sullen, irritable, and very sad child before me.

Who is at risk?

In the United States, it is estimated that one out of every 200 15- to 19-year-old girls suffers from anorexia. This makes it the third most common chronic condition among adolescent girls, behind obesity and asthma.[1] Once considered a disease of white, affluent women, anorexia now crosses all racial, socioeconomic, and gender lines.[2] Ten percent of the people diagnosed with anorexia are males, and according to the American Psychiatric Association, the incidence of anorexia among Hispanic and Caucasian adolescents is almost the same.[3] And while no statistics exist, it is evident that eating disorders are affecting more young children than ever before.[4]

Diagnosis

The American Psychiatric Association has established four very specific criteria that must be met to "officially" diagnose someone with anorexia. If your child has two or three of these, but not all of them, she can't be diagnosed with anorexia. However, as I mentioned earlier, even if your child doesn't meet all of the criteria, she can still have a very serious eating disorder. Her mental and physical health is the important thing, *not* the exact diagnosis she is given.

I've listed the diagnostic criteria for anorexia in this way: first the official medical definition, followed by a "translation:"

1. **Refusal to maintain body weight above minimally normal ranges for age and height** (less than 85 percent ideal body weight, which is defined as median body mass index for age and height). This means your child must weigh less than 85 percent of her ideal body

weight. The doctor or nutritionist uses standardized charts to cal-culate ideal body weight, taking into account gender, age, and height. Because it does not factor in muscle mass or how far someone is into puberty, this criterion may not be accurate for very athletic teens or for teens who are early or late in going through puberty.

2. **Intense fear of becoming fat.** This is just as it sounds. You may notice that your child says things like, "I hate being fat." Someone with anorexia has fears and feelings about fat that are far more extreme than the average person's concern about gaining weight.

3. **Disturbance in the way in which one's body weight or shape is experienced.** This refers to the fact that someone with anorexia sees herself as fat even when others see that she is truly mal-nourished. This is commonly referred to as body dysmorphia. This disturbance may be focused on a certain body part such as someone being distressed if her stomach comes in front of her hip-bones or if her thighs touch.

4. **Absence of at least three consecutive menstrual periods in females who have achieved menarche.** If a young woman has started to menstruate, she needs to miss three periods to be diag-nosed with anorexia. Technically, a girl who has never had a period cannot satisfy this criterion and, therefore, cannot be diag-nosed with anorexia. However, some psychiatrists will flex this cri-terion for girls who have never menstruated. There are no comparable criteria for boys.

Types of Anorexia

If your child has been diagnosed with anorexia, her doctor will also iden-tify what type of anorexia she exhibits: either restricting type or binge-purge type. Again, I've included the American Psychiatric Association's definition, followed by an explanation:

1. **Restricting type: During the current episode of anorexia ner-vosa, the person has not regularly engaged in binge-eating or purging behavior (i.e., self-induced vomiting or the misuse of laxatives, diuretics, or enemas).** If your child has the restricting type of anorexia, she will restrict food but will not vomit or take any medications to get rid of the food.

2. **Binge-purge type: During the current episode of anorexia nervosa, the person has regularly engaged in binge-eating and/or purging behavior (i.e., self-induced vomiting or the misuse of laxatives, diuretics, or enemas).** In addition to meeting the four criteria for anorexia, someone with this type of anorexia will also binge and/or vomit or take medications to rid himself or herself of food. This may seem surprising since many people think that people with anorexia don't eat and people with bulimia always vomit. However, there is quite a bit of crossover in behaviors.

Warning Signs of Anorexia Nervosa

○ Dramatic weight loss, often concealed by wearing large/baggy clothes

○ Preoccupation with weight, food, calories, fat grams, and dieting

○ Refusal to eat certain foods, progressing to restrictions against whole categories of food (e.g. no meat, no carbohydrates, etc.)

○ Preference to eat alone or may make excuses to get out of family meals

○ Frequent comments about feeling "fat" or overweight despite weight loss

○ Anxiety about gaining weight or being "fat"

○ Denial of hunger

○ Development of food rituals (e.g. eating foods in certain orders, excessive cutting or chewing, rearranging food on a plate, unusual food combinations)

○ Excessive use of low-calorie condiments such as salt, mustard, and artificial sweetener

○ Consistent excuses to avoid mealtimes or situations involving food

○ Excessive, rigid exercise regiment, despite weather, fatigue, illness, or injury

○ Withdrawal from usual friends and activities

○ Attitude that indicates weight loss, dieting, and control of food are becoming primary concerns

○ Depression and irritability

Prognosis

Full recovery from anorexia is not easy, and many people struggle with ongoing body image disturbances and disordered eating behaviors throughout their lives. Fortunately, with early treatment, your child's chance for full recovery is likely to be increased.[5] But it will take a lot of work—for you as well as for your child. Although adolescents with anorexia generally have a better prognosis than adults and many recover quickly, it can take up to five years to fully regain their mental and physical health. The medical literature states that 45 percent of children and adolescents with anorexia recover, 30 percent improve but still struggle and relapse, and 25 percent experience anorexia as a chronic illness for many years. It is estimated that 10 to 15 percent of adolescents with anorexia nervosa will die.[6] The major factor that influences someone's chance of recovery is the length of time they have anorexia.[7] This means that time is of the essence; the sooner your child gets appropriate, intense treatment, the better her chances are for recovery.

BULIMIA NERVOSA

My son is slightly overweight, but I caught him throwing up: how could this be bulimia?

BULIMIA NERVOSA, COMMONLY referred to as bulimia, is a complex psychological disorder, characterized by binging and purging. Bulimia often begins during the late teen or early adult years, which is later than the onset for anorexia. You may have difficulty detecting that your child has this eating disorder because people with bulimia do not necessarily look underweight and, in fact, may even be overweight. Also, in many cases, binging and purging are performed in secret; parents, therefore, may not be aware their child is exhibiting this behavior until they realize food is quickly disappearing from the pantry or notice the bathroom always has a disturbing odor.

Binging is defined as eating large amounts of food in a short period of time with a sense of loss of control. Someone with bulimia often binges on foods they consider "forbidden" or "bad." This is followed by feelings of guilt, resulting in an attempt to purge the food and calories. Contrary to popular belief, not all people with bulimia vomit as a method of purging. Excessive exercise, as well as the abuse of laxatives, diuretics, and/or enemas, is also considered to be a purging behavior.

Bulimia often begins as a desire to lose weight because of body dissatisfaction and/or low self-esteem. The binge eating may begin after a period of restrictive eating or even anorexia. The medical risks of bulimia are numerous. Even at normal weights, people with bulimia may have serious medical complications. These can include fluid or electrolyte imbalances, amenorrhea (loss of periods), cardiac complications, gastric bleeding, severe malnutrition, and even death (see chapter 4).

Who is at risk?

While anorexia usually develops in the early to mid-teen years, bulimia more often develops in the later teen to young adult years. In the United States, it is estimated that between three and ten out of every 100 college-aged women suffers from bulimia.[8] As with anorexia, bulimia crosses gender, socioeconomic, and racial lines.[9]

Diagnosis

According to the American Psychiatric Association, someone must satisfy four specific criteria to be diagnosed with bulimia. If your child has these behaviors, but doesn't meet all of the criteria to be diagnosed with bulimia, she still has a serious eating disorder. And she still is at great medical and psychological risk. The criteria to diagnose bulimia are as follows:

1. **Recurrent episodes of binge eating, characterized by eating an excessive amount of food within a discrete period of time and by a sense of lack of control over eating during the episode.** Different people define binges in different ways. One person may call a sandwich a binge while to someone else a binge may be a large pizza or an entire bag of potato chips and three sandwiches. The common thread is that people suffering from bulimia are eating what they consider a large quantity of food and are feeling the frantic sense of being out of control.

Warning Signs of Bulimia Nervosa:

- ○ Frequent weight changes
- ○ Bathroom use after meals
- ○ Shower, bath, or running water after meals
- ○ Lethargy and fatigue
- ○ Frequent mood swings
- ○ Periods of fasting and/or excessive exercise
- ○ Secrecy
- ○ Isolation
- ○ Hiding of food
- ○ Unexplained disappearance of food
- ○ *Lots of* food wrappers at the bottom of the trash
- ○ Chronic complaints of sore throat, upset stomach, diarrhea, or constipation

2. **Recurrent inappropriate compensatory behavior in order to prevent weight gain—such as self-induced vomiting or abuse of laxatives, diuretics, enemas, or other medications (purging); fasting; or excessive exercising—occurs, on average, at least twice a week for three months.** In order to be diagnosed with bulimia, your child must binge and purge (as defined in criteria 1 and 2) at least twice a week, and this must happen for at least three consecutive months. If your child binges and purges once a week or less or if she has been doing this for less than three months, she cannot be diagnosed with bulimia. Instead, she will probably be diagnosed with eating disorder not otherwise specified (see below).

3. **Self-evaluation is unduly influenced by body shape and weight.** In order to meet this criterion, your child must be very focused on (and harshly judge herself on) her weight and/or body shape (i.e., the shape of her thighs or how big her belly is).

4. **The disturbance does not occur exclusively during episodes of anorexia nervosa.** This criterion may be a bit confusing. It means that if a child is diagnosed with anorexia binge-purge type (as defined above), she cannot be diagnosed with bulimia as well. Therefore, a child who meets all of the criteria for anorexia and bulimia will be diagnosed with anorexia binge-purge type and not bulimia.

Types of Bulimia

There are two basic types of bulimia: purging type and non-purging type. The American Psychiatric Association defines them as:

1. **Purging type: During the current episode of bulimia nervosa, the person has regularly engaged in self-induced vomiting or the misuse of laxatives, diuretics, or enemas.** In order to be diagnosed with this type of bulimia, your child needs to physically rid herself of the food by vomiting or through the use of medications.

2. **Non-purging type: During the current episode of bulimia nervosa, the person has used other inappropriate compensatory behaviors, such as fasting or excessive exercise, but has not regularly engaged in self-induced vomiting or the misuse of laxatives, diuretics, or enemas.** In order to be diagnosed with this

type of bulimia, your child needs to "undo" the binge without physically ridding herself of the food. As mentioned above, this can be done by methods such as exercising excessively or fasting.

Prognosis

Significantly fewer studies have been conducted to examine the prognosis for people with bulimia than for those with anorexia, and none of these studies have exclusively looked at adolescents. Current research, however, suggests that 50 percent of people with bulimia will recover, 30 percent will have recurring symptoms and 20 percent will have a chronic course of full-blown bulimia. The mortality rate for bulimia appears to be much lower than that for anorexia. It is estimated that 1 to 3 percent of teens with bulimia will die of their disease, compared to up to 10 to 15 percent of those with anorexia.[10] It is presumed that, as with anorexia, a child who receives treatment soon after the disease begins will tend to do better.[11]Therefore, if you think that your child has bulimia or bulimic behaviors, it is crucial to get her help as soon as possible to give her the best chance of recovery.

EATING DISORDER NOT OTHERWISE SPECIFIED

I know something's wrong with my child.
If it's not anorexia or bulimia, what can it be?

EATING DISORDER NOT otherwise specified (EDNOS) is a rather awkward but accurate description of an eating disorder that does not meet the strict diagnostic criteria for either anorexia or bulimia. One reason for this is because the criteria used to diagnose anorexia and bulimia was formulated for adults, not children. For example, a teenager with EDNOS may meet most of the criteria for anorexia but *still* not weigh less than 85 percent of her ideal body weight; someone else may meet many of the criteria for bulimia but purge only once a week.

Younger children and preteens are commonly diagnosed with ENDOS because they fail to meet—both physically and psychologically—the diagnostic criteria for either anorexia or bulimia. I am seeing a definite increase in the number of younger children with eating disorders, some as young as 8 years old. There are many theories as to why so many young children are getting eating disorders but no definitive answers. Is it because puberty is starting earlier? Or because advertisements encourage 8-year-old girls to look "sexy" and dress like Britney Spears? Is hearing so much about obesity having a boomerang effect? Let's look at a few examples of patients from my practice who were diagnosed with EDNOS:

- 14-year-old Stephanie had always felt that she was overweight. According to the chart at her doctor's office, she was at the high end of normal. The summer before entering high school, she decided to go on a diet. She lost 20 pounds by cutting out fat, eating 800 calories a day, and running three miles a day. Her body and mind were affected by these extreme weight loss measures. Stephanie was diagnosed with EDNOS because, despite her large weight loss, she didn't meet the weight criterion for anorexia.
- 18-year-old Juanita had been on diets "her whole life," but she was fully committed to making it "work" this time. She cut out all sweets and fats from her diet and began eating mostly fruits and vegetables. She did well with her diet during the week because she was busy with school, but on the weekends it was difficult. Usually one day on the weekend, she would break down and eat the "forbidden food." Once she started, the floodgates would open and she would end up eating for an hour straight. Afterward she would feel guilty and angry with herself. To make up for this binge, she would vomit and then not eat for the rest of the weekend. Juanita was diagnosed with EDNOS because she did not meet the criterion for bulimia of binging and purging at least twice a week.
- 16-year-old Daniel was on the wrestling team in the 130-pound weight class. He knew that it would be difficult to maintain that weight throughout the season but felt that he would be more competitive in that class than in the 135-pound weight class. He tried to eat healthfully and work out. He put on quite a bit of muscle during the wrestling season, which made it even harder for him to weigh in at 130 pounds. Daniel found that the only way to continue to weigh in at 130 pounds was to fast for two days and take a diuretic (water pill) prior to each meet. Daniel was diagnosed with EDNOS because he didn't meet several of the criteria for bulimia and anorexia.
- 10-year-old Melissa got food poisoning during a family vacation

in Mexico. She was very ill, especially during the long flight home. Her pediatrician treated her, and follow-up tests showed the infection was gone. Melissa, however, continued to complain about severe stomach pain and nausea after meals. Gradually, she began eating less and less, saying she was afraid that her stomach would hurt if she ate any food. When Melissa did eat, she would lay on her bed afterward, holding her stomach and crying. When all of the tests run by the gastroenterologists came back negative, she was referred to a psychiatrist, who diagnosed her with EDNOS.

Warning signs of Eating Disorders Not Otherwise Specified (EDNOS)
○ Obsessive exercising
○ Constant dieting
○ Sudden changes in diet such as completely eliminating an entire food group (meat, sweets, carbohydrates, fried food).
○ Starting out overweight but rapidly losing significant weight by not eating and over-exercising, then continuing to diet.

Keep in mind that the medical risks of EDNOS are at least as great and sometimes greater than those of anorexia or bulimia. Some of the criteria used by the American Psychiatric Association to diagnose *Eating Disorders Not Otherwise Specified* are as follows:

- Meeting all of the criteria for anorexia nervosa, except that the person's menstruation is regular or they have never had a period
- Meeting all of the criteria for anorexia nervosa, except that the person's weight is in a normal range (despite significant weight loss)
- Meeting all of the criteria for bulimia nervosa, except that the frequency of binging and purging is less than twice a week or for a duration of less than three months
- Purging after eating small amounts of food, with the absence of binging
- Repeatedly chewing and spitting out (but not swallowing) large amounts of food

Some doctors, however, will ignore the official criteria and diagnose a young girl with anorexia, even if she hasn't started her period. The important thing is that she gets the right treatment, and it's likely to be the same whether her medical record describes her condition as anorexia or EDNOS.

THE FEMALE ATHLETIC TRIAD

*My daughter has a muscular physique and energy to compete.
How can she have an eating disorder?*

OVER THE PAST few years, the incidence of the "female athletic triad," a separate category within EDNOS, has dramatically increased. This "triad" consists of amenorrhea (loss of menses), bone loss, and disordered eating. As elementary school, junior high, and high school sports become more competitive, young athletes are asked to push their bodies harder than ever before. This can push young girls beyond the point of safety, causing such a low fat-to-muscle ratio that they stop having menses, lose bone mass, and put their hearts at significant risk. One mother I worked with was shocked to learn that her daughter's swimming coach had told the girls that well-trained athletes don't get their periods. There should be no confusion about this: it is never normal for a girl to lose her period, regardless of her athletic abilities or performance. Male athletes can also suffer from eating disorders and be diagnosed with EDNOS; however, no separate subcategory exists for them.

The female athletic triad most often develops in young women who participate in sports that emphasize a lean body or the maintenance of a low body weight such as cheerleading, ballet, cross-country running, ice skating, gymnastics, and lightweight crew. The pressure to be thinner and more physically fit may be internal or it may come from others. Coaches with unrealistic expectations may pressure players to lose weight or train too intensely. Because of the increase of the female athletic triad, the International Olympic Committee's Medical Commission (IOCMC) recently took a position on the subject, encouraging coaches to "increase understanding of nutritional principles and how they impact health and performance." The committee suggests annual preparticipation screening to identify early signs and to develop coach and team education programs that "reduce the incidence of the drive for thinness and subsequent unhealthy eating behaviors."

Girls do not need to participate in an organized sport to develop the female athletic triad. It's possible to become obsessive about recreational exercise such as excessively going to the gym or running. In order for your child to be diagnosed with the female athletic triad, she would need to have:

- Amenorrhea (loss of at least three consecutive periods)
- Osteopenia (loss of bone density)
- A distorted body image

Diagnosing this syndrome can be difficult and bewilder even the most observant parents. Susie, a 16-year-old soccer player, is a good example of someone with female athletic triad. At first glance, Susie appeared to be fine: her weight was in a low but acceptable range, and she looked toned and muscular. She was working out five to six days a week with the soccer team and running on her own on the weekends and some evenings. When she got home from practice, she would have dinner with her family, eating the same amount as her parents and 10-year-old sister. The truth, however, was that Susie's nutritional intake did not compensate for the tremendous amount of energy she expended.

Although Susie did not look emaciated, her body's fat-to-lean tissue ratio was so low that she was, in fact, severely malnourished and her body was shutting down. Her periods had stopped the second month of soccer season, but she didn't think it was a problem: she was an athlete and she heard that some athletes don't menstruate, so she never mentioned it to anyone. Susie's mother was shocked when her daughter had to be hospitalized for a weakened, malnourished heart. The medical risks faced by a woman with the female athletic triad can be as great or greater than those faced by a woman who just stopped eating.

Regardless of your child's diagnosis, chances are you will be asking yourself how this happened. The next chapter tackles parents' most common questions.

2

THE QUESTIONS EVERY PARENT ASKS:

Why My Child?
What Did I Do Wrong?

Laney's Story:
All her friends were dieting, and they're okay—
why did our daughter get an eating disorder?

Laney's mother made an appointment at my clinic because she suspected something wasn't right with her 14-year-old year old daughter. A very social and active girl, Laney always got good grades and was enjoying her freshman year in high school. But her mother was concerned about her constant dieting. She told me it started when Laney and her two best friends decided to try out for the cheerleading squad and wanted to lose weight to be more competitive. They cut out "junk" food and began walking around the track instead of eating lunch. Initially, they all lost some weight.

Laney's friends and family told her she looked great; her mother praised her for eating healthy food and having so much willpower. After the tryouts, Laney's friends began to add chips and pizza back into their diets and eventually stopped their lunchtime walks. But Laney began to restrict her diet more. She significantly cut down on breads and cereals and became a vegetarian. She also changed her lunchtime walks into lunchtime runs.

Her parents began to worry: she was looking pale and gaunt and began withdrawing from her friends. Always a cheerful and happy child, Laney seemed very moody. Although she still excelled at school, she seemed to have lost her joie de vivre.

When Laney came into my office, she was thin and pallid. Her hands and feet were cold and her heart rate was very low. When I explained to her parents that she needed to be admitted to the hospital because of a weakened heart, they couldn't understand why this happened to Laney. Why had her "diet" gotten out of control while her friends' did not? What did they do wrong? Shouldn't they have noticed sooner that things were going wrong? How could they have praised her for losing weight when she was going down such a dangerous path? How did this happen?

Why my child? This is generally the first question most parents ask me when their child is diagnosed with an eating disorder. Their second question is usually, "What did I do wrong?" Your child's eating disorder most likely developed because of a complicated combination of factors and is not anyone's fault: it is not your fault or your child's fault. Recognizing that your child has a serious problem is the first step; it's time to stop looking back and trying to second-guess yourself; it's more important to begin looking forward and focus on how to help your child fight her eating disorder. As the mother of one of my patients told me, "The more I stopped feeling guilty about causing my daughter's eating disorder, the more I was able to move forward and focus on her recovery." The best way to move ahead is to learn as much as possible about your child's disease.

Most eating disorders start as ordinary diets—a teenage boy wants to get in shape for cross-country or a girl wants to buy a bikini for spring break. But at some undefined point, the child stops controlling the diet and the diet takes control of the child. One parent described it as "alien force taking charge of my child's eating." It is almost impossible to pinpoint when a diet shifts into an eating disorder, which makes it difficult for parents to recognize.

Parents often tell me they suspected something was "different" with their child but it was such a subtle, gradual change it was difficult to define. "Ellen's mood swings were so tricky—I figured she was hormonal or anxious about starting high school," one mother told me. "I talked to my friends who also said their daughters were unpredictable. But their kids didn't get an eating disorder—why Ellen? I keep trying to figure out what I could have done differently." If you're feeling like Ellen's mother, you're not alone. Many parents feel responsible for their children's eating disorders. I can't emphasize enough that you are not to blame for you child's disease. You'll need all of your energy to help your child beat her eating disorder and letting go of your personal blame is a good way to start.

In working with parents, I've found that it helps to understand why some children are at higher risk for developing an eating disorder. Despite considerable research in this area, the cause of eating disorders is still unknown. However, what we do know is that developing an eating disorder is influenced by a combination of factors: psychological, developmental, social, cultural, genetic, and neurochemical (brain chemistry). Just one of these factors alone will not cause an eating disorder, but a combination of these elements can increase the possibility of developing one. Often, the lines between these different factors blur: for instance, personality traits are psychological as well as genetic; cultural influences and social pressure often overlap.

The following offers a brief summary of the major risk factors for the development of an eating disorder. If you would like more in-depth information, appendix C lists books specifically written about these complex topics and appendix A and B list links to the most reliable Web sites focusing on eating disorders.

PSYCHOLOGICAL FACTORS

PSYCHOLOGICAL FACTORS, INCLUDING low self-esteem, anger, and the feeling of loss of control can increase a child's risk of developing an eating disorder. Sometimes eating disorders develop as a way to suppress feelings of loneliness or anger; at other times they may be reactions to low self-esteem or feelings of inadequacy.

Certain psychiatric diseases such as major depressive disorder, anxiety disorder, and obsessive-compulsive disorder can also increase someone's risk of developing an eating disorder.

DEVELOPMENTAL FACTORS

EATING DISORDERS USUALLY start during puberty, a time of tremendous physical changes as well as increased social and sexual pressures. Adolescents are often uncomfortable or embarrassed with the changes that their bodies go through during puberty:

- Girls have a significant increase in body fat and develop fat pads on their stomach, thighs and buttocks.
- Boys are likely to have a significant increase in height and change in their body shape.

Parents sometimes mention that their daughter, who was self-confident in elementary school, suddenly became insecure as she entered her teens. Others recall how their once independent and high-spirited son suddenly wanted to be exactly like his friends in junior high. In adolescence, the insecurity and desire to conform can exacerbate a teen's discomfort with his body. This is also a time when young people begin to recognize themselves as sexual beings, and start taking interest in potential romantic partners. Since teenagers are still figuring out who they are, your child's image of attractiveness may be strongly influenced by his peer group and societal ideals.

All of these changes and pressures can cause a teen to feel dissatisfied with his body. Research confirms there that is a strong association between body dissatisfaction and the development of eating disorders.

SOCIAL FACTORS

A CHILD'S SOCIAL experiences and family situation can also affect his risk of developing an eating disorder. When friends or family are dieting or are very concerned about their weight, this can magnify a child's own feelings of body dissatisfaction. Certain types of family dysfunction, such as poor communication or another family member's health concerns related to obesity, may also increase a child's risk as well. Other social factors include being teased about one's weight or having a history of physical or sexual abuse.

Your child's choice of activities may also play a role. Involvement in sports or activities that emphasize a lean body such as cheerleading, gymnastics, ballet, or modeling may increase the pressure to be thin. The higher the level of participation, the more pressure there is from teammates and coaches to "get in shape." With competitive athletics beginning in elementary school, it's not surprising that I am treating more 8- and 9-year-olds with eating disorders.

CULTURAL INFLUENCES

Eighty percent of women who responded to a survey in People *magazine said images of women on television and in the movies made them feel insecure.*

AMERICANS ARE BOMBARDED with almost 3,000 advertisements per day and many of these promote a clear message about beauty.[1] Our society's narrow definition of beauty, which is "you must be thin to be beautiful," is reinforced by television shows and movies. It is fascinating to observe how this message has changed in the last fifty years. According to world-renowned author and lecturer Jean Kilbourne, Marilyn Monroe, the epitome of beauty and sexiness in the 1950s, wore a size 16 dress; today's celebrities, such as Lindsay Lohan, Nicole Richie, and Jennifer Aniston, wear a size 2 or even a 0 and the average fashion model is thinner than 98 percent of American women.[1]

The media's obsessive promotion of the "thin ideal" can increase a child's risk of developing an eating disorder. Research has shown that women who are exposed to advertisements with thin models (as opposed to average-sized models) have increased feelings of depression, stress, shame, guilt, insecurity, and body dissatisfaction—all factors that put someone at risk of developing an eating disorder.[2]

NEUROCHEMICAL (BRAIN CHEMISTRY) FUNCTIONS

RESEARCH SHOWS THAT different chemicals found in the brain, such as serotonin, dopamine, and neurepinephrine, affect hunger, mood, and behavior. Scientists believe that these chemicals may influence the development and course of certain psychiatric illnesses such as depression, anxiety disorder, and obsessive-compulsive disorder. There is now evidence that these chemicals may also play a role in eating disorders.[3]

GENETICS

GENES ALSO INFLUENCE a child's risk of developing an eating disorder. This doesn't mean that you can "inherit" an eating disorder, but you can have a genetic make-up that increases your chance of developing one.[4] Relatives of people with anorexia and bulimia have a seven to twelve times greater chance of developing an eating disorder.[5]

PERSONALITY TRAITS AND OTHER ISSUES
AFFECTING EATING DISORDERS

DIFFERENT TYPES OF eating disorders have been associated with specific personality traits. For instance, people with anorexia tend to be perfectionists while people with bulimia tend to be more impulsive. This doesn't mean your child necessarily has these personality traits, it just means people with eating disorders are more likely to have them.

Common traits of people with anorexia:
- Desire to please others
- Difficulty communicating negative emotions such as anger and sadness
- Perfectionism
- Has to always be in control
- Poor self-esteem

Common traits of people with bulimia:
- Impulsive
- Engages in high-risk behaviors
- Novelty seeking
- Poor self-esteem

WHAT CAN TRIGGER AN EATING DISORDER?

ALL OF THE factors above can put a child at greater or lesser risk of developing an eating disorder. One factor alone, however, will not suddenly create a child's eating disorder; in most cases, an eating disorder develops from a combination of factors and is often triggered by a specific event or situation. Once started, however, eating disorders can create a self-perpetuating cycle of physical and emotional damage. This is only a partial list of potential triggers, but it could give you an idea about a situation in your child's life that may have triggered his eating disorder. (If you believe a specific incident may have affected your child, mention it to his therapist.)

- Changes in environment
  - o Moving
  - o Parents getting a divorce
- Changing schools
- Losses
  - o Death of a relative or friend
  - o Loss of a friend due to a move or a fight
  - o Breakup with a romantic partner
- Wanting to be healthy or thin for a special event
  - o Prom
  - o Summer or spring break trips
  - o Fat caliper testing at school
- Trauma (may be a small one)
  - o Being teased about weight
  - o Not getting asked to a dance
  - o Not making a sports team

There is no one thing that has caused your child to develop an eating disorder. It is a combination of factors—factors neither you nor your child could control. But you can control how you handle the situation from this point on: accepting the truth is the first step in helping your child through his illness; the second step is moving forward. In the next chapter, I'll show you how.

3

ACCEPTING THE TRUTH AND MOVING FORWARD

Beth's Story
The secret world of bulimia

When Beth, a 17-year-old high school senior and member of the varsity swim team, came to my office, she was adamant that she was fine and her parents were totally overreacting. Beth's parents had made an appointment at the eating disorders clinic because they were convinced she had a serious problem. Over the past few months, they began noticing that Beth was increasing her workouts, staying after practices to do a few more laps or lift weights. She told them this was necessary in order to get in shape for the state finals. At first, Beth's dad encouraged her, figuring swimming could lead to a college scholarship. But soon he suspected Beth was taking it too seriously. She rarely got home in time for dinner anymore and would just make something to eat and take it up to her room. Beth's mother began realizing that several times a week food would disappear from the pantry—a whole bag of chips, a loaf of bread, a box of cookies in one night. Yet how could it be? Wasn't she always saying, "I'm an athlete. I wouldn't poison my body with that kind of food." She couldn't figure out where else it would have gone since Beth's older sister was away at college. The previous week, right before going to bed, Beth's mother told me she walked past the bathroom and heard disturbing noises. She slowly cracked open the door and found Beth leaning over the toilet, making herself throw up. It was at that point that she realized all of these signs might be part of a much larger problem.

One of the most difficult things for any parent is saying the words, "My child has a serious disease." With an eating disorder, as with cancer or any other life-threatening illness, it's not unusual to go through denial and anger before admitting the truth. This is especially difficult if your child has an eating disorder because it's a confusing combination of psychiatric and medical complications. And because, unlike other diseases, it may seem as though your child is *choosing* to be sick. As a parent just entering the frightening world of eating disorders, you may find it helpful to approach what you need to do in three stages: first accept that your child has an eating disorder, next speak to your child about the problem, and then begin to take action.

ACCEPTING YOU CHILD'S CONDITION

TRUST YOUR PARENTING instincts. The critical first step in helping your child overcome her eating disorder is realizing—and then accepting—that there is a serious problem. Sometimes this realization comes over a period of time as your child continues to diet after you feel that she is too thin. Other times, there's the sudden shock of walking into the bathroom and catching your son making himself throw up. Either way, once you understand—and admit—there's a problem, the next logical step is getting help. This might seem simple but, unfortunately, it probably will be more difficult and complicated than you expect—or even imagine. To begin with, unlike some other medical conditions, there is no blood test that confirms your suspicions. Additionally, eating disorders are complex and not always easy to identify. All too often, pediatricians and family doctors are not trained in the diagnosis and treatment of eating disorders. They may not see the problem or understand the severe medical consequences. Be concerned if your child's doctor

- Doesn't acknowledge there's any problem and implies that you're overreacting
- Tells you that it's just a phase
- Tells you to take your child home and make her eat

If you feel that your child has an eating disorder, trust your instincts. The lists of possible symptoms of eating disorders on pages 9, 13, and 15 may help you to identify some of the warning signs.

HOW TO BRING UP THE SUBJECT

Starting a dialogue

Initially expressing your concern to your child may be daunting. If just asking your moody teenage daughter to clean her room is met with hostility and rolled eyes, the idea of talking about her eating disorder can seem overwhelming. She may adamantly deny it; she may be totally unaware that she even has an eating disorder; or she may tell you it's none of your business and being thin is the only important thing to her.

Before talking to your child about the situation, take time to plan your strategy. For a more positive and successful conversation, think about what would be the best time, setting, and approach. Remember: you are not trying to cure your daughter's eating disorder or convince her to eat. However, you do want to communicate that you are worried about her health, that you love her, and that you want to help her. Spending some time planning for the discussion may ease some of the stress of this difficult conversation. Try to avoid a battle of wills—you know this doesn't work, especially with teenagers. Make sure to emphasize that no one is to blame. Your conversation must not be confrontational. If you are divorced or separated, it is critical to discuss what it going on with your child's other parent and try to include them in the initial conversation. Regardless of your personal situation, you must try to present a united front to your child.

Choosing the right time

The distractions of everyday life can be demanding, which is why you should dedicate a block of uninterrupted time. This not only allows you to give the conversation your full attention, but also signals the seriousness of your concern to your daughter. Allow enough time to give this conversation the importance it requires. Select a time that is relatively free of constraints and preferably openended. You don't want to have to stop your daughter from expressing her concerns or feelings because you must get to a meeting or pick up her brother at soccer. You will also want to select a time that is emotionally calm. It is not productive to have this conversation after a heated interaction. Your daughter will not listen to you if you try to start the conversation after she stomps away from the dinner table because of a conflict over food.

Planning the setting

Select a location in your house, where you will not be disturbed and that is comfortable and quiet. Because this is a conversation that will no doubt evoke intense emotion from your child, privacy is important so she can express herself freely and not feel stifled (try to find a time when other family members are not home).

Communicating your concerns

Refer to specific situations that have concerned you, using as many "I" phrases as possible: "I am concerned because I found three empty cookie containers in the trash" or "I am very worried because you haven't been eating with the family." These "I" statements are often perceived as less accusatory than "you" statements such as, "You have to stop vomiting after meals," or "Why don't you just eat?"

Explain why these specifics concern you: "I get worried when you don't eat because not eating can cause medical problems." Use examples to explain why you believe these situations indicate a problem exists that requires medical evaluation. Of course, you'll need to modify the conversation to suit your child's age.

Avoiding a battle of wills

Expect that there will be some resistance to getting help. It is possible that your child doesn't think she even has a problem. She may wonder why you are making such a "big deal" about "nothing." She may become defiant and angry or totally withdraw. If there is resistance, remain calm (easier said than done) and continue to restate your concerns. It is likely the conversation may end without any resolution. Don't expect your child to agree and say, "Sure, mom. Thanks so much for wanting to help me." In fact, many of the parents I work with report that their children will insist they are fine. If this happens, it is important to explain that as a parent it is your responsibility to make sure she is safe; therefore, you need to make an appointment. Tell your daughter that you will let the doctor evaluate the situation. Both of you—for very different reasons—may be hoping that he will prove you wrong. But as you will read later in this book, part of your child's illness is being unable to "escape" from her anorexia.

Avoiding blame or giving simple solutions

Remember that eating disorders are very powerful psychiatric diseases that control how a person thinks and acts. Your child is not restricting food or throwing up to be defiant or to cause you or anyone else pain. This is something out of her control. It is crucial for her to know that you are not angry with her, but rather, you are worried and want to help her. Try not to give simple solutions such as, "If you just eat it will all be okay," or "Just don't eat so much at night and you won't feel the need to throw up." Avoiding statements such as these will demonstrate to your daughter that you understand it isn't simple and you aren't expecting unrealistic results.

Help!
How Do I Start the Conversation?

BARBARA SWENSEN, a former pediatric nurse practitioner at Children's Hospital in Seattle who now specializes in helping parents communicate better with their children, offers the following advice on ways to talk to your child about his or her eating disorder.

BE UNITED AND PREPARED!

Planning how and what you are going to say is extremely important. It's equally critical to have both parents in attendance—whether you are together or divorced—to present a united front. Even if your child's other parent is out of state, try to convince him or her to be part of this conversation.

Agree on who will start and/or who will lead the talk:
It may depend on who communicates best with your child or who is more comfortable in this role.

Write out or develop an outline about the following:
○ How you will begin the talk
○ How to support the parent who plans to do the talking

○ How you will respond to likely objections or resistance
○ Your specific plan for follow-up care (before you set up the talk, research different options that you can present to your child)
○ Your plan for regular talks

Edit each other's proposed talking points: This helps to make sure you're in agreement.

Practice the talk with each other: It may feel awkward but it's worth the effort. Have the written points in hand or in a pocket for quick reference when you're actually talking to your child.

STARTING THE CONVERSATION

Because you have a good plan and have rehearsed what you're going to say, you will have more confidence and can be calm and factual, not emotional. Here is a brief outline and script for what you might say:

Inform your child that you have "something important" you want to talk about. She may roll her eyes or ask what it's about. She may follow you around and bug you. This is okay. What you're trying to do is not create a surprise or be confrontational.

Always give advance notice
○ The pre-warning should be no less than five minutes and no longer than one hour
○ Resist the demand to "talk right now"

State the time and place for the talk:
"Your dad and I want to talk to you about something important. Let's meet in the family room in fifteen minutes."

THE TALK

Begin with an "I" or "we" statement:
"I have noticed that you recently lost a lot of weight."
"We are aware that you are throwing up after meals."

State your concern:

"We are very worried about you."

"I have been very concerned about you lately."

Pause: Allow your message to sink in, don't rush ahead.

Identify your exact concern clearly, directly, and succinctly:

It's common to beat around the bush and hope a child will fill in the blank. Being specific is more effective.

"We see that you are not eating enough to be healthy."

"We are concerned that you have anorexia."

Pause for a response:

Notice your child's expression and/or listen to the verbal response. Listen to what your child says or identify what you see in your child's expression (anger, fear, or sadness are likely) and then paraphrase it *back* to her. This type of reflexive feedback is not judgmental because it reports what you observe or think she might be feeling.

"It sounds like you don't think our concerns are valid."

"You seem angry and would like us to leave you alone."

"You seem frightened that we think you have an eating disorder."

Explain your plan for further evaluation:

"Your mother and I need to have a professional opinion about our concerns." (This puts the focus on what you want and away from your child.)

"I know you don't agree with me but I need a doctor or therapist to give me their opinion."

"It's my job as your parent to make sure you're okay, and I need to get some professional insight about my concerns."

Don't be sidetracked from your need for a professional opinion:

At this point, your child may start giving reasons and explanations for why this is unnecessary or crazy. You need to stand strong.

"Whether or nor you agree with us, we need to get a professional opinion."

Try to offer a choice of professionals:
This could be your child's pediatrician, an eating disorders specialist, or a therapist. However, if you suspect your child's health is already compromised (dizzy spells, weakness), make an appointment with a physician.

Summarize:
If your child has agreed she needs help, then repeat your shared concern ("I'm glad you recognize there might be a problem, and I'll let you know when I've set up an appointment"). If your child denies there's a problem, you might say, "I understand that you don't think there's a problem—but we still want a professional opinion about our concerns."

Parting words:
Whether your talk ended with agreement, anger, tears, or stonewalling, make sure to tell your child how much you love her, that you are concerned for her health and will always support her.

Set up a plan for regular talks. One talk is never enough, so establish a regular check-in right away.

TAKING ACTION

ONCE YOU'VE COME to the difficult conclusion that your child does have an eating disorder, it is time to take action. The most important thing to remember is *you cannot do this alone.* Your child's doctor cannot do this alone. A therapist cannot do this alone. It is absolutely critical to assemble a team of medical, psychological, and nutritional professionals, who together will treat your child. After working with hundreds of children and their families, I cannot stress enough the importance of organizing a team and developing an appropriate plan of action.

Like a sports team, your child's treatment team will need a "manager." And this responsibility is going to fall to the person who cares the most and knows the most about your child—you. It is up to you to assemble and coordinate the treatment team. I wish I could tell you it won't be a lot of work or take a lot of time. I can tell you it will become a part-time job. A strong treatment team is a key factor in moving your child into recovery. The individual members of the team need to share a common goal: to help your child overcome her eating disorder and a common philosophy on how to do it. Don't panic—all the steps you need to do are found in this book and it will give you both the information—and the confidence—you need to help your child fight this disease.

What next? You've taken the first step of what will be a long journey. As a parent with a sick child, it's logical that your next questions will be: Where do I go from here? How can I make my child well? Before learning how to help your child, it's essential first to understand the medical risks related to your child's disease as well as what your child is experiencing. This will help you better manage and appreciate the complexities of putting together a multidisciplinary treatment team.

4

THE MEDICAL RISKS
OF EATING DISORDERS

Lucas's Story
How can my son look so healthy but be so sick?

Dr. Harris, a local pediatrician, called me because she was very worried about a 16-year-old boy named Lucas. Lucas had come to see her for his annual school physical, but Dr. Harris immediately sensed something was very wrong. Lucas, a quiet and shy boy, was not very athletic and always one of the shorter kids in his class. Over the summer, he decided to get bigger and stronger and embarked on a program of exercising and "eating healthy." Since he was out of school, Lucas spent most of his day exercising: running, swimming, lifting weights, or rollerblading. He eliminated "junk food," including fries, chips, pizza, and soda, from his diet. His parents were thrilled to see their son be so disciplined about his health; they supported his efforts and bought him a set of weights for his room. Dr. Harris noted that Lucas had grown several inches over the past year and his weight was stable. But on further questioning, she discovered something that concerned her: Lucas was exercising more than four hours per day; and, although he was not counting calories, he was trying to eliminate all fat from his diet. After Dr. Harris probed a bit deeper, Lucas admitted that he almost passed out several times while running. He also said he often became dizzy when he stood up. When Dr. Harris examined Lucas, she noted that his heart rate was 42 beats per minute, which is very low. She also observed that his hands and feet had a bluish tinge and were cold. She was very concerned that his heart was not functioning correctly and immediately admitted Lucas to the hospital, where he was put on a heart monitor because of his increased risk of an irregular heartbeat. Dr. Harris's concerns were valid: Lucas did have a weakened heart and a serious eating disorder.

Eating disorders can have serious effects on every organ system in the body and, in some cases, may result in lifelong or even fatal consequences. The statistics are unnerving: adolescents with eating disorders are twelve times more likely to die than adolescents without eating disorders, and 10 to 15 percent of adolescents with anorexia will eventually die from complications of their disease. This is the highest mortality rate of any psychiatric illness and higher than some forms of cancer.[1]

Although the medical complications described below are serious and scary, most can be reversed by attaining—and maintaining— a healthy nutritional state. Full medical recovery, however, can take years. Therefore, if your son has been diagnosed with an eating disorder, or if you think he might have one, it is crucial that a physician, preferably someone who specializes in treating teenagers with eating disorders, examines him. Even if your child's primary care doctor maintains your son does not have an eating disorder, go to a specialist if you suspect he has a problem. Eating disorders, as we've discussed, may be difficult to diagnose and some pediatricians may not be familiar with all of the symptoms. Please refer to appendix B, which lists resources for finding a specialist.

Most of the medical complications described below are related to malnutrition. In this book, malnutrition is defined as a state of improper nutrition, not just being underweight. Using this definition, a child can be of normal weight—or even overweight—and be malnourished if his proper nutritional balance is disturbed by not eating enough.

EATING DISORDERS AND THE HEART AND CIRCULATORY SYSTEM

THE MALNUTRITION CAUSED by an eating disorder can seriously affect your child's cardiovascular system. As the heart becomes malnourished, it gets smaller, weaker, and less able to function at its normal strength, causing a range of problems: a slowed heart rate, decreased blood pressure, an irregular heartbeat, heart murmurs, heart attacks, and sudden death. Some behaviors that accompany eating disorders—such as vomiting or using medications to purge—may further damage the heart.

Signs of a heart problem may include fatigue, weakness, dizziness, passing out, poor circulation, and cold or blue extremities. People with eating disorders may not show any obvious physical symptoms, even though their hearts are severely weakened. In fact, they may still be engaging in normal activities, including rigorous exercise. Although heart problems seem to appear suddenly and without warning, they actually have been developing over a long period of time, because the body tries to protect the heart by using up all of its other reserves before depriving the heart of energy. Therefore, someone must be significantly malnourished before the heart is affected; and the heart must be significantly damaged before losing the ability to function normally.

Fortunately, the good news is most heart damage resulting from malnutrition or purging can be reversed when a patient returns to and maintains a normal nutritional state. If the malnutrition or purging isn't identified in time, the following conditions may develop:

Low heart rate

People often think that a low heart rate is a sign of physical fitness. This is true to a certain extent, but a very low heart rate, especially in the presence of malnutrition, actually indicates weakening of the heart muscle, not fitness. A heart rate of less than 50 beats per minute (while awake) in a malnourished person is a sign of a weakened heart. In fact, several studies have shown that, on average, well-trained athletes have heart rates between 52 and 60. A malnourished, weakened heart that is unable to keep up a normal rate has a greater risk of developing an irregular heart beat or suddenly stopping.

Irregular heart beat

A weakened, malnourished heart is at risk of developing an irregular heart beat, called an *arrhythmia*. An arrhythmia can prevent normal blood flow through the body and may put the heart at greater risk of a heart attack or suddenly stopping. In severe cases, the patient's heartbeat may become so irregular that it is unable to effectively pump blood.

Low blood pressure

When a heart becomes malnourished, it is unable to beat with its usual force, causing a drop in blood pressure and reducing its ability to pump blood against gravity. When someone stands up, their heart must pump harder to get blood up to their brain. If a heart is weakened, it may be unable to do this, which results in a further drop in blood pressure as well as an insufficient amount of blood reaching the brain, which may cause dizziness as well as fainting.

Heart murmurs

As a malnourished heart shrinks, it may bend the rings of cartilage that hold the valves that regulate the flow of blood. Think of the valves as being like one-way doors and the cartilage like the doorways. If the doorways bend, the doors won't seal correctly, causing blood to leak in the wrong way through the one-way door and creating the extra sound or "murmur." If severe enough, this condition can result in the poor delivery of oxygen to the body, resulting in the destruction of body tissue.

Heart attacks and sudden death

Significant malnutrition as well as low levels of certain salts in the blood can cause someone to suffer a heart attack or to have their heart suddenly stop. When someone with an eating disorder restricts calories, vomits, or abuses laxatives or diuretics, they are at risk of disturbing the delicate balance of salts in the blood, which may result in a heart attack or sudden death.

EATING DISORDERS
AND HORMONES

MALNUTRITION, AS WELL as purging, can turn down or turn off a part of the brain, called the hypothalamus, which controls the release of hormones throughout the body. When this occurs, the body will decrease the release of hormones such as estrogen, testosterone, and growth hormones, resulting in low sex hormones and low growth hormones. This can cause loss of menses, arrest of or failure to begin puberty, and delayed growth.

BONES AND GROWTH

To UNDERSTAND HOW eating disorders affect the bones, it is helpful to understand how bones develop. Bones are constantly being broken down and reformed (the medical term for this is *remodeling*). The availability of minerals (such as calcium) and the presence of the sex hormones (estrogen in women and testosterone in men) are two major factors that encourage bone formation over bone destruction. During our younger years, more bone is formed than is broken down, making bones denser and stronger. Minerals in the bones, such as calcium and phosphorus, give bones their strength.

During adolescence, we reach two milestones for our bones: peak bone density and peak bone length (full adult height). By the time we reach our early twenties our bones no longer have the natural ability to get denser or longer. Somewhere in our forties, we get to the point where more bone is being broken down than formed. An eating disorder during childhood or adolescence has a significant impact on what happens to someone later in life, affecting bone density and height.

Loss of bone density

Adolescence is a critical time for skeletal development because, as previously noted, during this period, peak bone density is attained. Malnutrition from an eating disorder can cause the normal pattern of bone growth to reverse: instead of greater bone formation and less bone destruction, someone who is malnourished will have greater bone destruction and less formation. This puts them at risk for developing weakened bones (osteopenia or osteoporosis), which also increases the risk of broken bones.

A decrease in sex hormones (estrogen and testosterone) is the major reason why someone who is malnourished will have bone loss. The sex hormones affect the bones in two major ways: they inhibit bone destruction and they promote the absorption of calcium. If someone can't absorb calcium, his or her bones can't grow denser and, in fact, will decrease in strength and density. This is compounded by the fact that when someone is malnourished, he will not have adequate calcium in his diet. If there is not enough calcium present, and what is there can't be absorbed, bone loss—and osteoporosis—is very likely.

The duration and degree of malnutrition significantly influences the amount of bone loss a child may incur.[2] Because children usually do not experience a significant loss of bone density in the first year of their eating disorder, early treatment is critical. Unfortunately, once bone loss occurs, it usually is not reversible.[3] Although we usually think of girls as being at risk, some studies have found that boys may be at even greater risk of osteoporosis.[4] Loss of menstrual periods in girls is an indication of low estrogen and, therefore, signals a significant risk of bone loss.

Impact on Adult Height

Children and adolescents who are malnourished may delay, or never reach, their expected adult height. In a malnourished body, the bones do not receive enough nutrition to grow longer because all of the body's energy is being used simply to stay alive. This will cause a stunting of growth. Malnutrition may further stunt someone's growth by decreasing the production of growth hormone, which stimulates the bones to grow longer. Girls and boys who develop severe eating disorders while they are still growing may never reach their full adult height.

THE DIGESTIVE SYSTEM

THE EFFECTS OF malnutrition on the digestive system can be severe: the stomach can fail to deliver food properly to the intestines and the intestines themselves can fail to move food through properly. This overall slowing of the digestive system can result in many complications such as patients' feeling very full with minimal food intake, acid reflux, and severe constipation. A loss of the ability to sense hunger or fullness and the development of abdominal pain may also occur.

When people are malnourished, their liver can also go through changes. Although it may seem counterintuitive, the liver can develop fatty infiltrates—large fat deposits that may impair liver function. All of these effects on the digestive system are reversible with an extended period of proper nutrition.

Medical consequences of purging

Some people with eating disorders try to rid themselves of food (and calories) by purging, which can be in the form of self-induced vomiting, excessive exercise, or an excessive use of laxatives and/or diuretics. Not only does purging contribute to malnutrition but it also can create other serious medical complications.

VOMITING

Vomiting can have serious effects on the digestive system from the teeth all the way down through the intestines. Repeated vomiting brings up harsh digestive acids into the esophagus and mouth, eroding the tooth enamel, gums, and the lining of the esophagus. With repeated forceful vomiting, it is possible to tear all the way through the esophagus or stomach. The hand or instrument used to induce vomiting can cut or tear the fragile lining of the mouth and throat; and the repeated pressure and acid from purging may also cause the esophagus or stomach to tear open, causing bleeding, which may be life-threatening.

The salivary glands may also be affected by purging. When these glands become overstimulated from vomiting, they can enlarge and form a mump-slike swelling in the cheeks.

Induced vomiting may also cause a loss of the natural "gag reflex"—the protective reflex, which keeps food, liquids, and vomit from entering the lungs. If foreign substances do enter the lungs, they can cause choking, severe difficulty breathing, pneumonia, and even death. The enlargement of the salivary glands and the loss of the gag reflex will probably reverse over time, but damage to the teeth, esophagus, and stomach may not.

EXCESSIVE USE OF LAXATIVES

Excessive laxative use may result in severe constipation and a reliance on artificial stimulation of the bowels in order to have a bowel movement. In extreme circumstances, the intestines may become so impacted with stool that they can rupture. Laxatives can also disrupt the balance of salts in the blood, sometimes to life-threatening levels (see below for more information about effects on the blood).

THE BRAIN

Malnutrition affects the brain on several levels: psychologically, behaviorally, and physically. Although these areas are closely linked, they are being presented separately to help you better understand your child's condition.

Psychological/Behavioral impacts

Despite the fact that many children and adolescents with eating disorders maintain good cognitive function well into their disease, in extreme cases, they may develop "organic brain syndrome." This is characterized by a "slowing" of brain function that causes significant cognitive difficulties. People with organic brain syndrome may display slowed thinking, in which they take longer to respond to questions than expected; forget what you told them right after you said it; and have difficulty with decision making. There are also psychological symptoms that occur when someone's brain is malnourished. These include extreme shifts in emotions, depression, anxiety, and obsessive-compulsive like symptoms. Rigid thoughts and rituals regarding food and meal preparation also frequently develop.

Physical impacts

Imaging scans of brains of malnourished people show an actual decrease in the amount of brain tissue.[5] Although we know malnutrition can change chemicals in the brain as well as blood flow to the brain, there is much controversy as to whether a malnourished brain will recover fully with proper nutrition. Some studies conclude that physical damage to the brain reverses if a patient returns to and maintains a healthy nutritional state; other studies, however, imply that some people continue to have some neurological problems, such as social dysfunctions and spatial problems, throughout their lives.[6]

THE REPRODUCTIVE SYSTEM

BECAUSE MALNUTRITION AND purging can decrease the production of sex hormones (estrogen and testosterone), an eating disorder can stop sexual development, preventing puberty from starting or being completed. In girls, this can result in failure to begin menstruation or a loss of menstrual periods; boys may cease to have wet dreams or experience a loss of erectile function. Fortunately, there doesn't seem to be any effect on future fertility as long as the person has attained and maintained a healthy nutritional state.

BLOOD

THE HEMATOLOGICAL (BLOOD) system is also affected by malnutrition. All of the major types of blood cells—red blood cells, white blood cells, and platelets—may be affected. In most cases, once healthy nutrition is achieved, these conditions will be reversed.

Red blood cells

People with malnutrition may experience a drop in the number of red blood cells, called anemia. This can lead to fatigue and pallor.

White blood cells

The production of white blood cells is also impaired with malnutrition. Because the body uses white blood cells to fight infections, someone who is not producing enough white blood cells may be more susceptible to infections from both bacteria and viruses.

Platelets

Platelets allow the blood to clot. When someone is malnourished, the number of platelets in the blood may decrease, which causes easy bruising, bleeding gums, and nosebleeds.

Salts in the blood

Malnutrition, vomiting, and the use of laxatives and diuretics can alter the delicate balance of salts in the blood. These salts are responsible for many bodily functions such as making the heart beat correctly and balancing body fluids. A disturbance in the salt balance can cause medical complications such as heart attacks, arrhythmias, seizures, and death.

SKIN AND HAIR

THE LACK OF fats, vitamins, and minerals in people with malnutrition can cause visible damage to the skin, hair, and nails.

Skin

When someone is malnourished, the skin often becomes dry and flaky. Cuts and bruises don't readily heal and acne and rashes may develop. Because of a lack of body fat, a downy "fur" called lanugo may begin to grow on the body as an attempt to conserve heat and energy. People who purge may also develop calluses on their knuckles, where their knuckles hit their teeth. This is called Russell's Sign.

Hair and nails

Malnutrition may cause someone's hair and nails to become dry and brittle. Their nails may develop pits and the hair on their head may thin and fall out. People with malnutrition do not usually develop bald spots, but their hair may become noticeably thin, dry, and brittle.

REFEEDING SYNDROME

Medical Complications of Improper Renourishment

Although I frequently mention that proper nutrition can halt or reverse many of the medical conditions created by an eating disorder, there are also very real dangers involved in how a child is "renourished." This probably seems contradictory: if a child is starving, why wouldn't you just give him lots of food? The answer is that feeding a malnourished person too fast can have dangerous, life-threatening repercussions. It can result in a sudden drop of certain electrolytes (salts in the blood), causing problems with heart, lung, and muscle functions. Liver and kidney damage can also result. If not properly managed, refeeding can also cause a significant increase in fluid in the blood vessels, which may result in puffy hands, feet, and ankles, fluid in the lungs, heart failure, and even death. Therefore, it is extremely important to "refeed" severely malnourished people in a medically supervised environment.

OTHER BODY SYMPTOMS CAUSED BY EATING DISORDERS

FATIGUE, COLDNESS, AND dizziness are problems commonly seen in people with eating disorders. These are due to an overall lack of nutrition and possibly inadequate amounts of body fat. In some people, starvation releases chemicals in the brain called endorphins, producing a type of "high." When this occurs, people seem to have a normal or even increased energy level despite being extremely malnourished.

PREDISPOSITION FOR ACCIDENTS

ACCORDING TO THE National Institutes of Health, accidents—from automobile crashes to sports-related mishaps—are the leading cause of injury and death among adolescents and young adults. Adolescent brains are still developing and their judgment is not always sound. Combine this with the side effects of malnutrition, and the propensity for accidents increases dramatically. Because malnourished people are more likely to be weak, dizzy, and uncoordinated, they are at an even higher risk of being involved in an accident. They also have a higher risk of passing out, which further increases their risk of injury. While some accidents may be minor, such as cutting or burning oneself out of clumsiness, passing out while driving a car can be extremely serious.

There's no question that the above medical risks associated with eating disorders are terrifying; of course, no child will have all of them. However, the sooner you can intervene and help your child to overcome her eating disorder, the less damage will occur. To truly support your child it can be helpful to try and understand what your child may be thinking and feeling. Chapter 5 provides some insight from children who have suffered from eating disorders themselves.

5

PRIVATE THOUGHTS

What Kids Say about Their Condition

"I don't want to 'get better.' Without my eating disorder, who am I?"
—Karen, 14 years old

•

"If I let myself eat, I know that I will never be able to stop."
—Josh, 16 years old

•

Ana's Creed

I believe in Control, the only force mighty enough to bring order to the chaos that is my world.

I believe that I am the most vile, worthless, and useless person ever to have existed on the planet, and that I am totally unworthy of anyone's time and attention.

I believe that other people who tell me differently are idiots. If they could see how I really am, then they would hate me almost as much as I do.

I believe in perfection and strive to attain it.

I believe in salvation through trying just a bit harder than I did yesterday.

> *I believe in bathroom scales as an indicator of my daily successes and failures.*
>
> *I believe in hell, because I sometimes think that I am living in it.*
>
> *I believe in a wholly black-and-white world, the losing of weight, recrimination for sins, abnegation of the body, and a life ever fasting.*
>
> "Ana's Creed" often appears on "Pro-Ana" Web sites. The authors of these sites state that they believe that anorexia is a lifestyle choice and not a disease. (Chapter 12 has information about Pro-Ana Web sites). This clearly illustrates the rigid black-and-white world of eating disorders—a place where things are either good or bad, or right or wrong. It also shows how people with eating disorder use their disease to control their lives.

It's difficult to fully comprehend the nightmare of living with an eating disorder. It is heartbreaking to hear a lovely 15-year-old girl say, "I know that this could kill me. I would just rather be dead than fat." Then there was 13-year-old Jamie who said, "It's not just a glass of milk. It is liquid with calories and that is about as terrifying as it gets."

People with eating disorders often describe their illness as a "voice" or another "person" in their head. This voice usually starts off fairly quietly, saying things like, "Look how strong you are for not eating breakfast. Don't be weak by eating that sandwich for lunch. You can stay strong." However, as the eating disorder progresses, the voice often becomes louder and more angry saying things like, "You are so fat and that toast is going to make you even fatter. You'd better throw it up now!" Eventually, as the disease becomes more and more consuming, people describe the eating disorder as taking over how they act and think. Individuals report feeling mentally and physically drained from the incessant thoughts of food and weight that the eating disorder invokes. Others describe the experience of having an eating disorder like being in a "tunnel" where there is no escape.

Carla, who battled with anorexia for three years, said, "Every time I look in the mirror I see my thighs get larger. I can look, turn around and then look again and they will have grown." Carla was 5 feet 4 inches and weighed 80 pounds.

The following recollections, letters, and essays are written by young women with eating disorders. They eloquently describe this inner battle between the eating disorder and its victim. Because these are personal accounts, the names have been changed to protect the authors' privacy when requested.

Heidi's Diary
Struggling with Bulimia

Diary entry, April 23, 2003

Dear Mom,

For some reason I have regressed exponentially in the past few weeks . . . regressed to what seems like the deepest pits of hell. I would trade my bulimia for cancer, AIDS, any illness . . . anything but this. "It" consumes me. I can only devote half of my time to my studies, my friends, myself . . . the other half is selfishly gobbled up by this ravenous thing living within me. Or at least, that is what I hope . . . . that it is "a thing" living within me . . . something I can possibly exorcize from my body someday. Maybe it's not a thing . . . maybe it's me. How can I escape myself? What an awful thing to fear, to hate, to shun . . . my very own being, until death do we part.

Each day that passes, I slip farther and farther away from who I am, who I used to be, who I want to be. It is permeating every aspect of my life . . . taking over everything. Soon there will be nothing left . . . it is killing me.

I don't know what more I can do. Life is so painful, so lonely, such a miserable existence. I'm so tired of fighting.

I trust you, Mom, to keep this to yourself. Please do not show dad or anyone . . . I am exposing a part of myself that is more internal and private than anything I know. Please do not ask me about/make reference to this on the phone or in person.

Love,

Me . . . and It

Heidi recently wrote the following essay:

I remember writing this letter in my diary to my mom. Of course, I never sent it to her. But looking back, I think it was the first step on the long road to recovery. It was my way of finally acknowledging what I'd known deep down for years: I could not beat this "thing" alone. Having an eating disorder is more than taking a diet to extremes. I know now that an eating disorder is not a choice—but I really didn't understand it when it was controlling me.

Many people consider eating disorders to be a problem rooted in food and weight. In reality, at least for me, the struggle around food and weight was really about loneliness, comfort, power, fear, and control. All these primal emotions are simply masked, in turn, by one of the most primal human drives: eating.

Now when people ask what drove some of my initial eating disorder thoughts and behaviors, I'd be lying if I didn't include "weight loss" as one of the motivators. I did begin the cycle of restricting-binging-purging in the false belief that losing weight would bring me some semblance of happiness. Somehow, controlling the number on the scale, along with inducing the numbness that comes with a binge, did offer a certain amnesty from what I dreaded most: reality—and all the emotional wounds, stressors, and feelings of powerlessness that came with it.

I can't pinpoint the specific moment or day it happened but it was as if a switch flipped on some specific part of my brain and simultaneously turned off the switch to my personal willpower and, in some way, to my freedom of choice. When I wanted out of the vicious, self-perpetuating cycle of my bulimia, I had no control. Something so powerful—more powerful than anything I'd ever known—had taken over my mind.

The eating disorder was all consuming—every second of every day. Although I would put on a front that I was present in the moment or in the conversation at hand, this wasn't the case. I was always worrying about how I'd get out of the next meal or where and when I'd be able to find a place to binge/purge in private. I was possessed by incessant mental calculations of how many calories I consumed; how many calories I purged; how many calories I needed to burn at the gym. It was always there ... gnawing at my consciousness, or at best, simply lingering in the back of my mind. Ultimately, my passion for life and the things I once enjoyed simply vanished into nothing. My entire life evolved around the bulimia. It took priority over family, friends, and me.

As much as I wanted to rid myself of this "thing" that plagued my mind, body and soul, something kept me holding on to it. I believed there was a way to have both my life and my disorder so that I didn't need to face my issues, my problems, and most importantly, my emotions. For me, the eating disorder took care of all of that. It allowed me to avoid the anxiety or stress from taking finals, enabled me to cope with potential rejection from boys, and blocked out any emotional pain from my past, which included abuse and rape. I, or rather, my disorder, rationalized that sacrificing my physical self was the trade-off to protect the ache in my soul.

I continued to make that "trade-off" for years because, unlike anorexia, bulimia does not necessarily reveal itself externally. I didn't look emaciated; in fact if someone looked at me they wouldn't necessarily describe me as thin. Despite my outward picture of normalcy—good grades, involvement in the school orchestra, ability to hold down a part-time job—internally, I was in a living hell filled with secrets, lies, and deceptions.

My parents didn't catch on until I was fully entrenched in my disorder. And when they did, their first instinct was to try and "fix" the problem by endlessly asking me what was wrong and telling me to eat. Their initial attempts to help were met with anger and further withdrawal. Feeling perpetually alone and misunderstood, I sank even deeper into my disease and became further isolated from my family, especially my mother. Our household—once filled with playful teasing, laughter, family games, and pleasant dinner conversation—became infected with the tears, screaming matches, stress, worry, frustration, and anger. I passively watched my relationship with my mother, my father, and my two younger brothers shatter.

Throughout all of this, I was not blind to the pain I was causing my family. I just didn't care. Although the eating disorder numbed out painful, negative emotions it also took away any love, joy, and happiness. My mother and father tried to be patient with me but eventually, their frustration began to show through and turned to anger. And who could blame them? I flippantly disregarded any extensions of help and stubbornly clung to something that was slowly killing me.

In retrospect, I do realize that my parents' anger was not directed at me but towards the eating disorder and what it was doing to their daughter. At the time, however, I internalized my parents' anger as yet another indicator of what an awful, unworthy waste of space I had become.

Although I know it's difficult, if not impossible, for someone without an eating disorder to truly understand what the sufferer goes through, I also cannot begin to fathom how emotionally and physically draining the experience must be for parents. I know that my parents initially blamed my bulimia and self-destruction to personal flaws in their parenting. What we all learned through therapy is that there is nothing they could have done—from my childhood through early adolescence that would have prevented my eating disorder.

Ironically, while an eating disorder is no more a choice than leukemia or Alzheimer's, recovery is indeed a decision one chooses to make. It *requires* an intense personal desire for life without the eating disorder and a willingness to completely surrender to those who want to help.

It is important to recognize that recovery is not an end state, but rather a journey with both high and low points. If I experience a setback, I know what I have to do to get back on track and keep moving in the right direction—towards goals, relationships, self-love, happiness: things I could never have in my disorder.

It isn't easy. And oddly enough, there are times when I even "miss" my illness; when taking responsibility for my actions seems more daunting than simply acquiescing to the voice that still lingers in my mind from time to time. I am always mindful of underlying emotions and triggers that might ruffle the waters. I tell my story so that you—parents, friends, and siblings—may gain insight to this awful disease from the sufferer's perspective. In turn, I hope this may foster a supportive environment to help your loved one in his/her difficult struggle. More importantly perhaps, I tell my story so that I may remember—remember a time when my life was not my own. Some days are easier than others; but at least it's my life I'm living now.

The following poem appeared in *Healing Hearts Magazine* (Vol. 2, October 2005), published by Lucile Packard Children's Hospital at Stanford.

I Will Get Better Soon
Shelly (Age 14)

Hi, my name is Shelly, about a year ago I
had gotten a disease, and now I am not a pretty sight . . . My hair is
Falling out, and my skin is drifting away. I used to be beautiful
But I am not today. I can't ever be out with friends or family,
Because I am always too tired, and I have no energy. I have all these
Moods that I just can't control, I used to have a smile on my
Face and my heart was made of gold. It shined in the day, and

Brightened up the night sky, now all I ever think about and wonder is
Why? Why this had to take control of my life and mind, and all I ever
Think about is all the magical and wonderful dreams that disease made me
Leave behind. All my love and joyful thoughts I had for things, and all
My fantastic goals and heart-warming dreams. Dreams of growing up to be a soccer
Star. Dreams of letting my heart run free, and going really far. I could go to
Hawaii or even the moon . . . because I've not given up yet, I know I'll
Get better soon. I am always so sad and even depressed, but when I think about
It, I think god gave this to me, kind of as a test. A test for me to realize
All the things I have to love, and how God and his angels are protecting me with
My loved ones above. And to realize how lucky I am, and how much
I have coming towards me too, if I look deep in my heart, and fight
As hard as I can, and start loving the real person that I truly am.
I will try to learn to love who god made me to be, because you only
Have one life, so you better live it free. And soon living with your heart living wild
And strong, and follow god's hands and your own soul, and you'll never go
Wrong.

Before ED (that's what I decided to call my eating disorder) took over my mind and body, I was a happy, high-spirited, goal-oriented, success-striving Olympic-bound athlete. ED has taken over my mind, thoughts, and my life. And although I am fighting with all my heart and soul, my road is still long and hard. I know with God's help and the love of my family and friends, I will win this war with ED. And as my poem says, if my heart stays strong, and I follow God's will, then I'll never go wrong. Never.

Adrienne's Memories of Anorexia

I am now 22 years old, but I remember (though I'd like to forget) September 1996. In my head, that month is collapsed into flashes—moments that at once feel familiar and unfamiliar, as memories do. Some of the details are fuzzy, but to be certain I'm 12 years old, my body is starving, my pulse is slowing, my hair is falling out, and my skin is drying and tightening and bruising. Some of my memories are recurrent—like one where I wake up in the morning, crawl out of bed, and as soon as I'm standing upright, everything around me turns black. It's as if my head is swimming in a black sky.

It's a dizzying feeling to remember. I write this as a grown-up woman, and these flashes of memory seem distilled from reality, like dreams. Yet these fragments from my past hang in my mind. Because even as a grown woman, when sit down to eat, I feel the repercussions of my younger self. I still feel confused and ashamed.

And then these memories visit me:

I remember tasting the sweet chemical-laden air of a hospital room while sitting on the examination table, thighs pressed against the smooth white paper covering it. Mother stands against a wall opposite of me staring at my legs, and I wonder why she has to look at me the way she does; but this question has an obvious answer and I know what that is. She wants to find a cure. So before the pediatrician enters the room, she shakes her head, sighs, and mutters, "We've got to fix this . . . thing. We've got to get rid of this . . . this bad situation you have." She says "bad situation" instead of *anorexia*, the word that embarrasses her, brings her shame, and makes her cry at night. "I didn't want it to come to this," she goes on. "I didn't want to bring you to a doctor. But what I've discovered is that you don't know what's best for you anymore. You've lost your ability to think." Then I come back, "Mother, I can think," only instead of reassuring her, I upset her, so her voice gets shrill and she says, "Well, I've been reading and I know what's happening to you. Your brain is eating itself!"

And, too, in memory, I hear my mother's voice on Monday mornings. "It's weigh day," she says, "so you need to take off those sweats, get into my room and onto the scale." And the way to respond to her, to make her think I haven't prepared for this moment, is to say, "Oh yeah, it's Monday," as if I've lost track. But I've not lost track at all. I could *never* lose track. And in my head, I practice saying, *Believe me, Mom, I tried to gain a pound for you this week, but all I could do was maintain my weight.* But here's the secret she doesn't know: I drank nearly a gallon of water in my bedroom closet before stepping on that scale, and I haven't peed in twelve hours.

• • •

I promise, I say to myself, *I'll gain weight.* I've made a thousand promises in my head, and morning after morning, I've said to my reflection in the mirror: *starting today, I'll be different. I'll eat just the right amount of the right things, and after that, I'll figure out what I need to do for everyone to love*

me—and not love me out of pity, but love me because I'm beautiful and thought-
ful and generous and kind.

A violent headache flashing against my eyes, I remember:

The psychologist with the yellow legal pad searching for answers. Was it the sexual abuse? A father who drank? A mother's expectations? Pressures at school? Or just the media's celebration of thin women?

The girls in the school choir class asking, between songs, "Do you eat?" And me searching my brain for excuses. *Well, of course I eat, but the doctor says I might have hyperthyroidism, which means my metabolism is working extra fast; and, oh, actually, I was swimming in this lake last summer, and I swallowed this parasite and it made me really sick and I'm just now recovering and gaining back the weight I lost. But trust me, I eat.* And then the choir girls saying, "Well, we just wondered, because everyone's saying you're anorexic."

Hair falling out.

Lying in bed, on my side, bruises blooming where the insides of my knees touch.

Daydreaming about my funeral. Would *anyone* cry?

I'm a grown woman now and healthy, but in the perennial present of memory, anorexia doesn't go away. This is not my mother's fault. And it isn't my father's fault. For that matter, I am not a victim. What anorexia amounts to is a failure at perfection and the delusion of control. It's a slight twist in character, and recovery has meant seeing through different shades, accepting the gap between what is and what I sometimes think should be, and striving for balance within. The truth is that the most vexing part of this illness, for me, has had nothing to do with food. Ten years after recovery I still panic when confronted by someone else's displeasure or unhappiness, as if I'm the cause of it. I'm painfully aware of the faces around me and I absorb every change of emotion I see in people's eyes and mouths. Sometimes I even blame myself for a stranger's frown.

Of course, I'd much rather talk about someone else's relationship with food instead of my own. Except somehow I've convinced myself, just long enough to write this, and hope that by revealing my own troubles someone else might be unshackled.

Cora's Story:

Letter from a 21-year-old woman to her eating disorder

Dear It,

You have been the best abusive but loving friend I have ever known. You are a part of me. You make me whole. However, you are not who I am, not who I want to become. I have loved you just as much as you have hated me. I trust you to help me through the storm. Yet you are responsible for the storm in the first place. How do I avoid a storm I like so very much? You are my best friend and have been for so very long. You have stuck with me through tears. You never leave my side. You are strong. So strong you overpower me at times and block out my own voice. You are a leech. Sucking the very life from my soul. Yet you help heal the wounds that hide before my very eyes. You are my friend. You provide hope that one day you will help me achieve my unreachable goal of perfection. Even when I doubt you and your intentions you grow stronger. Each time I gain strength to even attempt to fight what really feeds you is when I am overcome with depression and anxiety and feel like the world is going to fall apart around my very life. Then, this is when you move in even more and possess me even further. Yet I allow you to. So in a way it's my fault. I see who you really are. I see the pain you have caused everyone around me. I see this, yet I don't know this. I still see you as this beautiful dream that fills my imagination. You are a picture of perfection, to me. Can you see this? Can you see what I see? Through my eyes you can do nothing wrong. My emotional mind tells me that in order to control myself and my emotions I desperately need you and can't do it without you. I desperately need you and everything you do for me. My intellectual mind shows me that indeed you really have helped me but there are other ways to deal with my problems than to hang on to you. You are not a healthy coping mechanism. You are killing me bit by bit 'til I am just a shell of a body without a soul. Physically I may exist but mentally I will be so absorbed in my relationship with you that there will no longer be a part of me that exists just for me. It will all be just for you alone. I am afraid that I grow closer and closer to you with each passing day. My soul cries out for help but for so long I am afraid to give you up. What will become of my life without you? I fear that when you leave me I will no longer be complete, no longer be whole. I fear that once you leave me I will contain a hole deep within me that only you can fill. You can fill the void in my soul. What will become of the hole? Will it stay empty? Will it fill with loneliness? Can I be accepted without you? Can I be accepted without being whole? Will I be the person I was before I met you, It? I can't seem to let you go. I deserve to have such an abusive friend as you are. I am an inherently bad person. I deserve to be abused by you. I could have done better in my life. I feel like my life is over without you. I could never have achieved higher. I could have performed better. I could have made my parents proud of me. Then I had to go befriend you. The only thing I have to do to please you is to listen and obey you, which I find ever so easy to do. I wish it could be as easy to please myself as it is to please you. But then again nothing is good enough for you. You have carried me through the pits of despair when I should have been learning to walk on my own two feet. Where does that leave me? Crawling when I should be walking. Who shall help me walk when I am so afraid of falling? You have been the shoulder to cry on, the voice in my ear, the teacher that I have been taught by. One of the hardest things that I will ever do is desert my best friend and convince myself that I am better living without you. To be on my own. It will take time to get over you and a huge amount of strength and courage. But deep down, past the superficial mask I wear, I know there is enough strength to beat you and everything else that might come along.

Your faithful servant,
Cora

Anonymous Essay Posted Online

The following account of a young woman's struggle with anorexia has been excerpted from an eating disorders Internet bulletin board and offers a glimpse into the life of someone living with an eating disorder.

Anorexia is not an illness, it's a person. I call her Anna. Anna comes to live inside your body with you. You're still in there, too—but she is always stronger.

I don't remember the exact day she arrived but I remember suddenly realizing that the actions of my body were no longer my own, and wondering who it was that was making these decisions for me. After I'd eaten, Anna would make me feel so terrible that it was easier to let her choose when and what we ate. When I was out with my friends, or ready to eat with my family, I told them I wasn't hungry, or I was allergic to foods, or I felt ill. Anna would just sit there and laugh at me trying to convince everyone. It was okay for her; she lived in my body but couldn't feel my hunger, or my pain. She didn't care that my hair fell out, that my bones creaked or that my teeth were loose.

Eventually I ran out of lies, so I made sure I never had to be with people when they were eating or drinking. I didn't like it—it was Anna's choice. It was her that got on the scale every day, and punished my body if another pound hadn't been knocked off. I wanted to tell everyone that it wasn't me that had done this—but how could I expect them to believe me when they didn't know about Anna?

And then I gave up the fight with Anna and I let her have my body to herself. People sat and watched and talked about me as if I was the one refusing food and being hostile and rude. I resented them all. Had they just forgotten who I was? Did they not remember that I loved food and that I was fun and sociable?

There were a few people that knew it wasn't me. They were the ones that would eventually fight to get me back, and would eventually realize that they had to fight Anna to get to me. Though they didn't know it then. Back then they thought it was me.

I didn't want to die, but I would sooner have left my body than share it with Anna. I felt it start to happen. I lost the ability to walk more than a few feet before having to lie down. I had to summon all my strength just to go on breathing. My hair would come out in handfuls from my head and my nails had started to fall out. All the time Anna just watched and laughed— and I waited. It was almost a relief knowing that soon I'd win over her—and that she couldn't survive without me.

It was at this point that Anna showed herself to my family. They said they knew I couldn't fight her on my own, but they said that together we'd be stronger, that we'd send her away, and that I could take my body back for myself. I didn't believe them. For two years I'd fought and fought. I'd watched her take my body and kill it slowly and painfully while all I could do was sit by and watch. How could I change that now? I didn't know how to eat food anymore. I didn't know how to feel hunger anymore. I didn't feel anything anymore.

It took time for them to reach me. It was a constant battle, with Anna trying to push me back every time I found a bit of strength. But this time there wasn't just me there to greet her. I had the strength of my family, and the doctors with their medication. She'd still creep up on me when I was alone, but I knew how to deal with her now.

My body began to look normal again. And then one day I woke up first, and had my first taste of life, albeit for just a few minutes, without her in my body. Then it was a few more minutes, then an hour, and then a whole day.

That was a year ago. And now I look at my body and know that I control it. I won't lie and say she's not there. I don't know if she'll ever be totally gone. But now her being there serves a purpose. As long as she's there, I will draw strength from her. She will serve as a constant reminder that with the love and belief of my family's strength—and their belief in mine—I defeated her.

Anorexia can choose anyone's body to invade. At first it's hard to identify that it's not you, but her that is controlling you. But once you know she's there, you can accept that it's not your fault that you're acting against your will. Once you accept this, you can, with help, fight the other being living inside you. The most important thing to remember is that although many people will not understand that there is someone else using your body and killing your soul, someone will. And when that someone does, they can fight with you to get rid of the impostor. Don't ever let her win.

Each of these essays and reflections describes the negative voice that speaks to someone with an eating disorder, the powerful messages that begin controlling the person's behavior and, ultimately, life. What also comes through is desperation to get well and the desire, even if it a faint cry, to be free of the eating disorder's influence.

Everyone's eating disorder is different. What your child is experiencing may or may not be like those described above. What ever your child's experience, respect that it is beyond her control and, no doubt, as upsetting and terrifying to her as it is to you. But as mentioned earlier, knowledge is power, especially when treating eating disorders. Now that you have more information and knowledge about eating disorders, it will be easier to move to the next step—organizing your child's treatment team.

PART TWO

YOU KNOW THERE'S A PROBLEM:

NOW WHAT DO YOU DO?

. . . .

"We can't do this alone." It was the same inner voice that told me my 11-year-old daughter, Sarah, was slipping away from us during those early days of trying to fight her eating disorder. Every day my wife and I would try something new. But with every step we took forward, the eating disorder seemed to take two leaps. We were desperate—two parents struggling to save their child, a child whose life we feared would be lost without intervention. We had no idea what to do, and we knew time was running out. Sarah's physical and mental health deteriorated so fast that we had to admit her to an eating disorders unit of a major hospital. Lucky for us, it offered a preassembled team of professionals who could help our daughter: top-quality physicians to monitor her vital signs; psychologists and social workers to compassionately probe her confused and troubled young mind; nutritionists to help undo the damage of hearing that fats are always unhealthy and thinner is unequivocally better. While Hillary Clinton's book, *It Takes a Village*, had nothing to do with eating disorders, I think she was onto something. If your child has an eating disorder, you can't help her alone. Some parents seem to think that asking for help equates to an admission of parental shortcoming. But putting together a treatment team—and asking for help—is not an indictment of your parental ability. It is an endorsement of it.

> Four years later, my 15-year-old daughter is in a stage of recovery that borders on the miraculous. I marvel at the distance she has come, and I know we couldn't have done it without a team of caring professionals. It took a village.
>
> —A father's essay

IF IT IS apparent that your son or daughter has an eating disorder, it is likely that you're now anxiously asking yourself, "What do I do now?" At this point, it's understandable why many parents are very frightened and overwhelmed. You, however, have already taken the first step by recognizing that your child is sick.

In this section, I'll help you take charge of the situation by providing an overall strategy for putting together an effective treatment plan. I will walk you through every step of the process, beginning with how to select the right team of professionals to support your child.

With this information, you will be empowered and able to take a proactive role in your child's treatment and recovery.

6

GETTING HELP:
Organizing Your Child's
Treatment Team

Martina's Story:
How could eating healthy turn into an eating disorder?

Martina came to see me at the urging of her middle school counselor. The counselor, who had met with Martina to review her next semester's class schedule, thought Martina looked incredibly thin and seemed very tired. She also remembered seeing Martina sitting alone at lunch, no longer hanging out with her usual group of friends. When she checked the attendance records, she noticed that Martina had been frequently absent. She called Martina's mother because something didn't seem right. Martina's mother admitted that Martina had been withdrawn and moody but chalked it up to being a teenager. She agreed Martina was losing weight, but thought it was because she was trying to eat healthy. Martina had always been a picky eater and recently decided to cut meat out of her diet, and her mother thought being a vegetarian was the problem. She was quite adamant that Martina didn't have an eating disorder, but agreed to bring her to see me anyway. After examining Martina and determining that her weight loss was from inadequate nutrition, I explained that the label didn't matter—Martina required help: she had lost considerable weight, seemed depressed, and needed help developing a healthy eating plan. This would require working with a medical doctor, a therapist, and a dietitian. I told Martina's mother that she couldn't do this alone. It would be wise to begin putting together a multidisciplinary treatment team.

THE BENEFITS OF A MULTIDISCIPLINARY TREATMENT TEAM

The Critical Components: Medical Doctor, Therapist, Dietitian, and YOU

Because your child's eating disorder is a psychiatric illness with severe medical and nutritional consequences, treatment is more complex than for many other diseases. Your daughter requires a different health-care professional to treat each aspect of her disease. We call this a "multidisciplinary treatment team," and it should include, at least, a medical doctor, a therapist, and a registered dietitian. *You* are also a critical member of your child's treatment team. Your role is to support your child and facilitate communication between team members (see pages 71 to 75 for specifics).

I cannot emphasize enough the importance of locating professionals who specialize in eating disorders. Treating these diseases requires specific skills and understanding. Ideally, you want team members who work with children or teens *and* specialize in eating disorders. This, however, may not be an option so at least try to find people with one of these specializations. Having one person on the team who specializes in eating disorders can make a significant difference. The concept of a "team" is critical. This means everyone needs to have a common approach to treatment and be in frequent communication with each other. As you will see below, each member of the team will focus on a different aspect of your daughter's illness.

The medical doctor

The physician will evaluate and manage any medical complications caused by your daughter's eating disorder. She should be a pediatrician; adolescent medicine specialist (which is a subspecialty of pediatrics or internal medicine); family practitioner or an internist (this is not the best subspecialty because these doctors usually only take care of adults). Chapter 7 provides more specifics.

The therapist

The therapist will work with your child and possibly your whole family on the issues and behaviors that surround her eating disorder. Chapter 8 will give you specifics about who is qualified to treat your child and different therapeutic approaches.

The registered dietitian

The registered dietitian will evaluate your child's nutritional needs and deficiencies. She may set up a specific meal plan, depending on the type of treatment or refeeding that is required. You will learn more about the dietitian's role in chapter 9.

HOW TO PUT TOGETHER AN EFFECTIVE TREATMENT TEAM

IF YOUR COMMUNITY has an eating disorders clinic, all of these professionals will probably be in one place. Unfortunately, only a handful of eating disorder clinics exist in the United States and many of these have waiting lists. So, it's very likely that you are going to have to compile and possibly manage your child's treatment team. Yes, it is a daunting task, but by reading this book you will have all of the information and tools you need to put together an effective multidisciplinary treatment team for your child.

One of the best ways to find an eating disorder specialist is to get a recommendation from your child's primary medical doctor or from a trusted family member or friend who has experience in this area. If you are unable to get a recommendation, there are other places that you can turn. Appendix B contains a list of Web sites with eating disorder specialists.

There is no particular "order" to identifying the members of a treatment team. Any team member who you find first can probably refer you to other providers, although in my experience, a medical doctor, psychiatrist, or psychologist who specializes in eating disorders may have the best network of referrals. The biggest challenge is finding people who work with children or teens *and* understand eating disorders.

Choosing the right treatment team is crucial for your child's treatment and recovery. Interview in person, if possible, each of the potential providers to be sure he or she has the right credentials and is an appropriate fit for your child and your family. You know your child better than almost anyone. Just because someone recommends a particular provider does not mean that he will have the right chemistry with your son; perhaps your daughter will be more comfortable with a woman therapist; maybe you just don't "click" with the dietitian. All of these things are important to consider. Listen to your gut. If you are not comfortable with a provider, he is probably not the right one for you. To be successful, you'll want to find team members not only who you feel comfortable with but also who will work well together.

INTERVIEWING POTENTIAL TEAM MEMBERS

WHEN YOU GET a referral for a doctor, dietitian, or mental health provider, your next step is to make a short appointment to meet each person. Explain to the receptionist what you are doing and ask if you can set up an appointment or speak to him or her on the telephone. Expect to pay a fee, especially for an appointment. You will be looking for several things: the person's credentials, philosophy, experience, and ability to engage your child. If you hope to have your child's care covered by insurance, be sure to check with your insurance company to be certain the provider is on your plan. You should also ask the provider to make sure they do, in fact, take your insurance. (See Section 5 for more information on insurance issues.)

The following questions are appropriate to ask medical, psychiatric, and nutritional providers. Be sure to write down the answers—if you're interviewing several people, it's easy to forget who gave which answer. If a provider is unwilling to speak with you for an "interview," this is a big red flag.

- **Are you licensed?**
    - o You want to be sure that every provider on the team is licensed. This does not guarantee that they are good at what they do, but it does increase the odds, as they are licensed to practice their profession.
- **How many adolescents with eating disorders have you treated?**
    - o Some providers will say that they have experience in treating eating disorders, but on further questioning you will find out that they have treated one or two people. You would ideally like to find someone with more experience than that, but this is not always possible.
- **What eating disorders do you most often treat?**
    - o If you have a child with bulimia and the dietitian mostly treats children with anorexia, you might want to find someone with more appropriate experience (again, if possible).
- **Do you have any subspecialty training in eating disorders?**
    - o This can include a formal clinical fellowship or a weekend or week-long training seminar.
- **What is your philosophy about treatment?**

○ There are different approaches to treating children and adolescents with eating disorders, which include family-based and individual treatments. With younger children, family-based treatment is usually the most appropriate.

- **What kind of involvement will I have in my child's treatment?**
  ○ You want to make sure that you are comfortable with your level of involvement in your child's treatment. I would be very cautious about a provider who says that you should have no involvement. I would also be sure that all of the providers on the team encourage and welcome parental involvement and view your role similarly.

- **Can you recommend other providers who you usually work with?**
  ○ This is a good way to get a team where some members already know each other and work together.

COMMUNICATION: THE KEY TO A SUCCESSFUL TREATMENT TEAM

MANAGING YOUR CHILD'S treatment team requires time and persistence. Your most important job is to make sure that all of the team members are communicating with you and with each other. Everyone on your child's team knows what to do—the most difficult thing is to make sure everyone knows what the others are doing.

Members of the team not only need to communicate with you and with each other—most important, they must be consistent in what they communicate to your child. It is critical that they all present your child with consistent messages. If your daughter observes there is dissention among team members, she may be tempted to manipulate the situation.

Children controlled by eating disorders may try to "split" team members in order to avoid treatment. Your son may mislead his medical doctor, by saying, "My therapist said that it is best for my mental health if I exercise." This may not be true; the therapist may have said your son could begin moderate exercise after he gained two pounds. Or he might inform the dietitian, "My medical doctor says I'm doing really well and don't need to gain any more weight." Again, this may not be the whole truth. To avoid splitting the team, all team members must be on the same page, send out consistent messages, and communicate with one another. If they do not agree on a treatment plan, they should discuss it among themselves before talking to your child.

This worked very well with one of my patients, Brianna, and the members of her treatment team. Brianna's psychologist, Trisha, called to ask me what I thought about allowing Brianna to run three times a week. She felt allowing Brianna to exercise might help decrease her purging. Although Brianna had gained some weight and her vital signs were beginning to improve, I was not planning to restart any exercising for several more weeks. But in talking with Trisha, it seemed like a good idea if it would decrease Brianna's purging. I, however, was not comfortable allowing her to run three times a week. What about walking for thirty minutes, three times a week? When I got off the phone with Trisha, I called Bruce, Brianna's dietitian, to ask what he thought about allowing Brianna to walk for thirty minutes, three times a week. He was fine with it as long as Brianna had an extra snack on the days that she walked. This illustrates how a team can work together to help a patient. We had all communicated and come up with a solid plan, which was presented to Brianna, who was excited about being able to walk, which did seem to help with her recovery.

There are several effective ways to establish and maintain communication among your team. These include:

- Setting up a monthly phone conference with the entire team. This may be spaced out as your child improves.
- Asking that the providers speak to or e-mail each other after each visit or fax their notes to the other providers after each visit.

Although we have emphasized the importance of fostering good communication among team members, it's also important to allow the team to develop its own rhythm and procedures for working together. If, however, you feel that communication is breaking down or if you believe your child is getting mixed or contradictory messages, then it's important to step in. (Please refer to the box on page 73 for tips on how to handle some common situations.)

Compiling and managing your child's treatment team will take time and effort, but it is the best way to help your child regain her mental and physical health. Information in the following chapters will help you select the right providers and then move ahead to your first appointment and what to expect during treatment.

How Team Members Communicate

When you select a member of your child's treatment team, ask how he or she plans to communicate with the other providers (some of us like to use e-mail, others prefer sending written reports). If necessary, one of the members may suggest a conference call. Make sure to sign any release forms that allow each member to share information with the rest of the team. If you believe there is a communication problem or team members are not sending consistent messages, then you will need to take charge.

What If Our Team Isn't Working?

YOU WERE SO relieved to finally get a team together to help your child—you interviewed all of the members, liked each one individually, and knew they had worked together before. But after two weeks:

Dilemma: Your daughter says she hates the dietitian; you hate to admit it, but you're not comfortable with what she is telling your daughter.
Solution: Always trust your instincts. I do not recommend switching providers cavalierly, but if you truly are not comfortable with what one of the providers is saying and you do not feel better after discussing it with them, you may need to find a new provider. Be aware that your child may be ambivalent about treatment and therefore may find reasons to dislike all providers so always evaluate the situation for yourself.

Dilemma: The medical doctor doesn't communicate with the other team members.
Solution: It is important for one of the providers on your child's treatment team to take on the role of team leader to facilitate communication within the team. Although this job often falls on the therapist, other team members may take the lead—it often depends on the individual personalities as well their relationship with your child. However, if one member of the team is not communicating

with the rest of the team, you can try to help facilitate the communication. In the above scenario, ask your child's doctor if he has been in touch with the other providers. If not, ask if he can fax his notes to the other providers after each visit. If he is unable or unwilling to do so, ask if he can copy his notes and you can take them to the other providers.

Dilemma: The therapist and the doctor seem to be contradicting each other.

Solution: The first step is to determine if they are really contradicting each other or if they are just focusing on different parts of the same problem. For instance, the doctor expresses concern that your daughter is not gaining enough weight, but the next day, your family therapist says that your daughter is having difficulty dealing with the weight that she has gained. Although these may sound contradictory, they actually are different aspects of the same problem. Both team members believe your daughter needs to gain weight, and both are concerned about her lack of progress. They are just stating it from different angles. Her doctor, who is viewing the situation from a medical perspective, is concerned that she is not gaining enough weight. The therapist is viewing it from a psychological perspective and sees that your daughter is really struggling with her weight gain. Both are legitimate concerns. If, however, you identify a real contradiction, you need to resolve it. This can be accomplished by speaking with the individual team members and trying to clarify the contradictory recommendations or by setting up a team meeting or a conference call.

7

WORKING WITH YOUR CHILD'S MEDICAL SPECIALIST

Amanda's Story
When dieting gets out of control

Amanda, an outgoing 16-year-old, came to my office with her father, who explained that his daughter spent vacations with him but lived with her mother during the school year. When he picked up Amanda at the airport, he was delighted to see that his once awkward preteen girl had blossomed into a beautiful 15-year-old teenager. "She looked so grown up I barely recognized her," he said. Amanda proudly told her father she had been on a serious diet to lose weight so that she would look good in a bikini for summer vacation and their trip to Hawaii. She said she only ate healthy food and had totally given up sugar and processed food. However, her father had noticed that Amanda ate almost nothing at meals, saying she wasn't hungry. She also seemed withdrawn and depressed, staying in her room. A few weeks after she arrived, when Amanda's dad was looking for a magazine he accidentally threw in the trash, he came upon empty cookie boxes, dozens of candy wrappers, and empty bottles of laxatives. He had discovered Amanda's secret—binging and purging.

Although an eating disorder is a psychiatric disease, because of the related medical consequences, it is crucial that your child be under the supervision of a physician. Make every effort to find a doctor who has experience treating eating disorders because some conditions created by these illnesses are subtle and may be easily missed by a less experienced practitioner. Very few physicians have specific training in eating disorders, with the possible exception of some adolescent medical specialists. To help you find a specialist, we have provided information about locating a doctor with these qualifications in appendix B.

If you live in a small or isolated community and do not have many options, the best thing to do is find a provider—whether it's a pediatrician or someone in general practice—who seems interested in eating disorders and is willing to learn and communicate. You might ask if he would be willing to look at information in this book (explain it has been written by a physician who specializes in eating disorders). He can also get information about the medical risks of eating disorders and what tests to perform from Web sites of some of the leading medical centers with eating disorder programs.

Once you have identified a physician, you will schedule your daughter's first appointment. Understanding what to expect will prepare both you and your child, ease some of the anxiety, and help you get the most from her initial appointment.

HOW CAN I PREPARE MY CHILD FOR THE FIRST APPOINTMENT?

As a PHYSICIAN trained in adolescent medicine, I can confirm that children—especially teenagers—do not look forward to seeing a doctor. Even if they've been comfortable with their pediatrician or family doctor, a visit to a doctor because of a concern about an eating disorder can be very difficult. The drive from your home to the doctor's office will probably be tense, especially if your daughter is adamant that there's no problem. Explain to her that you're just worried and then describe the behavior that concerns you: not eating, vomiting, using laxatives, etc. Reinforce that you understand why it might be difficult for her to talk to you about this, and tell her that this is okay. But encourage her to let the doctor know if there is anything going on so he can make sure she is healthy. The following section will help you tell her what to expect.

WHO SHOULD ATTEND THE FIRST APPOINTMENT?

IDEALLY, BOTH PARENTS—even if there is a divorce or separation—should attend the medical evaluation. If a child lives part-time in two households with an involved and supportive step-parent, then all three of you should attend. This may be uncomfortable but it's crucial to your child's health. Everyone needs to understand the medical risks and hear the doctor's assessment of the situation. Each parent will have different concerns and different questions; and—I cannot emphasize this enough—it is essential for all involved parents to be on the same page. Siblings should *not* be there if at all possible. Your energy and attention should be focused on your "sick" child. Information about how to support your other children can be found in chapter 15, What about the Rest of Us?

WHAT WILL HAPPEN DURING MY CHILD'S FIRST VISIT?

YOUR CHILD'S INITIAL medical evaluation will be similar to an annual physical, except that there will be an even greater focus on her nutrition, eating behaviors, and exercise. This may create tension and be emotional, especially if your child is still denying she has a problem. The doctor will do a complete physical examination to investigate if there are any other medical reasons for her symptoms; to look for medical complications of her eating disorder; and to determine if any other medical factors need to be addressed.

You and your daughter should each have time alone with the doctor to express any private concerns and ask any sensitive questions. If the doctor does not offer each of you an opportunity to meet with her privately, you should ask for this. Your daughter might be uncomfortable or shy about asking for this herself. As parents, we like to think our children will tell us anything but, unfortunately, this is not always the case, especially with adolescents. Because your child may be more comfortable about disclosing sensitive information to the doctor in private, assure her that whatever she tells the doctor is confidential. Encourage her to be honest—the doctor needs to know everything that is going on so she can evaluate the medical risks. If your child assumes that what she says will go back to you, she may be less forthcoming.

There is a fine line between withholding important information from parents and breaking a patient's trust that what they say is confidential. I often ask parents to trust me and assure them that if things are going down-hill, I will let them know. If I told parents every time their son said he purged or used laxatives, then he would never tell me anything and thus it would be far more difficult to assess his medical risks. I, however, will strongly encourage a patient to speak with his parents if I believe there's something they need to know. Usually, the patients agree to this.

If one of my patients adamantly refuses to tell his parents and he is in acute danger of spiraling downhill, I will tell them but also give the child the opportunity to be there if he chooses. For example, when 17-year-old Jenny first came to see me, her parents knew she was binging and purg-ing. They, however, were totally unaware she was occasionally using lax-atives as a way to purge. At the end of her initial evaluation, I met with her parents and reviewed my concerns about Jenny's health and presented my recommendations for her treatment plan. Although I suggested they remove all laxatives from the home, since they may be used to purge, I did not divulge that Jenny was abusing laxatives. Over the next several visits, Jenny's laxative use increased. I was getting more concerned about this and the effect on her body. When Jenny told me that she felt her use of laxa-tives was getting out of control, I encouraged her to discuss this with her parents. Although she was afraid her parents would be disappointed in her, she agreed to let me tell them about the laxatives with her in the room. If I had divulged Jenny's laxative use to her parents at the first visit, I am con-vinced she would never have told me about her increasing use of laxatives, which could have resulted in serious medical complications.

WHAT SHOULD I BRING TO MY CHILD'S FIRST APPOINTMENT?

IT WILL BE very helpful to the doctor if you can bring the following parts of your child's medical record:

- Immunization record
- Growth charts from the pediatrician. This will help him get an overall sense of her growth and nutrition. Has she been getting taller? Has her weight fallen off?
- All records from any specialist that your child has seen for her mal-nutrition, vomiting, or other eating disorder symptoms, such as

a gastroenterologist or an endocrinologist. You can request records from the doctor's office and will probably have to sign a medical record release form. Try to call at least a week before the appointment in case the specialist's office needs time to copy the records.

- Results of any lab tests that your child's pediatrician ordered.
- Bottles of any prescription medications, nonprescription medications, or vitamins that your child is taking.
- Any pertinent family medical and psychiatric history from your child's other parent if he or she is unable to attend the medical evaluation. If your child is adopted and you have any information about his biological parents, bring this as well.
- A list of questions that you want to remember to ask the doctor; some parents use a spiral notebook to keep track of each visit.

WHAT QUESTIONS WILL THE DOCTOR ASK?

THE DOCTOR WILL take a very detailed medical, social, and dietary history. She will also ask questions about exercise, purging, medication use, and physical symptoms. It's likely the doctor will delve into areas of your child's and your family's lives that you may consider private. The answers to these questions will be crucial in your child's assessment and treatment planning. She will probably ask about peer relationships, school, family issues and problems, including emotional or physical abuse. This extensive history will help her figure out what is going on with your child and determine if any other issues may be of potential concern. It is important for the doctor to assess if your child may be involved in other dangerous behaviors, such as drugs, alcohol, shoplifting, cutting, or risky sexual behaviors.

One of the most valuable parts of an adolescent's initial medical visit is the psychosocial history. This is done using a tool called the HEADSS exam. The acronym HEADSS is described below. Your child's doctor uses this as a general guide for talking to your child about the following situations:

H(OME): Who lives at home? Do you feel safe there?

E(DUCATION): What's going on in school? Have your grades changed? What do you like and dislike in school? Are you skipping classes, having lots of sick days, or have you been suspended?

A(CTIVITIES): What do you do when you're not in school? Who are your friends? Do you have a best friend? Are your friends aware of your eating issues and if so, have they been supportive? Do any of your friends have eating disorders? Have you been in trouble with the police? Do you or your friends ever shoplift?

D(RUGS): Do you use drugs, cigarettes, or alcohol?

S(EX): Are you sexually active? How many partners have you had? Are you using birth control?

S(UICIDE): Are you having thoughts about suicide? Have you ever attempted to commit suicide? Have you ever cut or burned yourself on purpose?

This is not a formal "test" or measurement and there are no right or wrong answers. Asking these types of questions helps to give the doctor background to add to his medical evaluation.

WHAT TO EXPECT DURING THE PHYSICAL EXAMINATION

YOUR CHILD'S DOCTOR will perform a thorough physical examination to rule out any other causes of her symptoms. It is also an opportunity for the doctor to look for medical complications caused by her malnutrition or vomiting. Great attention will be paid to examining her heart, lungs, abdomen, skin, extremities, and nervous system.

First, however, she will be weighed: this should be done undressed, in a gown, to give the most accurate weight. Her vital signs will then be checked. These include her heart rate (pulse), blood pressure, temperature, and rate of breathing (respiratory rate). I always take my patient's vital signs two different ways: first when lying down and then when standing up. This allows me see how well the person's heart is able to accommodate to the change in position.

Your child's doctor will then plot her height and weight on a growth chart. This will allow him to see how her weight, height, and body mass index (BMI) compare to others of her age and gender. Where a child's weight falls on the growth chart is not always indicative of how she is doing medically or the degree of her illness. It is often surprising to parents when their child is at a seemingly healthy weight but is actually "malnourished" and sick. This can happen if a child or teenager was initially overweight and lost considerable weight in a short period of time or exercised extensively and, therefore, developed a high muscle-to-fat ratio (high muscle mass, very low body fat). It can also occur if a child purges, because she is not getting the nutrition from the food—the food is coming back up.

WHAT TESTS WILL THE DOCTOR WANT TO DO?

THE DOCTOR WILL probably want to conduct several tests to further evaluate your child's health. These may include:

EKG (ALSO KNOWN AS AN ECG): An EKG is a tracing of the electric impulses of the heart and reveals if the heart is beating correctly. Stickers, placed on your child's chest, arms and legs, will be attached to wires that, on the other end, are connected to a machine. The only electric impulses going through the wires go away from your child's body. This test is painless and often done in the doctor's office.

URINE DIP TEST: This in-office test of the urine measures if a child is drinking too much or too little water; it can also detect abnormalities that may indicate other problems, such as kidney dysfunction or diabetes.

BLOOD TESTS: The following blood tests will probably be preformed; the results of some tests may be back in a few hours while others, such as those looking at hormone levels, may take more than a week.

(a) A blood chemistry panel will examine the salts in your child's blood and can also give an indication of how some of your child's internal organs, such as her liver and kidneys, are functioning.

(b) A complete blood count (CBC) will show the quantity of the different types of blood cells. This will allow the doctor to look for anemia or other blood deficiencies.

(c) A thyroid function test evaluates how her thyroid is functioning. The thyroid has a role in controlling a person's metabolism (how slowly or quickly they use up calories).

(d) Other hormone tests will look for imbalances that may be causing symptoms such as loss of periods.

(e) Other nutritional tests can determine if she has any specific nutritional deficiencies that need to be corrected. These might include low vitamin levels or a deficiency in certain types of fats that need to be corrected.

DEXA BONE DENSITY SCAN: This test measures the density of your child's bones and can determine if any bone loss has occurred. It is similar to an x-ray. Your child will lie on a table and the x-ray machine will move over her, taking the pictures. There are no injections, dyes, or other invasive measures used. The radiation from the DEXA scan is similar to that of a chest x-ray.

WILL MY CHILD BE GIVEN ANY MEDICATIONS?

ALTHOUGH MANY MEDICAL complications may develop because of malnutrition and purging, most of these can't be fixed by taking medications: only proper nutrition and not purging can improve your child's health. There are, however, medications that can relieve some of the symptoms created by an eating disorder.

HEARTBURN AND ACID REFLUX can be treated with medications that decrease the acidity of the stomach contents. Some doctors will prescribe these medications to all patients who purge in order to reduce the damage that the acid can do to the esophagus, mouth, and teeth.

CONSTIPATION, caused by poor intestinal motility and poor dietary intake, can be treated with increased water intake and a high-fiber diet. If this doesn't relieve the symptoms, a fiber supplement such as Metamucil can be added. A stool softener—or in very rare cases a laxative— will only be prescribed if it is absolutely necessary. Laxatives are truly a medication of last resort because of their potential for abuse.

AMENORRHEA (the loss of menstrual periods) is not generally treated with medication. Even though oral contraceptive pills (birth control pills) may bring about the return of menses, they do not stop or diminish the damage being done to a girl's bones. Unfortunately, they only give someone a false sense of being healthy and make it more difficult to determine when your child's body is beginning to make hormones on its own.

WHAT HAPPENS NEXT?

AT THIS POINT, the doctor will have some idea about your child's medical condition but may still need to get test results back before making specific recommendations. It is most likely you will be asked to schedule a follow-up appointment for the following week.

If the doctor is the first specialist you've seen, ask her for referrals to a therapist and registered dietitian. If you already have these team members in place, you should provide her with their names and contact information.

Occasionally, a doctor will need to admit a child to the hospital on an emergency basis. This happens if the child's vital signs are medically unstable; if the salts in her blood are severely altered; if her heart is not functioning correctly as noted on an EKG; or if she is having very concerning symptoms, such as passing out. Alternatively, the doctor may ask a child to return in one or two days if she suspects something is wrong but doesn't believe the situation requires immediate hospitalization.

WHAT TO EXPECT AT FOLLOW-UP VISITS

THE DOCTOR PROBABLY will want to see your son regularly, possibly every week. At these appointments, she will probably do the following:

CHECK WEIGHT: Your son should be weighed, undressed in a gown, to give the most accurate weight. Your son's weight indicates how he is doing nutritionally. Doctors have different philosophies about sharing this information with parents and patients. When deciding whether or not to share weekly weights, the team needs to take into account your child's age, diagnosis, severity of the disease, and type of therapy being used.

Sharing a patient's weight on a weekly basis can help a child and his parents see if he is making progress. This can be very beneficial for parents who are taking charge of refeeding their child since it tells them if their child is eating enough and allows them to adjust their child's nutrition as needed. It also works well for older teens who are taking control of their own nutrition. One of my 19-year-old patients told me that even though it was difficult to hear, "You gained 2 pounds this week," the information helped her stay on her treatment plan. Sharing weekly weights can also help patients gradually deal with their weight gain. It may be easier for someone to learn he has gained 2 pounds each week—and process this gradually with his therapist—than to suddenly find out he has gained 18 pounds over the past two months.

Week-to-week weight changes, however, can be very upsetting and anxiety provoking for some patients, in which case the team may decide not to share weekly weights. Dealing with weight in this way does require significant trust. A patient needs to trust that his doctor is not going to let him gain weight too quickly and does not want him to keep gaining more and more weight indefinitely. Both of these are very common fears of people with eating disorders. It also takes trust on the parent's part. If I don't share weights with my patient, I will not share this information regularly with the parents. It is not productive to tell a patient that we are not focusing on his weight but rather on overall health, only to have his parents follow me out of the room to secretly ask about his weight gain. In many cases, however, I will periodically update the parents on weight progress.

A good example of this was Jinny, a 15-year-old girl with anorexia. She was very focused on her weight, and I didn't give her weekly updates. But after each appointment, her mother would follow me out of the room with her notebook, ready to write down a weight, promising, "It's okay, I won't tell Jinny." I finally told her this was not healthy for Jinny and her actions were undermining my efforts to help her stop focusing on her weight. We came up with a solution: since she really needed to know her weight progress, I would meet with her once a month to review her progress. Yes, I would share her weight with her, but she had to accept that it would only happen once a month and not at her daughter's appointment.

In either case, the doctor should not focus on weight but, instead, focus on the ultimate goal of getting your child's body to a healthy place where she can grow, develop normally, maintain a normal heart rate, normal blood pressure, and regular menstrual periods.

TEST URINE: This will indicate your child's level of hydration. Sometimes people with eating disorders limit their fluid intake, which can cause them to get dangerously dehydrated. More frequently, they may overhydrate as a way to feel less hungry or to increase their weight before a weight check at the doctor's office. We refer to this as "water loading." The urine test may also suggest that a child may be purging. Although it's not a precise indication for purging, it may raise concern that there might be a problem.

CHECK HEART RATE AND BLOOD PRESSURE: These usually are checked both lying down and standing up to give a good indication of how your child's heart is functioning.

CHECK BODY TEMPERATURE: This indicates if he is able to maintain an adequate body temperature.

ASK ABOUT SYMPTOMS SUCH AS DIZZINESS AND FATIGUE AND CONDUCT A MEDICAL EXAM: This can help to determine if your child is developing any other medical complications from his eating disorder.

ADDITIONAL LABORATORY TESTS: Some of the tests that were performed during the initial evaluation may be repeated periodically.

While the physician on the treatment team will be dealing your child's medical issues, it is equally important to evaluate her emotional health. The next chapter focuses on how to find a therapist.

8

WORKING WITH YOUR CHILD'S PSYCHIATRIC PROVIDER

Ashley's Story:
Why Did She Stop Eating?

The first time I met Ashley she had just been admitted to the hospital's eating disorders unit. She was in bed, surrounded by stuffed animals and hooked up to a heart monitor. Extremely thin and very weak, Ashley looked like a large doll. I checked her chart—she was 8 years old. Her mother, who was sitting in a chair crying, asked me, "How could this happen?" She told me that Ashley, a quiet and reserved child, had recently developed unusual food rituals, cutting everything into tiny pieces and then barely eating anything at meals. Ashley kept repeating that she wasn't hungry and her mother should stop forcing her to eat. Concerned that her daughter was becoming ill, Ashley's mother took her to the family's doctor. He was shocked by her low weight and very concerned by Ashley's weak heart. He immediately had Ashley admitted to the hospital and thought she would require intensive therapy as well as a nutritional plan to slowly refeed her malnourished body. Ashley's mother couldn't believe her daughter was so sick she had to be hospitalized. She mentioned that the family had moved the previous summer but Ashley seemed to be happy and adjusting to her new school. Could this have triggered Ashley's eating disorder?

Eating disorders are complex psychiatric illnesses that require expert treatment, so it is critical for your child to obtain intensive psychological treatment from a professional with experience in this area. Without appropriate psychiatric help and treatment, eating disorders can become lifelong illnesses. To regain a healthy relationship with her body and with food, your daughter may require long-term treatment, which may continue long after her body is considered medically healed. The average length of psychological treatment is two to three years.

I cannot over-emphasize the importance of finding a mental health professional who has experience working with children or teens with eating disorders. Several types of mental health professionals are qualified to work with your child: This person can be a psychiatrist, a psychologist, someone with a master's degree in social work (MSW) or a marriage and family therapist (MFT). If psychiatric medications are indicated, your child will need to see a psychiatrist (only an MD can prescribe drugs); some psychiatrists do therapy as well as medication management while others may just manage the medications and leave the therapy to another provider.

How do you decide whom to call? My suggestion is to base your decision on the person's training and experience with eating disorders and how you think he or she will connect with your child; sometimes, your decision may come down to whom is available. A trusted friend may recommend a great psychologist but if the psychologist doesn't have any experience with eating disorders, it may be better to work with a social worker who specializes in treating eating disorders. It is extremely important to find someone with training and/or experience in treating adolescents with eating disorders.

After you select your child's therapist, you will set up an initial appointment for her to meet with your daughter and evaluate what type of treatment will be most effective. There are several psychological approaches to treating eating disorders. As with many diseases, one approach does not work for everyone. The type of treatment chosen for your child will depend on many factors, such as her age, her eating disorder diagnosis, your family situation, and any other coexisting medical or psychiatric issues.

Your daughter will most likely begin her psychiatric treatment with outpatient therapy. She, and possibly your family, will attend therapy sessions on a regular basis, usually once or twice a week. The frequency will depend on what the therapists thinks is necessary. Question anyone who initially suggests anything less than once a week.

DIFFERENT PSYCHIATRIC APPROACHES

FAMILY THERAPY AND individual psychodynamic therapy are the most common therapeutic approaches recommended for children and teens with anorexia. Cognitive behavioral therapy and interpersonal psychotherapy are the most common approaches used to treat bulimia. Sometimes a combination of these is recommended. Group therapy with peers dealing with eating issues is often used in addition to individual or family therapy. Although group therapy may be helpful, there are no studies proving its efficacy. The four main therapeutic approaches used to treat children with eating disorders are briefly described below.

Family therapy

This type of therapy regards the family as a strong force in the adolescent's recovery. In family-based treatment, the entire family—especially parents—is involved in the treatment program. The focus of family treatment is to support the parents in refeeding their child by providing guidance about how to encourage the child during mealtimes and how to handle issues such as weight gain and exercise. If there seems to be an obstacle to refeeding, this type of therapy may delve into areas of how the family unit functions. Areas such as how family members communicate, relate to one another, and solve problems will often be explored. Siblings are often asked to participate in these sessions.

Family therapy works well for many children and adolescents, especially those who have been ill for less than two years. It, however, requires that the parents be united in their view of the treatment.

Individual psychodynamic psychotherapy

Individual psychodynamic psychotherapy focuses on helping a teenager deal with the difficult emotional and developmental tasks of adolescence such as becoming more independent and developing an individual identity. It can also help the teen learn how to identify and deal with difficult and often scary emotions, such as anger and depression. This type of therapy is based on the philosophy that disordered eating behaviors are being used as a way to cope with or suppress these difficult emotions. The therapist can help patients recognize and deal with these emotions in a productive manner. In this type of therapy, issues around body weight and shape are addressed only in the context of being poor coping mechanisms that need to be replaced by healthier ones.

Interpersonal psychotherapy (IPT)

Interpersonal psychotherapy addresses difficulties in a patient's relationships with important people in their life, such as parents, siblings, or peers, and it explores how the eating disordered behaviors are being used to deal with these issues. The therapy, therefore, examines these relationships and helps the patient to improve them by working on their verbal and nonverbal communication. There is also a focus on developing skills to cope with relational difficulties. This type of therapy does not directly address the eating disordered behaviors or issues around body shape or weight.

Cognitive-behavioral therapy (CBT)

Cognitive-behavioral therapy is a common treatment for eating disorders, especially bulimia nervosa, and can help correct poor eating habits and change thoughts about food, eating, and body image. It also may improve self-esteem, depression, and social functioning. A form of individual psychotherapy, CBT emphasizes the critical role of thoughts in our feelings and actions. Treatment focuses on changing thoughts in order to change behaviors. Therefore, if your daughter is experiencing unwanted feelings and behaviors, the therapist will help her identify the thinking that is causing these feelings and behaviors and then replace them with ones that lead to more desirable reactions. Utilizing a structured process, the therapist helps the patient set goals. Homework is typically assigned to help patients internalize the skills discussed in treatment.

HOW CAN I PREPARE MY CHILD FOR THE
FIRST APPOINTMENT?

YOUR SON MAY have preconceived ideas from watching television or movies about meeting with a therapist. Explain that the therapist just wants to talk to him and it's an opportunity to talk to someone in confidence. You may want to explain to an older child that it is often helpful to have an outside perspective from someone who doesn't have the emotional investment of a friend or family member. With younger children, it's often helpful to refer to the therapist as a "talking doctor." The therapist may ask to set up a separate appointment with you and/or your family. Do not expect any feedback from your child about his sessions and do not ask for specific information if he doesn't want to talk about it.

What should I bring to my child's first appointment?

- Before your appointment, write down any questions or concerns you have about your child and his eating disorder.
- If you can remember, write out a timeline of how his eating disorder progressed. When did you notice he started cutting down on food or vomiting. Does this behavior relate to something specific in your child's life (a divorce, rejection from a sports team, etc.)?
- Bring any medications your son is taking.
- Bring any pertinent family medical and psychiatric history from your child's other parent if he or she is unable to attend the psychiatric evaluation. If your child is adopted and you have any information on his biological parents, bring this as well.

WILL MY CHILD REQUIRE PSYCHIATRIC MEDICATIONS?

THERE ARE, UNFORTUNATELY, no drugs that "cure" an eating disorder. Psychotropic (psychiatric) medications, however, are sometimes prescribed to treat related factors. The specific medication prescribed is related to the problem being addressed.

There is often an overlap between eating disorders and other psychiatric disorders such as depression or anxiety. Sometimes the eating disorder comes first and the other symptoms develop as a result. Other times, the depression or anxiety predate the eating disorder. If the eating disorder came first and the depression actually results from being malnourished, the symptoms will quite possibly subside with renourishment. Medications frequently are not prescribed in these instances because psychotropic medications tend not to work well in significantly malnourished people. If the eating disorder was preceded by the anxiety or depression, a psychiatrist may feel that a psychotropic medication could be of help.

If a therapist believes your daughter would benefit from a psychotropic medication, she will refer her to a psychiatrist for evaluation because only medical doctors can prescribe these drugs.

If More Intensive Psychiatric Treatment Is Required

THERE ARE TIMES when a child requires more intensive treatment than therapy once or twice weekly can provide. In this case, your child's therapist may recommend either an intensive outpatient program (IOP) or a partial-hospitalization program (PHP). These options should be explored before even considering inpatient residential treatment, which is when a child lives full-time in a residential treatment center (these are discussed in detail in chapter 11).

A good example of this type of situation is illustrated by one of my patients, 13-year-old Sandy. As soon as Sandy was diagnosed with an eating disorder, her parents put together a treatment team. After three months, her physician reported that Sandy had not gained any weight and her therapist confirmed that she was still purging several times a week; he also suspected she was using laxatives. The team held a conference call and decided Sandy would benefit from attending an intensive outpatient program to give her more concentrated therapy and nutritional support. Although many IOPs and PHPs are available, only a limited number treat those under 18 years of age.

INTENSIVE OUTPATIENT PROGRAMS (IOP)

An intensive outpatient program (IOP) usually consists of different types of group therapies as well as a group meal. Generally offered after school, IOP sessions usually are scheduled several times a week for several hours. For example, your daughter might attend an IOP from 4 PM to 7 PM. on Monday, Wednesday, and Friday. Depending on the program, she may continue to work with her regular therapist and see her regular doctor and dietitian as well. IOPs are sometimes offered by residential treatment centers as a way to transition patients back home; others are stand-alone programs.

PARTIAL HOSPITALIZATION PROGRAMS

Also referred to as "day programs," partial hospitalization programs (PHPs) are intensive daylong treatment programs that a child usually attends eight to twelve hours a day, five to seven days a week. These programs either operate separately or are offered by centers that have psychiatric inpatient or residential care. They may also be used as a transitional or step-down program for patients being discharged from a residential treatment program.

PHPs often include individual therapy, group therapy, and observed meals. They may also offer other therapeutic activities, including art therapy, recreation therapy, and exercise such as yoga. By providing a safe, therapeutic environment for a child with an eating disorder, PHPs create opportunities to focus on recovery, bonding with others, and readily receiving support and guidance. People usually do not work with their home treatment team during the time they are engaged in treatment at a PHP. Many of these programs also offer some type of family involvement.

You've now met the first two members of a multidisciplinary team—the medical doctor and the therapist. In the next chapter, you will see how the third member—the registered dietitian—ties your child's treatment together by helping you determine what and how much your child needs to eat in order to regain her health.

9

WORKING WITH YOUR CHILD'S
REGISTERED DIETITIAN

Erica's Story
Discovering the Missing Piece for Recovery

When Erica's parents brought her to my office, they couldn't understand why their 12-year-old daughter didn't have any energy and seemed weak. Since being diagnosed with an eating disorder, she was seeing a therapist twice a week and making good progress. According to her parents, Erica was trying to eat more and was motivated to get healthy so she could go to summer camp. Her father kept saying, "But look at Erica—her weight is normal, she's not skinny, and she's eating plenty of food." Why was her health not improving? After talking to Erica and her mom—who was desperately preparing all of her daughter's favorite foods—the problem was very clear: although Erica was eating, she wasn't getting the right nutrition or eating enough to compensate for being malnourished for the last year. Erica needed to add a dietitian to her treatment team, someone who could help her mother plan nutritious meals to feed her malnourished body.

Parents are often surprised to learn that not all people with eating disorders are underweight. People with eating disorders may be underweight, normal weight, or even overweight. Regardless of where you child falls in the weight spectrum, it's almost guaranteed that his health has been affected and he needs to be renourished in order to improve his health. Properly renourishing a child with an eating disorder involves more than just getting him to eat. What, how often, and how much your child eats is extremely important. For this reason, nutritional therapy needs to be an integral part of your son or daughter's multidisciplinary treatment plan. A registered dietitian is the person who will help you and your child with this important part of your child's treatment.

Parents often ask me what the difference is between a nutritionist and a registered dietitian. There is a major difference: anyone who feels that they are qualified to give out nutritional advice can call himself or herself a nutritionist; however, a registered dietitian is trained to meet specific educational and professional standards.

The dietitian's role on the treatment team will depend on the type of therapy your child is receiving. If your family is engaged in family therapy and you are taking on the task of refeeding your child, the dietitian's role will be more of a consultant. She can answer your nutritional questions and help you to make sure you are on track with your child's nutrition. If your child is engaged in individual therapy and therefore taking more control over his own nutrition, the dietitian may provide help by analyzing and adjusting his intake. Regardless of the role, the dietitian is an important part of the treatment team.

When choosing a dietitian for your child, make every effort to find one who specializes in eating disorders. Even if your son is active in sports or your daughter has been diagnosed with female athletic triad, do *not* go to a sports nutritionist. It may seem like a logical thing to do but it's quite the opposite: a sports nutritionist is not trained to help children with eating disorders, but rather, to help athletes. This often involves diets that are not appropriate for people with eating disorders, particularly children and adolescents.

WHAT TO LOOK FOR WHEN INTERVIEWING A DIETITIAN

As EVERY PARENT knows, communicating with children requires special skills—talking to an 11-year-old is very different from negotiating with someone who is sixteen. For this reason, it's important to find a dietitian who not only specializes in eating disorders but also has experience working with preteens and adolescents. In addition to developing rapport, the dietitian needs to have knowledge about adolescent growth, nutritional needs, and cognitive development. Interview the dietitian before bringing her on to your child's treatment team to make sure she has the proper credentials and—equally important—is someone your child will be comfortable working with.

WHAT WILL HAPPEN AT THE FIRST APPOINTMENT?

YOU AND YOUR daughter may meet with the dietitian together or separately, depending on the dietitian's approach. Your daughter's weight and height will be measured and plotted on a growth chart. During the initial evaluation, the dietitian will take a detailed diet history from your child and analyze her daily food intake, looking for specific deficiencies such as poor protein, dairy, or fat intake. She will explore any food restrictions or eating rituals and also ask about eating disorder behaviors such as binging, obsessive exercising, vomiting, and using diet pills or laxatives.

The dietitian's goals

Once the dietitian has determined your daughter's nutritional status and any dietary deficiencies, her next step will be to develop the nutrition portion of your child's treatment plan. The purpose of a nutritional plan is to help your child consume a diet that is well balanced and provides appropriate energy. How long it takes to improve your daughter's nutrition will depend on what your child has been eating, the severity of her eating disorder, and her level of motivation. The dietitian will then work in conjunction with the treatment team to support you and your child in carrying out this plan.

Nutrition plans

Your child's nutrition plan will take into consideration her age, degree of malnutrition, her eating disordered behaviors (does she purge, exercise, abuse laxatives), and any physical symptoms (constipation, reflux, lactose intolerance). There are several different types of nutritional plans that a dietitian might recommend:

- **Parent food journal:** You will be asked to feed your child what you feel is right and then log what she eats in a journal. The dietitian can then evaluate what your child is eating and help you to adjust it as needed. Some dietitians will give you guidelines; others may ask you to start out on your own and then offer suggestions.

- **Patient food journal:** Your daughter will be asked to eat what she feels is right and record it in a journal. Depending on the dietitian's approach, your daughter either will be given free rein or will be asked to eat a certain number of meals, which is usually three meals and two to three snacks per day. Your child and the dietitian will then review her food journal and make adjustments as needed. This type of nutritional plan is primarily used for older adolescents and for adolescents with bulimia.

- **Portion plan:** The dietitian will prescribe a specific number of portions from different food groups (grains, proteins, dairies, fruits, vegetables, and fats) that your child is required to eat every day. You and your child will create daily menus that fulfill all of the prescribed portions. Although this type of nutritional plan can help develop a balanced meal plan, it may encourage a patient's obsession with numbers (see below).

- **Counting calories:** The dietitian will prescribe a specific number of calories that your child is expected to eat each day. In my experience, it is not uncommon for this type of plan to backfire. People with eating disorders are often obsessed with numbers such as numbers of calories, number of portions or cutting food into a particular number of pieces. I often have patients who initially were limiting themselves to 500 calories a day or purging anything over 750 calories a day. Asking someone with an eating disorder to eat a certain number of calories can encourage this obsession.

FOLLOW-UP APPOINTMENTS

You AND/OR YOUR child will probably meet with her dietitian weekly or every other week. At each visit the dietitian will:

- Monitor your child's energy intake
- Assist you and/or your child in adjusting her nutrition as needed
- Provide education to help you and your child understand her nutritional requirements, make wise food choices, increase variety in her diet and practice appropriate food behaviors
- Possibly recommend dietary supplements to meet your child's nutritional needs

NUTRITIONAL SUPPLEMENTS

AS A WAY to help your child regain nutritional balance, the dietitian may recommend certain nutritional supplements. To avoid serious interactions, make sure to inform the dietitian if your son is taking any other nutritional supplements, even if these are medicinal herbs, over-the-counter vitamins, or medications prescribed by the doctor or therapist. The following list includes some of the most common supplements prescribed for children with eating disorders.

Multivitamins

If your child has been diagnosed with an eating disorder, it's very likely she's not getting adequate vitamins or minerals. In a study conducted at Massachusetts General Hospital and Boston Children's Hospital, more than half of patients with eating disorders did not meet the recommended daily allowance (RDA) for vitamin D, calcium, foliate, vitamin B_{12}, zinc, magnesium, and copper. A standard multivitamin with minerals is a good idea; make sure the label indicates it has approximately 100 percent of the RDA. Your child's dietitian may have suggestions about specific brands.

Calcium

Although the loss of bone mass in patients with eating disorders is primarily a result of low sex hormone levels (estrogen and testosterone), not getting enough calcium also contributes to this problem. It is often recommended that young people with eating disorders take a calcium supplement.

Zinc

Most multivitamins have zinc but not enough for someone who is malnourished. For this reason, zinc supplements are often recommended. Research suggests that people with eating disorders are often deficient in the mineral zinc, which can cause delayed growth and sexual maturation, slowed wound healing, decreased appetite, and loss or impairment of smell and taste.

Vitamin D

Vitamin D is essential to efficiently absorb calcium, which is critical for normal bone development and the prevention of osteoporosis. Ergocalciferol (vitamin D) may be prescribed if your child is found to be deficient.

Working together as a team, you, the medical specialist, therapist, and dietitian will develop a multidisciplinary treatment plan to help your child move toward recovery. Your role as a member of the team is to facilitate communication and make sure the team is on the same page in terms of your child's treatment plan.

In my experience, working with a treatment team is the most effective way to take charge of your child's eating disorder. A coordinated effort to heal your child physically, mentally, and nutritionally can be the path to recovery. Sometimes, however, a child requires more than outpatient treatment. She may be deteriorating medically or failing to progress psychologically. At this point, the treatment team will begin to evaluate if a more intensive level of treatment is necessary. The next section examines when either hospitalization or inpatient residential treatment might be necessary, and what you can do to make the most appropriate choices for your child.

PART THREE

EXTREME SITUATIONS

· ·

The most difficult year of my life started on my birthday when my daughter's best friend was diagnosed with anorexia. My 14-year-old daughter Shani was very upset when her friend was later admitted to a residential treatment center. When Shani asked to see her psychologist, I thought it was because she was distraught about her friend. Little did I know that my daughter was actually concerned about her own health.

We located a psychologist who specialized in treating eating disorders. After meeting with Shani for less than fifteen minutes, she brought me into the room and said there was "no doubt" in her mind that Shani had anorexia. Shani began seeing the psychologist every week and we also set up a meeting with a dietitian, who explained the physical symptoms my daughter had been experiencing. I also learned from Shani's bone density scan that she had osteopenia, the precursor to osteoporosis. At that time, I believed that her friend's trip to a residential treatment center would deter Shani from that path and she would do what was necessary to get well at home.

Over the course of the next month, I started to see her change. Every day, Shani wrote menus of what she would eat and counted every calorie that would go into her mouth, including her vitamins. If she ate more than her self-restricted 1,200 calories, she would do crunches or run in place to burn the extra calories. She started to isolate herself from her friends, spending as much time as possible in her bedroom.

Two months after her diagnosis, Shani had lost another four pounds. The dietician told me to add a nutrition supplement called Ensure for extra calories . . . this is when I moved from being "mom" to the deeply hated "food police." Despite my best efforts, she refused to drink the supplement. Shani knew that if she didn't drink the supplement, she would be too weak to go to school, a condition that her psychologist and I had established. One morning, Shani looked at me and said, "I am not going to drink the Ensure, and I am not going to eat any more food." At that point, I knew the decision to send her to a residential treatment center had been made.

Finding a residential treatment center was not an easy task. I researched centers and programs recommended in books as well as searched the Internet. The programs Shani's psychologist suggested were too far away, and I really wanted to have her as close to home as possible. While on an eating disorder Web site, I stumbled upon a center that was only about five miles away. I called and spoke to the executive director for about forty-five minutes. He seemed to understand our situation and invited me to visit their program the next day. I asked her dad (we are divorced) to meet the director and take a tour, and then we took Shani to visit. We felt this program offered enough flexibility to individualize Shani's treatment and would allow us to be an ongoing part of her recovery. Before making a decision, we checked the references from other parents whose children had attended the program.

The day we left Shani there was very sad and difficult for us. There was, however, some sense of relief, since I knew Shani was now in the hands of professionals. We missed Shani terribly. After a long seven weeks, the time finally came for Shani to begin the step-down program. We were all thrilled but also a bit concerned about how it would work to have her at home. We were prepared with meal plans, food exchanges, and scheduled times for her to eat her three meals and three snacks. Shani continued to attend group therapy at the residential treatment program. I coordinated and attended all of her appointments with the doctor, dietician, psychiatrist, and psychologist, and the family and group counseling sessions.

As I write this, Shani has been home for two months. Dealing with day-to-day issues continues to be a challenge. Fortunately, Shani is now healthy enough to be a cheerleader again, but she is closely monitored, with clearly defined parameters and consequences, just in case the eating disorder starts to rear its ugly head again. I am hopeful that Shani will be back at school and flourishing in the fall. In the meantime, I am home full-time, dealing with Shani's continuing recovery from the ever-present nightmare called an eating disorder.

Barbara
San Diego, California

I STRONGLY BELIEVE THAT the best place for most children and adolescents with eating disorders is at home, with their parents. You are your child's best support and can positively influence your son or daughter's recovery. Unfortunately, despite everyone's best efforts and intentions, a child with a severe eating disorder may require medical hospitalization or a long-term stay at a residential treatment center.

Both of these options are only used in extreme cases, such as when a child's life is in danger or after all other treatment options have been explored and failed. Fortunately, the number of children with eating disorders who require medical hospitalization or inpatient residential treatment is small. Should your treatment team recommend either one of these options, the following chapters will help you understand medical hospitalization and inpatient residential treatment.

10

HEALING THE BODY AT
A MEDICAL HOSPITAL

Trevor's Story
A treatment team recognizes a serious medical problem

Fifteen-year-old Trevor was being followed by his pediatrician, psychologist, and dietitian for his anorexia. His parents had put together this treatment team when he was diagnosed with anorexia a year earlier. He had been doing well until August and started backsliding a few weeks before school started. His parents and his treatment team knew Trevor was anxious about starting high school. His mother noticed he had started to restrict his eating again and once school started, he was spending a lot of time studying and began pulling away from his friends and family. It was a familiar pattern and his therapist, doctor, and parents were all becoming concerned. His doctor, who he saw every week, noticed that Trevor's weight was declining and contacted Trevor's therapist with this information. Because Trevor's heart rate was low, he set up an appointment for two days later. Trevor's heart rate had dropped even lower, so he called me to admit Trevor to the hospital.

When someone is hospitalized because of medical complications related to an eating disorder, it usually involves an emergency admittance and means there is serious medical danger. Fortunately, only a small percentage of children with eating disorders require medical hospitalization. The goals of medical hospitalization are twofold: to get your child medically stable and to be sure there are no other causes for your child's symptoms. A medical hospitalization will usually last only until your daughter is medically stable. The exact length of the hospitalization depends on the reason for of her admission, the degree of her malnutrition, and how compromised her body is. Although a hospitalization will stabilize your daughter's medical condition, it will not resolve the underlying problems of her eating disorder. And after being discharged, she will still require an intensive, structured plan of outpatient therapy, nutritional counseling, and ongoing medical supervision.

If your child is admitted to the hospital for medical complications of an eating disorder, it is likely you will be shell-shocked and numb. Even if you suspected something was wrong, the fact that your daughter has a life-threatening illness is often unimaginable, especially because she may have been feeling fine and engaging in her usual activities until right before admission. (You can refer to chapter 4 for more information about related medical risks.) However, eating disorders don't happen overnight—it is more than likely that your daughter's eating disorder has been developing for some time. The following sections will explain why your child may require hospitalization as well as help you navigate through the often overwhelming hospital experience. The more you know, the better you can support your child.

WHY HAS MY CHILD BEEN HOSPITALIZED?

Medical admission criteria

The American Academy of Pediatrics and the Society for Adolescent Medicine has established specific criteria for when a child with an eating disorder needs to be hospitalized. These generally relate to life-threatening conditions, including unstable vital signs, abnormal laboratory results, and severely low weight, all of which must be closely monitored and treated in a hospital setting. (Please refer to chapter 4 for specific information about medial risks related to eating disorders.) A physician will usually use the following criteria to determine if your child requires a medical hospitalization.

- **Severe malnutrition (weight is less than 75 percent of the child's ideal body weight):** At this extreme state of malnutrition the body can no longer properly perform its basic functions. Someone who is this severely malnourished is also at a greater risk of having significant cardiac problems. Hospitalization for someone this malnourished is important because they need to be closely monitored, and refeeding a severely malnourished person needs to be managed very carefully. If a severely malnourished person is refed too rapidly, damage to the liver, heart, and other organs can result.

- **Bradycardia (heart rate is less than 50 beats per minute):** A heart rate this slow during the day while awake is not normal. In someone who is malnourished, it indicates that her heart is not getting enough nutrition and therefore is too weak to keep up a healthy rate. This increases someone's risk of arrhythmias (irregularities in the heart's rhythm), which may lead to sudden cardiac death.

- **Hypotension (blood pressure is less than 90/45 mmHg):** Very low blood pressure indicates that the heart is weakened and unable to beat strongly enough to circulate blood adequately throughout the body. A weakened heart is at an increased risk of arrhythmias (irregularities in the heart's rhythm) and sudden cardiac death.

- **Hypothermia (temperature is less than 36.3° C/97.3° F):** Hypothermia occurs in part because of reduced "insulating" body fat and in part because of the body's overall lack of energy. It is an indication that the body is too malnourished to perform the basic function of heating itself to a normal temperature.

- **Orthostatic changes (decrease in blood pressure or increase in heart rate when transitioning from lying to standing):** Orthostatic changes are a sign that the heart has significantly weakened. The weakened heart is unable to beat strongly enough to make up for the body transitioning from a lying to a standing position (the pull of gravity requires the heart to beat harder to get blood to the brain when one is standing), and so it attempts to compensate by beating faster. This is reflected as a drop in blood pressure and/or an increase in heart rate.

- **Prolonged QTc Interval (a measurement of a specific part of the heart beat on the EKG):** This condition, which can be detected by an electrocardiogram (EKG) reading, carries with it an

increased risk of sudden cardiac death. If the interval is too prolonged, the risk of sudden cardiac death becomes so severe that
the patient will need to be taken to the intensive care unit.

- **Hypokalemia (low potassium level in the blood):** When the body
  does not have enough potassium, it affects all muscle functioning,
  including that of the heart. Without enough potassium, the heart
  may be unable to beat correctly, and there is an increased risk of
  sudden cardiac death.

- **Hypophosphatemia (low phosphorus level in the blood):** When
  the body does not have enough phosphorus, muscles are not able
  to function properly. The two muscle groups of greatest concern
  are those of the chest wall and heart. An adequate amount of phosphorus is also needed for blood to deliver oxygen to the tissues.
  Therefore, without enough phosphorus, there is an increased
  risk of an arrhythmia (irregular heart beat), sudden cardiac death,
  and damage to the body from lack of oxygen.

Typically, someone will initially exhibit one or two of these signs. However, as the patient is observed and refed in the hospital, more of these signs
often become apparent. The list of admission criteria above is not all-
inclusive. There are other conditions, such as acute food refusal, passing
out, and vomiting blood, that also may require immediate hospitalization.

If your child needs to be hospitalized due to a medical complication of
her eating disorder, it is possible that she may be admitted to a specialized
eating disorder medical or medical/psychiatric unit if there is one nearby.
However, as there are a limited number of these types of units around the
country, it is more likely that she will be admitted to the general medical
or pediatric unit of your local hospital and cared for by her regular doctor.
Your child's doctor may decide to transfer her to a hospital with an eating
disorders unit—even if it is in another state—if he feels that the local hospital is unable to meet her needs.

As soon as your child is admitted to the hospital, she will have an EKG
(electrical tracing of the heart) and several blood tests, unless these tests
were recently conducted at your doctor's office and do not need to be
repeated. The initial blood tests will check you child's blood count, salts
in her blood, liver, kidney, and thyroid function as well as hormone levels.
Depending on your child's condition, the tests may be repeated daily or
every other day.

WHAT HAPPENS AT THE HOSPITAL?

Every hospital has its own protocols and every patient has different needs. The following description is based on how I typically treat patients who are admitted to the comprehensive care program (our medical inpatient eating disorder unit) at the Lucile Packard Children's Hospital at Stanford. It will give you a general idea of what happens during the medical hospitalization.

The doctor recommends hospitalization:
10 AM Monday

Diane, a 12-year-old girl, has been consistently losing weight for the past two months. Extremely concerned, her pediatrician keeps encouraging Diane's parents to "try to make her eat more." He has been seeing her every other week but today notices that her heart rate has dropped to 45 beats per minute. This is a serious sign that Diane's health is deteriorating, and he recommends that she be admitted to the hospital. Diane lives in a small town three hours north of Stanford University. Her doctor calls me to find out if we can take her on our inpatient unit. I accept her for admission, but request that she be transported to the hospital by ambulance because her heart rate is so low. Diane's mother accompanies her in the ambulance. Her father follows in the family car after going home to pack some of Diane's personal posessions.

Diane arrives at the hospital: 4 PM Monday

When Diane arrives on the unit, her nurse, Beth, greets her. Beth helps Diane to get settled in and gets some of her basic medical information. Diane is then weighed naked in a hospital gown. This gives us the most accurate weight.

As the attending physician, I meet with Diane and her parents after she is checked in. I do the same type of history and physical examination that is described in the initial outpatient medical visit section. I then order an EKG to check for an irregular heartbeat and a battery of blood and urine tests to determine if anything else might be contributing to her malnutrition and low heartrate. (These tests will also let me know if any other medical complications have been caused by her malnutrition.)

Diane is then connected to a heart monitor that will stay on her twenty-four hours a day. The monitor transmits information to the nurse's station so they can monitor her heart rate and see if her heartbeat looks regular. If Diane has an abnormally slow or fast heartbeat or an irregular heartbeat, an alarm will go off to alert the nurses to come in and check to make sure she is okay. She is put on bed rest and required to stay in bed until her heart rate improves.

At this point, Diane's overnight heart rate is a major concern. Although everyone's heart rate drops when they are asleep, because Diane is so malnourished and her heart is weakened, we are concerned that her heart rate may go dangerously low (into the twenties or thirties) overnight. She will remain on bed rest until her heart begins to recover, which can take from a few days to several weeks.

The first forty-eight hours: (Tuesday and Wednesday)

During the first forty-eight hours of Diane's hospitalization, she meets the other members of the hospital treatment team. They come in one by one to meet with her and do individual evaluations and include:

THE PSYCHOLOGIST AND PSYCHIATRIST: After the psychologist and psychiatrist meet with Diane and her parents and learn about Diane's individual and family issues, they agree on a diagnosis: anorexia nervosa. Although they determine Diane doesn't require any psychiatric medication at this time, a plan for psychological treatment is set up while she is in the hospital. They also talk to Diane's parents about what might be going on with Diane psychologically and explain what having anorexia means.

THE REGISTERED DIETITIAN: The dietitian meets with Diane and takes a diet/nutrition history. Using this information—plus her height, weight, and the results of her blood tests—she designs a refeeding plan to slowly renourish Diane without overwhelming her malnourished body. (See refeeding syndrome in chapter 4.) Diane's mother is confused and says, "I don't understand—my child is starving and you are not feeding her enough. She was eating more than this at home." I explain that refeeding someone who is malnourished can be very dangerous. We must do it slowly while carefully monitoring how their body is responding. If we refeed Diane too quickly, she can develop problems with her heart, her liver, and the salts in her blood.

I use the first forty-eight hours of her vital signs to determine how compromised her heart really is. The first night in the hospital, Diane's heart rate goes down to 42 beats per minute. However, on the second night it goes into the midthirties. Often, patients' heart rates look better on the first night than they really are. This may be due to the adrenaline rush that accompanies an emergency hospital admission. Once they get settled in, we get to see how their heart is really functioning.

By the end of the first forty-eight hours, Diane's treatment team will have a solid treatment plan in place for her.

Phase one of hospitalization: Bed rest

Diane remains on bed rest until her heart rate improves and she is able to maintain a minimally normal body temperature. This can take anywhere from days to weeks depending on how compromised the heart is. For Diane it takes one week. During this time, Diane remains connected to the cardiac monitor and her vital signs are checked frequently. She also has blood tests done every few days to look for abnormalities in the salts in her blood and any problems with her liver or kidney function. These can be signs of refeeding syndrome.

A psychologist begins working with Diane to help her to understand her illness and deal with her fear of gaining weight. The dietition monitors Diane's weight progress and nutrition and adjusts her meal plan daily.

Phase two of hospitalization: Getting out of bed

After being in the hospital for one week, Diane's heart rate improves and she is allowed to get out of bed. Initially, Diane is restricted to a wheelchair to move around the inpatient unit. As her nutritional status and vital signs improve, Diane's activity level slowly increases. By the time she is discharged, Diane will be allowed to walk around the unit to get from one place to another, perhaps from her room to the dining room but nothing too far. Diane remains connected to the cardiac monitor at night because we are still concerned about how low her heart rate drops while she is sleeping. As Diane becomes more active—such as getting out of bed—her body will demand more of her heart and, therefore, her heart rate is at risk of dropping more at night.

Diane continues to have her vital signs checked several times a day, although less frequently than when she was on bed rest. The salts in Diane's blood and her liver and kidney function continue to be monitored through blood tests. The frequency depends on the severity of Diane's malnutrition and the presence of any abnormalities that have already been identified.

Mealtimes at the hospital

As Diane's body becomes better nourished, the dietitian who developed her nutritional plan adjusts it to meet her changing caloric and nutritional needs. Because refeeding is started slowly, initially it may seem that Diane is not getting enough food. However, her nutritional plan will be evaluated and adjusted on a daily basis. By the end of her hospital stay, it may appear that she is being asked to eat too much. It is important to recognize that when someone becomes malnourished they begin to "eat" their own body. They initially burn fat, but end up destroying muscle and other important body tissues. As they begin to renourish themselves, these destroyed tissues must be repaired. This repair work takes a lot of energy (calories). Therefore the caloric needs of someone who is malnourished can be very high.

A nurse or other staff member observes Diane during all meals and records exactly what and how much she eats. Diane's parents are encouraged to have meals with her so they can learn from the staff how to help Diane get through meals and become familiar with her nutritional plan.

Discharge planning

As Diane progresses through her hospitalization, her hospital treatment team begins to plan for her discharge. They help her parents understand their role in Diane's outpatient care and set up an appropriate outpatient treatment team. (Please refer to chapters 12 to 15 for information on strategies to help your child at home, during meals, and at school.)

Final phase: Discharge from the hospital (Tuesday)

After just over two weeks of hospitalization, Diane receives permission to be discharged. She has met the following discharge criteria: her vital signs have been stable for two full calendar days (including her heart rate on the cardiac monitor overnight), her weight is greater than 75 to 80 percent of her ideal body, and her electrolyte levels (salts in the blood) are in the normal range.

When Diane receives permission to go home, she is thrilled and her parents are excited and relieved. What they need to realize is that although their daughter is stable enough to go home, their challenges are just beginning. Diane is still medically fragile and her eating disorder has not been "fixed." The real work will begin when they get home.

Please note that the above scenario is based on what I generally do on the eating disorders unit at Lucile Packard Children's Hospital at Stanford. This scenario will help give you a basic idea of what happens when a child is hospitalized. Every hospital will have different protocols and every patient has unique requirements.

ADVOCATING FOR YOUR CHILD IN THE HOSPITAL

Even at the best hospitals, you will need to advocate for your child. Ask questions if you don't understand something and use this book as a way to open dialogues. You can ask for additional assistance in the following areas, especially if your daughter is not in an eating disorders unit and the staff may not be aware of the nuances of treating these diseases.

Monitoring meals

Hospitals are understaffed. If your daughter is in a unit where meals are not observed, ask what time meals are served and if you are allowed to be there to eat with your daughter. This way you can help your daughter through her meals and be sure that she is eating what she is supposed to. If a child is left alone, she may flush food down the toilet and pretend that she's eaten a meal. You might want to "help" the nurse by informing her what your child has eaten or not eaten so she can accurately record it.

Managing pain

Starvation and refeeding can result in abdominal pain. Some of this pain is caused by asking a gastrointestinal system that has shut down to handle large quantities of food it is no longer used to. And some of it is due to the incredible anxiety caused by eating and not purging. Regardless of the cause, pain is pain; if someone says they are in pain, efforts should be made to provide comfort. This, however, does *not* mean decreasing nutrition because "it hurts to eat." Nutrition is what will ultimately make your child physically better. As her body gets used to having regular meals, the pain will lessen. During the time that her body is getting used to eating, there are a few things that you can do: request warm packs for your child to hold on her stomach after meals, which may relieve some of the discomfort; ask the nurse or attending physician if an occupational therapist (OT) can do relaxation exercises or guided imagery with her; request a physical therapist (PT) to do biofeedback, which trains kids to be able to consciously relax their muscles, such as their abdominal muscles, when they tense after meals or when they are in pain.

Medical Staff You Will Meet on a Hospital Unit

ATTENDING PHYSICIAN

A doctor will see your child every day while she is in the hospital. Depending on the hospital, this doctor may be your child's pediatrician or a doctor who works specifically for the hospital. You can speak with the doctor about your child's medical condition, progress, and any symptoms she is experiencing. The attending physician will discuss your child's progress with her primary doctor.

PSYCHIATRIST OR PSYCHOLOGIST

A therapist may work with your child on the emotional and psychological issues surrounding her eating disorder. If the team believes psychiatric medications may be helpful, a psychiatrist will then evaluate your child. For information about psychiatric medications, see chapter 8.

DIETITIAN

A dietitian will assess your child's nutritional status and nutrient needs, develop a dietary plan, and follow your child's nutritional progress throughout her hospitalization. Depending on the hospital, she may be able to help you arrange outpatient nutritional care.

NURSE OR NURSE'S AIDE

The nurse or her aide will take your child's vital signs, bring her medications, and possibly help her with meals. You should speak to the nurse if your child isn't feeling well, if you or your child needs to speak with a doctor, or if you have questions about your child's treatment. If your child is on an eating disorders unit, the nurse may also supervise meals; if not, you should ask the nurse about mealtimes so you can be available to eat with your child.

OCCUPATIONAL THERAPIST (OT)

The OT can do relaxation exercises or guided imagery with your child to help lessen her anxiety and to help with after-meal discomfort.

PHYSICAL THERAPIST (PT)

The PT can help your child in several ways. If your child is on prolonged bed rest, the PT can do passive range of motion stretches. This can help to relieve stiffness and may even decrease your child's desire to move around. The PT may also be able to do some biofeedback, which teaches her to consciously relax her muscles and may help with some of the abdominal pain that accompanies refeeding.

OTHER HOSPITAL STAFF

Depending on the size of the hospital, your daughter may also work with an art therapist, a recreation therapist—who organizes activities for patients—and a credentialed primary or secondary school teacher. The teacher will keep in touch with your child's school, help with homework, and support the transition back to school. Most hospitals also have a chaplain available to meet the spiritual needs of patients and their families. You can ask a nurse about this.

WHAT YOU CAN DO DURING YOUR CHILD'S
MEDICAL HOSPITALIZATION

Rest

Your daughter is hospitalized, and I'm going to tell you to rest. I realize this probably doesn't make much sense, but one of the best ways to help your child is to use this time to conserve energy and get prepared for her return home. When a child is sick enough to require a hospitalization, parents often feel defeated, demoralized, and utterly exhausted. During your child's hospitalization, you need to take the time to rest, renourish your own spirit, rebuild your support network, and renew your confidence in your ability to parent a child with an eating disorder. The more you take care of yourself now, the more energy you will have to spend when your child returns home.

Every hospital offers different levels of parental involvement. When your child is admitted to the hospital, ask what is expected and what is allowed in terms of your involvement. Then, be as involved as possible in your child's inpatient care. It is also helpful to take advantage of any parent education or support activities that may be offered. But this is also the time to take care of yourself—the road ahead will be emotionally demanding and, at times, physically draining.

Set up or reevaluate your child's outpatient treatment team

Start planning for your child's discharge the day she is admitted. If you don't already have a treatment team in place, make this your first priority. When your child is discharged from the hospital, it is critical that you have a strong outpatient treatment team in place, consisting of at least a medical doctor, dietitian, and therapist. Since identifying and interviewing potential team members is time-consuming, you can do this while your child is in the hospital. If you already have a team in place, you should be communicating with each member—or setting up a conference call or joint meeting—to try to determine if there need to be any changes in the outpatient treatment plan.

Having a child with an eating disorder can be very stressful for everyone in your family. It not only taxes individuals but can also create tension in the relationships between family members. While your child is in the hospital, you may want to arrange for some emotional support for yourself as well as for your spouse, other children, and any other family members in the home. This support may come in the form of individual therapy, family therapy, and/or support groups. You and your spouse may also want to consider couples therapy, since your relationship needs to be stronger than ever to help your child battle her eating disorder.

THE TRANSITION HOME

THE TRANSITION HOME from the hospital can be a stressful time for the entire family, which is why advanced preparation is very helpful. Your child is going to have to face eating her meals in a different environment (some kids "allow" themselves to eat in the hospital because it's out of their control but revert to earlier behavior when they return home). She will be facing the reality of having gained weight in the hospital and also may be stressed about being behind in school.

All of these factors may cause a child to have even more difficulty with eating or purging after she is discharged from the hospital. Krista, a 15-year-old girl with anorexia, is a good example of this. She was in the hospital for almost three weeks and during that time gained eight pounds. When she got home, Krista could no longer fit into her size 2 clothes. While her parents were thrilled with her weight gain, Krista felt she had "failed" at being anorexic and stopped eating again. She was readmitted to the hospital one week after her discharge. Her parents couldn't understand why being in the hospital didn't "scare" their daughter enough to get better. They didn't realize that although she had been medically stable enough to be discharged, Krista was still very medically fragile and psychologically sick. She needed the intensive support of her entire treatment team to get better.

Before your child comes home from the hospital, begin planning what you will need to do to help her recovery when she gets home. This information can be found in chapters 12 to 15.

11

HEALING THE MIND AT A
RESIDENTIAL TREATMENT PROGRAM

Jennifer's Story
Being at Home Wasn't Working

Jennifer, an accomplished cellist who was attending college on a music scholarship, had been my patient when she was in high school. A lovely and articulate young woman, Jennifer had struggled with anorexia but her treatment team felt she was in recovery and ready to attend college out of state. She was living in a sorority, had a boyfriend, and a 4.0 grade-point average. When she came home for the summer, her mother was shocked by Jennifer's appearance. She had lost at least 15 pounds and looked like a skeleton. Her mother immediately called the members of Jennifer's old treatment team, who began seeing Jennifer again. But at the end of the summer, Jennifer's health was not improving. From the outside, Jennifer's college experience looked positive but she couldn't handle the pressure. Jennifer told me that although she was always the best musician in high school, in college she found herself in a program with other students who were just as good if not better than she was. She said she felt she was losing control. Her mother said Jennifer refused to eat and stayed in her room all day, too weak even to practice the cello. Jennifer's mother didn't know how to help her daughter anymore. The treatment team agreed that there was no way she could go back to college in this condition and were recommending that Jennifer be admitted to a residential treatment program where she could work on some of her emotional issues and renourish her body. Her mother was terrified that Jennifer would lose her place at college and end a promising career. I looked her mother straight in the eye and asked her what was more important: a healthy daughter or a dead cellist.

A residential treatment program was definitely the right choice to help Jennifer. She took a one-year leave from college. She spent three months in a residential program and six months at home with her parents taking some classes at a local community college.

When a celebrity is diagnosed with an eating disorder, news reports often imply that she is whisked away to a spa-like treatment center, only to emerge a few months later "cured." Unfortunately, this representation is totally misleading. Although residential treatment programs can help patients work through some of the issues surrounding their eating disorders and behaviors of their disease, it does not "cure" them. A very small number of people with eating disorders—about 5 percent—actually go into residential treatment. Because finding out about this type of treatment is often difficult, I am providing in-depth information about residential treatment for parents whose children may end up needing it.

Residential treatment programs do provide 24-hour support for patients who are unable to make progress in the outpatient setting by offering extensive psychological and nutritional services in a safe and monitored environment. The primary goal of admitting a child into a residential treatment program is to get the child back on track to resume working with her multidisciplinary treatment program at home. In nearly all cases, a child enters a residential treatment program because nothing else is working.

A child should be admitted to a residential treatment center only after the treatment team has exhausted all other options. Residential programs are a bridge, but not an answer to helping a child with an eating disorder. I often share the following analogy with my patients: fighting your child's eating disorder is like pushing a wheelbarrow up a hill. You, your child, and her treatment team are pushing and making some progress and then the wheelbarrow gets stuck on a rock. No matter how hard you push, it doesn't budge. Residential treatment will help you get the wheelbarrow over the rock; however, you still need to push the wheelbarrow the rest of the way up the hill.

There is no question that admitting a child to a residential program will be difficult for you and your child. It can be heart-wrenching to be separated from your child, even if your home life has been a struggle; and it is frightening to send your child to live someplace else, especially if the center ends up being far from home. On the other hand, if your child has been suffering for a long time, you may actually feel slightly relieved that she will not be at home. This is perfectly understandable. Don't feel guilty—you are mostly likely exhausted and worn out.

PHILOSOPHIES, FACILITIES, AND APPROACHES

EVERY RESIDENTIAL TREATMENT program will be different in its philosophy, size, and physical setup. Most programs require a two- to three-month stay and cost on average $900 and $1,000 per day—that comes to a staggering $30,000 a month. (Information about how to get your insurance company to help you pay for eating disorder treatments is covered in chapter 16.)

Facilities can range from a few teens in a suburban private home to large, sprawling facilities in the country, to more institutional housing attached to a hospital. None are luxury spas. One of my patients, 16-year-old Mandy, was upset when I went to visit her after she was admitted to a residential treatment program located in a comfortable but modest house in the suburbs. This program was not what she expected. She was under the impression that inpatient treatment would be more like a resort or at least as nice as her family's upscale house in a much more affluent neighborhood. Mandy's parents were thrilled to find this program even though it was a five-hour drive from their home, a trip they made every weekend without fail.

Although there are a number of residential treatment programs across the country, only a limited number care for children who are under 18 years old; a recent study also found that less than 25 percent of them take boys. Carefully consider the type of program that is appropriate for your son or daughter. While some programs accept people of all ages, it may not be appropriate for your 14-year-old daughter to be with women in their forties or fifties who have been batting this disease for decades. On the other hand, seeing people who have struggled with this disease for many years may be helpful for some kids. My personal belief is that it is better for younger teens to be in a program that specializes in adolescents; if this is not an option, make sure to find out what programs they do offer and how many teens they have worked with. As I mentioned above, finding a program that accepts adolescent boys is more difficult.

The first step in looking for a residential program is to ask the members of your child's treatment team if they can recommend any local facilities. Appendix B provides information about places that offer referrals for residential treatment programs across the United States. It is appropriate—and recommended—that you ask a residential treatment program for references from parents whose children have been through the program.

Every residential treatment program has a unique approach that reflects the training and interest of its director, founders, or affiliated organization. There is no standard for how a program should operate, but you must make sure that the overall philosophy fits your child's personality and meets her medical needs. Some may emphasize spiritual or religious elements. All residential programs, however, should have a medical doctor, a nurse, a therapist, a psychiatrist, and dietitian on staff, although they may not be onsite or available full-time. While most programs require that a child be medically stable, some can be an alternative to hospitalization if they are equipped to monitor and treat medical complications. Intensive psychological counseling is a major component of residential treatment. Most programs focus on increasing a child's motivation to heal as well as increasing her ability to stand up to the thoughts, feelings, and impulses that maintain the eating disorder. Family therapy should be a component of every residential program, either in person or with sessions conducted on the phone. The staff at the residential program should also be in contact with members of your child's home treatment team.

Getting enough nutrition and dealing with food issues is a significant part of the treatment; therefore, mealtime is critical at any residential treatment program. Meals will be monitored by staff and developed for each resident by a dietitian. At one successful program, a therapist eats with patients at every meal and all residents are required to sign an agreement to finish 75 percent of what is on their plate. As patients become more confident and comfortable with eating, they progress to increasing levels of independence, which will include choosing their meals or eventually shopping and cooking food with the help of staff. Before a child is discharged, parents usually have meals with their child and may receive specific meal plans and instruction on how to supervise and manage meals at home.

The daily routine at a typical residential treatment center might include group therapy sessions, one-on-one therapy, medical evaluations, nutritional counseling, and social or leisure activities. In most cases, residents share a room. Depending on a child's situation, bathroom visits initially may be monitored to prevent purging. This might mean a staff member is inside the bathroom or stands outside the door.

HOW TO EVALUATE THE RIGHT PROGRAM FOR YOUR CHILD

BECAUSE EVERY RESIDENTIAL treatment program has a unique focus, it's important to carefully evaluate a program so that it will be the right fit for your child. If a program has a religious or spiritual focus, this should reflect your family's values and be comfortable for your child. If your child requires medical supervision, this also will be a factor. It's likely that you will have to make some trade-offs based on geography and availability. Although it is ideal for your child to be at a program that's fifteen minutes away from home, it should not be the only criterion.

Call the director or whoever is in charge of admission on the phone and then make an appointment to visit, even if it is a six-hour ride or in another state. It is very important, unless you have a referral from someone whom you trust completely, to personally visit the facility before your child is admitted. Consider asking a relative or friend—someone you trust and who knows your child well—to visit an out-of-town facility if you are unable to go personally.

When you are evaluating residential treatment programs, don't be misled by their recovery claims. Remember, these centers are businesses and not charitable organizations. There have been no systematic studies performed that measure the success rates of residential treatment programs, so be wary when a program director reports that they have a 90 percent recovery rate. This information is usually based on surveys the program has sent to past patients, and the results are very biased because people who are doing well are more likely to respond to the survey.

Questions to Ask about a Residential Treatment Program

- Is the facility accredited or licensed? Some states have strict licensing requirements while others have very little oversight. Be very cautious about sending your child to an unlicensed facility.
- Does the treatment philosophy correlate with your family's personal beliefs?
- Does the facility have a pediatrician or adolescent medicine specialist providing medical care?
- Is psychiatric care delivered by a board-certified child and adolescent psychiatrist?
- Do they use evidence-based therapies such as IPT or CBT (see chapter 8 for descriptions of these therapies).
- What type of family therapy and support is provided? Individual family therapy, multifamily support groups, parent training? Does the program offer therapy or phone therapy if you are not local?
- If teens and children are integrated with adult patients, are the groups and activities age appropriate?
- Is the facility equipped (onsite) to treat any chronic medical conditions that are not related to his or her eating disorder, such as diabetes, as well as those related to her eating disorder (e.g., severe malnutrition, low heart rate).
- How frequent is parent contact with the treatment team?
- What sort of education is provided? Is there an onsite school? Are individual tutoring and school liaison available?
- Is the facility associated with an eating disorder organization?
- Does the staff attend eating disorder conferences?
- How long have various staff members been working there?
- Ask them to describe mealtimes. Does a therapist eat with the residents?
- What types of programs do they offer for transitioning a patient from residential to outpatient status?

If possible, I recommend that you and your child visit a treatment center together. The parents of one of my patients were able to identify two facilities that seemed appropriate. They first met with the director at each program and then made appointments for their daughter to visit. "Cara definitely liked one better than the other. She felt more comfortable with the director and liked the house," the dad explained. "I think the fact that she had some input and was able to choose made her more willing to go."

When Residential Treatment
Is Not Appropriate

MRS. JOHNSON CAME to see me when her 17-year-old daughter Alison was diagnosed with bulimia. Alison had been hospitalized and would be released the following week. Although she recognized the importance of organizing a multidisciplinary team for Alison, she told me she couldn't possibly juggle so many medical and therapy appointments with a full-time job, two other busy kids, and a husband who traveled a lot. Mrs. Johnson said her daughter was moody and there was a lot of tension in the house. So instead of organizing a treatment team, she thought it might be better—and more effective—to find a residential treatment program for Alison. She also decided it would be good to get her daughter away from friends who were a bad influence. She told me about a colleague's son, who recently returned from a residential treatment program for drug addiction, and said the boy was doing great. What Mrs. Johnson didn't understand is even after Alison comes home from a residential treatment program, she wouldn't be "cured" and would still require multiple appointments with the doctor, therapist, and dietitian as well as ongoing supervision. And Alison would still have an eating disorder.

Mrs. Johnson's misconception about residential treatment is not unusual. Residential treatment programs exist to help a child who is failing outpatient treatment. And unlike live-in programs for addiction, there is no way to physically "detox" someone who has an eating disorder. Once she understood that residential treatment was not the answer for her daughter, Mrs. Johnson decided to take a leave of absence from work. In Alison's case, going to a residential treatment program was unnecessary. Working with her treatment team, she was able to regain her health and began understanding some of the issues that caused her eating disorder.

WHAT TO DO DURING YOUR CHILD'S STAY AT A RESIDENTIAL TREATMENT PROGRAM

MANY PROGRAMS HAVE weekly or biweekly family therapy sessions or may offer phone sessions for families that are not local. It is very important to find a program with parent participation, and it is critical that you take advantage of these opportunities. Make an effort to join any parent support groups; I have found that parents benefit greatly from sharing their experiences and supporting each other. It's comforting not to feel alone or isolated.

You and your family will need to be as prepared and rejuvenated as possible when your child returns home—there is a lot of hard work ahead. When your child is in an inpatient facility, use the time to rest and to re-evaluate your current treatment team by asking the following questions:

- Was something not working?
- Why didn't it work?
- Should you consider changing any of the members?
- Make appointments to speak with team members to discuss your child's situation and to ask why they think your child ended up needing residential treatment. What might they and you do differently when she comes home.

The next section offers information on how to plan ahead, figure out what needs to be set up when she is released, and begin exploring outpatient programs that can make the transition easier.

THE TRANSITION HOME

WHETHER YOUR DAUGHTER has been gone thirty days or three months, the transition home can be challenging. Most programs will help you and your child address these challenges as they prepare your child to move back home. Three months may seem like a long time, especially if your child is out of state and you cannot visit regularly. But I strongly advise that you begin planning your next steps as soon as possible. A large percentage of adolescents do make significant progress in residential treatment programs, accepting their disease and coming home ready to battle it. Unfortunately,

I have also observed many of them quickly slip back into their eating dis-ordered behaviors. Therefore, you need to be prepared to build on your child's progress as soon as she returns home.

Some residential treatment programs make the transition home smoother by "stepping" kids into intensive outpatient or partial hospital-ization programs. (Specific information about these types of programs appears in chapter 8.) Both of these programs allow people to gradually move back into their regular home life in increments. Your child may start off just spending the night at home but having all of her meals at the treatment cen-ter. Then, she might have dinner and sleep at home but return to the pro-gram for breakfast and lunch. It's a good process to acclimate your child back into her regular home life and for you to manage having her back.

The next section offers practical advice on how to support your child's treatment at home, manage meals, and make school a safe and healthy environment.

IT'S UP TO YOU:

STRATEGIES TO HELP PARENTS PROMOTE RECOVERY

....

My Daughter Has What?

Halfway through the eighth grade, when my daughter Michelle was fourteen, she decided to lose a little weight and started changing her eating habits. Her motivation was to look great for the eighth grade's formal graduation and dance. People began noticing Michelle's weight loss and told her how wonderful she looked. She was getting a lot of attention from her peers as well as adults. I found myself glowing with pride and filled with happiness because it seemed my daughter was reaching a goal that she had set out to accomplish. And I have to admit she did look fantastic. She had always been a little chubby and was transforming into a lovely, slim young woman. Wow!

High school was an exciting time, with many new friends, more challenging classes, competitive sports and thoughts about college. My daughter was driven to succeed—conscientious, hard-working, always expecting more of herself. Although I noticed that Michelle's weight kept dropping, I presumed it was because she was involved in more competitive sports. At one point, she seemed a bit sad and withdrawn but I figured it was teenage hormones. The summer after Michelle's freshman year, I began noticing a compulsion about appearance, about food, about being perfect. When classes began in September, it was evident—and surprising—that she couldn't keep up with all of her homework. I was finally beginning to think something was wrong with my beautiful, successful daughter. I scheduled an appointment with the pediatrician. He suspected she had an eating disorder because her vital signs were so low and recommended she go to an eating disorders clinic as soon as possible. As soon as possible? I told him that sounded serious. He said it was. My heart was pounding. How can this be? I was sure his diagnosis was wrong. As soon as the eating disorders specialist examined Michelle, she put her on complete bed rest in the hospital. I couldn't believe it. How could my daughter—a good student, great kid, and high achiever—have a life-threatening disease from an eating disorder? After eighteen days of treatment our daughter was released to my care. We left the hospital, confident that this experience had enlightened us, brought our family closer together, and cured our beautiful girl.

We put together a treatment team, and Michelle started seeing a physician, therapist, and dietitian. Life at home wasn't easy—she would have meltdowns and talk about being "fat" when she couldn't fit into clothes she used to wear. Meals were the hardest, but we followed the dietitian's advice. Michelle went back to school and was voted homecoming princess for her class. What an honor. She was so happy. I assumed everything was fine and the worst was behind us. I was so wrong. Several months later, my daughter confessed to her therapist that she had been forcing herself to throw up and would hide heavy magnets in her clothes to weigh more at checkups. Less than a year after being released from the hospital, she was readmitted for "severe anorexia." She was there for twenty-eight days.

She is now home again. This time, I know it will be a long road to recovery. I'm feeling more cautious but remain optimistic that this time it will work. And I'm determined to do everything I can at home so we won't have to send her to a residential treatment program.

— A mother's reflection

You've taken the first critical steps toward helping your child by identifying her eating disorder and organizing a treatment team. I wish I could tell you the hard part was over. Realistically, however, you are now at the beginning of a very challenging, often frustrating journey. Even with an experienced and supportive treatment team in place, it still comes down to you. There's no place like home. This is especially true for a child with an eating disorder. Hospitalization will stabilize her medical condition; a residential treatment program can help her accept, understand, and begin to control her eating disorder; but the best possible place to restore her mental and physical health is at home. Ultimately, your child's recovery depends on what happens when she is living with you at home. "I don't think I can do this," one father admitted to me. "It's already been so exhausting with Laura in the hospital—the idea that she's coming home is too much to contemplate." I will tell you what I told this apprehensive father: "It won't be easy but you can do it with planning and patience. Supporting your child at home is like running a marathon: your need to set a slow and steady pace. Take note of your successes however small they might be, and take care of yourself along the way."

One of the most difficult aspects of helping a child with an eating disorder is accepting that you will need to be tough and, when necessary, uncompromising. I know this sounds harsh. As a parent, your instinct is to protect your child. Seeing your child in pain, whether it is emotional or physical, is one of the most difficult things a parent can experience. Parents want to make their children happy: when your daughter pleads not to be admitted to the hospital, the temptation may be to postpone her admittance. If she cries and says "eating hurts," you may be inclined to take the food away instead of making her sit at the table until she finishes. It is crucial that you are strong and consistent. Your son may shout, "I hate you" for making him go to a therapy appointment. Remember, your actions are based on love. Eating disorders have a mortality rate greater than some types of cancer. If your child begged you not to get chemotherapy to treat cancer, you would make him go to the hospital for treatment and be there to support and comfort him. The same action is necessary when you are helping your child through the treatment for his eating disorder.

By using the tools and strategies in this section, you can create a safe haven at home, learn to cope with how your child's eating disorder is affecting you and your family, and find ways to support him at school.

12

SUPPORTING YOUR CHILD AT HOME

> ## Ginny's Story
> ### The challenge of coping every day
>
> **Ginny's mother left** this message on my voice mail: "Dr. Carlton, I just don't know how to help Ginny—I can see that she's trying to fight against the anorexia but she is surrounded by things that test her will. Her friends at high school constantly talk about their diets, she sees skinny actresses on television and ads for diet products in magazines. Last night at dinner she threw her food on the floor and screamed we were trying to make her fat. I can't lock her in her room, but I just don't know what to do." Ginny's mom is not alone. It's tough trying to help a child who is working on fighting her disease but is constantly undermined by society. I called Ginny's mother back and discussed some strategies on how to help her daughter ease the struggle.

Whether your daughter has recently been diagnosed with an eating disorder by her primary care doctors or is coming home from the hospital, it's important to prepare yourself emotionally as well as modify your household to help her effectively battle her eating disorder.

All of the advice in this section is general and needs to be adapted to your child's personality and circumstances. I have developed these practical tips after years of treating children and teens with eating disorders. Not everything will work for every person or every family, but these tips will assist you in the ongoing process of helping your child overcome her eating disorder. Many of these topics will be brought up in therapy, either in family sessions or individually with you or your child. If you have concerns about any of these areas, make it a point to discuss them with your family or child's therapist.

CREATING A SAFE HAVEN

UNFORTUNATELY, WE LIVE in a society obsessed with weight and body image. The constant parade of ultrathin models on billboards and in magazines can exacerbate your child's eating disorder. While this one factor did not cause your daughter's eating disorder, it can be a powerful force that hinders her recovery. Society's acceptance of comments such as, "You look great, have you lost weight?" furthers the view that our bodies are out there for public scrutiny. Although you can't shelter your daughter from the outside world, you can take steps to make your home a safer place for her.

Get rid of it! The scale

Your daughter may feel a great need to weigh herself frequently, in some instances numerous times a day. This obsession can be very upsetting and anxiety provoking but difficult to control. Therefore, it is a good idea to put the scale away or simply get rid of it. Of course, she will have access to scales at other people's homes, but make your house a safe place.

Remove any temptations: Medications

Having certain medications around your home can also cause difficulties for your child with an eating disorder. It is not uncommon for people with eating disorders to use diet pills or herbal "energy boosters" to suppress their appetites, diuretics to decrease their weight, or ipecac or laxatives to purge. Although these very common medications are often considered safe, they can be very dangerous or even deadly if abused by people with eating disorders. Even if you do not believe your daughter is taking any of these medications, I still strongly recommend that you remove them from your home. It can be very tempting for a child with an eating disorder to use or abuse these medications, even if they have never used them before. Yes, your daughter will absolutely have access to them at friends' homes, the grocery store, and drugstores; you cannot control the world but you can—and need to—make your home a safer place for your daughter.

If you need any of these medications for your personal use, keep your supply in a place that your daughter does not have access to, even if this means at your office or a neighbor's house. If we're talking about diet pills, please seriously examine why *you* are taking them.

What is she reading? Diet books and fashion magazines

When I check out at the grocery store, I am always amazed that more of us don't have eating disorders. Almost every magazine cover in the checkout aisle has diet tips or has articles congratulating celebrities for their successful weight loss or chastising them for going to the beach and exposing cellulite. This can easily fuel an existing eating disorder as described in chapter 1.

Decreasing your daughter's exposure to these images and messages can help her fight her eating disorder. If you subscribe to magazines that glorify underweight celebrities, give diet tips, or promote an unhealthy body image in any way, I recommend that you cancel your subscription or switch the address so that it is sent to your office. Diet books or books promoting specific diet or exercise plans are best removed as well. What do you do if the subscriptions or books belong to your daughter? This gets into a more touchy area. While I still believe it is destructive for her to be exposed to these messages, you do need to consider her privacy. Discuss your concerns about the appropriateness of this reading material with her and with her therapist. I do not recommend going behind her back and canceling the subscriptions or throwing away her books.

What's in the fridge? Food choices

I am a strong proponent of the philosophy that there are no "good" foods or "bad" foods. As with most things, whether something is an appropriate choice depends on the circumstances. If a child has diabetes and, therefore, must limit his sugar intake, a brownie might not be an appropriate snack choice. To make it easier and remove the temptation, his family might agree not to keep brownies in the house. Because of your daughter's eating disorder, certain foods will not be the best choices for her. For instance, since she is trying to renourish her malnourished body, "fat free," "sugar free" and "diet" foods are not appropriate choices. Keeping inappropriate food out of the home can help her make better food choices.

Although this may be difficult for other people in your family, it is crucial for your daughter's health.

What did I say? Monitor your references to weight and diets

Because our society is obsessed with being thin, comments about people's weight or current diet trends have become part of our daily conversations. How often have you said or heard: "Wow, you look great, have you lost weight?" or "Have you seen Jane, I think that she's put on a few pounds?" or "Bert looks so fit. Did you know he's been on the Atkins diet?" There are thousands of things that your daughter will be exposed to during a typical day that have the potential to exacerbate her eating disorder, and you can not protect her from all of them. You can, however, make your home as safe a place as possible. To do this, try to avoid discussing the following topics around your daughter:

- Your own weight and/or your desire to gain or lose weight
- Fad diets
- Good foods or bad foods (For example: "I was so bad, I ate a brownie at lunch, but it's okay because I'll eat less or go to the gym tomorrow.")
- The weight or physical fitness of celebrities, friends, or family members
- The amount of food your child with an eating disorder is being asked to eat
- Your child's weight or target weight. How, you may be wondering, is it possible to avoid this? What you want to focus on is her health as opposed to her weight. Weight is a very sensitive topic for someone with an eating disorder. Although your child may be working very hard to regain her health, it can actually be very upsetting when she learns she has gained weight. What is a positive for you will actually seem like a negative to your child. Also, weight might not be the best indication of her health. Remember, people with serious eating disorders can be underweight, normal weight, or overweight. It is their health that we are concerned about. Also avoid discussing your child's target weight, which is simply your doctor's estimation of what your child will need to weigh to have a properly nourished body. I usually don't share this with my patients because it may set up false

expectations. For instance, if I tell a teenage girl that that her target weight is 130 pounds, she may reach it but still not have her period or still have poor vital signs. It will then be very difficult for me to get her to gain the additional weight that she needs to be healthy. Additionally, it could undermine the trust we established because she may feel I lied to her when I told her she needed to get to 130 pounds.

It can be disturbing when we really listen to what we say and what is being said around us in relation to food, weight, and nutrition. Even if you try to avoid these topics, it is inevitable that things will slip out that you wish you didn't say. Don't worry. By being conscious of what you are saying in this area and trying to avoid comments that will trigger her eating disorder, you are doing the best thing you can for your daughter. Remember, you cannot change all of this overnight. It is a process that takes time.

MANAGING PHYSICAL ACTIVITY

When a child is diagnosed with an eating disorder, her doctor will often recommend that she cut back or totally stop physical exercise. In many cases, a child with an eating disorder will feel fine, so she may not understand why the doctor is so concerned about physical activity. There is a very good reason for this recommendation: exercise can be dangerous for someone with a weakened, malnourished heart. Additionally, the nutrition your child consumes needs to be used to renourish her weakened, malnourished body, not burned off by exercise.

Restricting or eliminating exercise can be devastating for children and adolescents with eating disorders, especially if it is a significant part of their daily routine, social life, or self-image. Children in elementary school often live for recess. Adolescents may identify themselves by the sports they play and by being part of a team. In some cases, a child with an eating disorder has incorporated exercise into his or her disease, using it as a way to "undo" eating. This might take the form of running five miles a day to burn off the calories she consumed; or in more extreme situations, someone will use exercise as a way to purge by eating large amounts of food and then running ten to fifteen miles to "undo" the binge. Regardless of the degree of exercise your child engages in, taking it away can produce extreme anxiety.

Be aware that people with eating disorders may do "covert" exercise, even if they have been warned against it. Your daughter might do hundreds of pushups or crunches in her room at night. You son might quietly run in place or sneak out of the house to go running or to the gym.

Exercise restrictions

So, now you are in the situation of telling your child she must eat foods she associates with getting "fat" and also stop or limit exercise, both requests go against everything her eating disorder is telling her to do. Here are a couple of suggestions on how to support your child through the time when she is not allowed to exercise:

1. **Reiterate why exercise can be dangerous:** "I know you miss running but your heart is too weak. If you stress it by running, it could stop and you could die."
2. **Set up a plan to restart exercise and use it as an incentive:** Discuss with the treatment team what needs to happen before your child can resume exercise. Once this plan is set up, help your child keep an eye on the goal. "I know that this is so difficult and you are getting antsy, but if you have two more good doctor visits, you can add in twenty minutes of exercise three times a week. Won't that feel good?"

Competitive sports

If your child plays competitive sports, having to give up a place on his or her team can be extremely upsetting and difficult. For teen athletes, sports are often a large part of their individual identity as well as their social circle. A sport may also be their focus for college or the source of a scholarship. It is important to keep focusing on one issue: your child's health. You may have to help your child identify other things that she is good at and can enjoy if sports are temporarily not an option.

Some children like to support their team by watching practices and games, although for others this could be upsetting and frustrating. Make sure to tell your child's therapist if she seems to be especially depressed about not playing her sport. One of my patients, a young woman who performed professionally with a regional ballet company, had to stop dancing due to malnutrition. Dance had been her whole world since she was six years old, and she became extremely depressed without the personal joy it brought her. When the art therapist at the hospital began working with her, my patient not only discovered that she enjoyed painting but that she was very talented. Of course, it couldn't possibly replace ballet, but it did give her something else to focus on.

If sports are very important to your child, use the possibility of getting back on a team as an incentive for her to get healthy. Looking a year ahead is too daunting for most teens but you can use team sports as a larger goal and then set up smaller steps—such as beginning to exercise a few times a week—as more immediate benchmarks. Again, before setting up this type of incentive program, consult with your child's treatment team.

Gym memberships

What to do about gym memberships can be very tricky. If you have a family membership, it may be impossible to put one person's use on hold. If only your child is a member, then I strongly recommend that you temporarily suspend the membership, which will save you from paying for the membership and ensure your child is not covertly going to the gym. Most gyms will do this with a doctor's note. Some teens have weights or other exercise equipment in their rooms or the garage. If your child has exercise equipment in his room and has been asked not to exercise, I suggest that you discuss removing the equipment with your child and his therapist.

Even if your son has permission to exercise, you must take into consideration his medical condition and what types of exercise are appropriate. For instance, if you know he has bone loss or if it is even suspected, he should not participate in activities that carry a high risk of falls or injuries, such as skiing or mountain biking. It is also advisable to discontinue all exercise if he complains of dizziness.

MONITORING SOCIAL AND FAMILY ACTIVITIES

UNLIKE MANY OTHER serious illnesses, a child with an eating disorder may feel physically fine even though her body is weakened and compromised. While it is good to try to keep things as normal as possible, there are certain activities that you will probably need to modify or stop. The activities considered to be safe will change as your child's treatment progresses. If exercise is prohibited, you must also evaluate other types of activities that expend a lot of energy. School dances, trips to the amusement park, or jaunts to the mall probably are not appropriate if your child needs to conserve energy. Even a school visit to a science museum might be too much for some children. Before your child engages in any of the above activities, you should discuss it with her treatment team.

As with meals, curtailing your child's activities will probably involve taking back some of your child's independence, which will be especially difficult for teenagers. Use your judgment (not your child's pleading) to decide what activities are appropriate. Make sure to read the section in chapter 4 about the risk of accidents because activities, such as skiing, horseback riding, and driving a car may be dangerous for someone who is malnourished.

HANDLING "STICKY" CONVERSATIONS

LIVING WITH A child with an eating disorder can sometimes be equated to walking across a minefield. You are never quite sure when something is going to explode. Sometimes you may accidentally say something that causes an unexpected reaction. You might tell your daughter that she looks pretty in the pink dress and she will freak out because it's something she used to wear when she was "fat." Other times, you might be reading a book or watching TV when your son comes in with a really difficult, loaded question such as:

- Am I fat?
- Why do I have to eat more than anyone else in the world?
- Why can't I exercise? I'm fine, I feel fine, and the doctors obviously think that I'm fine; they let me out of the hospital.

Although there is no way that you can avoid all these confrontations, you can use certain tactics to decrease the chances of conversations turning into battles.

1. Remain calm. Once you lose your cool, the situation is bound to escalate. There is no question that this is much easier said than done. When you feel that you're about to loose your cool, give yourself a time out. This may involve leaving the room.
2. Focus on your child's medical condition, not her weight. What we want is for her to have regular menses, a strong and healthy heart,

healthy bones, and a healthy body. This is accomplished with good nutrition. If you enter into a conversation about her weight or body shape, it will almost always end badly.

3. If your child asks questions that you are not sure how to answer, do the best you can and then write them down. At your child's next appointment, ask her therapist or doctor to discuss them with her (and you).

When your child asks you a loaded question, it's helpful to have a mantra that you can say to yourself in stressful moments. For example, think to yourself, "I am a good mother/father." This is absolutely true—you are reading this book and doing the best you can to help your child. Remember this! Repeat these words to yourself in moments when you feel overwhelmed. Additionally, think of a phrase that you can repeat to your child when she asks questions that reflect her eating disorder. One example might be: "You need to eat to live." Attempting to persuade your child that she is too thin or using logic and reasoning will not be effective.

What Do I Say or Do . . .

EVEN THOUGH YOU'VE been talking to your child about serious and uncomfortable issues for years (remember when he asked you how babies were made?), it's not unusual to feel flustered about how to respond to questions or situations that relate to his eating disorder. At times, you may feel like you're walking on eggshells, especially when a child becomes defiant or abusive.

Remember that to your child you are probably the safest person in the world. He is "giving" to you all the terrible and scary feelings he has inside of him. Because he is looking to you to see how you will respond to his feelings, you must model for him a safe and strong response. This will send the message to your child that if *you* can handle all of the awful feelings he is experiencing, then *he* can handle these feelings as well. Having a child with an eating disorder is scary; but you can't let him know this. Just as you would try to remain calm and present a positive exterior to a child who had cancer, it's important to do this for a child with an eating disorder. If your child sees you becoming overly upset, this sends the message that his words and behaviors can control you, and this is a very scary feeling for a child. The responses suggested below require tremendous energy but can help you master difficult moments.

- **Paradoxical response:** This technique gets at the scared and anxious emotions that are at the root of your child's behaviors. By responding to the emotions and not reacting to the behaviors, you will "soften" the moment. Examples of paradoxical responses include: "I love you," or "We are in this together," or "I am here for you." Although you might assume this approach will not work with cynical teenagers, I have found it to be very effective. Remember, your child is sick. Sometimes what might backfire with a healthy child may be exactly what a child with an eating disorder needs.
- **Externalizing response:** This technique helps separate your child from his eating disorder, putting you and your child on the same team against the disease. For example, you can say, "That is the eating disorder talking, I want to talk to (child's name)."
- **Verbally disengaging:** In moments of stress, it is sometimes best to disengage, walk away, and address your child in a calmer moment. This does not mean ignoring his behaviors. For example, you can try acknowledging that your child is upset (e.g., "I see you are upset right now."); addressing his behaviors (e.g., "We do not use that language in this family."); and taking control of any appropriate follow-up (e.g., "We will talk about this together after dinner/later tonight.").

Helpful Responses to Questions

BELOW IS A list of common questions and some strategies on how to handle them.

"AM I FAT?"

While it is tempting to try and engage your child, using a paradoxical response will be more effective. Although it may feel awkward, try to respond with something like: "I know this is so hard for you. I am here to help you in any way I can." Any conversation about weight or size will not be productive.

"NO, I WON'T EAT!"

Do not enter into a power struggle over food. If your child does not eat, verbally encourage her to try but do not yell or become upset. Think of a phrase you can repeat to your child, such as, "You need to eat to live." There is no benefit in attempting to persuade your child that she is too thin. Using logic and reasoning with her is likely to be a frustrating experience because of her malnourished and, therefore, cognitively compromised state. Sometimes it helps to set goals for your child. You and your child's treatment team may agree that she could begin mild exercise if her next three visits indicate good vital signs and weight gain.

"WHY DO I HAVE TO EAT MORE THAN ANYONE ELSE IN THE FAMILY/WORLD?"

This is likely to be a true statement. Because of the fragile state of her body, your child's nutritional requirements are extremely high and she probably does need to eat more than anyone in the family. Engaging in a conversation about the quantity of your child's portions can often end badly. One response to this question might be reminding her that food is her "medicine" and she must eat what the doctors prescribe to regain her health. You may also try the paradoxical or externalizing responses described above.

"I FEEL FINE. WHY CAN'T I EXERCISE?"

Since the damage that has been done to your child's body is internal, it is not always easy for her to understand that she is extremely sick. Instead of answering the question directly, stress how wonderful it is that she's feeling so well even though she is sick. Then explain that once her weight (or blood pressure or heart) meets the doctor's expectations, she will be able to exercise.

"I WON'T GO TO THE DOCTOR/THERAPIST . . . AND YOU CAN'T MAKE ME."

Remember that due to her eating disorder, your child is emotionally much younger right now than her chronological age. You may, therefore, need to apply some of the basic "cajoling" techniques you used when she was very young. These might include giving her a choice, such as "You can go on your own to the car or walk with me." Or it might take the form of giving ten- to fifteen-minute warnings before the appointment to help reduce her anxiety and increase her compliance. Planning something fun, such as going to a movie, after the appointment may help to motivate your child to be cooperative.

MANAGING OTHER DIFFICULT SITUATIONS

What to tell close friends and relatives

PARENTS OFTEN ASK me what they should tell people who ask what is going on with their child. Since your child will be having many doctor, therapist, and dietitian appointments and may even be hospitalized, people will know something is happening. It's best to have a plan about what you will say to avoid being blindsided when someone asks why your child is missing so much school or has dropped off the soccer team.

Before deciding what to say and to whom, it is very important to discuss it with your child. Your daughter might be fine with you telling everyone about her eating disorder or she might not want anyone to know. I strongly advise you to respect her wishes. However, this doesn't mean that you shouldn't state your opinion as well. I always encourage my patients to be as open as possible about their eating disorder. I never want to make them feel this is something to be ashamed of or hidden. In many cases, they think their eating disorder is a big secret and are quite surprised when they discover that many people actually already know about it.

KEEPING SECRETS

A FEW YEARS ago I was caring for Tammy, a 17-year-old young woman on a competitive gymnastics team. After she was admitted to the hospital for a very low heart rate, her coach asked to visit and she made plans for him to come on a Saturday afternoon. He had to drive two hours to get to the hospital. But just before he arrived, Tammy changed her mind. She didn't want him to visit because she didn't want him to know about her eating disorder and it was obvious she was on an eating disorders unit. "I don't want him to know about this," she said. "It would be too embarrassing with the other girls on the team." She asked me to tell him that she wasn't feeling well and to send him away.

I did respect her wishes but instead of sending him away, I asked the coach if he would mind waiting in the cafeteria for about half an hour. I went up to the unit and told Tammy her coach was having coffee in the cafeteria. I then asked her if she thought the girls on her gymnastics team knew about her eating disorder, what might happen if they did know, and why she was afraid of telling them. We came to the agreement that she would test the waters. She would tell her coach and see if he would be a good support for her. She trusted that he would respect her privacy if she didn't want anyone else to know. In the end, the coach told her that everyone already knew she had an eating disorder. He emphasized that they loved and supported her. The next weekend, eight girls from her gymnastics team made the two-hour trek to the hospital to visit. They spent the afternoon making inspirational signs to put on Tammy's walls to support her recovery. After they left, Tammy told me what a relief it was to not be hiding this secret any more. In fact, two of her teammates even disclosed their eating disorders to her that day.

Sometimes, however, even after considerable discussion, there may a person who your child is not comfortable with telling them about her eating disorder. I strongly recommend respecting this. Some of my patients choose to tell these people that they have a "heart condition," which is usually true because this is medical consequence of their eating disorder. Over time, with your support and that of her therapist, your daughter may feel ready to disclose her eating disorder to a wider range of people.

If your daughter is hospitalized, friends and relatives will probably call you to find out how she is doing and what is going on. Before these calls begin, ask her what information she does and does not want shared. This way, you are prepared with something to say from the start. It is important to be consistent. The people who care about your child are likely to discuss her situation, so telling Aunt Mildred your daughter has a heart condition and Aunt Ellen it's really an eating disorder can damage relationships and put your daughter in an awkward position.

HIDDEN DANGERS: PRO-ANA/PRO-MIA WEB SITES, ONLINE CHAT ROOMS AND SOLIDARITY BRACELETS

IMAGINE A WEB SITE that encourages drug addicts to support their habit. Or one that tells teens with alcohol problems that drinking is a lifestyle choice and then offers tips on how to trick their parents into thinking they're sober. The Internet is full of Web sites that do exactly this for people with eating disorders. Known as Pro-Ana (for anorexia) or Pro-Mia (for bulimia) Web sites, they support a disturbing subculture where people with eating disorders encourage each other and share tips. Many of these Web sites do post warnings that they should not be viewed by anyone who is in recovery or who is considering recovery. These messages, however, can indirectly appeal to or even encourage someone with an eating disorder.

Although efforts by the National Eating Disorders Association (NEDA) have successfully shut down some of these sites, there's a flourishing underground of pro-Ana and pro-Mia Web sites. MySpace, a popular networking Web site frequented by many teens also has private links that support eating disorders. Visiting any of these Web sites may trigger your child's eating disordered behavior by showing "thinspiration" photos of models and celebrities, giving tips about how to lose more weight, or fool people into thinking that she is eating, even if she is not. Some sites even

The Thin Commandments

If you are not thin, you are not attractive.

Being thin is more important than being healthy.

You must buy clothes, cut your hair, take laxatives, starve yourself, do anything to make yourself look thinner.

Thou shall not eat without feeling guilty.

Thou shall not eat fattening foods without punishing oneself afterwards.

Thou shall count calories and restrict intake accordingly.

What the scale says is the most important thing.

Losing weight is good/ Gaining weight is bad.

You can never be too thin.

Being thin and not eating are true signs of willpower and success.

The "Thin Commandments" are often posted on Pro-Ana Web sites.

send e-mail messages reminding members to "remain strong" and not eat. Just as I always recommend that parents know where their child goes when she leaves the house, you should also know where your child goes when she surfs the 'net. I recommend that you go online and visit these sites to better understand what dangers are out there for your daughter. I am purposely not listing any specific pro-Ana or pro-Mia sites for you to visit because they change frequently. You can find these sites, which may be disturbing, as well as articles about the subject by googling "Pro-Ana," "Pro-Mia" or "thinspiration." You can also determine if your child is going to the sites by tracking her online history.

SECRET CODES:
PRO-ANA/PRO-MIA BRACELETS

PRO-ANA AND PRO-MIA Web sites not only encourage people to nurture their eating disorders, but have helped to spawn a subculture of color-coded bracelets: red is for anorexia; purple signifies bulimia; and green is for binge eating. The following excerpt is typical of those found on Pro-Ana Web sites:

> Have you ever wondered if a skinny girl you see walking down the street is anorexic? Now, there is a way to find out!

> Let us all unite! We need to recognize each other and how would we do that—with a bracelet.

> It's simple and fashionable. If you have ever wondered if someone was anorexic, now all you have to look for is a red, beaded bracelet. This will help us tell the world and each other that we are proud of who we are. We are proud to be striving for perfection.

> Join us! Make a bold statement that you are strong. Proclaim Ana is your goddess!

This message was posted on another Web site where girls were discussing their bracelets: "Yeah, you can just wear a red band of string or even a hair thing. You can snap on your wrist when you get hunger pains. It works for me."

If you notice your daughter wearing one of these bracelets, the best strategy is to ask her about it and let her know that you know what it means. In an unemotional and nonconfrontational tone, you might say: "I notice you're wearing a red bracelet. I know this can signal that you have anorexia." Pause and see what she says. It's likely she will deny there's any connection. "Mom, you are so paranoid," she may angrily respond. "It's just something I saw at the mall and thought was cool." Don't be thrown by her response but emphasize that it does concern you. If it doesn't mean anything symbolic, ask if she would mind not wearing it because it does mean something to you. By saying this, it lets her know you are "onto" it but don't make it into a major issue. This is something you should discuss with her therapist.

While some aspects of eating disorders are secretive, mealtime is when many issues explode. What used to be a happy time—when family members could discuss their day or describe what happened at school—often turns into an ugly battleground between parents and their child. The next chapter offers ways to make mealtime easier for your family and more positive for your child.

13

FOOD FOR THOUGHT:

Planning, Preparing, and Supervising Meals

Karen's Story:
A Mother's Mealtime Nightmare

Karen, the mother of a 14-year-old daughter with anorexia, described mealtime as "utter chaos." She told me about one dinner that started out okay. At least her daughter, Jenny, joined them at the table. Karen was serving chicken, rice, and asparagus. However, she had put butter on the asparagus. Jenny took a little chicken and a little asparagus. As soon as she saw there was butter on the asparagus, she refused to eat it. Karen, happy her daughter was willing to eat anything, immediately jumped up to steam some more, which she would serve to Jenny without butter. Jenny then noticed that the chicken had been cooked with the skin on. "What have you done?" Jenny demanded. "Even if I remove the skin, the disgusting fat has already steeped into the meat." Because Karen had cooked all of the chicken, she offered to run to the store to get more if Jenny would eat it. Jenny said that she would. Karen immediately jumped up again and drove to the store. At least her daughter was going to eat something! When she returned, the rest of the family had finished eating. Jenny was still sitting there with an untouched piece of asparagus and the chicken on her plate. Karen quickly broiled a piece of skinless chicken for Jenny and put it on the plate with the plain asparagus. She then reheated her own dinner and sat down to eat with her daughter. Jenny looked at the new food on her plate, cut the asparagus into tiny pieces, and ate three bites. "I'm full," she declared, and went to her room to study. Karen was left alone at the table feeling defeated.

Helping your child eat nutritious meals is one of your most important responsibilities; it can also be one of the most challenging. Planning meals in advance, having a routine, and remaining calm and unwavering are keys to successful meals and, ultimately, to your child's recovery. The major pitfall is being unprepared and scrambling at mealtimes, which not only undermines your child's eating, but also can be stressful for you.

It is important to feed your child and not to, as one mom put it, "feed the eating disorder." This occurs when parents give in to their child's disease. They run to the store to buy nonfat cottage cheese because their daughter says that she will eat that, but won't eat the yogurt that's in the refrigerator. You can avoid "feeding your child's eating disorder" by good planning, remaining as calm as possible, and establishing a routine.

It is very possible that your child's treatment team will recommend that all of your child's meals are initially supervised, including those at school. This is to help encourage your child to eat and to make sure that her body is being nourished—that she is not throwing the food away or pretending to eat it. Having regular meal times as well as regular family meals can help make things a bit easier.

Feeding a child with an eating disorder is not normalized eating. It is a process that will eventually result in your daughter's independent intuitive eating. The optimal end result is for your daughter to be able to eat when she in hungry, stop when she is full, and make well-balanced, nutritious choices.

Although the following information reflects the advice I generally give to my patients and their families, you should ask your child's treatment team how to specifically handle your child's mealtimes.

MEAL PLANNING

Careful planning is the key to containing chaos during meals. One of the most effective things you can do is to establish a routine so that you and your child make a specific meal plan each day. This meal plan delineates how all of his portions or nutritional requirements will be fulfilled. By doing this, issues of what to eat will not come up at mealtimes and can be decided at a less anxious time. This also creates a grocery list to plan meals for the entire family, encouraging communal meals. Someone with an eating disorder needs to eat at least five times a day: three meals and at least two snacks. Planning these ahead can resolve many conflicts and determine in advance exactly what your child needs to eat.

MEAL PREPARATION

ALTHOUGH IT MAY be helpful for a child to be involved in planning her meals, initially it may not be advisable to involve her in their preparation. This includes shopping, cooking, and serving. Why, you might ask, isn't this a good idea? The father of one of my patients described an awful trip to the grocery store. He and his daughter Beth were going to have dinner together and after lots of discussion agreed that she would eat a very specific organic vegetarian burrito from a local grocery store. At the store, she went to get her burrito when he was getting food for himself. When they met up at the check out line, her hands were empty. She tearfully explained to him that she really had intended to get the burrito but when she looked at the label, she discovered that it had 600 calories and 18 grams of fat. There was no way that she could eat it. In the initial stages of recovery, it is often easiest if a child, as I always put it, "has the food magically appear in front of her." This involves you shopping for the food, cooking it, and putting the required portion on her plate. When your daughter is doing better and shows she is capable, then you can and should involve her in these activities.

MEALTIME SUPERVISION AND ENCOURAGEMENT

MEALTIMES WITH SOMEONE who has an eating disorder can be extremely difficult and volatile. Your child's frustrations, fears, anxieties, and anger may surface during meals. Remember these two strategies: stay calm and don't be afraid to ask for help.

The term *meal supervision* may bring up visions of a mother sitting and staring at her daughter as she eats. This is not the optimal way to do things. I recommend eating with your child and having family meals whenever possible. If you are supervising your child's lunch, make sure to eat your own lunch at this time. Imagine what it would be like to sit with someone who was monitoring everything you ate but didn't eat anything themselves. One of my patients, a 12-year-old boy, confided that it was unnerving when his mother came to school to supervise his lunches. "She just sits there and watches me chew. I hate it," he said. When I asked his mother about this, she told me her son's lunch schedule at school was earlier than she liked to eat. We came up with a compromise: she would bring a snack with her so that she could participate in her son's meal.

Very often, a child will become even more anxious about eating once she begins treatment. This happens because asking your child to eat increasing amounts of food directly challenges her eating disorder. Adding your involvement in the feeding process can make meals a very difficult time. Try to provide firm yet supportive assistance during meals and be watchful after meals. This is important: up to 50 percent of people with anorexia will purge at some point during their illness. You don't need to be paranoid but do keep a watchful eye about where you child goes after meals. Some parents initiate board games after meals or watch a TV program with their child to help to reduce some of the anxiety of having eaten. Positive encouragement is the key—just keep telling your child she is doing great. There, unfortunately, are no shortcuts. What you will need to do is be patient, gently persistent, and supportive.

Because mealtimes can be stressful, it is helpful to set up a schedule with your partner or a friend or relative so that you aren't responsible for every meal, and make an advance plan about who will supervise your child's meals if you aren't available. If a good friend offers to help supervise meals, take her up on it! Don't wait for a crisis; ask if she would be willing to relieve you one night a week. Then, set up a time to "train" her. You want to be sure that she knows what to feed your child and how to supervise her. Warn her that your child may try to hide food or pretend to eat. One of my patients cleverly deceived her grandmother, who had dinner with her every Tuesday night, by putting most of the food into her pocket. Do not ask your child's siblings or friends to take on this responsibility.

Encourage eating by using natural consequences and setting goals

You can't force a child to eat but you can make the natural consequences of not eating very compelling. Explain your decisions *only* in terms of nutrition and medical complications. These are natural consequences, not punishments. Remain calm and unemotional. Here are some examples of natural consequences:

- If your son won't eat, then he can't drive his car: it's dangerous for someone who is malnourished—and therefore weak and possibly dizzy—to drive a car.
- If your daughter won't eat, she can't go to school because the exercise of walking around school without the proper nutrition could jeopardize her health.

Let your mantra be something like: "As your mother, I love you and it is my job to keep you safe. It isn't safe for you to (fill in the blank)." It is essential that all caregivers understand and agree to these rules, even if your child lives in two households. As I discussed in the section about the treatment team, consistency and communication are crucial to help someone fight an eating disorder. You cannot let the child controlled by the eating disorder split the team.

Using incentives is another strategy that can motivate your child through mealtimes. Some common incentives that I have used with my patients include resuming exercise, going to the prom, or taking a trip. When setting specific goals, it is important they are realistic and relatively small. Telling a teenager in April that she can rejoin the crew team in September if she has consistent weight gain through August is not helpful. The payoff is too far away. Instead, explain she can add twenty minutes of mild exercise three times a week if she has consistent weight gain for three consecutive weeks. Even though the payoff is smaller, it is much more immediate, and therefore more attainable. Work with your daughter's treatment team to set safe and attainable goals.

There will probably be times when none of the above strategies work—times when your child doesn't care about anything as much as she cares about not eating. It is during those times that you will need to remain strong and calm. Remember that it is the eating disorder that you are fighting, not your child, and continue to calmly encourage her as best you can.

You can create a supportive and nurturing environment at home—a place where you can monitor your daughter's behavior and remove those things that may trigger her eating disorder. But you can't keep her locked inside. Coping with the outside world can be very stressful, especially at school. In the next chapter, we will explore ways to help her manage challenges at school.

14

CREATING A SAFE AND HEALTHY ENVIRONMENT AT SCHOOL

Kevin's Story
Solving a Lunchtime Dilemma at School

Thirteen-year-old Kevin was mortified when I told him that he would have to eat lunch with his mother every day at school. He said the kids at his junior high already teased him about being a "geek" and he knew this would be really embarrassing. Because of his eating disorder, he also had to drop out of PE and would need to sit in the library, which he thought would make things even worse. I suggested that his mother call the school counselor to see if she had any suggestions. She called back the next day with good news: since Kevin's PE class was immediately before lunch, the counselor suggested that Kevin go home for lunch during PE period and come back to school in time to hang out with his friends who liked to play chess. Even better, the counselor said on days his mom couldn't get him, she would supervise his lunch in her office.

It is very uncomfortable for a child, especially a teen, to be singled out among his peers as being different, and this discomfort is exacerbated by the stigma of having an eating disorder. Your child's therapist will be able to help you and your child decide the best way to handle this situation. By anticipating the following issues and handling them proactively, it's possible to avoid embarrassment, academic difficulties, and conflict with school personnel.

WHAT TO TELL FRIENDS, TEACHERS,
AND ADMINISTRATORS

YOUR CHILD'S SCHEDULE is likely to be disrupted by doctors' appointments as well as by being separated from friends during lunchtime. And people will ask why. I often recommend letting a child make his own decision about whom he tells. This gives him some control over the situation. I do, however, believe it's important to point out the benefits of having the support of a trusted friend or teacher. Because eating disorders are common and most people recognize the signs, it is quite possible that his peers and teachers already know that he has an illness. As a parent, it is important to support your child's decision but not express a desire to hide the eating disorder from teachers or peers. This can exacerbate your child's feelings that this is something to be ashamed of and it is his fault.

If PE classes are a state requirement, you may need a note from your child's doctor in order to drop this class. Parents have called me in a panic that the school will not let their child graduate because of missing PE credits. Contact your doctor and ask him to fax or send a letter. I have never had a child not graduate because he or she could not take PE.

If your child initially chooses not to disclose his disease, you will need to decide what you will tell people who ask. I do not recommend lying but there are ways to state the truth without going into detail. You can explain his altered schedule or school absences by citing some of the medical complications of the disease. "He can't take PE and needs to see a doctor on a weekly basis because he has a problem with his heart." "He has a stomach problem and must eat many small meals throughout the day."

Absences from school

In my experience, it is helpful to make an appointment with a school counselor to make him or her aware that your child is dealing with a medical issue and will be having ongoing appointments that may cut into the school day. If your child agrees, I recommend explaining the full situation to the counselor and bringing along a copy of this book in case he has questions. Knowledge is powerful—if people understand what your child is going through, they can be more supportive.

Between the doctor, the dietitian, and the therapist, your child can have as many as three to four appointments a week. You may want to try to arrange appointments on one day so that your child's schedule is less disrupted; this, of course, will depend on the availability of the members of your child's treatment team. You may be able to rearrange your child's school schedule to free up one afternoon per week for appointments. When you have set up an appointment schedule, let the teachers know so that your child can find out what classwork or assignments he will be missing.

Your child may be missing classes on a weekly basis to attend doctor, therapy, and nutrition appointments. He may also miss an extended period of school if he is hospitalized for the medical or psychiatric complications of his disease.

If your child is hospitalized for an extended period of time or requires treatment in a residential treatment program, he will probably miss a significant amount of school. Most hospitals and many treatment programs have teachers on site or a contract with a local school. You will need to speak with the hospital/treatment program teacher to see how the schoolwork that your child does there can transfer back to his school.

HOW TO HANDLE
SCHOOLWORK-RELATED ISSUES

Not only will your child probably be missing classes, but, in some cases, malnutrition may lead to slowed thinking. It can be very frustrating for someone who was a good student in the past to suddenly have difficulty with schoolwork. Many parents have described their straight-A daughters as still getting straight-As after they developed an eating disorder; however, instead of taking three hours to do their homework each evening, they are taking four or five hours. If you feel that your child is having difficulty with her schoolwork, getting behind in school, or that the amount of schoolwork is putting so much stress on her that it is exacerbating her eating disorder, talk to your child's teacher and/or counselor to see what they can do to support your child. This might include allowing her extra time to complete assignments or take tests. You may also want to discuss this with her therapist, who can help you work with the school to make accommodations.

SUPERVISING LUNCH AND SNACKS

YOUR CHILD'S TREATMENT team may recommend that all of your son's meals be supervised, including lunch and/or snacks at school. This can be a tricky situation to manage, both logistically, if both parents work, and because your child—especially a teenager—will not want to be seen having lunch with his mother every day. It may be possible for a teacher, counselor, or nurse to supervise your child if you are not available. You may, however, need to ask a relative or an adult friend your child trusts to help you with this. I strongly recommend that the supervisor be a responsible adult and not a sibling or peer.

PHYSICAL EDUCATION AND SPORTS

A DOCTOR MAY restrict your child's physical activity until he has gained weight, decreased or stopped his purging, and/or has a good heart rate and blood pressure. If your child is instructed to refrain from physical activity, he will probably need to drop or temporarily not participate in physical education class and also refrain from participation in sports teams. As noted earlier, this can be very emotional for children who are active in school sports and define themselves as athletes. It may be possible for your son to watch practices or go to games and sit on the bench. This should be discussed with the treatment team and the coach, who needs to understand the situation. For some children, watching on the sidelines may be extremely difficult; for others, it might be an incentive to get better.

Helping your child navigate the turbulent waters of home and school is critical to recovery; another essential component is taking care of yourself and your family. The next chapter provides information on how one child's eating disorder can impact the whole family, as well as suggestions for self-care during this difficult time.

15

WHAT ABOUT THE REST OF US?

Annie's Story
The impact of an eating disorder on a younger sibling

Annie, the 10-year-old sister of one of my seriously ill patients, started having nightmares and began throwing temper tantrums when her mother left the house. Annie's mother, understandably, was very concerned and asked me if this might be related to her older sister's hospitalization for anorexia. She admitted that the family had been totally focused on their older daughter and Annie was spending a lot of time with a babysitter and at the neighbor's home. At my suggestion, she took her younger daughter to a psychologist, who determined that the little girl was depressed and afraid her mother would leave her. Annie began regular therapy and her mom instituted a special once-a-week outing with her. Over the next couple of months, the nightmares and tantrums resolved.

A child's serious illness impacts every member of the family and almost every aspect of family life. In order to really support your child, it is essential that you take care of yourself. It's also important to be aware of how the situation is affecting your other children. Caring for a sick child can be overwhelming and take over every aspect of your life. You can't be a good support for your child if you do not take care of yourself. This is the only time in this book that I say you *must* do something. You *must* take care of yourself. You need to sleep well, eat right, and do some type of activity that relaxes and recharges you at least *once a week*. This might be getting a massage, taking a walk, going to a movie, or going out with friends.

THE IMPACT ON YOU—THE PARENTS

PARENTING A CHILD with an eating disorder can be one of the most overwhelming and difficult things you will ever do. This can take a toll on your physical and emotional well-being, your relationships with your friends and family (including your partner), and your job.

Be sure that you take the time to take care of your own health. Remember, if you get sick, you will not be able to be there for your daughter. Be sure to eat right, which also sets a good example for your daughter, rest, exercise, and take care of any personal medical issues. Do not put your own health on hold. This might be a good time to have an annual physical to make sure the added stress is not impacting your blood pressure or causing other risks. Your emotional health is also important. You and your partner may want to consider therapy or joining a support group for parents of children with eating disorders. Make sure you continue to go out with friends and do the things that recharge you, whether it's having a massage, taking a hike, or going to the movies.

Even the strongest marriages can suffer from the stress of having a sick child. For your child's well-being, you and your partner must be united and consistently act as a team.

It's okay to disagree about your child's treatment but don't do this in front of her. If you feel your relationships is being tested or if, as a couple, you would like some outside help in dealing with your child's illness, couples counseling could be very beneficial.

At the very least, plan a date night once or twice a month as a way to keep your relationship solid. This can be going out to dinner, taking a walk, or just getting a latte—anything that allows you to be together and talk.

You and your partner are going to spend considerable time taking your child to appointments as well as supervising meals. In order to care for their child, some of my patient's parents have been forced to cut back on the amount of time they work. It may be possible to take time off for family medical leave. Your company's human resources manager can provide you with a form to request family medical leave, which your child's doctor will need to fill out and you can submit. Of course, many families may not financially be able to take medical leave, especially single parents.

Regardless of your situation, please take care of yourself. You can't help your child if you are not emotionally and physically healthy. This is the time to lean on family and friends.

- When people ask if they can do anything, say, "Yes!" And then ask them to help with something specific, such as relieving you once a week at dinner.
- If possible, get someone to help you on a regular basis—not just during a crisis—so that you're not always scrambling to find someone to cover you.
- Look for support groups online or at your local library, community center, church, or synagogue.
- Ask your child's team members if they can direct you to support groups or put you in touch with other parents.

HOW SIBLINGS ARE AFFECTED

YOUR DAUGHTER'S EATING disorder can take a tremendous toll on everyone in the family, especially her brothers and sisters. All of a sudden, the focus of attention is shifted from all of the family members to one family member. You and your partner not only have less time for the other kids, but probably less patience as you may be emotionally drained from fighting with and caring for your child with an eating disorder. Because of this situation, siblings often become angry with the brother or sister who has an eating disorder.

Some siblings may begin acting out to get attention; get in trouble at school; become involved with drinking and drugs; or begin shoplifting. Others fade into the woodwork, withdraw and become depressed. If you are not working with a family therapist, you may want to consider it. Otherwise, it may be helpful for the siblings to see a therapist of their own. This will give them the opportunity to deal with some of the emotions they are having in response to the changes in the family.

Depending on the ages of your other children, there are a few things you can do to be supportive.

- Be honest about what's going on and explain the nature of their brother or sister's illness. Emphasize that even though their sister may look fine, she is very sick.
- Explain to younger children that they can't "catch" an eating disorder.
- Try to spend quality one-on-one time with each of your other children.
- Attend activities, such as sporting events and recitals. This may require that you tag team with your partner or another relative, with one of you attending an event while the other is with your child with the eating disorder. If you are a single parent, ask a relative or good friend for help.
- Consider getting therapy for your other children, especially if you notice behavioral (acting out) or emotional changes.

It's difficult not to seem like you are favoring the child who is sick. If your child with the eating disorder can no longer do certain chores—such as mowing the lawn or taking out the trash—for medical reasons, it is best not to assign those jobs to your other children. They can, however, be given less physically demanding chores such as folding laundry or watering plants.

Navigating the world of eating disorders is not easy and requires extraordinary effort, whether it's trying to have peaceful meals or working with your child's school. Negotiating with your insurance company to pay for your child's care can add to an already challenging and frustrating situation. The next chapter offers strategies for getting your insurance company to pay for your child's treatment.

PART FIVE

TACTICS TO GET YOUR INSURANCE COMPANY TO PAY FOR TREATMENT

"They said WHAT? They will not authorize treatment? There has to be a misunderstanding; they just don't appreciate the severity of the situation. All I need to do is speak to someone at our insurance company to sort this out."

This was my reaction when I heard that our insurance company had refused to authorize care for my daughter's life-threatening eating disorder. My husband and I were stunned and thought it was a mistake. However, it did not take us long to realize that it was not a mistake but a common practice and that getting insurance to authorize the appropriate level of care for someone with an eating disorder is almost always a challenge and very often impossible.

Seven years ago my husband and I were told that our daughter Anna was in critical condition and needed immediate care or she would almost certainly die from her eating disorder. The knowledge that our daughter had an illness that could kill her was shocking, but our fears were somewhat lessened by the fact that she was in a highly regarded program that offered specialized care for anorexia. We were confident that she would recover fully and go on to live a life free from anorexia and we believed our insurance company would join us by providing the best care available. After all, we had a "Cadillac" plan and believed it would protect our family in the event of serious illness. Imagine our shock and horror when we were told to take Anna home because our insurance company would not authorize the treatment her doctors recommended stating that it was "not medically necessary."

This was the beginning of our long and tortuous battle with our insurance company over coverage for our daughter's treatment for anorexia. At a time when our family should have been 100 percent focused on helping Anna stay alive we were distracted by filing appeals and fighting with insurance. We had almost no knowledge of how to fight this battle and very little help or support. We felt alone, confused, and most of all scared that we would lose Anna to anorexia. Tragically, Anna died on February 17, 2000, as a direct result of her eating disorder.

Sadly, our story is all too common and we hear from people every day who share very similar experiences. Insurance companies continue to discriminate against people with eating disorders and severely limit access to care. There is still limited information and help available for families when they encounter insurance delays, denials and withholding of care. When I found out that Dr. Carlton was writing a book to help families and that included in the book would be a chapter on insurance issues, I was thrilled. Our family does not want anyone to go through what we did, and we thank Dr. Carlton for giving families the tools they need to help them navigate through the insurance maze.

Kitty Westin, president
The Anna Westin Foundation

YOUR CHILD HAS a life-threatening illness and your insurance company refuses to pay for the recommended treatment. It may be hard to believe, but many parents find themselves wrestling to get their child's treatment covered. In fact, many insurance companies frequently refuse to cover the cost of treatments related to eating disorders, especially those related to residential treatment programs.

The good news is that most insurance denials can be overturned—if you have the right strategy and are willing to fight. It does take a lot of time, effort, and sometimes money (if you hire a lawyer) to fight an insurance company. And, of course, there's no guarantee. Unfortunately, the majority of eating disorder–related insurance denials occur at some of the most crucial moments—when a child requires residential treatment and is therefore very sick, and her parents are often feeling very desperate.

I have helped many parents fight their insurance companies and get their children the treatment they desperately need. This section offers specific strategies to deal with your insurance company effectively and maximize the likelihood that they will cover the costs of treatment. Dr. Edward Tyson, one of the country's leading experts on insurance issues as they relate to eating disorders, has provided much of the information included in this section.

16

MAXIMIZING INSURANCE
REIMBURSEMENT

A	TTEMPTING TO GET your insurance company to cover the costs of
	your child's treatment for her eating disorder can be a frustrating expe-
rience, one that leaves you feeling angry and powerless. Because eating disorders are psychiatric diseases with medical complications, they can fall
into the abyss between your mental health and medical coverage. Therefore, getting insurance companies to pay for your child's treatment can be
very complicated and difficult.

The goal of this chapter is to help you realize that although you may need
to fight your insurance company, you are not powerless. And you are not
alone. The strategies in this chapter are intended to help you get your insurance company to work with you. Insurance companies are not "evil," but
their employees often have no expertise in eating disorders and, therefore,
cannot understand why the requested treatment is so critical to your
child's life. It is your job to educate them as well as to make them
understand—in a civil but determined manner—that you are not going
away until this lifesaving treatment receives approval. There is no question
that residential treatment is very expensive; I know parents who have gone
into bankruptcy in order to give their children appropriate treatment. It
is impossible to comprehend that an insurance company would deny
treatment if your child was dying of cancer; yet eating disorders can be
equally if not more life-threatening. The information in this chapter is general. Every state has different insurance laws, every insurance company has
different procedures, and every individual policy provides different benefits. Therefore, it is crucial that you become familiar with your policy, the
rules of your insurance company, and the laws in your state.

Although getting coverage for residential treatment can be a major problem, most outpatient services, such as physicians, therapists, and dietitians, are usually covered by insurance. Surprisingly, you actually might need to fight to get reimbursed for having your child treated by an eating disorders specialist. Medical hospitalizations are also generally covered, as long as your child's doctor handles the billing and any insurance issues appropriately. Unless your physician is an eating disorders specialist, he may be unfamiliar with how to effectively file claims. Tips for this are given below.

CLAIMS FOR MEDICAL CARE

When doctors submit bills to insurance companies or request tests, they use specific "billing codes," which tell the insurance company what the doctor is treating. If your child is being seen for a medical visit or hospitalized for medical complications of her eating disorder, it is important that the doctor use the **medical billing code,** *not* the code for an eating disorder. For instance, the doctor might be focusing on your daughter's malnutrition, weight loss, or abdominal pain at her outpatient visit. Or, her hospitalization may be due to bradycardia (low heart rate), hypotension (low blood pressure), or hypophosphatemia (low phosphorus in the blood). There are two important reasons why the doctor needs to bill for **these conditions**, not for anorexia or bulimia: first of all, insurance companies generally have better reimbursements for medical rather than psychiatric illnesses; and secondly, billing for an eating disorder diagnosis is more likely to be paid out of her mental health benefits. You do *not* want to use mental health benefits to pay for medical care because you will need these benefits to cover your child's psychiatric care.

Sometimes, even if your child's doctor bills correctly, the claim for your child's medical hospital admission may be denied. Your child's doctor will usually handle this situation, which may require a "doc-to-doc" phone call between your child's doctor and the doctor at the insurance company. The doctor at the insurance company has the authority to approve the claim on the phone during the doc-to doc.

In my experience doing countless "doc-to-docs," I can report that the claims are almost always approved. To improve the chances of your child's doctor getting approval for a hospital stay, he should focus on the following in the doc-to-doc:

- Your child's medical complications, not the eating disorder.
  - "No, she has not been admitted for anorexia. She is in the hospital for bradycardia and malnutrition. She does have anorexia, but I am not a psychiatrist and that is not what I am treating or billing for."
- The specific reasons why your child needs to be admitted and the consequences if she does not receive treatment immediately.
  - "Laura has been admitted for severe bradycardia. Her heart rate is 35 overnight and this carries with it an increased risk of sudden cardiac death."
- Specific practice guidelines or studies to back up the treatment decisions. Remember, the doctors at the insurance company are not eating disorder experts and often do not know the medical risks or the standards of care. Lists of practice guidelines are listed in appendix F.
  - "According to the treatment guidelines set out by the American Academy of Pediatrics and the Society for Adolescent Medicine, adolescents with malnutrition should be admitted to the hospital for heart rates less than 50. Laura's daytime heart rate is 45."
- The urgency of the situation. He should use words like *critically ill, life threatening, requires immediate help, cannot wait.* Unfortunately, many people do not recognize that eating disorders can be medically devastating. It is important that the doctor at the insurance company understands your child has a life-threatening illness. Your doctor must emphasize that she has been admitted to the hospital on an emergency basis because of specific, potentially life-threatening complications of her malnutrition, vomiting, laxative use, etc.

  Your child's doctor should get the name, specialty, and medical license number of the medical director he is speaking with. The medical director needs to understand that if he denies this claim he is going against the medical recommendations of the team of specialists treating your child and his name and medical license number will be in her medical record.

STRATEGIES TO EFFECTIVELY DEAL WITH
AN INSURANCE COMPANY

DEALING WITH YOUR insurance company can be a frustrating experience. If you are lucky, you might get a very helpful person who understands your situation right from the start. Unfortunately, it is more likely you will end up spending hours on the telephone, speaking to many different people, most of whom will give you the run-around, and getting nowhere. Keep the following strategies in mind whenever you are dealing with your insurance company, whether you are making your first exploratory call or appealing a denial.

- **Remain calm:** This may not be easy but always be polite and keep the tone of your communication professional. Keep your cool, especially if the person on the phone becomes impatient with you. Using an aggressive tone or threatening language can make people defensive and less likely to listen or want to help solve your problem. Being calm does not mean you have to be dispassionate about a decision that is putting your child in harm's way.

- **Document everything:** Keep a notebook and religiously record all correspondence, including phone calls, e-mail, and mail. Always record the date and time of all calls and the names of the people you speak with. Write up a summary of every conversation. Always identify the name of person you spoke with as well as what department she is in and her direct contact number. If possible, tape-record your conversations but within the context of the laws. Tell them you are taping it. Ask if they are recording your conversation and, if so, ask them to preserve the tape.

- **Diligently follow up:** Send a fax or letter summarizing all conversations. This is a hassle but if it is not done, the company can always say that they have no record of what you are claiming and it's essential that you keep track of all communication.

- **Use return receipt:** Send all letters "return receipt requested" or at least by a service that requires a signature on receipt. This shows you are insistent on communication and will not be ignored.

- **Get written confirmations:** Whenever someone agrees to anything, ask the person on the phone to send you a confirmation in writing. If you don't receive this confirmation, send a letter yourself confirming what was agreed. It is not uncommon for someone at an insurance company to verbally approve something and then reverse it.

Insider Tips on How to Deal with Your Insurance Company

MARYANN STUMP, vice president of strategic and consumer innovation at Blue Cross and Blue Shield of Minnesota, acknowledges that the industry is complicated and confusing and needs to be revamped to better serve consumers. Although every insurance company operates differently, she offers these tips on how to successfully deal with an insurance company in regards to your child's eating disorder.

1. Call as soon as you identify your child has an eating disorder to understand what your plan does or does not cover. Find out in advance what the policy will cover in regards to residential treatment, even if you don't anticipate your child will need inpatient treatment.
2. Ask if there is a patient advocate or a patient representative who can help you understand and identify your options.
3. Develop a relationship with one person (it helps to "make a friend").
4. Ask the person who handles insurance claims at the clinic or provider's office who she deals with at your insurance company; ask for a name and a direct phone number.
5. Don't assume a plan will cover 100 percent of your child's treatment; it all depends on the plan your employer has selected.
6. If you work at a large company, talk to the person in human resources who handles insurance issues. She can find out who to speak with as well as what the policy covers.

You are in a better position to appeal rejected claims if you've done you homework in advance and know what your insurance covers.

HOW TO GET PREAUTHORIZATION FOR
RESIDENTIAL TREATMENT

IF YOUR CHILD'S treatment team decides that she requires residential treatment, you will need to get this immediately preapproved by your insurance company. This means that unless you are able to pay for this treatment out of pocket, you will need to wait for your insurance company to approve the claim before your child can get the recommended treatment. There are things you can do to expedite the situation.

1. Determine your insurance policy's mental health benefits. Often these benefits include a specific amount for outpatient treatment (which you may have already used) as well as an amount (or number of days) for inpatient treatment. The booklet that comes with your insurance policy will have this information; do not rely on information on the company's Web site because this will not be specific enough. If you don't have the booklet or don't understand what is in it, call the number on your insurance card and ask for a "case manager" or the "medical director" assigned or your child's case. It is unlikely the person who answers the phone will have the knowledge or authority to really help you. When you speak with the case manager or medical director, you will need to get answers to the following questions:
   o Find out how many inpatient mental health days your policy provides.
   o Understand what percentage of the costs they pay.
   o Find out if your insurance company contracts with any residential eating disorder programs and what these programs offer and whether or not they are appropriate for your child.

2. When you have the answers to these questions, you will then need to apply for preapproval from your insurance company. Sometimes your request might be straightforward. For instance, you might have sixty mental health inpatient days and your insurance company contracts with a program that is perfectly appropriate for your child. Other times, you might need to ask the insurance company to make an exception. There are certain exceptions that are standard and are very reasonable to ask for. Here are two of the most common exceptions:

- **Substitution of Care:** A substitution of care means if you have one hundred days of medical inpatient treatment per year, the insurance company can substitute it for one hundred days of psychiatric inpatient care if your child needs this and you want it. The insurance company may deny this at first but they can do it. This can make a major difference in getting approval for residential treatment.

- **Single-Case Agreement:** If your insurance company does not contract with an appropriate facility, or if the facility they do contract with is full, it is your right to ask them to make a single-case agreement with an appropriate facility. This means that the insurance company will negotiate a special one-time arrangement with a facility they normally do not contract with. If they do contract with an appropriate facility that has openings, but is just not your first choice, it is unlikely that your insurance company will negotiate a single-case agreement. You really need to have a compelling reason to ask them to do this. I have seen insurance companies make single-case agreements with out-of-network facilities if there are long waitlists for contracted facilities or if they do not contract with facilities that specialize in treating adolescents with eating disorders. However, you may have to make some compromises. I was caring for a 17-year-old girl from an Orthodox Jewish family. Everyone involved in her care agreed that she needed to go to a residential eating disorder program; however, the only program that the insurance company contracted with was Christian-based. After weeks of arguing with the insurance company over the appropriateness of this facility, her parents decided that she so desperately needed help that they would send her there even though they had very different spiritual beliefs.

If you have identified a residential program that seems appropriate for your child, ask the director of that program to talk to your insurance company. He probably deals with insurance companies on a regular basis and understands all of the issues.

It can be excruciating to watch your child struggle and deteriorate as you wait for faceless, nameless people in some large organization to determine if they agree with the specialists who know and are caring for your child. I have had patients get approval the next day and one case that took eight months, during which time the child was hospitalized numerous times. Because every insurance plan is unique and every company has different policies, it is impossible to offer specific information about what to ask. The most important advice I can offer is to really understand your policy and what the insurance company is obligated to provide for your child. Ask for help from your company's human resources department since they are the ones who contract with the insurance company. Keep calling your insurance company—don't be a pest but do be persistent.

WHAT TO DO IF YOUR CLAIM IS DENIED

IF THE INSURANCE company denies your claim, you will likely just receive a form letter that states your request for insurance coverage for residential treatment has been denied. This letter often states the requested services are either "not a covered benefit" or "not medically necessary."

If you receive such a letter, there are very specific steps that you can take. According to eating disorder insurance advocate Dr. Edward Tyson, you should not formally appeal the decision, which is what the letter will suggest. Instead, you should immediately call the insurance company. When you call, you must speak with someone who has authority to reverse the denial, which will most likely **not** be the person who takes your call. Instead, insist on speaking with a case manager or the medical director, who do have the authority to reverse the denial. The goal is to get someone to overturn the rejection and avoid a formal appeal. There are three important things to remember when speaking with an insurance company: be prepared, be firm, and be persistent.

Be prepared: Before you make the call, have the following in front of you:

- The actual policy with the key parts underlined
- The specific recommendations of your child's treatment team
  - "Jennie's treatment team says that she needs a minimum of sixty to ninety days in a program that offers a tiered approach, with intensive residential and transitional components that focus on the care of adolescents and young adults with eating disorders."

- A written list of the reasons why this denial should be overturned
  - ○ "According to my policy, I am entitled to these benefits. I have ninety days of inpatient treatment."
  - ○ "According to Jennie's treatment team this treatment is medically necessary because:"
    - ○ "She has spent one hundred days over the past twenty months in the hospital because of damage to her heart."
    - ○ "She is developing irreversible osteoporosis from her malnutrition."
    - ○ "They are convinced that she will have lifelong medical complications or possibly die without this treatment."

Be firm: Politely demand the following:

- Specific criteria they are using to deny your claim
- A letter with a detailed explanation for the denial; do *not* accept the standard form letter.

As mentioned earlier, do not get angry. Explain you believe an error has been made and that you believe it needs to be reversed. For example, you might take the following approach:

There seems to have been in error in denying my request for residential eating disorder treatment for my daughter, Jennie. My policy clearly states that Jennie has one hundred days of medical inpatient treatment. I know that I can have a substitution of benefits and use these days for mental health inpatient care for Jennie, especially since her physician and therapist strongly believe that residential treatment is needed to save her life. She had been in an intensive outpatient program but is still struggling. Her doctor is very concerned about how her severe malnutrition is causing ongoing and possibly irreversible damage to her heart, bones, brain, and internal organs. Please tell me what it is I need to do to get the substitution of benefits. Jennie's life is in danger and I really need your help in figuring out how to get her into residential treatment as soon as possible.

Be persistent: Insurance companies count on people giving up after the first or second appeal. Make it clear from the beginning—you are *not* going away. If your claim is rejected because the insurance company deems there is no "medical necessity," insist on speaking to the medical director, who will be a physician. Some insurance companies are reluctant to divulge the name of the medical director. This is inexcusable. **Do not accept anyone other than a medical director for these disputes.** It will be helpful for your child's doctor to speak with the medical director as well. Remember, if the insurance company's doctor maintains there is no medical necessity for this treatment, he is going against the advice of a team of professionals who know and are caring for your child. If he believes their recommendation is not valid, he needs to have very compelling reasons. Again, documentation is critical for your case. Continue to keep records of every phone call and every correspondence.

Translating Insurance Company Jargon: What Are They Talking About?

INSURANCE COMPANIES HAVE created their own language. The following terms are often found in documents relating to eating disorders:

Medical Necessity: The term *medical necessity* is often used in the insurance world. It is not uncommon for someone's coverage for eating disorder treatment to be denied because of "lack of medical necessity." Medical necessity means "the need for continued care as determined by the best clinical judgments of the physician in charge and the other physicians and team members in consultation." Insurance companies often use their own judgment as the basis for necessity, not that of the attending physicians and team members caring for the patient. However, some states do have rulings indicating that the treating physician, not the insurance company, should determine medical necessity.

Disputes about medical necessity require communication between the treating physician and the insurance company's medical director. These are usually phone conversations and commonly referred to as a doc-to-doc. This is an excellent opportunity for the treating physician to pin down the insurance company as to how they are actually making decisions in your daughter or son's case.

Independent Medical Review: Your insurance company may offer you an *independent medical review* (IMR) in lieu of an appeal. In an IMR, an independent physician evaluates your claim and makes a decision as to how it should be handled. This may sound good, but unfortunately, sometimes the "independent" physician is actually paid by the insurance company. Also, sometimes the physician does not have enough expertise to make an informed recommendation. This can especially be true when it comes to eating disorders. If you are considering an IMR, be sure to ask the case manager or medical director of the insurance company if the physician who will be doing the IMR has an expertise in eating disorders and if the insurance company is paying him to do this review. Another risk of IMRs is that if you agree to an IMR, you sacrifice your right of appeal. It is very important to ask the case manager or medical director handling your claim about this. If they say that you will not be sacrificing your right of appeal by having an IMR, be sure to get that in writing. Only consider an IMR if you know the reviewer is truly skilled in eating disorders and is truly financially independent of the insurance company.

Qualified Approvals: Avoid a situation where an insurance company gives you a *qualified approval* for a residential treatment center. A qualified approval is usually given on the phone after a parent advises the insurance company that he has identified a residential treatment program for his child and a bed is available. This means you could take your child to a program across the county, admit her, and then learn three days later that they won't cover it.

In Network Requirement: Some insurance companies will insist your child go to one of their *in-network* facilities. This does not mean it is a better facility or even appropriate for your child. It only means your insurance company has an arrangement with the facility and negotiated rates in advance. If all of the in-network facilities are full, the insurance company is obligated to find you other options *and* pay any difference in fees.

If there is no appropriate in-network facility, then your child has the right to be sent to an appropriate facility that is out-of-network. However, you will need to provide the insurance company with compelling evidence as to why the in-network facility is not appropriate. This could mean that the program does not specialize in treating adolescents with eating disorders.

HOW TO FORMALLY APPEAL YOUR CASE

IDEALLY, YOU WILL find a resolution by talking to the medical director or to his or her supervisor, the executive medical director. At most insurance companies, the executive director is as high in the bureaucracy as a member can go to ask about reversing a rejection. Unfortunately, very often it is necessary to formally appeal the decision.

If it does come to this, it is probable that you will be entering into a long and frustrating process. Just remember, you are not asking for anything that you have not paid for. You and/or your employer pay for this coverage and the insurance company has agreed to pay for certain services delineated in your policy. You have lived up to your end of the deal and paid them the money, now they have to live up to their end and pay for the services—in this case, residential treatment for your child.

In order to get your insurance company to provide the coverage promised in your policy, your next step is a formal appeal. The letter you initially received informing you of the denied claim will explain the procedure for appeal. Each insurance company has a different process and every state has different regulations. You should be able to determine the regulations for your state through the insurance commissioner or attorney general's office. A recent study in Texas showed that 70 percent of denials for psychiatric treatment for eating disorders are overturned if they are fought long and hard enough. Don't give up!

Some companies use a committee to make a determination during a formal appeal. If a committee will make the decision, ask who will be on the committee and about the members' expertise in eating disorders. At many insurance companies, the committee will vote on your appeal and the majority will win, regardless of the individual committee member's expertise, knowledge, or experience with eating disorders.

Make sure that whoever is making the final decision has all of the pertinent information. You will want to send them what I call an appeal pack, along with the forms required by your insurance company for the appeal (they will either send you the forms by mail or you can download them from the company's Web site). This will help the insurance company to understand the urgency of the situation and see your child as a person, not just a case. This should be sent directly to the medical director of the insurance company, with return receipt requested. The appeal pack should include:

- A calm, polite letter giving the specifics about your child's case (a sample letter is included in appendix E).
  - The tone of this letter should be rational, not emotional. Appeal to the business side of the person reviewing your case. Absolutely do not let your frustration or anger come through. Consider writing two letters: in the first, say exactly what you feel, and then *tear it up*. Next, write the letter you will actually send.
  - Emphasize that you know that they want to do the right thing; do not intimate that they are trying to "screw you."
  - Put a timeline in your letter with a phrase such as, "I expect a reply in one week."
  - Carefully proofread the letter and have someone else read it as well for typos and grammar. Some insurance companies actually will automatically deny any appeal that has typos or mistakes.
  - The following people should be carbon copied:
    - The president of the insurance company
    - Your lawyer
    - The attorney general in your state
    - The Insurance Commissioner in your state
- A photo of your child if she is significantly underweight, which can emphasize the severity of the situation.
- The American Psychiatric Association's guidelines for the treatment eating disorders, which you can get at http://www.psych.org/psych_pract/treatg/pg/EatingDisorders3ePG_04-28-06.pdf
- The summary of the Minnesota lawsuit for the wrongful death of Anna Westin from www.annawestinfoundation.org/insurance.htm

- A letter from your child's doctor stating the specifics of her case and why he thinks the increased level of care is needed. Be sure he includes what he believes will happen if your daughter doesn't get this increased level of care. (A sample letter is included in appendix E.)
- A statement of statistics about the mortality rates of eating disorders and the greater efficacy of a full course of treatment versus shorter treatment, with references from the medical literature (see Appendix E).

I know this may sound overwhelming and possibly discouraging. But you can successfully challenge your insurance company and get them to pay for treatment. It's just a question of knowing how to work the system. The following case study is a good example of what some parents must go through to get the right treatment for their child. At least in this case, the final outcome was positive:

After Dena's fourth hospitalization, her therapist and I sat down with her parents to discuss our concern about how fragile Dena's heart and body were becoming. We were afraid that she was not progressing and that her health would continue to deteriorate without more intensive intervention. We recommended that Dena's parents look into residential treatment programs. They agreed with the recommendation and, after a week of evaluating local programs, came up with two different programs that seemed like a good fit for their daughter. They called their insurance company to start the preapproval process. Although their policy allowed thirty days of inpatient mental health benefits, neither of the programs they asked about were in network. The insurance company only contracted with a facility in another part of the state that cared for both children and adults. Although she did not want to send her child so far away, Dena's mother was very concerned about Dena's health. Not wanting to rule out any options, she called the in-network facility, only to discover that it was full with a three to four month waitlist.

Dena's mother immediately called her insurance company and insisted that time was of the essence and her daughter couldn't wait three to four months. The insurance company said they would try to find another option but it would take time. Dena's mother said her daughter didn't have time and needed immediate help. Unfortunately, she was right. Seven days later Dena was readmitted to the hospital. Her treatment team immediately wrote a letter to the insurance company, clearly delineating all of Dena's medical complications, her ongoing medical risks and their professional opinion that if Dena did not receive appropriate, intensive treatment *now*, her life was in danger. Two weeks later, Dena's mother received word that the insurance company had made a single-case agreement with one of the facilities that she had chosen.

Web Sites with Helpful Insurance Suggestions/Information

Securing Eating Disorders Treatment: Ammunition for Arguments with Third Parties:
> http://www.nationaleatingdisorders.org/nedaDir/files/ documents/ handouts/SecrTxAm.pdf
> *National Eating Disorders Association (NEDA), Margo Maine, PhD.*

Insurance Court Papers and Coverage Advice:
> http://www.annawestinfoundation.org/insurance.htm
> *Anna Westin Foundation, Kitty and Mark Westin, (952) 361-3051*

Getting Help and Treatment: Medical Insurance
> http://www.palereflections.com/ getting_help.asp?page=insurance
> *Pale Reflections Eating Disorder Community,*
> *E-mail: postmaster@pale-reflections.com*

Another case, which shows that it is possible to successfully reverse an appeal, involves the parents of a severely ill 17-year-old girl who confronted their insurance company and won. Their daughter had been hospitalized numerous times, including one week at a cost of $60,000 while they were waiting for approval for residential treatment. Their first claim for residential treatment was rejected because the facility they found, which had availability and was well-suited for her situation, was out of network;

when they appealed, it was rejected because the insurance company stated the program did not provide 24-hour skilled nursing, even though her physicians did not believe this was necessary. The parents contacted the medical directors who made the initial denials, demanding to know their credentials and the specific policies and guidelines they were using to reject the claim. They threatened legal action. In the end, the insurance company approved 100 days of residential treatment at the out-of-network facility.

Every day, I talk with parents who are caught in an insurance nightmare. If you find yourself in this situation, do not despair. Using the information in this chapter you will have the tools you need to fight for the coverage you are entitled to receive.

FINAL THOUGHTS

IT IS EASY for me to tell you to "take charge" of your child's eating disorder. If you've finished this book, you know that the road ahead will be difficult, frustrating, and challenging—words you have seen repeated throughout this book. But I also want to emphasize the positive side of the equation: the children who recover from their eating disorders and go on to lead happy and normal lives; the parents who have been through hell but send me photos of their daughter's wedding or son's graduation from college; and my personal satisfaction of seeing patients move forward in their recovery.

When I first meet with the parents of a child who has been diagnosed with an eating disorder, they usually are in shock and disbelief. Fortunately, their child is in at a place that specializes in eating disorders and offers educational programs for parents. The goal of this book has been to give you the knowledge, comfort, and guidance that I strive to provide to the parents I meet. And, most importantly, I hope that it had given you the confidence to take charge of your child's eating disorder.

ACKNOWLEDGMENTS

WE ARE ESPECIALLY grateful to the parents who generously shared their experiences and to the young adults who told their personal stories, in the hope of helping others battling these devastating diseases. We would like to thank everyone who contributed their expertise to this book, including Kitty Weston, Dr. Edward Tyson, Barbara Swensen, Steven Schaeffer, and MaryAnn Stump. Dr. Carlton would like to thank to Dr. James Lock and Dr. Iris Litt for their continuing support and encouragement. She would also like to thank everyone at Lucille Packard Children's Hospital who helped with the development and support of the Parent Education and Support Program, especially Dr. Harvey Cohen.

The authors would like to extend a special thanks to Renée Sedliar at Marlowe & Company for championing this book, as well as for her patience and thoughtful insights. Finally, thanks to our agent Neil Salkind for recognizing that this needed to be written and for his superb matchmaking skills.

APPENDIX A

INTERNET RESOURCES

Alliance for Eating Disorder Awareness
Educational information including hotline phone numbers, referrals for treatment, and recommended reading.
www.eatingdisorderinfo.org

Andrea's Voice
Personal stories, advice, and helpful resources.
www.andreasvoice.com

Anorexia Nervosa and Related Eating Disorders
Information, parent advice, and resources.
www.anred.com

Eating Disorders Coalition for Research, Policy and Action
Policy information and advocacy involvement relevant to eating disorders
www.eatingdisorderscoalition.org

Eating Disorders Information, Inc.
Tips and support groups for parents coping with an eating disorder in the family.
www.edsn.asn.au/Families.htm

Empowered Parents, *Abigail Natenshon*
Resources, information, and advice for parents; family approach to treatment.
www.empoweredparents.com

Kristen Watt Foundation

Resources and information to help parents gain understanding of eating disorders and what to do when/if faced with this issue.
www.KristenWattFoundation.org

Milestones Eating Disorders Support

Online support group for families/friends/sufferers to discuss experiences and resources related to all eating disorders.
http://health.groups.yahoo.com/group/milestonesinrecovery

National Association of Anorexia Nervosa and Associated Disorders (ANAD)

Nonprofit organization offering information and services.
www.anad.org

National Eating Disorders Association

Information, referrals, services.
www.edap.org

New York Online Access to Health (NOAH)

Basic care, community support, and risk factors to guide parents and physicians.
www.noah-health.org/en/mental/disorders/eating

Pale Reflections

Support groups for parents and teens, professional information, treatment finder.
www.pale-reflections.com

The Something Fishy Website on Eating Disorders

Information, support, personal stories, and resources for family, friends, and sufferers.
www.something-fishy.org

Troubled With: Eating Disorders

Advice for parent's on body image, ED warning signs, prevention, and roles in treatment.
www.troubledwith.com/Web/groups/public/@fotf_troubledwith/documents/articles/twi_topic_008629.cfm

APPENDIX B

REFERRAL RESOURCES FOR FINDING
EATING DISORDER SPECIALISTS

Online Referral Services

Academy for Eating Disorders
Directory of eating disorder professionals searchable by geographic area.
www.aedweb.org/public/EDsearch.cfm

Anorexia Nerovsa and Associate Disorders (ANAD)
Referrals to treatment and information.
www.anad.org; (847) 831-3438

Eating Disorder Association—United Kingdom
Database of eating disorder services by area (UK).
www.edauk.com/list/index.htm

ED Referral
International database of eating disorder services; provides referrals to
practitioners, treatment facilities, and support groups by area.
www.edreferral.com

Find-A-Therapist
International database of thousands of mental health professionals
including psychiatrists, psychologists, social workers, and counselors.
www.find-a-therapist.com/

National Eating Disorders Association (NEDA)
Nationwide helpline, outpatient/inpatient treatment referrals, and support
groups by area.
www.nationaleatingdisorders.org/p.asp?WebPage_ID=655; (800) 931-2237

National Eating Disorder Information Center (NEDIC)—Canada
Support groups and treatment services by area [Canada]
www.nedic.ca/giveandgethelp/helpforyou.shtml; 1-866-633-4220

Pale Reflections
Treatment finder for a range of eating disorder services and local support groups searchable by area.
www.pale-reflections.com/treatment_finder.asp

Something Fishy Web site: Eating Disorder Treatment Finder
Wide range of services searchable by location and treatment type.
www.something-fishy.org/treatmentfinder

Helplines and Referral Services by Phone

Bulimia and Self-Help Hotline
24-hour crisis line.
(314) 588-1683

Eating Disorder Treatment and Helpline
Confidential consultations, treatment options, and information on anorexia, bulimia, and all other eating disorders.
(866) 494-0866 (www.edhelpline.com)

Massachusetts Eating Disorder Association, Inc. Helpline
ED helpline staffed by trained/supervised individuals.
Monday–Friday 9:30-5:00 pm; Wednesday evenings until 8:00 pm
(617) 558-1881 (www.medainc.org)

The National Mental Health Association Information Center
Directs caller to their local Mental Health Association, who helps find community mental health services and self-help support groups in desired location.
(800) 969-NMHA (1-800-969-6642)

Rader Programs
Referrals to eating disorder specialists in the U.S. and Canada.
(800) 841-1515; (www.radarprograms.com)

The Renfrew Center

Referrals to eating disorder specialists in the U.S. and Canada.
(800) 736-3739; (www.renfrew.org)

1-800 THERAPIST Network

International mental health referral service.
(847) 831-3438; (800) 843-7274; (www.1-800-therapist.com)

APPENDIX C

RECOMMENDED BOOKS ABOUT EATING DISORDERS

Children and Teens Afraid to Eat: Helping Youth in Today's Weight-Obsessed World, Frances M. Berg, 2001
> This book is geared to parent, teachers, and health professionals. It provides research and guidelines for how parents can establish self-acceptance in their children. The author focuses more on health and well-being, and less on weight, when discussing eating disorders.

The Eating Disorder Source Book: A Comprehensive Guide to the Causes, Treatments, and Prevention of Eating Disorders, Carolyn Costin, 1997
> This book helps parents understand the complex interplay of biology and environment in eating disorders. The author incorporates nutritional, psychological, and biochemical aspects in explaining possible causes of eating disorders and lays out potential treatment approaches accordingly.

Just a Little Too Thin: How to Pull Your Child Back from the Brink of an Eating Disorder, Michael Strober and Meg Schneider, 2005
> This book is a guide for parents who are concerned that their child is on the brink of an eating disorder. It gives them warning signs to look for that they might not have noticed and provides them with strategies they can use to help turn things around before their child develops a full-blown eating disorder.

Eating With Your Anorexic, Laura Collins, 2004
> This book details one mother's experience battling her daughter's eating disorder using a family-based approach.

Help for Eating Disorders: A Parent's Guide to Symptoms, Causes and Treatment, Debra K. Katzman and Leora Pinhas, 2005

> This book, based on the eating disorder program at the Hospital For Sick Children in Toronto, helps parents to determine if their child has an eating disorder and gives them practical advice about how to be an active part of their child's recovery.

Father Hunger: Fathers, Daughters, and Food, Margo Maine, 1991

> This book talks about the emptiness ("father hunger") experienced by women whose fathers are/were emotionally absent while growing up. The author suggests that this emotional void often leads to unrealistic body image, yo-yo dieting, food fears, and disordered eating patterns. The book offers practical solutions to help readers understand and improve their father/daughter relationships and help families reconnect.

Help Your Teenager Beat an Eating Disorder, James Lock and Daniel LeGrange, 2004

> This book, written by two international experts in the psychological and psychiatric treatment of children and adolescents with eating disorders, provides detailed descriptions of how these children think, feel and act, and also provides parents with strategies to help their child fight their eating disorder using either a family-based approach or individual approaches combined with parental guidance.

Nourishing Your Daughter, Carol Beck, 2001

> The author focuses on eating disorder prevention and gives advice on how parents can help their children have healthy relationships with food and their bodies.

The Parents' Guide to Childhood Eating Disorders, Marcia Herrin and Nancy Matsumoto, 2001

> This book highlights warning signs for eating disorders and advises parents on how and when to seek professional help. The book also provides tips for how parents can establish a healthy relationship with food and a positive body image in their teens to reduce the risk of relapse.

Reviving Ophelia, Mary Pipher, 1995
> The author, a therapist who has worked extensively with young girls, reveals firsthand evidence of the damage that can be caused by growing up in a "girl-poisoning culture." This book offers parents compassion and strategies for surviving their child's eating disorder.

The Starving Family, Cheryl Dellasega, 2005
> The author uses family case studies to address how parents and siblings can cope when a loved one has an eating disorder. The book looks at how eating disorders can impact siblings, marriages, and careers and provides guidance for the entire family. Real-life mothers and fathers share their eating disorder wisdom drawnfrom their personal experiences.

Surviving an Eating Disorder, Michelle Siegel, Judith Brisman, and Margot Weinshel, 1997
> This book helps family and friends better understand eating disorders and provides strategies for approaching recovery. The author provides helpful information and guidelines for the psychological, medical, and financial aspects of treatment.

When Your Child Has an Eating Disorder: A Step-by-Step Workbook for Parents and Other Care-Givers, Abigail Natenshon, 1999
> This interactive workbook provides practical resources and information to help the parent better understand their child's eating disorder. The book analyzes treatment options and discusses the role of the parent in the recovery process.

Your Dieting Daughter, Is She Dying for Attention?, Carolyn Costin, 1997
> This book serves as a how-to-cope guide for family members. Topics include symptoms, underlying psychological causes, and separate preventative advice for parents. The author describes the "social milieu" of eating disorders to help parents understand the kinds of pressure their daughters are under and to provide them with the necessary knowledge to work with their child in the recovery process.

Book Catalogs

Eating Disorders Arena
Wide range of Eating Disorder books produced by Psychology Press and Brunner-Routledge, a publisher of mental health and professional psychology books and journals.
www.eatingdisordersarena.com/

Gurze Books Eating Disorders Resource Catalog
Free catalog of eating disorder books and videos.
www.gurze.com; (800) 756-7533

APPENDIX D

SAMPLE INSURANCE LETTERS

Example of a Follow-up Letter from Parents

Date

Jane Doe
Case Manager
Insurance Company
City, State, Zip code
Phone number
Fax number

RE: Anne B. Smith
      Insurance policy number
      DOB: 8/8/88

Dear Jane Doe:

This is a follow-up letter to summarize our phone conversation today at 3:15pm. If you have any dispute about what I say transpired, please notify me in writing (by mail or by fax) within two (2) business days of receipt of this letter. If I have not received a response by that time, then that will be tantamount to your acceptance of what I state in this letter.

In our conversation you stated that your company was denying the coverage for our daughter Anne's treatment at the West Coast Eating Disorder Treatment Center. Your stated reason for that denial was that her treatment was "not medically necessary." I asked you to give me the name, title, and expertise regarding eating disorders of the medical director who has made the claim that this treatment is not medically necessary. You refused to give me that name in spite of my telling you that as a fully paid member I do have the right to know who in that company is making life-or-death decisions regarding my daughter. You stated also that this was "company policy."

I, again, am asking to know what medical director made that decision and all contact information for that person, including address, direct phone number, and fax number. I am also requesting his or her qualifications to render a decision in this matter.

Your company's delays already have cost my daughter much-needed treatment time. These delays in treatment have resulted in a further deterioration in her condition, ultimately extending her recovery and making it more difficult and more expensive. As time is of the essence and my daughter's life is at risk, **I can only allow a maximum of three (3) business days for a response.**

I may be contacted at any time at the following numbers:

Sincerely,

Your name

Example of an Appeal Letter from Parents

Date

Jane Doe
Case Manager
Insurance Company
City, State, Zip code
Phone number
Fax number

Re: Tina Smith
      Insurance ID#
      Date of Birth

Dear Jane Doe:

My wife and I would like to take the opportunity to provide additional information and documentation about our daughter's desperate need to receive inpatient treatment at NAME OF TREATMENT CENTER.

Tina's life is in serious danger. Her treatment team, composed of an eating disorders specialist, a psychotherapist, and a registered dietitian, agree that Tina immediately requires inpatient treatment at a residential treatment program that specializes in the treatment of adolescents and young adults with eating disorders. Partial hospitalization has been unsuccessful. Tina refuses to eat anything except an apple and maybe lettuce, and then insists on exercising to burn off the few calories she has taken in. Our lovely, once vibrant 5'2" daughter now weighs less than 80 pounds. She has been hospitalized four times in the last six months. Tina is desperately ill and has told us she wants to get better but is caught in the nightmare of her eating disorder. Although she is now medically stable, the treatment team believes it is likely Tina will require medical hospitalization again if she does not get help at NAME OF TREATMENT CENTER.

We were very excited to learn that NAME OF TREATMENT CENTER has an available bed. Although we recognize that it is not in your network, the only facility in your network is not appropriate for Tina because it does not specialize in treating adolescents. Our daughter is only 12 years old and we, along with her treatment team, strongly believe she needs to be at a facility that only treats women under 18. Her therapist also feels very strongly that she should *not* be in a facility that has women in their forties and fifties who have struggled with eating diseases for many years (please see the attached copy of his evaluation). NAME OF TREATMENT CENTER only treats adolescents and is less than two hours from our home so that we can participate in their intensive family therapy. It also has an intensive out-patient program, which will make it easier for Tina to transition home.

Tina's treatment at NAME OF TREATMENT CENTER was denied due to it being an out-of-network facility. We would like to appeal this denial. We are prepared to seek legal counsel if INSURANCE COMPANY is unwilling to approve the treatment our daughter desperately needs and that both her physician and therapist have recommended. The cost of sending her to NAME OF TREATMENT CENTER will be far less than the cycle of recurrent medical hospitalizations that she is currently stuck in. More importantly, it will put Tina on the path to recovery and give her back her life.

Thank you for the opportunity to appeal. We look forward to hearing from you.

Sincerely,

Your Name and Contact Info

Example of a Letter from a Physician

Date

Jane Doe
Case Manager
Insurance Company
City, State, Zip code
Phone number
Fax number

Re: Tina Smith
      Insurance ID#
      DOB: 01/01/88

To Whom It May Concern:

We are writing this letter to summarize our treatment recommendations
for Tina Smith.

We have been following Jane in our eating disorder program since April 12,
200X. During these past two years, Tina has had six hospitalizations for
medical complications of her malnutrition including profound bradycardia,
hypothermia, and orthostasis.

Her hospital admissions are listed below:

Admission Date—Discharge Date	Profound bradycardia
Admission Date—Discharge Date	Profound Bradycardia and hypothermia
Admission Date—Discharge Date	Bradycardia and orthostasis
Admission Date—Discharge Date	Bradycardia
Admission Date—Discharge Date	Orthostasis
Admission Date—Discharge Date	Bradycardia

In all, Tina has spent 111 days of the past two years in the hospital due to
cardiac complications of her malnutrition.

Tina's malnutrition is damaging more than her heart. The following medical issues have complicated her course:

1. Secondary amenorrhea since August 200X. This prolonged amenor-
    rhea has the potential to cause irreversible bone damage leading to
    osteoporosis in her early adult life.

2. As above, significant risk for osteopenia. Bone density results are pending examination.
3. Essential fatty acid deficiency, which can impact all organs, most especially her neurocognitive function.
4. Hypophosphatemia
5. Constipation, delayed gastric transit, and abdominal pain
6. Leucopoenia
7. Hypoalbuminemia

Despite receiving intensive outpatient medical, nutritional, and psychiatric treatment, Tina's medical condition has continued to deteriorate. She has had consistent weight loss since January 200X and is currently 83 percent of her estimated minimal ideal body weight (the weight where the nutritionist estimates she will regain regular menses). Her white blood cell count and serum protein and albumin levels have been steadily decreasing as well, because of her extraordinarily poor nutritional intake.

Due to Tina's poor nutritional progress and continued medical complications despite receiving intensive outpatient treatment for anorexia nervosa, it is our strong recommendation that she needs more intensive psychiatric and nutritional treatment. The type of treatment that Jane needs is offered only in a residential treatment program specializing in eating disorders. We recommend a minimum of a sixty- to ninety-day stay in a program that offers a tiered approach, with intensive residential and transitional components that focus on the care of adolescents and young adults with eating disorders. Tina requires intensive daily psychiatric, psychological, and nutritional treatment by therapists well trained in the treatment of her disease. She will be best served by a program that is age appropriate for her, and not a program for much older adults. In such a tiered program, Jane could get the residential treatment that she so desperately needs, and then show that she can maintain any progress in a transitioned setting. We do *not* recommend treatment in a non–eating disorder specific behavioral treatment center, as Tina has a severe case of anorexia and deserves subspecialty-level care. Some examples of such programs would include (name a few appropriate programs).

Anorexia nervosa is a deadly disease with a 10–15 percent mortality rate and 15–25 percent developing a severe lifelong course. We believe that without the intensive treatment of a residential program, Tina's malnutrition, and the medical complications that it causes, will continue to worsen, and Tina will be at significant risk of developing lifelong anorexia nervosa or dying of her disease. We understand that in the past, your reviewers have denied Tina this level of care.

This is the only appropriate and medically responsible care plan that we can recommend for Tina. We truly believe that to offer her less is medically negligent, and trust that you will share our grave concern for Tina's needs and approve such care to assist in her emotional and physical recovery.
Thank you for your thorough consideration of this matter. Please feel free to contact us with any concerns regarding Tina's care.

Sincerely,

NAME OF DOCTOR

APPENDIX E

THE INSURANCE APPEAL PACK

In addition to a letter and many forms required by the insurance company, include the following:

I. **American Psychiatric Association (APA) Guidelines for the Treatment of Eating Disorders**
www.psych.org/psych_pract/treatg/pg/EatingDisorders3ePG_04-28-06.pdf
Important medical findings reviewed in the APA guidelines
   - Physical consequences of eating disorders include all serious sequelae of malnutrition, especially cardiovascular compromise.
   - Prepubertal patients may have arrested sexual maturity and growth failure.
   - Even those who "look and feel deceptively well," with normal EKGs may have cardiac irregularities, variations with pulse and blood pressure, and are at risk for sudden death.
   - Prolonged amenorrhea (less than six months) may result in irreversible osteopenia and a high rate of fractures.
   - Abnormal CT scans of brain are found in less than 50 percent of patients with anorexia nervosa.
   - Bulimic behaviors may result in electrolyte, fluid, and mineral imbalance; may be presenting cardiac risk; gastric irritation and bleeds; large bowel abnormalities; dental enamel erosion; peripheral muscle weakness, cardiomyopathy, and hypometabolism. These consequences may be present despite normal weight.
   - Bulimic patients of normal weight may also be severely malnourished and have serious nutritional deficiencies.

II. Court cases to site as precedent for medical coverage of eating disorders

From ANAD Web site

www.anad.org/site/anadweb/content.php?type =1&id=6976

- *Simmons v. Blue Cross and Blue Shield of Greater New York*, 1989
  - o Starvation resulting from anorexia nervosa is a physical state which should be covered by medical benefits.
- *State of Minnesota v. Blue Cross and Blue Shield of Minnesota*, 2001 (for the wrongful death of Anna Westin)
  - o Blue Cross/Blue Shield agreed to allow an independent panel of three experts to review denials of coverage. The majority decision is binding upon the insurance company if the policyholder is part of a state-regulated managed care system. (Unfortunately, those covered by a self-insured plan in Minnesota are not subject to state laws and therefore, for them, the panel's decision is only advisory.)
  - o After receiving a claim, Blue Cross will make an immediate decision as to payment within twenty-four hours for urgent care and within two business days for nonurgent care.
  - o Blue Cross/Blue Shield agreed to increase access to psychiatrists and other therapists and significantly increase coverage for intensive treatment of eating disorders, which, until then, it had rarely covered.
  - o Blue Cross had to reimburse families who paid for care out-of-pocket. The company also agreed to consider claims by families who did not participate in the lawsuit, but who believed they were inappropriately denied coverage.
- *Mannheim v. Travelers Insurance Company* (United States District Court): Until the patient is at least 85 percent of target weight, treatment is medical and should be covered by medical benefits, even if treatment takes place in a psychiatric hospital.

III. Important studies/research to cite:

- Individuals who were 90 percent of their ideal body mass index (BMI) or less at the time of transfer from residential treatment to a day hospital program were more than ten times more likely than someone above 90 percent of their ideal BMI to fail day hospital treatment and require either readmission to an inpatient unit or discharge against medical advice.[1]

- For individuals less than 90 percent of their ideal BMI, there is a strong economic advantage for continued inpatient treatment, because it avoids the immediate relapse and readmission of more than one-third of those individuals.[1]

- Over the past fifteen years the treatment of eating disorders has gone from longer hospitalizations for disease management to short hospitalizations for acute stabilization (average length of stay in 1984 was 149.5 days and in 1998 was 23.7 days). This shift to short hospitalizations has been accompanied by a significant rise in hospital readmissions (0 percent readmissions in 1984 and 27 percent readmissions in 1998). This can significantly increase the duration and cost of treatment.[2]

- Patients with anorexia who are discharged while still underweight had a 50 percent chance of readmission versus a 10 percent chance of readmission for those discharged after full weight recovery.[3]

- Patients with anorexia who are discharged while still underweight are more likely to have poorer clinical outcomes and a more chronic disease course. This increases their risk of osteoporosis and other lifelong adverse medical outcomes.[3]

- Assuming treatment consisting of inpatient weight restoration with a gradual step-down to a partial hospitalization program and then outpatient treatment, the treatment of anorexia is cost-effective when looking at cost per year of life saved, as compared to many other medical interventions.[4]

- 10–15 percent of people with anorexia will die from their eating disorder. This is the highest mortality of any psychiatric illness.[5]

- The risk of death for people with eating disorders is increased with longer the duration of the illness.[5]

- 1–3 percent of people with bulimia will die.[6]

- The longer someone has bulimia, the worse the outcome.[7]

- If children and young adolescents with anorexia do not receive intensive intervention, severe and permanent stunting of growth will occur.[8]

- People under the age of 15 with strong eating-disordered attitudes and a low rate of weight recovery during admission, need a longer hospitalization and a period of weight maintenance before discharge. Upon discharge, they require a step down to intensive therapy in a day program.[9]
- If girls with eating disorders do have stunted growth, catch-up growth is possible. However, to achieve this, they need continuous long-standing weight gain. The sooner this is achieved the better, because the capacity for growth will eventually decline.[10]

References:

1. Howard W.T., Evans K.K., Quintero-Howard C.V., et al. (1999) "Predictors for success or failure of transition to a day hospital treatment for inpatients with anorexia nervosa." *Am J Psychiatry* 156, no. 11: 1697–702.

2. Wiseman C.V., Sunday S.R., Klapper F., et al. (2001) "Changing patterns of hospitalization in eating disordered patients." *Int J Eat Disord* 30 no. 1: 69–74.

3. Baran S.A., Weltzin T.E. and Kaye W.H. (1995) "Low discharge weight and outcome in anorexia nervosa." *Am J Psychiatry* 152, no. 7:1070–2.

4. Crow S.J. and Nyman J.A. (2004) "The cost-effectiveness of anorexia nervosa treatment." *Int J Eat Disord* 35, no. 2: 155–60.

5. Walsh J.M., Wheat M.E., and Freund K. (2000) "Detection, evaluation, and treatment of eating disorders the role of the primary care physician." *J Gen Intern Med* 15, no. 8: 577–90.

6. Keel P.K., and Mitchell J.E. (1997) "Outcome in bulimia nervosa." *Am J Psychiatry* 154, no. 3:313–21.

7. Keel P.K., Mitchell J.E., Miller K.B., et al. (1999) "Long-term outcome of bulimia nervosa." Arch Gen Psychiatry 56, no. 1: 63.

8. Lantzouni E, Frank G.R., Golden N.H., et al. (2002) "Reversibility of growth stunting in early onset anorexia nervosa: a prospective study." *J Adolesc Health* 31, no. 2: 162–5.

9. Castro J., Gila A., Puig J., et al. (2004) "Predictors of rehospitalization after total weight recovery in adolescents with anorexia nervosa." *Int J Eat Disord* 36: 22–30.

10. Swenne I. (2005) "Weight requirements for catch-up growth in girls with eating disorders and onset of weight loss before menarche." *Int J Eat Disord* 38, no. 4: 340–5.

APPENDIX F

GUIDELINE FOR PHYSICIANS FOR RESPONDING TO DENIAL FOR "LACK OF MEDICAL NECESSITY"

by EDWARD TYSON, MD

If your insurance company is unwilling to pay for appropriate treatment for your child, ask your physician to intercede on your behalf. Unless the doctor specializes in eating disorders, he may be unfamiliar with the challenges these diseases present with insurance companies. You might consider providing him with the following information, which has been written for physicians by a physician, who specializes in eating disorders and in insurance issues related to this disease. Don't feel intimidated about showing this to your child's doctor; none of us enjoy hassling with insurance companies and most of us are delighted to receive advice that can help our patients and us.

The physician should:
1. Communicate by phone, which allows you to directly connect with the doctor who is denying treatment you have recommended.
2. Immediately ask if the person you are speaking to has the authority to overrule the prior denial.
3. Introduce yourself at the beginning of the conversation with the reasons why you can speak authoritatively on this particular case. Emphasize your expertise and knowledge of the patient's history, and summarize the necessity of residential treatment.
4. Explain that you want to familiarize yourself with who is sitting in judgment on your patient's case; then ask about their training, certification, experience in eating disorders, whether they are members of any national ED professional organizations or if they present on the subject.

5. Summarize your understanding of why your patient was denied the care, preferably quoting the reasons they stated.

6. Address any errors of fact about the patient's history, their assessment of her/his condition, or appropriate levels of treatment. Take each one of these points and offer direct proof or evidence as to why their conclusion is inappropriate for this patient at this time.

7. Make sure the medical director knows that you are going to hold him responsible for any decisions he makes.

8. Ask how the decision to deny the claim was made.

    a. Did they review the records and chart? You should know ahead of time whether or not they asked for and received copies of the medical records.

    b. Did they review the recommendations from the treatment team?

    c. Did they review the consultant's assessment?

    d. Are they aware of practice guidelines regarding management and treatment of eating disorders?

    e. Are they aware of practice guidelines regarding the special management and treatment of adolescents with eating disorders? Have they followed them?

9. Refer to guidelines and position papers from the Society for Adolescent Medicine, the American Academy of Pediatrics, the Canadian Pediatric Society, and the most up-to-date Guidelines from the American Psychiatric Association. You can also refer to the Web sites for NEDA (www.edap.org) and AED (www.aedweb.org)

10. Although it is less powerful and takes longer, if you must do this by letter, write the letter to the medical director assigned to the patient's case. Send the letter by fax, e-mail, and by mail, return receipt requested.

Edward P. Tyson, MD, an eating disorders specialist practicing in Austin, Texas, is recognized as one of the country's leading experts on insurance issues as they relate to eating disorders. Instrumental in helping families who have been denied insurance converge for their children, he is board certified in Adolescent Medicine and Family Medicine. Dr. Tyson has practiced medicine for more than twenty years and has specialized in eating disorders for the past decade.

APPENDIX G

RESOURCES FOR PHYSICIANS

Guidelines for Identifying, Treating and Managing Adolescent Eating Disorders (ED) in the Primary Care Setting

American Academy of Pediatrics (AAP) Guidelines

This policy statement devised by a subcommittee of AAP sets guidelines for the management of eating disorders in the primary care setting. The statement outlines the roles of pediatricians in various treatment settings (i.e., subspecialty practice, hospital care, day program).
http://pediatrics.aappublications.org/cgi/content/full/111/1/204

American Academy of Family Physicians (AAFP) Guidelines

This article provides an overview of the guidelines set forth by the American Psychiatric Association (APA) in treating adolescents with eating disorders of varying degree and nature.
www.aafp.org/afp/20000701/tips/15.html

Society for Adolescent Medicine (SAM) Guidelines

This position paper outlines current research in the field of eating disorders and treatment approaches for the primary physician. Insurance barriers to care are also discussed.
www.adolescenthealth.org/PositionPaper_Eating_Disorders_in_Adolescents.pdf

National Institute for Clinical Excellence (NICE) Guidelines, United Kingdom

This document contains guidelines for the identification, treatment, and management of eating disorders for individuals at all ages and at all levels

of care. The core interventions recommended by NICE are evidence based.
www.nice.org.uk/page.aspx?o=cg009niceguidance
www.nice.org.uk/page.aspx?o=cg009quickrefguide *(abridged version)*

Informational Resources/Articles for the Physician

"Children and Adolescents With Eating Disorders: The State of the Art"

This review article outlines the issues relevant to the care of the adolescent
patient with an eating disorder (ED), specifically highlighting roles and
responsibilities of the primary care physician. The article summarizes current knowledge in the field to arm the physician with appropriate strategies
to best care for the eating-disordered adolescent. Important topics and
guidelines for the physician to be familiar with include: the pathogenesis
and etiology of EDs; prevention and screening tools for ED diagnosis; risk
factors for disease; nutritional issues in the adolescent patient; appropriate
use of a multidisciplinary team in the management and treatment of EDs;
and obstacles in managed health care and reimbursement that the physician may face in providing eating disorder services.
http://pediatrics.aappublications.org/cgi/content/full/111/1/
e98#-otherarticles

"Diagnosis of Eating Disorders in Primary Care"

This review focuses on recognition and diagnosis of eating disorders in primary care. An overview of diagnostic tools (medical tests and questions for
patient history) provides the physician with resources to improve early
intervention and/or possibly prevent the illness from progressing to a
more severe or chronic state.
www.aafp.org/afp/20030115/297.html

"Eating Disorders from a Primary Care Perspective"

This position paper from the Medical Journal of Australia (MJA) discusses
key interventions for early recognition and treatment of adolescent eating
disorders. Case studies provide examples of behaviors and symptoms that
the physician should recognize as ED warning signs.
www.mja.com.au/public/mentalhealth/course/12wilhelm.pdf

Academy for Eating Disorders (AED)

This Web site has current research on treatment approaches and information for professionals as well as AED position statements on issues related to eating disorders.

www.aedweb.org

NOTES

CHAPTER 1

1. Fisher M., Golden N.H., Katzman D.K., et al. (1995) "Eating disorders in adolescents: a background paper." *Journal of Adolescent Health* 16, no. 6: 420–37.
2. Fisher et al., "Eating disorders; Keel P.K., and Klump K.L. (2003) "Are eating disorders culture bound syndromes? Implications for conceptualizing their etiology." *Psychological Bulletin* 129, no. 5: 747–69; Kjelsas E., Bjornstrom C., and Gotestam K.G. (2004) "Prevalence of eating disorders in male and female adolescents (14–15 years)." *Eating Behaviors* 5 no. 1: 13–25.
3. Pritts S.D., and Susman J. (2003) "Diagnosis of eating disorders in primary care." *American Family Physician* 67, no. 2: 297–304.
4. Rosen D.S. (2003) "Eating disorders in children and young adolescents: etiology, classification, clinical features, and treatment." *Adolescent Medicine* 14, no. 1: 49–59.
5. Fisher et al., "Eating Disorders"; Rosen, "Eating disorders in children."
6. Walsh J.M., Wheat M.E., and Freund K. (2000) "Detection, evaluation, and treatment of eating disorders the role of the primary care physician." *Journal of General Internal Medicine* 15, no. 8: 577–90.
7. See note 5.
8. See note 6.
9. See note 2.
10. Keel P.K., and Mitchell J.E. (1997) "Outcome in bulimia nervosa." *American Journal of Psychiatry* 154, no. 3:313–21.
11. Keel P.K., Mitchell J.E., Miller K.B., et al. (1999) "Long-term outcome of bulimia nervosa." *Archives of General Psychiatry* 56, no. 1: 63–9; Quadflieg N., and Fichter M.M. (2003) "The course and outcome of bulimia nervosa." *European Child and Adolescent Psychiatry* 12, Suppl 1: I99–109.

CHAPTER 2

1. Andrist L.C. (2003) "Media images, body dissatisfaction, and disordered eating in adolescent women." *MCN: The American Journal of Maternal Child Nursing* 28, no. 2: 119–23.

2. Andrist, "Media Images"; Pinhas L., Toner B., Ali A., et al. (1999) "The effects of the ideal of female beauty on mood and body dissatisfaction." *International Journal of Eating Disorders* 25, no. 2: 223–6.; Stice E., Schupak-Neuberg E., Shaw H.E., et al. (1994) "Relation of media exposure to eating disorder symptomatology: an examination of mediating mechanisms." *Journal of Abnormal Psychology* 103, no. 4: 836–40.

3. Kaye W.H., Frank G.K., Bailer U.F., et al. (2005) "Neurobiology of anorexia nervosa: clinical implications of alterations of the function of seratonin and other neuronal systems." *International Journal of Eating Disorders* 37, Suppl: S15–9; discussion S20–1.

4. Strober M.R., Freeman R., Lampert C., et al. (2000) "Controlled family study of anorexia nervosa and bulimia nervosa: evidence of shared liability and transmission of partial syndromes." *American Journal of Psychiatry* 157, no. 3: 393–401.

5. Lilenfeld L.R., Kaye W.H., Greeno C.G., et al. (1998) "A controlled family study of anorexia nervosa and bulimia nervosa: psychiatric disorders in first-degree relatives and effects of proband comorbidity." *Archives of General Psychiatry* 55, no. 7: 603–10.

CHAPTER 4

1. See chapter 1, note 6.

2. Mehler P.S. (2003) "Osteoporosis in anorexia nervosa: prevention and treatment." *International Journal of Eating Disorders* 33, no. 2: 113–26.

3. Golden N.H. (2003) "Osteopenia and osteoporosis in anorexia nervosa." *Adolescent Medicine* 14, no. 1: 97–108.

4. Ibid.

5. Swayze V.W., Anderson A.E., Andreasen N.C., et al. (2003) "Brain tissue volume segmentation in patients with anorexia nervosa before and after weight normalization." *International Journal of Eating Disorders* 33, no. 1: 33–44.

6. Mehler, "Osteoporosis in anorexia nervosa"; Katzman D.K., Christensen B., Young A.R., et al. (2001) "Starving the brain: structural abnormalities and cognitive impairment in adolescents with anorexia nervosa." *Seminars in Clinical Neuropsychiatry* 6, no. 2: 146–52.

INDEX